Cat's Pilgrimage

 Cat's Pilgrimage

Marilyn Bowering

 Harper*Flamingo*Canada

Cat's Pilgrimage
© 2004 by Marilyn Bowering. All rights reserved.

Published by Harper*Flamingo*Canada,
an imprint of HarperCollins Publishers Ltd

No part of this book may be used or reproduced
in any manner whatsoever without the prior
written permission of HarperCollins Publishers
Ltd, except in the case of brief quotations
embodied in reviews.

First Edition

HarperCollins books may be purchased for
educational, business, or sales promotional use
through our Special Markets Department.

HarperCollins Publishers Ltd
2 Bloor Street East, 20th Floor
Toronto, Ontario, Canada
M4W 1A8

www.harpercanada.com

National Library of Canada Cataloguing in
Publication

Bowering, Marilyn, 1949–
Cat's pilgrimage: a novel / Marilyn Bowering. –
1st ed.

ISBN 0-00-200523-9

I. Title.

PS8553.O9C38 2004   C813'.54   C2003-905626-0

HC 9 8 7 6 5 4 3 2 1

Printed and bound in the United States
Set in C&C Galliard

for Michael, Xan
    and Companion of the Well, Linda,
and in memory of sweet Raphael

There were three angels who came from the North,
One bringing Fire, the other brought Frost,
The other he was the Holy Ghost

From the Devon charms,
noted by the Reverend
Sabine Baring-Gould, 1910

nor is heaven as is alleged
nor is hell as is asserted
nor is the good eternally happy
nor is the bad eternally unhappy

Oran, traditional

Prologue

i. The Cat, the Dog and the Donkey

The cat met the dog and the donkey on a road. The road was beside a river, or a path of stars.

"It took you long enough to get here. Where have you been?" the cat said.

"I've been in the ice in the mountains," the dog said.

"I've been on the moor watching an empty house," the donkey said. "And you, where have you been?"

The cat turned away. He gazed at the dark path ahead of him. "Most recently at a lake."

The dog and the donkey looked at each other. The donkey spoke. "You know we're not supposed to lose sight of the stones!"

The cat, Cutthroat, cleared his throat. It felt as if there were ash in it.

"It's about Jones, isn't it?" the donkey said. "You can't just consider what you want, Cutthroat. What if everyone did that? Anything could happen!"

"Yes," Cutthroat said, "that's what I'm hoping."

"What would you like us to do?" the dog said.

"Keep your eyes open, look for opportunities, use your experience . . ."

"But we've never done this before," the donkey said.

"I'm only asking, Knowall."

"What difference does it make?" the dog said. "If it will make Cutthroat happy."

"You don't know what this means to me, Breaker." Cutthroat blinked rapidly. "You won't be sorry." He looked down at his paws. There was mud and blood on them. How hard it was to repay a debt. How difficult to be a friend.

The white dog was already a distant frost streak carving the sky. Knowall and Cutthroat gazed after him. The donkey brayed unhappily. "Are you certain about this?" she said.

The cat took a deep breath. "Yes."

ii. Cutthroat

What I was doing when Jones died:

    Nothing.

    Guarding a green stone.

    Waiting for orders.

What I should have been doing:

Whatever it took to keep Jones safe.

Breaking the rules.

iii. *A Promise,* a tale told by Jag to Cathreen

A river winds round the world. You can't see all of it now that the continents have drifted apart. Once upon a time, though, you could follow its current even through the oceans, which were much shallower then. They called it the Amazon, the Mackenzie, the Nile, the Tigris, the Limpopo, but it was all the same river. The river brought news from one part of the world to another. If you put a leaf in the river, at some point it would return to you.

The river began in the sky. It flowed, milky white, along a great swathe of stars, then fell over the edge in a stream of moonlight to the earth. It was along this river that souls travelled to be born, and along the same river, in the moon's shadow, that they returned after death. As far as I know, that's still how it works. There was a full moon when you were born, Cathreen, and like your mother says, I'll probably die in the darkness. Not for a while, though, so don't worry. It doesn't bother me. I'll be going back up to the stars, and when that happens, I'll be looking down at you and you'll be looking up at me, and one way or the other, you and me will always be together.

Some people will try to tell you that the river and the earth are separate. Don't you believe it. The river carries pieces of the earth as silt and moves them along: the earth, bit by bit, is moving through time. This means that wherever you are, you're home: some piece of where you're standing has already been where you've been, and that leaf you dropped in a river long ago is on its way.

Wherever I am, you can come to me. Wherever you are, I'll find you.

When you were small, you told me a story about unicorns. You said they could fly, and that the reason there aren't any anymore is because they refused to get into the ark when Noah asked them to. They flew around and got tired and drowned; you said their spirits lived for ten days and then they died, and their bones are buried in the sand at the beach where I took you and your mother fishing. I asked you how you knew this. You said you *didn't* know it at first, but after you started to tell me, you knew it was true. Cathreen, you don't have to listen to what anybody else says because you already know it all inside of you.

My sister, Jen, and I used to climb this hill near where we lived in England. At the top of it was a tower. You could stand up there and think you were looking down at the whole world. It made you feel powerful, like there was nothing you couldn't do if you wanted to. Then, as it grew dark, mist would come swirling up from the ditches and marshes and make it all look different. You didn't know anything after all! You'd hear these strange sounds, people and horses, and dogs baying: big swirling shapes like dust and green and gold—ghosts driving themselves straight into the side of the hill. I'd start shivering and stand close to Jen, but I never said anything. You don't always have to discuss things to understand what's going on.

But we'd keep standing there because after a while the mist would settle down and then you'd see the stars, millions of them, so near you could reach up for a handful and pull them to your chest, but you didn't want to. You wanted them to be up there forever. The sky was huge. We don't have skies like that here. We have mountains and trees and scenery. It's like living in a goddamned tourist brochure.

So, Jen would put her coat down and we'd lie on top of it and gaze up. She taught me the names of the constellations like our dad had taught her before he took off to wherever he went to. Ireland maybe, I was never sure. I didn't know him, Cathreen, and your grand-mother died at my birth. The sky would turn and you'd feel so small and dizzy and privileged, going slowly around on the spinning earth like a plate inside a big dish; you were an ant but you were right at the centre, part of everything that was important, and some nights that river of stars would flow right out of the sky on top of you and you'd feel those souls travelling up and down it, some just practising dying or being born in their dreams, others stepping out for real. I'd think about the green-and-gold ladies and gentlemen on horseback, and the dogs, and wonder if they were part of it too. Jen would tell me stories about the fairies who were once angels in heaven and about the three stones lost from Lucifer's crown and how people still searched for them and about this hill where we were lying being close to the place the stones tried to get back to given half a chance because that's where they'd first fallen. And I'd think how much money I'd get if I ever found them, and what I'd buy for Jen and what I'd do to Colin Printer who was already nosing around her even though he was old and stank because he never washed; and we wouldn't need him or his free trips to the seaside or Sunday drives in his Vauxhall. Jesus, Cathreen. Sometimes I could feel so good. Then we'd go back to the house we lived in and drink cocoa and Jen would be happy until Colin came in.

It takes so little to make people happy, Cathreen, remember that.

Good night, Sweet. Sure I'll see you in the morning. Every morn-ing for the rest of your life. Honest. Forever. I promise.

Time is the shadow of a swift bird which ever moves.

Stella Langdale,
writing to K. E. Maltwood

One

Cathreen

From the trees to the right of the docks, you could see the dirty sand of the shore and its overhanging shrubbery, the branches heavy with dead, unshed leaves. A light wind rippled across the surface of the little lake. Other than that, there was only bright moonlight and the block-shaped shadows cast by floats and their pens where Cathreen, long ago, had learned to swim. Cathreen followed the others from the trees, across the parking lot and then continued alone towards the pilings below the boat shed, letting the dizziness take her. Mud sucked at her running shoes. Minuscule waves lapped dully. She had to pee. She looked behind her. The others were laughing and talking, pushing each other ahead. When they reached the water's edge, somebody stumbled and half fell in. She heard a girl shout, "Fuck! You'll pay for this!" She slogged between the pilings, climbed a short bank, tripped over a log, her nostrils filled with the odours of rotting vegetation, undid her jeans and squatted.

What are we doing here? This sucks. Look the fuck at that! The voices of newcomers, piling out of a car; the thump of bass from a radio, then the engine turned off. She kept low in the grass between brambles and struggled to pull up her jeans. The lights from the car, still on, illuminated a path to the lake. "Hey, Fawn," a boy at the lake edge called, "wanna be my girl?" A girl pulled herself away from whoever had hold of her arm and propelled herself across the grass to the sand. It was darker there, where the others had gathered in a knot, but Cathreen could see her friends Judy and Toni step forward to speak to the girl. The girl, Fawn, staggered a little as if dazed or drunk. When no one was looking her way, Cathreen blundered down the bank, but stopped short when she saw a wrecked bicycle frame half-buried in the sludge. "That your bike, Toni?" she bawled. "You get it for your birthday?"

"Fuck off, Cathreen," came the reply. "You keep it." She heard Toni say to somebody, "Take your shoes off, hon."

Cathreen swayed, staring down at the twisted wheels and broken spokes, the dismembered body of somebody's ten-speed. Nobody rode a ten-speed. It was a piece of junk, even before.

The stink of algae and dead water suddenly turned her stomach. She moved nearer to where the water slurped at the pilings, the dull pulse of the wavelets like some slack mouth at the timbers. She had a sudden vision of herself, her father and mother and her parents' friend Tink sitting around a beach fire, looking out at Jag's fishing skiff anchored just offshore along the coast. Wave after wave crashing in. Cathreen blanked out the picture. She wasn't a little girl anymore.

"Get on over here, now, Cathreen," she heard Toni shout. Cathreen could see the glow of Toni's cigarette brighten as she drew on it; high cloud had cancelled the moon.

"What? Just a minute!" The vodka and Sprite she'd been drinking roiled into her throat. A surge of self-pity flowed through her, then she felt her scalp prickle, shivers walk up and down her spine, and she bent to the water to spew.

She stood up in time to see a boy emerge from the parked car. He stepped hesitantly towards the others down the pathway of head-lights. Toni's cigarette fell into the water with a hiss. "Hey!" Toni yelled. "It's Timmy! Hey, Tim!" As Cathreen neared her friends she heard Toni say, in a low voice, to the people who had come with the girl, "Why'd you bring the fag?"

"Hey, Fawn," Timmy said, "let's go." He stood outside the half-circle the others had formed around the girl. Now Cathreen could see that the girl was up to her knees in water.

"She can't go yet," Judy whined, "she's got my shirt. I need it, I'm cold." Judy put her arms around herself. "Brrrr."

"Yeah, and that's my scarf. I asked for it back," Kora said.

"You said you didn't want it," the girl said. Her words were slurred. As the clouds moved aside and the moon flowered, Cathreen could see her face. She didn't really know her. She was new at school. She'd come down to the gully once to talk to them and had given them cigarettes. Toni had laughed at her afterwards. "Did you hear that crap? 'I have this thirty-five-year-old boyfriend on the Internet,' she'd mimicked. The girl was tall, with wavy brown hair, and on the heavy side. Her face was slack, but she was blinking rapidly, as if she were trying to catch up.

"Come on, Fawn," Timmy said.

"You smell something?" This was Chris, usually quiet, but he'd been drinking with Cathreen earlier at the picnic tables outside the scout cabin up the lane, and then they'd gone into the woods to smoke weed. He bent his head and started sniffing. "Yeah, there's something." The others laughed. Cathreen stepped away when he sniffed at her, and he kept on going. Fawn, in the water, was slowly unwinding the scarf. Chris stopped at Timmy. "It's here. It smells like shit. Fag shit."

"Joe," Timmy said to one of the boys he'd come with, "we should go."

"That your boyfriend?" Chris said to Joe.

The boy shrugged. "Fuck you, he said. "I'm out."

Timmy followed and it looked like the others who'd come with them would go too. Fawn whimpered; Timmy looked back. Fawn was trying to break through the line of bodies.

"No, you don't, bitch!" Judy shouted. "Get her, don't let her leave! My shirt! I want it now." Toni, Judy and Kora walked the girl into deeper water.

The girl took off her jacket. "Timmy?" she said. He stepped forward to catch it as she threw, but Chris reached up, snagged it, then let it fall in the water. "Oops!" he said.

"What's going on?" Cathreen said. "Somebody tell me what's happening." Nobody paid her any attention, so she reached down and splashed a handful of water over her mouth and eyes. It was icy and stank but it helped to clear her head. What were Toni and the others doing? There were too many people around the girl now for Cathreen to see much. They were all laughing. She staggered through mud and water and pushed her way through the crowd.

Judy had the shirt in her hand and the girl stood there in her jeans and bra, her arms clutched around herself. She was white skinned and flabby. She let her long hair drop forward to hide her face.

"Hey, slut," somebody said, "take it all off!"

"Yeah! Let's see what you've got!"

Timmy ran along the dock and jumped in beside Fawn. He took her by the hand and started pulling her with him to the floats. Cathreen remembered what it felt like to walk along them in bare feet. They were made of plastic, and fitted together like a jigsaw. The ridges where they interlocked tickled.

"Shit, you're spoiling the fun!"

"Fucking fag, what does he care."

Cathreen said to Chris, "I thought we were going swimming."

"Hey! That's a good idea." He started forward into the water.

"No! At the pool! That's where we said we were going."

He looked at her blankly. "You go on, we'll catch up."

It was a bit of a walk—back to the cabin, along to the main road, then a hike across the bridge and up the hill. But there was lots of traffic, and street lights. She'd be safe enough.

Cathreen started off but her feet squelched and she stooped to shake water out of her shoes. When she looked up again, Fawn and Timmy were still in the water. The others had formed a cordon along the shore and the dock. Somebody on the shore threw a pebble. It struck the girl in the forehead. "Please!" she cried out, as she put her hands and arms over her head. Why didn't they stop? The girl would have got the point, whatever it was. Sean, whom Cathreen knew— he'd been at the cabin too—jumped up from where he'd been sitting on a log and picked up a handful of stones. They rained down over the two in the water, like hail. There was blood on the girl's face and Timmy looked frightened. There were more stones, bigger ones, and more blood.

"What are you doing! Stop it!" Cathreen cried. She knew she should do something more, but she was drunk and frightened too.

Another girl pushed her way through the crowd and stood facing them, thigh deep in the lake. "That's enough, leave them alone now. If anybody touches them again they'll have to deal with me!" She looked like she knew what she was doing. Good idea, thought Cathreen, about time, I'd like to go home now, please. Forget the pool. She was feeling crappy and there were people blocking her exit, milling around, undecided. She waited. Some of them left.

She tried to find Chris, but couldn't, then she checked in her jacket pockets for her money. It wasn't there. Timmy and Fawn had climbed out of the water. Fawn sat sobbing on the floatway while Timmy poured water out of his shoes and set them neatly to one side. Blood ran from the side of his head onto his clothes. Cathreen walked back towards the boathouse pilings where she thought she might have dropped her wallet. She searched there, and then through the bushes along the shore. When she came back into the shadows below the pilings where an upturned rowboat lay tied to a stump, a grey cat jumped onto the timbers beside her. Cathreen stared at the slits of its green eyes then away as Toni called out, "Anybody got a pair of fucking scissors? We should cut her hair."

Cathreen heard the flick of a lighter, saw a tongue of flame spurt up. "Shit," Toni said as she looked at her watch. "We've got to go now, Jude, or we'll miss the bus. I told my mom I'd be home by twelve." They passed not far from Cathreen without seeing her.

Fawn heaved herself to her feet; Timmy was throwing up on the other side of the dock. Cathreen could see that Fawn had her arms crossed over her chest as if she were trying to hold herself in. The cat on the joined timbers near Cathreen mewed and Fawn looked over at it, squinting.

When Cathreen reached the gate at the main road, she saw Judy and Toni about fifty yards ahead. Since they'd left without her—

obviously they didn't give a shit—she thought she'd wait for Chris, but then she saw him come out of the woods behind her and start to walk back down the hill towards the lake. Cathreen called, "Where're you going? Want to walk with me?" He waved at her, but said nothing. Cathreen watched after him and saw someone coming up the lane to join him. Was it Sean? Or one of the girls? Kora, maybe? Cathreen blinked away the water that kept slipping into her eyes and blurring her vision, then she hurried to tail after Toni and Judy. She really didn't feel like being alone.

"Hey, Cat, what are you doing? We lost you," Toni said when she caught up to them.

"I thought you were taking the bus," Cathreen said. Everything was spinning. Her throat burned with stomach acid. She shouldn't have tried to run.

"We fucking missed it," Toni said. "There isn't another one for an hour. I'm going to call my mom."

"You coming with us?" Judy said. She bent and squeezed water out of the bottoms of the legs of her jeans. "We're gonna walk to the pool and phone her mom from there."

"Maybe she could give me a ride too," Cathreen said. "I'm not feeling well. I could really use a ride." The cat from the lakeside brushed against her legs. She looked down at it, surprised. It twisted insistently in and out between her feet so that she had to keep sidestepping to get away from it. The cat looked a little familiar. "Got a new friend?" Judy said, laughing at her. It had turned her around completely so that she was facing the way she'd just come. She felt dizzy again. She thought she could see Chris and Sean or whoever it was passing between the trees, nearing the lake. From up here, on the road, through a screen of alder, you could see that the lake was one of several—sump holes, really, mosquito traps, full of duck shit. When she'd swum there before, she'd got duck itch. She wondered, vaguely, if Fawn and Timmy were going to be all right, and took a step or two as if she might go back to check, but Toni was watching her and said, "Don't sweat it, Cat. Don't interfere."

Judy giggled nervously and twirled her hair with her fingers. "Let's go. It'll be all right," she said.

Something was bothering Cathreen. She felt itchy and jumpy and like there were small fingers and fists pulling at her hair and at her ears trying to make her look down at the lake. As if she could really see it, through a bunch of trees. Fucking stress. She didn't want it. It wasn't her business. She had a headache and her mouth tasted like shit. The cat mewed, sprinted past her and ran to the gate and down the hill, stopping several times to look back at her. Then everything was quiet. Like there was ice in the atmosphere and if she did the wrong thing, like breathe, she would break it and have to bear the consequences. So she held her breath until the feeling went away.

"There must have been a good reason for that," Cathreen said, glancing at Toni, "otherwise you wouldn't have done it."

"Fucking right," Toni said.

When Toni's mother came to pick them up at the pool, Toni got in the front and Cathreen and Judy in the back. Toni said, "It took you long enough to get here." Her mom said, "What do you mean? I didn't even finish my Scrabble game!" Toni put on a CD and turned it up loud. Her mom said, "Oh, please!" but didn't make her turn it down. She did say, "Don't think I can't smell the toothpaste, don't think I don't know it means you've been drinking." On the drive back to Cathreen's after they'd dropped off Judy, they noticed Chris,

Sean and Kora hitching a ride from across the road, just past the Chinese restaurant.

"Aren't those your friends?" Toni's mom said. "Should I pick them up?"

"Shut up!" Toni hissed from the front.

Cathreen waved but her friends didn't wave back. "What do you think happened after we left?" she said, leaning forward so that only Toni could hear her.

"Shut up, asshole," Toni said, almost yelling at her. "Will you shut the fuck up!"

"I won't have swearing in the car," her mom said. "I came all this way to get you. The least you could do is to show some respect."

"You shut the fuck up too," Toni said.

Cathreen kept her eyes closed. She was seven years old, sitting up in bed in the dark, her knees making hills under the blankets, the space between them a wide valley. She reached into the pool of moonlight farther down the covers and shaped out of it, as she had been taught to do at school with clay, a small figure. She placed the figure along with the others—people and animals—that were already gathered in her kingdom. She made small tents with her fingers and urged the creatures towards them. Her hands trembled and burned from the touch of their shining skins; the happiness she felt made her stomach and throat feel like they'd melted. Her hands had caught the glow, and her brown hair, when she lifted it into the moonlight, was shining. *They* told her everything.

She listened beyond the click and scrape of the apple trees outside her bedroom window for the sound of her father's car. When it came, the headlights slashed across her wall as he turned into the driveway, and she heard her mother open the front door and step out onto the porch to greet him. In a few minutes she caught the tune of their voices as they murmured together in the kitchen. If she could stay awake long enough, while the shining ones swayed up the moonlit cord that closed her curtains back to the night they had come from, her parents would come to say good night. Jag would bend and press his cheek to hers so that she would feel the stubble of his whiskers, and Helena would whisper from the doorway, "Don't wake her, she's tired," but then step into the room anyway to draw the covers up round Cathreen's shoulders and smooth out the hills and valleys, the tents, houses, castles, shops, fields, schools, rivers and lakes of the kingdom of the blanket—not knowing that she did so, but making everything ordinary again so that Cathreen could start over, the next night, whispering and being whispered to, full of secrets and joy, brimming with life.

Cathreen opened her eyes. She wasn't seven anymore. She was fourteen. But they were here, now, as they'd been for the past three nights, robbing her of sleep, dancing on the standing ends of the hairs on her arms, pulling sharply at the hair at her temples until her eyes watered, whistling into her ears, trying to make her listen, trying to make her think she was crazy. But she wouldn't think that and she wouldn't listen. She couldn't. She was too old. She was too afraid.

Cathreen got up, turned on the bedside light and fished in the desk drawer for her cigarettes. She opened the window so that she could blow the smoke outside. If she didn't, her mother, whenever she got back, would sniff the air, sneeze and complain about her allergies. Cathreen blew the smoke, hard, at the bare branches of a tree: the smoke swirled and spiralled and stopped the fine drops of rain that were falling, making out of them, for a second, a cloudy mirror. She saw her father's face in the sheen and spun round thinking, stupidly, that he might be coming into her room. He wasn't, of course; it had been nearly two years since she'd seen him.

The room had settled down. *They* had arranged themselves on the pillow, and some were quietly patting out a space for her next to them. *Cathreen, darling, we have to talk,* they said.

Cathreen dressed in jeans, running shoes, sweatshirt and her fleece and went outside. The air was still damp, but it had stopped raining. Mist had thickened into low cloud caught in the trees and on the pitched roofs of all the little shambling wooden houses on the road. She stood at the corner of the house in which she and her mother lived, lit another cigarette, leaned against the drainpipe and gazed out. The street was dark except for a light at Elsa's. Elsa, like them, owned her own house, but most of the others in the neighbourhood were renters. You could tell which they were, her mother said, because of the gravel and concrete instead of grass and shrubs in the yards, and by the stacks of soggy beer cartons, left for months, turning to pulp on the front steps. Renters, said Helena, didn't care how things looked.

Cathreen hated it all. But once, so Jag had told her, Pear Street had been a pleasant road with long stretches of fields spiking from it. And facing the road, their mailboxes at the end of long drives, had stood several nobly large, brightly painted farmhouses. Now, on the south side of the street, at the back of flimsy bungalows put up in haste decades ago, instead of fields there was a "park" consisting of three concrete bunkers linked by asphalted playgrounds. Two of the bunkers were washrooms and the third was an "activity centre" closed except for two weeks in summer, when it filled with screaming children. On Elsa's side of the street, in the spaces between the few remaining original houses, squatted flat-roofed concrete-block warehouses that were surrounded by chain-link fences, and behind these snaked a highway that had fattened over the years to digest more and more lanes of traffic, linking suburb to suburb.

In the "better" days Jag used to talk about—days Cathreen thought she could just recall—a field still ran along the old railway line on the far side of the highway. She and Jag had dozed in the grass there one summer afternoon when she was small, waiting for a train to come. She remembered bees treading the clover, the speckled shadow made by Jag's hat over his eyes and her excitement when her father had let her put her ear to the rust-coloured rail to feel the vibration of an approaching engine on its way west, out to the logging camps. They'd put a penny on the track for the train to flatten; she'd kept it, for years afterwards, for luck.

Cathreen dropped her cigarette, crushed it with her heel and started walking. Orange street light peed over the wet road, filling in crevices, leaving no shadows. There were no trees; there was no place to hide except in the blank houses themselves or behind the few scarred cars parked along the roadway. Nobody else was out. At night this was somebody's territory and people got agitated when you were on their turf and they didn't know why. But she wasn't scared. Nothing very bad could happen to her in her own neighbourhood in her own hometown, and she knew everybody there was to know anyway even if she wasn't in a particular gang. *Cathreen, my dear, something bad* has *happened,* insisted a voice in her ear, so close that she jumped and cried out, "Shut up!" Then she leaned forward and had to take several deep breaths to quell the nausea that followed; it was another minute before she could walk on, swinging her arms at her sides to look as if she owned the whole fucking world.

Why did you come out if you're so frightened? the stupid voice said again. To get away from you, she thought, biting her lip to hold the words inside. But the voice was more distant this time, and she knew she could push it further away if she wanted. She could probably push it away forever.

She had walked all the way to the bridge before she admitted to herself where she was going. Light spilled from the Chinese restaurant and pub, making the surface of the water below tremble like silk. Jag had told her once about a canoeing accident he'd been in: he'd said he'd felt dreamy after a while in the cold water, and as he'd grown colder, he'd thought someone was speaking to him. It had been like hearing the start of a story when you were falling asleep and you believed you were listening but next thing you knew you'd stepped off a cliff into a dream, and right after that you were safe and awake in the morning. He'd kind of liked it, he'd said.

Headlights flared from behind her, and Cathreen ran across the bridge and made a dive for the gate. She was through in an instant, running past the cabin and down the hill, gulping down bile when she found herself at the dock where she'd last seen Fawn and Timmy. She wiped her sweating hands on her jeans. She remembered, for no particular reason, that Toni had said, when she and Judy had made Cathreen return here with them after school, that Fawn had told the others, before they'd pushed her off the end and told her to swim, that she'd buy them cigarettes all year because she liked them. What an idiotic thing to say, and why was she remembering that now? What good would it do? Tears seeped out of her like she was this plastic bag that was leaking. She brushed them away. She'd hardly known Fawn. She'd never seen Timmy before in her life. The whole thing was, like, an accident, and she wouldn't cry for people she didn't know.

They'd come up to her at school yesterday and Judy had said, "You know that girl on Saturday night? That Fawn girl? She hasn't turned up. Nobody's seen her, and Kora's been saying that she and Sean and Chris went back. That it was Chris's fault because he doesn't like fags."

"Yeah, so what?" Cathreen had said.

"So, like, if they did what she said they did, you'd better come with us and help. We're in it, all of us."

"No way, man," Cathreen said.

"You were there. You were with us."

"I didn't even know them! It wasn't anything to do with me!"

"Yeah, but nobody's seen her and if she's, like, dead . . ." The words had floated away on the puffs of steam coming from Judy's mouth. It was getting colder. Cathreen shivered and hunched her shoulders. Toni had just watched her.

"What about Timmy?" Cathreen had said.

"Everybody knows he's a fag. They found him downtown in one of those fag places. He got beat up by one of those old guys he picked up. You know what I'm saying? The old guy even took his shoes." She looked hard at Cathreen. "He'll be in the hospital a long time. Like he's maybe a vegetable."

They'd taken the gully path from school to the rec centre, crossed the bridge and followed the path through the gate and past the cabin to the lake. It spread beyond them, a shadowed bowl, dotted at the edge with long grass and scrub fir. The thicker, more elegant cedar were behind them; alder thickets straggled over marshland all the way up the slope to the road.

"I don't get what we're doing here," Cathreen had said. They were on the narrow beach.

"The clothes," Toni said patiently. "We've got to find the clothes. That way they can't prove Fawn or Timmy were even here. They can't prove anything. When the cops came I said maybe Fawn ran away. I told them about the Internet guy. I said maybe she'd gone off with him."

"The cops came?"

"What do you think?"

"What clothes?" Cathreen said. She felt dull—nothing made any sense.

"Don't be a dumbass. The shoes and jacket, remember? We made her take off her shoes. Kora had wanted the jacket but she didn't take it. I already told you about Timmy."

Timmy's running shoes were on the float, neatly placed beside a mooring pole. Judy found Fawn's shoes in a tuft of weed and grass on the shoreline opposite the raft. "Wal-Mart, probably," she said, turning them over. "They're not even leather." In the darkness, Saturday night, Cathreen hadn't noticed the raft, had forgotten it was even there.

Cathreen shaded her eyes. The raft bobbed, fifty yards or so away, and Cathreen remembered that she'd never swum out to it. She wasn't good enough, and she was frightened of the thickets of weeds tangled not far below the surface. She'd had to stay in the pens where the lifeguards watched over them. "There's something on it," she said. "Look!"

"It's not human," Judy said. "It's nothing."

"It might be something," Toni said. "We'd better go see."

They'd untied the old rowboat from the stump, turned it over and dragged it to the water, scraping through the grit, and as they did so, Cathreen found her wallet. It was damp from its days and nights in the sand, but otherwise undamaged. The oars were tucked under the boathouse, resting on hooks screwed into a beam.

"I didn't think she'd come," Judy said as they rowed out.

"What do you mean?"

"We told her it was an initiation. You had to do it to join us," Judy said. "Then afterwards we'd all go swimming. Like we said to you, at the pool."

"You could say anything to her and she'd believe it," Toni said.

"But she didn't come with us," Cathreen said.

"We got somebody to ask. One of the guys in Joe's car. She came because she was a slut."

Cathreen stared at her. "You set her up?"

"She deserved it. Are you telling me you don't think she had it coming?"

"I didn't say that."

Toni said, "If it was me instead of Kora and Sean and them, I would have dealt with the clothes. I wouldn't have left all this shit behind to turn up."

"You're pathetic, you know that?" Cathreen had said. She hadn't known she was going to say it. She hadn't known where the words had come from. And then she was afraid: Toni was her best friend, Toni might decide not to like her.

Toni had looked surprised, but she'd nodded before she'd dropped her gaze. "Yeah," she said. "Don't I know it. I should have been with them."

They nudged against the raft and shipped the oars. Judy got out and rummaged through a black garbage bag of ropes that lay there; there was nothing else. "What do you think," she said, getting back in and looking out at the lake, "is she still out there somewhere or did she make it in?"

Toni had slipped the oars back into the locks. "We'd better keep looking for the jacket."

Nothing happened after Cathreen stopped crying except that the clouds slowly erased themselves and the mist trickled away in drops, leaving the sky open. It was darker now at the lake; beyond the black oasis of the scout camp, light from street lamps and houses leaked freely into the black nothingness. Month by month, as more subdivisions and shopping centres sprang up, the general darkness diminished. Cathreen watched the stars, muted and orange, until her eyes stung. A sudden movement in a nearby tree startled her. She swung round; the tree's branches were shaking. At some time, somebody had looped strips of toilet paper over them, so that now the strips hung torn and dirty and trembling. She saw the flash of green eyes from behind them, there was another flurry of activity, and then the grey cat she'd seen there before dropped out of the branches to the ground. The cat came straight over and rubbed against her legs. It had a white spot on one of its paws and a long tail held high. Cathreen picked it up. It didn't look particularly hungry or uncared for but it wasn't wearing a collar.

"What are you still doing here, Puss? Looking for rats?" The cat climbed out of her arms and onto her shoulder; it purred in her ear. She reached up and brought it back down to hold against her chest. "You should be safe and warm at home. Who do you belong to, I wonder." A half-memory of her mother, Helena, shooing a cat out of her car flickered through her mind. Where had that been? Helena hated cats. She'd never let Cathreen have one. Cathreen petted the short grey fur and scratched the notched ears. The cat kneaded its paws on her arm. She could feel static electricity in her fingers as she ran her hand down its coat. The cat jumped onto her shoulder once more and gripped tightly with its claws as she moved off carefully back up the hill. It had grown very cold; the nearest street light had burned out and there wasn't a car on the road. The stars swam overhead; she crossed the bridge, passed the Chinese restaurant and headed for home.

The cat followed, keeping mostly out of sight and running in quick spurts from shrub to shrub. Where there were no bushes or trees, it skulked behind parked cars, a pale patch emerging from time to time to dart through open spaces to shadows. The slick backs of the cars glistened, the road shone and stretched through the stillness alongside the marsh. It was a relief to turn away from the spongy landscape into the fixed wasteland of parking lots, shopping malls and intersections for the rest of the walk home. The small stucco or wooden houses elbowed to the sidelines by lanes of asphalted roadway were dark and quiet. Nobody played music or twitched back a curtain to examine their passing. It was as if the essence of the world had evaporated when she wasn't looking: she felt more and more cold and tired. She looked up through the haze of the halogen street lights. Up there were satellites and space stations, human beings cannonballing through the symmetry of the constellations. Up there were the stars. Cathreen tried to search them out as Jag had taught them to her on camping trips, the two of them the only ones awake, lying on the moist sand of a beach in their sleeping bags. She thought she could make out Ursa Major—that was easy—and Cassiopeia and the Lynx, and not far from that, Castor and Pollux, the twins. That's what she and Helena had called Jag and Tink when Tink was Jag's best friend. Twins. Like shit. Tink was Helena's boyfriend.

When Cathreen arrived home, the cat was still with her. A small cloud, backlit by the moon, slipped behind the roof: for a second it appeared as if the house were moving, sliding away from her and the grass of the postage-stamp lawn. Then the cloud popped out and the house steadied. The cat ran ahead along the cement walk to the front steps and up them onto the porch landing. The bulb in the porch light had burned out, there were no other lights showing, and the house sat in the recesses of its own shadows. If it hadn't been for the cat waiting, Cathreen might not have had the courage to enter the dense blackness and fumble for the house key hung on a nail behind the thermometer. Once the key was in her hand, though, she found she didn't feel like going in. She wished she'd called somebody before going out: maybe she could have stayed at Toni's or Judy's, although last she'd heard, Toni was going to move out.

The cat returned from wherever it had gone and pushed against the back of her legs. When Cathreen bent to pick it up, she noticed a grocery bag stuffed into a corner. It hadn't been there when she'd gone out. The cat flowed from her hands and went over to sniff at the white plastic. Cathreen picked up the bag and unlocked the door. She turned on the hall light and blinked. Her name and a brief message had been written with a marking pen on the outside of the bag.

The cat was waiting at the back door when she came out. She ignored it and pushed her way through the blackberry canes that had started to grow up since Helena had given up on the garden. There was a thicker band of bramble, wild rose, thistle and morning glory near the fence where Jag had set up the incinerator. It was hardly ever used.

Cathreen heard a scuffle and saw the cat emerge from a tangle of brush with a mouse in its mouth. "Nice going," she said, bending to pat it. "If you want to stay, you've got a job." She scrunched up the newspaper she'd brought from the house, put it on top of the morning glory growing in the rusty metal barrel and dumped the contents of the bag on top of it. She poured on the lighter fluid she'd found in Jag's drawer—still unemptied—in the bureau in Helena's bedroom, shooed the cat away and lit a match. There was a whoosh of flame, a puff of sparks going straight up and a stink of black satin smoke blotting the sky.

When she'd opened the bag, Cathreen had found Fawn's jacket: she'd recognized it as soon as she'd seen it. There were mud and water stains on it. It was a nice jacket, so nice she'd considered trying to wash it and save it, but whoever had left it on the porch for her would know she had it and she might get in trouble for nothing. It was a shame though. Helena didn't have the money to buy her a jacket like that.

Cathreen lay on the ground and watched the charred fragments of Fawn's jacket twist out of the fire and fly away. The cat came to sit on her chest; he groomed carefully between each toe on each paw. Some feeling she didn't fully recognize started to rise in her chest: if it hadn't been for the cat, the loneliness that was part of it would have overwhelmed her. But the cat was there, so she let the feeling rise, and suddenly all there was to save her was the cat's fur beneath her hand. Smoky, rank air bubbled in and out of her lungs. She felt she was drowning.

I am fourteen years old. I have no criminal record. I've been stopped by the police for possession of alcohol and once, at school, for carrying a knife. I never intended to use it. It was just a knife from the kitchen. Big deal.

My mother reported me once for being out all night. My father doesn't live with us. My mother works as a housekeeper. She keeps saying she's gonna take all these courses and graduate from university, but I don't believe her. Me and my mom get on fine. You'd better not call her or bring her into this! I know what they say happened but it doesn't have anything to do with me. I was just there like everyone else, and then I went home.

I wouldn't say Toni is my best friend, but she's a friend. We've known each other since elementary school. I know Chris and Sean and Judy. I know Kora. Yeah, sometimes we trade clothes, but you don't always want to be dressed by Value Village! Duh.

I didn't know the girl. I knew who she was. I don't know if people didn't like her. No, I didn't do anything, I was just drinking like I said. Somebody brought vodka from home. A girl. Her mom wouldn't care anyway.

I don't remember if the girl—Fawn—said anything. I was pretty buzzed. I don't know anything about Timmy. I didn't even know what had happened, I thought, like, they'd just walked off. Yeah, maybe somebody threw a few stones, but it was dark, it was hard to tell. Maybe I did go down there later on if somebody saw me. Or maybe it was somebody else. It's a free country, isn't it?

No, I haven't seen my father for a while. He's always writing and asking me to come and visit him. He's going to send me a ticket to England where he's living. Maybe I'll go. You can tell Fawn's family I'm sorry, but there wasn't anything I could have done. I wish it hadn't happened. If there's a problem for Timmy, I'm sorry about that too.

Look, all this is really upsetting, can't we stop?

It was like being in an airplane where, when you looked out one side it was night, with the moon in the sky, but the other side was bright with sunrise. She'd been on planes twice, once to go to her grandmother's funeral in Prince George, the other time to visit Jag in

Halifax before he left the country. Cathreen felt something like cob-webs on her arms and then she could stand upright although there was nothing particular to stand *on*. There *was* a sketch of a chill, frosty garden, its trees so fragile and transparent that she could see the stars through them.

Cathreen knew she was dreaming. The dreams had piled on top of each other like a library of heavy books for hours. Every now and then she'd surface to hear the cat purring contentedly beside her on the bed, but then she'd fall back beneath the weight of accumulating dream information. Her brain filled up with it, she could sense its efficient sorting. Once, when she'd awakened, she'd been aware that the cat was gone and that she could hear him in the kitchen eating from the dish she'd put out for him. Before she dropped through the library chute again—the slide that led to the dreams—the cat had returned to the bed.

Cathreen stood in the tracing of the garden and here she found Fawn, installed among the brittle white trees and looking bewildered. Her eyes unseeing, she walked slowly, her hands stretched out in front of her. Cathreen thought she also saw a ghostly Timmy, but when she looked straight at him, he wasn't there.

"She can't see you," Cathreen heard the cat, who had come to stand next to her, say. "She can hear sometimes, but mostly she believes she is down there, abandoned, hurt and alone."

"Down there" was instantly visible: Cathreen saw Pear Street and its few houses, and how it ran, like a narrow, jagged scar—the kind made by broken glass—through the spread flesh of warehouses, fences and security lights. A police car rushed along the highway, its red and blue lights flashing; knots of small settlements, neon and white jewels, were strung out along the road, but over at the lake, to the southeast, there were no lights at all.

She felt the thrill of its blackness: it drew her and she fell far too quickly towards it, but the cat jumped onto her shoulder and dug in his claws. That stopped her. She pulled away from the sinkhole of black water until she could see the whole town and the small pulsing flames of its lights far below. She went higher. The globe of the earth arranged itself into segments of colour. Her body felt hot and cold. She felt a sharp tug and she and the cat were in cold beyond cold.

"Do something!" she cried. "Help me!"

"Close your eyes," the cat said. She closed them, sobbing, sounding like a two-year-old, hating herself for it even if it were a dream. The cat gave a tart meow and with a bump they were back in the bed. It was daylight. The house creaked and stretched out its emptiness.

The phone rang from the kitchen. After the fourth ring, her mother's answering machine clicked in. "Cathreen?" It was Helena's thready voice. "You should be up. I hope you did your homework. Call me at work. I love you. Don't forget to eat breakfast and make a sandwich for your lunch. Let me know if you need a ride after school. Tink said he'd come and get you."

School. As if.

A hard ball of gum or glue was stuck in Cathreen's throat, making it difficult to swallow. Maybe she was coming down with something. She breathed in and out through her nose. The phone rang again.

"Cathreen? Please, if you're there, call right back. If you're not there, I want to know why." The answering machine clicked off.

Cathreen dressed and went into the kitchen. She plugged in the kettle, snipped open a sachet of instant hot chocolate and poured it into a cup. When the water boiled, she filled the cup and stirred the mix, and then she scooped the foam off the top with a spoon. She'd been going to make toast, but the first sip of hot chocolate made her gag. She dumped the rest down the sink.

A scurry of paws on the floor upstairs caught Cathreen's attention. Fuck. The cat was in her mother's bedroom. Helena would kill her. She'd start sneezing as soon as she went in there.

She was always complaining about the cat at Mrs. Hamilton's house, where she worked, and how her sinuses were raw because of it. Cathreen took the narrow stairs two at a time. The cat stood on Helena's bed with a mouse trapped between his paws. He let it go and scrambled after it off the bed, across the floor and round the open door of the closet. "All right, Tiger, do your stuff," Cathreen said. "Helena won't mind this time, it's in a good cause. I'll explain it to her, she'll understand." Cathreen swung the closet door open wide.

The cat leapt again and scattered Helena's neatly arranged collection of boots and shoes. There was a scuffle, then the cat emerged with the remnants of the mouse in his mouth and walked calmly out of the room.

Cathreen grabbed the flashlight from Helena's bedside table and shone it inside the closet. The plywood floor was streaked with blood; flecks of mouse fur speckled the shoes and plaster. She went into the bathroom for a bucket and cloth, shoved shoes and boots out of the way and started to scrub. When she'd done the floor, she took the cloth to the shoes, wiping them down and lining them up in what she hoped was Helena's order. One boot out of a pair—an ugly spike-heeled black leather construction that came up to Helena's knees—gave a papery crinkle at Cathreen's touch. Cathreen stuck her hand inside and fished. Well stuffed into the toe was an envelope.

She sat on the floor to examine it: it was addressed to her but it had been opened. Inside she found an air ticket, in her name, to London, some British money and a brief note and directions from her father.

"Dear Cat," the note read. "The ticket is good for a year. I don't have a phone so call and leave a message for me at the George and Dragon when you know when you're coming. If I can't meet you for any reason, take the bus to the village and go to the pub. They'll know where I am." The ticket had been issued two months earlier. Cathreen rocked back with shock. Helena hadn't said anything. She'd only shrugged her shoulders when Cathreen had asked why Jag had stopped writing. Cathreen would have wept, but she was too fucking mad.

In her room, she took her passport out of the drawer where it had remained ever since she'd made her mother help her apply for it after Jag had written to say he wanted her to come and visit. That had been months ago. She'd waited for him to send a ticket. She'd thought he'd forgotten all about her. She'd thought he didn't care. She put the passport with the ticket, money and a few clothes in a backpack and then went into the kitchen and removed Helena's new credit card from an envelope on the table. She'd only just got it. Cathreen signed it with Helena's name.

Helena had been sitting at the table with the lights off, her handbag, bus pass and mail in front of her in the moonlight, when Cathreen had come in a couple of nights back. Moonlight had whitened Helena's hands and glittered off a new ring. "You scared me," Cathreen had said. "I didn't think you'd be home." She opened the fridge behind her mother.

"You should have left me a note, Cathreen. I was worried."

"Sorry." She took a glass from the counter and poured juice into it.

"I called earlier and you didn't answer."

"Yeah, well, as you can see I was out. I go out sometimes. I have friends." She drank the juice and poured another one.

"We have an agreement. I let you know where I am and you do the same for me. It's called common courtesy."

"You don't have to tell me where you are. I know where you are, and I've a pretty good idea what you're doing."

Helena's thin face had crumpled. "That's not fair, Cathreen." She took a deep, steadying breath. "I know this has been hard on you, but life goes on, *my* life goes on. I've offered to stay here with you. Tink's asked you to stay at his place. We've been through this before. We're doing what you said you wanted. You said you wanted time to get used to the idea of me and Tink being together. Well, you've had some time. Now we're getting married, Cathreen. Tink's going to be your new father."

"I already have a father. I don't need another one. You've made your decisions, let me make mine. I don't want you hanging around just for me."

Helena sighed and twisted the new ring. There were bags under her eyes and her mouse blond hair was stringy. She wouldn't cut it because Tink liked it long. Fuck Tink, Cathreen had thought. Fuck you.

"I don't have to take the bus when I stay at Tink's. I can get to work faster. I've got more time to study. I don't get so tired."

"Yeah, you've said. Maybe a thousand times. You don't have to explain your life to me."

"Things are getting better, Cathreen. Mrs. Hamilton's given me a raise and asked me to start helping her catalogue her collection." She picked up an envelope from the stack of mail and waved it. "See?" She removed a card from the envelope and loosened it from the sticky strip that held it to a sheet of paper. "I even got my credit card back. I just have to sign it. The sky's the limit." Helena had beamed.

"Don't you know anything!" Cathreen had shouted. "How can you be so stupid! You have to pay it back, you know!" She'd run out of the kitchen and into her room. She'd lain on the bed, stomach heaving, eyes squeezed shut, half waiting for, half dreading her mother coming to talk to her. She'd waited for what seemed a long time. Nothing moved in the house, and then she could hear Helena's sad sighs as she did her rounds locking up for the night. She'd wondered why Helena bothered. They didn't have anything worth stealing.

She was lucky. There was room for her on a plane that afternoon. After making the reservation she called the number in Jag's letter and spoke to a woman at the George and Dragon. The woman said, "Just a minute, luv," and within seconds she was back with, "Here's your father, he's been filling in behind the bar." Jag was great; he didn't make her explain, he just asked where and when he should meet her. He sounded fantastic.

Before she left, she checked through the house to make sure the cat wasn't inside. It would have to find its way back to wherever it had come from. She couldn't take it with her. She put the food and fresh water dishes outside in the porch, just in case. "My mother's a bitch," she said out loud as she set the dishes down, "but maybe she'll feed you." She shut the door behind her but didn't lock it. She hoped somebody would break in: it would serve Helena right.

Mrs. Hamilton's house, where Helena worked, was on the way to the airport. Cathreen had the driver who'd picked her up hitchhiking drop her nearby. She waited until he was out of sight before walking up the drive. A meadow of gnarled Garry oak and then a stout hedge nearer the house masked the entrance. She climbed a short flight of stone steps and stood before a big black wooden door. As she thought about what she wanted to say to her mother, hesitating to knock before she had it right, she felt something shift in her pack and bump against her back. She set the pack on the ground and undid the flap. A grey paw with a white spot on it poked through the strings.

"What are you doing here?" she said as she let the cat out. It leapt instantly down the steps and raced round the back. Cathreen trailed after it. The house was stuccoed white, half-timbered, and bigger than Cathreen had realized the one time she'd come here with Tink to pick up her mother. That time, they'd waited in the front hall. Now, as she called to the cat and followed the flagged path to the back garden, she realized that the "cottage," as Helena called it, was at least three times the size of the little house in which she and Helena lived. What a waste. The old lady lived here by herself.

The cat was sitting on the back step. It turned and scratched at the door as she came up. "Come in, dear," Mrs. Hamilton said, smiling at her after she'd opened the door and picked up the cat. "I'll tell your mother you're here. She's just finishing something for me upstairs. Will you stay and have lunch?" Cathreen shook her head. "That's too bad." Mrs. Hamilton patted the cat and set it down. The cat padded away inside.

Cathreen stared. "Is he yours?"

"I hope he hasn't been bothering you," Mrs. Hamilton said. "His name is Cutthroat. I don't know what he gets up to half the time." She gestured Cathreen to a chair in the kitchen. "In any case, he seems to have his own friends." She left the room.

"You've a lot of explaining to do, Cutthroat," Cathreen said, watching the cat, splayed on a mat near the stove, groom himself. It *was* Cutthroat she'd remembered seeing Helena chase from her car that time she'd been here with Tink. He must have crept in again recently and come home with her.

Mrs. Hamilton poked her head round the corner. "My mother used to say that cat came with her, from England, in her baggage. He couldn't have, of course, but one of his ilk has always been with the family.

"Go on through into the living room, dear. Your mother knows you're here. She shouldn't be too long. You should find something in there to amuse you. I'm finally getting around to unpacking Mother's things."

The room Cathreen entered was long. It had tall windows, a brick fireplace and black beams dividing the high ceiling. Cathreen took a seat at a small desk and waited. The room was stuffed with furniture, rugs and heavily labelled travel trunks. Framed stained glass and paintings leaned against the walls. Also set against the walls, in between sculptures, tables, bureaus and chairs, were a number of free-standing glass-front cabinets. Most of these were full of objects, but several, with their doors open, were half empty: on the floor in front of these squatted sturdy cardboard boxes packed with newspaper-wrapped articles. As Cathreen looked around, examining the artwork, she noticed that there were zodiacs everywhere: a copper one hung in an alcove; a framed embroidery zodiac had its own wooden stand; there was a zodiac lampshade, and several ceramic zodiacs were set out on tables. Above the mantel hung a map of the heavens with the constellations of the zodiac outlined in silver. Helena had mentioned that Mrs. Hamilton had come from the same part of England as had Jag, and Cathreen felt a *frisson*—one of Jag's French words; he had lived, years ago, in Paris—when she saw on a zodiac map superimposed on a landscape the name of the village in which Jag had been born and was now living. She knew little about it, only what Jag had told her, but it was where he was now, and where he'd been when he'd sent her ticket. Jag used to recite a poem about the region around Glastonbury, his village: "To the valley of Avilion," she remembered, and something about there not being any clouds there.

After another twenty minutes or so of waiting, Cathreen had had enough. She could hear Helena laughing somewhere upstairs. How fucking long was she supposed to wait? Obviously, Helena didn't give a shit about her. Sudden, unsheddable tears brimmed in her eyes. She stood up, and let the chair clatter backwards. The cat shot out from behind a cabinet, stopped to regain its dignity, and groomed itself. She heard the front door open and shut, and the house went quiet.

A car door slammed. She went to the window when she heard an engine start up, and she saw the sleek black shape of Mrs. Hamilton's car escape down the driveway. She couldn't tell for sure how many people were in it, but she thought she caught a glimpse of Helena's dirty blond hair in the driver's seat. A stab of loneliness that quickly changed to anger made her stomach clench. Without thinking, she kicked at the wall, breaking off a small chunk of its plaster. Fuck them! Fuck them all!

The cat meowed. She saw it jump into one of the open cabinets. It caught her gaze, meowed again, jumped down and stood waiting. She shoved a chair aside with her arm and went over to have a look. On the shelves were heavy paperweights, vases and porcelain bowls; there were also a jade Buddha and several pretty pieces of jewellery arranged on velvet: one was a brooch in the shape of the head of a woman with hair made of snakes. She picked up the brooch and put it in her pocket. Again the cat meowed. It was standing before another one of the cases. A set of keys dangled from the lock and swung gently as if someone had left them there that minute. She turned the key and opened the cabinet. Inside were small carved ivory animals, several pieces of amber and a lump of crystal with an etching of a crouching tiger on it. As she reached for one of the intricately made animals, her hand knocked a rounded piece of green glass from its plastic stand. She touched it: it was smooth, almost warm feeling; when she handled it, it sat nicely in her palm. She lifted it to her eye and turned towards the light: she couldn't quite see through it, but it made the whole world look, somehow, like plants. She placed it in her pocket with the brooch, thought about it, and returned the brooch to where she had found it. She wasn't a thief. A piece of green glass, the kind of stone you'd find on the beach, didn't count as stealing. If there was a problem about it, or about a wall that could easily be fixed, Helena could go fuck herself.

The sky was grey and bleak, and the wind had shifted, banishing rain and bringing cold. At the rear of the long back garden, and up a set of steps leading to a field that stretched to the edge of the highway, was a tall spreading tree encircled by a low wall. Cathreen sat on the ledge with the tree between herself and the wind, and shivered, and puzzled over why she had bothered to come here at all. She wondered if Helena could lose her job when the loss of the little stone was discovered, and if she'd have to pay for the plaster repair. She decided she didn't care. It was Helena's fault anyway. Neither Helena nor her boyfriend, Tink—who had once been Jag's best friend, as she reminded herself often—had any real time for her: they were, in effect, forcing her to run away. "Assholes!" she yelled several times, as loudly as she could, but there was nobody to hear her and so she felt foolish and stopped.

She had opened her pack to check on her money when she heard cars drive up to the house and doors being opened and shut; she listened for the sound of her name being called, but there was only the churning of the wind in the tree's branches and the rustle of its sparse red leaves as they spun on their stems.

Cathreen glanced up as a gust of wind rippled through the branches and they dipped suddenly towards her: after a panic-stricken second she saw it was only the cat perched on the end of a limb that had made the twigs brush her face. It scrambled back up the trunk and eyed her.

When she looked round again, Tink was standing a few feet in front of her with his hands in his pockets. He wore clean clothes and a jean jacket, his nose and cheeks were reddened from the wind, a toothbrush stuck out of his breast pocket. He flashed his best smile.

"Hey, Cathreen, Helena's waiting," he said. "We're taking you out. Let's go."

Tink had short black hair that was going grey. He was stockily built, and muscular. He swayed from foot to foot—he was probably cold, but he'd always had trouble standing still. She'd known him since she was small; it was difficult to forget, sometimes, how much he'd once meant to her.

"Let her wait," she said, turning her face away. The cat slid down the tree and chased through the grass.

"C'mon, Cathreen, be nice. The old lady has given your mom the rest of the day off. I'm not busy and you don't look like you're doing much. Let's go spend some money. We'll get something to eat and cruise the mall."

"I've been waiting for her for hours," she said, still looking away from him. "She didn't hurry for me. She took off in the car."

"She came to get me—we were pouring cement. You can't reach me by phone when I'm on a job, you know that. She didn't know you were coming, but she's doing the best she can."

"You always say that," she said, glaring at him. "You always take her side." The cold had begun to hurt her skin. She rubbed her hands on her nose in an effort to warm it. A gleam of light broke through the cloud and polished a circle of the field, but it only emphasized the drabness around it—the thin grass, the grimy bushes, the tree at her back rattling its few leaves, virtually lifeless. She looked down at her feet. The grass had made them wet.

She heard Tink sigh. She put her sleeve to her mouth and blew; the warmth of her breath huffed back to her. She closed her eyes. "I found the ticket Jag sent me. Nobody told me about it."

Tink nodded. His eyes were puffy and sad. "We were going to tell you. Helena's a little worried about Jag. We thought it would be better if we all went over together. We've been saving up."

Her face jerked up. "Jag's fine, there's nothing wrong with him. Helena's just saying that because she's mad he doesn't love her anymore."

Tink's shoulders were hunched. "Your aunt Jen's husband, Colin, is dying, and I think Jag has some issues with that. There was a lot of trouble between them when he was young."

"Shut up! You just want to ruin things for me! All you care about is Helena! You'd say anything to make Jag look bad. He's my father!"

"We're all on his side, Cathreen, whatever you think." Tink tugged at his ear, his face wrinkled with distress.

"Don't bullshit me, Tink. You don't care about him anymore. You don't care about me, either. I'm just part of the package with Helena, and isn't that too bad? You wish I was out of the way. Helena made you come here, didn't she? You'd rather go out somewhere just with her."

"You're a good kid, Cathreen. Jag's lucky. I wish I had a kid that cared that much about me," Tink said. He dug in his pocket. "I almost forgot, I brought you a present." He held out a key chain;

attached to it were a small light, a compass and a whistle. He winked. "It's so I don't lose you."

When she didn't take it, he crouched down and snapped it onto the ring of her backpack zipper. "You never know, it might come in handy."

Tears came to her eyes again—couldn't she do anything but cry?—but she blinked them back and said, "You don't know anything about me, you don't know what I'm like."

A car horn beeped from beside the house. Tink swivelled his head to look. He turned back to her, his mouth pursed. "Maybe you're right. But I'm always here for you. If there's anything you need, just ask."

"I'd like you to go away now and leave me alone," she said. She was finding it hard to breathe.

"I had a pretty tough time as a kid, too, Cathreen." He examined his hands, which were scarred from construction work. "You know my mom was Native, my dad was white. Your mom understands what that's like up north. You don't fit in anywhere. But if you're lucky, you come through it, whatever it is. You find something inside yourself that won't let you go under. I want you to know that I'm rooting for you."

She couldn't speak for a few seconds and then she said, "Helena gave up on me a long time ago. That's why she's never at home. There's nothing anyone can do." She stood up. "I've got to go now. Tell Helena . . ." She bent and lifted her pack. "Tell Helena to have a nice afternoon."

Tink's compact figure rapidly shrank as he moved away down the steps and through the garden to wherever Helena was waiting for him. Cathreen was certain he'd already forgotten her. Her head ached. She glanced at her watch. She flipped through her wallet and counted the money she'd taken from the change jar in Helena's bedroom. She didn't need that much and when she got to England there was Jag's money. Once she started using the credit card, money wouldn't be a problem anyway. At least not for a while.

"Hey, Tink," she yelled after the figure that was almost out of sight, "I'm spending the night at Sharon's, okay?" He raised a hand in acknowledgement and walked on until she could no longer see him. He was out of her life forever, both he and her mother were. She broke off a twig from the tree and tucked it next to the green glass stone in her pocket—something to remind her of home. Then, with the pack on her back, she strode off across the field towards the highway.

Cutthroat

The flight attendants are in their cubbyholes reading ¡*Hola!* or sharing recipes or sex tips; you've had the chicken and the movie and you're wrapped up nicely in a blanket with your head resting on a pillow. I, in the meantime, have been jammed in—in the dark, with no food or water and little enough air—with T-shirts and underwear, a hairbrush, toothbrush and enough small implements of various types to make shish kebab. I hate airplanes—the noise, the dryness, the air swimming with viruses. My ears hurt; and I do think it was a waste to leave that much of your dinner.

It's time, now, Cathreen. You hold the green stone in your palm. So open your ears and your heart. Let's begin with bedtime stories to mend that frazzled brain of yours, or at least put something in it.

I climbed the tree of knowledge of good and evil in the Garden of

Eden and knocked down an apple for Eve. I ate the seeds in the core because I was hungry, and I licked dew from the leaves of the tree of life out of thirst.

I fled from Atlantis on the last ship.

I ate the heart of a Pharaoh after his death. I killed poisonous serpents.

I crossed the glacial ice of the Alps carrying three arrowheads and a small dagger in a leather pack on my back.

I sailed in King Solomon's ship, carrying treasure.

I licked sweat from the brows of the labourers at Stonehenge.

I was ship's cat in the tin trade with Joseph of Arimathea when he sailed west.

I was decked out in ribbons and flowers and tied to ears of corn in a field. I was placed under the last bundle of corn to be reaped and struck dead with flails.

I entered Jerusalem with Godfrey de Bouillon.

I was at Montségur.

I carried messages for Monmouth at Sedgemoor.

I slept with the sentries on the Plains of Abraham.

I escaped from the *Boston* at Nootka Sound.

I peered out of a tree at Alice.

I assisted Bligh Bond with his excavations.

I killed mice in the artillery tunnels at Naour.

But above all, I loved Jones.

To the island-valley of Avilion;
Where falls not hail, or rain, or any snow,
Nor ever wind blows loudly; but it lies
Deep-meadow'd, happy, fair with orchard-lawns
And bowery hollows crown'd with summer sea,
Where I will heal me of my grievous wound.

Tennyson,
Morte d'Arthur

Two

Jag

There are a number of ways you can wait for someone to die.

You can do it as if it didn't matter to you at all. You can pretend that every minute of the day isn't spent wishing you had the courage to thrust a knife through Colin Printer's black heart, as if there were anything else in life for you to do.

You can wake up in the morning and shove the nightmares back into their drawers and turn to the woman lying beside you and pretend that there is room in your heart for love.

You can allow yourself to remember one detail of what it was like to live in that house on the edge of the moor in the most beautiful spot in the world—before *he* was in it—just enough to fuel your hate, to get you through the next day.

You can think of nothing at all.

But in the end you make the only real choice you have and leave behind everything that keeps you sane so that you can get a little closer to the nightmare itself—it's what you know, you're on familiar ground, there won't be any more surprises.

Jag thought it was funny. Amazing what he'd let himself think. Astonishing how he'd dropped his guard since he'd learned that Colin had cancer. The kind you don't recover from. He jiggled his pack on his back so that the heavy boots wouldn't dig into his spine: he should have left all his gear behind, at the George and Dragon, to pick up later, but he'd thought this would be it, moving day. Colin had been dead for a week. Jag had collected the carton of ashes from the crematorium—he hadn't arranged a funeral, he wasn't a hypocrite—then he'd kept the appointment at the lawyer's office, expecting to have the keys to the house—Jen's house—handed over so that he could shift his stuff there and then. There wasn't any reason why not. It's not as if there were anybody else for it to go to—of Colin it could truly be said, he hadn't a friend in the world—and the house was Jag's, left to him by Jen; it had belonged to their parents before them. It was supposed to have been Colin's to live in only until he died. It simply hadn't occurred to Jag that Colin would have had the ability, while dying the death he deserved, to screw him out of it. Once the bad news had been delivered, he'd asked the lawyer if Colin had known he'd moved back to the village. The lawyer's eyes had skidded sideways. Maybe he was the jerk who'd let it slip. The lawyer was young, a scion of a scion of the old firm and didn't know fuckall. He'd have no idea how it had been.

Jag let his head fall back against the smooth bump of the sleeping bag tied to the top of the rucksack and looked up. The sky was marbled yellow and grey with smoke. The house, in front of him, was a similar colour, not warm, as he'd remembered, but fart yellow, like clay.

When he'd left the lawyer's office he'd walked straight up the high street and tossed the carton of ashes into the first available rubbish bin. He'd intended to strike out cross country until he met a main road and then flag down any bus that came along that was headed for a bigger town, and from there get to London, pick up Cathreen when she arrived and figure out what to do after that. But somehow he'd found that his shortcuts took him several streets over, so that he was passing the little stone cottage in which he'd been born. It sat in a hollow behind a low wall, with the moor pooled behind it. There were three chimneys, one at each gable end and the third at the back, above the kitchen. Two of the chimney pots were missing, several of the terra-cotta roof tiles had split off, one of the dormer windows was cracked, and the roses that Jen had planted to foam over the walls and trail under the eaves had grown wild, partly blocking the mullioned windows and the heavy plank front door.

Jag opened the little black iron gate and stepped into the yard. It was overrun with grass and weeds and strewn with broken glass, candy wrappers and plastic cups. Half a dozen torn-open black plastic bags of garbage, stacked on top of each other, leaked tea bags, beef bones and tin cans over what had once been Jen's front garden. Nobody had bothered to stop the newspaper or milk delivery: papers and bottles staggered from the front door along the walkway, reflecting the weeks of Colin's final illness. A neighbour would have done something—for anybody else.

Jag had come here before, of course, in the time he'd been waiting, but he'd never been as close as this. Even with Colin in the hospital he'd kept his distance. He'd stood by the little crabapple tree up the road, not so long that the neighbours would start wondering but long enough to imagine what it could be like to live here again. His mother and father had bought the house when they married; both he and Jen had been born in the big upstairs bedroom. His mother had died when he was born, and his father had stayed just long enough afterwards to get discouraged at his future prospects with two kids. He thought Jen had kept in touch with the old man for a while, but if there had been letters, he'd never read them. It was his house, his and Jen's. They'd done all right, they were getting by, looking after each other, heading for something better, until Colin moved in. Jag had thought, when Colin lay dying, that he was going to get a chance to roll back the years; he'd felt like a prisoner standing, unexpectedly, in front of an open window. He'd let himself dream. He'd decided which bedroom would be his and which Cathreen's when she came to stay with him; he'd even imagined another chance with Helena, a different Helena, of course, one who still loved him.

At the rear of the house, Jen's vegetable garden merged impercepti- bly with a field that belonged to a disused farm. At the far end of the field, a line of pollarded willows defined the edge of a rhyne. Beyond the rhyne were the wetlands, marshes, and drained land that ate up the rest of the landscape. He could feel the pull—that much remained the same—of these Levels, his old fallback and bolt-hole. He'd loved the loneliness out there, *his* ache undisturbed by the needs of others, the wildfowl—stirring, shaking and fluffing their feathers—his only company, the soft plash of their webbed feet as they entered shallow pools all there was for traffic. Some nights he'd stayed crouched in the withies in the cold rather than risk Colin's fists by coming in late: he'd felt secure within the barricade of their spiky moon-cast shadows, watching the marshfire that, in the early hours, before sunrise, rolled and jigged over the land. Nobody knew the things that he knew, had seen what he'd seen. Christ knew he'd never planned to leave it.

As Jag looked now, a solitary scruffy donkey chugged between the willows and stopped to tear up grass with its teeth. It lifted its head and brayed at him, making him grin. Jen had always liked donkeys. She'd kept one as long as he could remember until Colin had sold it. It was just as well, really—Colin would have killed it, worked it to death most likely.

Nearer the house, the remnants of Jen's hard work—the greenhouse, the small shed-roofed chicken house, the trough that had watered the donkey and the goat they'd kept for milk, the sum of the outbuildings and trellises and trees they'd laboured on throughout the seasons—were in ruins. A rusted, blackened incinerator slouched against the foundation of what had been a potting shed. The black earth, the good humus in which Jen had planted her crops, had been stripped away. Small pieces of flint and stone littered the surface of a thin, poor soil. Not even weeds grew in it. Jag kicked at the dirt and toed up charred wood and charred bones. It was an utter wasteland.

Heavy curtains had been drawn across the windows. Jag found, when he tried it, that the solid back door had been fitted with a deadbolt. He thought a minute, scouted around the periphery of the tumble-down sheds until he found a usable shovel and, glancing about to make sure no one was watching, shifted a pile of rotted lumber, broken furniture and bricks away from the house wall and began to dig.

The door to the coal cellar lay beneath a layer of earth and leaves threaded with pale roots. He scraped the entire covering away to reveal metal shutters; only one of these, when he tested them, was still snibbed from the inside. He lifted the other, cleared away cobwebs and dust, took a small torch from his pack, and lowered himself into the cavern.

The cellar was empty, but a coating of seasoned coal dust crackled under his feet as he probed his way with the light to the wooden slats of the bin. He climbed over them, located the door into the main part of the basement and tried the knob. The door was locked. Again, he took a minute to think, recalling each step of the process by which he'd fetched coal to feed the fires when he and Jen had lived here. There'd been a small sliding bolt at the upper edge of the door, on the outside, to keep it shut. Jag shone the light on the frame until he could see where the bolt passed into it. He took out his pocket knife, wiggled the blade through the crack and pried at the slender metal cylinder until he felt the bracket holding it give. Seconds later he was through the door and inside.

Once in, though, he could hardly wait to get out. The faint stench of dust, damp and mould with an underlying odour of rotting meat that he'd noticed right off on entering the coal cellar was now so strong that it made him gag. He dashed to the stairs, ran up them and shut the door behind him. He was in the kitchen. Rags had fallen from the frame when he'd opened the door, and he quickly stuffed them back into the cracks, then opened the window over the sink and took several deep breaths of fresh air. What was going on? The lawyer had told him that no one had been in the house since Colin had gone into hospital: it made sense that there'd be some smell of decay from food and garbage, but the stench downstairs was not from that, and it was clear, from the rags, that it had bothered Colin too.

When his stomach had settled enough to allow it, Jag began to examine the room. The remains of a small meal of breakfast cereal and tea sat on the kitchen table, but other than that, all was neat—the countertops clear, the sink empty and the cupboards tidily stacked with dishes and tins. Inside the fridge were milk, cheese, eggs, some pears gone soft, the remains of a roast wrapped up in plastic, half a bottle of white wine and something that looked like sweetbreads, greyish and swimming in a bowl of pink liquid. He closed the fridge door and continued his investigations.

On the floor in the front room, next to the television, was an arranged-by-date stack of magazines and newspapers. On the walls were photographs and certificates from Colin's school-teaching career. There wasn't anything in the room of himself or Jen—not that he'd really expected there would be, not out in the open. Not a picture or ornament or stick of furniture that Jag remembered remained. The arms of the new chairs and sofa were protected with plastic, the antimacassars laid over the backs of them were white and clean. Colin's slippers reposed, side by side, retaining his footprints in the fleece lining, next to a footstool.

Jag headed upstairs to the bedrooms. It was in one of these he'd last seen Jen, ill and distraught, her brown hair lank around a face bruised and swollen with weeping. He remembered his feeling of hopelessness, pushed down a surge of panic and made himself go to that room first. It was empty. All that remained in it was Jen's prized fitted carpet—the first she'd been able to afford—faded to a paler blue. Although the dust of the last weeks veiled the windowsills, it was clear that the room had been kept clean. No dustballs cloaked the corners, and the wallpaper had been scrubbed so often that the flocking had worn thin. Why had Colin bothered, unless it was an attempt to excise all memory of her—that she and Jag and Jen's child had ever been? Jag had a quick vision of Jen in her nightgown, kneeling on the bed, begging him to help her. He went back to the hallway.

Although he swung open the door, he could not make himself enter Colin's room. The very air across the threshold throbbed with pain and suffering. The bed was unmade, the sheets and pillows spotted with blood; unstoppered bottles of urine stood in brown and yellow ranks on the floor. There were stained cloths, clotted basins and containers of tablets on the two night tables, a list of telephone numbers taped beside the phone; the contents of the chest of drawers were strewn everywhere: Jag imagined Colin clawing through them to find his last clean clothing before the ambulance came. Still, behind the disarray caused by illness, he was aware of Colin's usual orderliness: furniture squared to the walls, no rugs or cushions, no comfortable chair, no pictures—nothing *extra*. Once again there was nothing to show that the house had been his and Jen's, none of the bits and pieces he'd half hoped might still be inside somewhere—no photographs, or Jen's stitchery, or her books, or her jewellery.

There remained only one other room in which he wanted to look, and that meant a return to the basement. The night that Jag had left, everything he'd owned in the world had been in his room: a few photographs of his parents, his model airplanes, collections of stamps and stones and coins, his books, his clothes, his *dreams*. Once, in the night, he'd awakened in that lowering basement to see lights, like the smallest of candles, moving through the air; he'd been filled with happiness for no other reason than that they were there. He'd known enough not to mention this to anyone, not even Jenny, but had imagined for a while that they were the fairies, once fallen angels, that Jen had talked about in her stories, and that they had singled him out for some reason.

Jag returned to the kitchen, and feeling depressed and not a little fearful that there, too, Colin might have cleared everything away, pulled out the wadding from around the door, held one of the cloths over his nose and went down.

Colin himself had framed in the room off the laundry area. The space was only about seven foot square. It had no windows. Jag had put his bed in it and squeezed in a desk. His clothes were hung on nails. He'd done his best by painting the walls white, but Jen had been appalled when she'd inspected it. "He can't stay here, it's like a prison cell!" she'd said to Colin. Colin had replied, with a smile, that it was important for a boy of Jag's age to have privacy. To Jag, on his own, he'd said, "Don't you come upstairs even to use the toilet, you little prick, you can use the sink down here." Jag had taken to using the coal-cellar door as his exit and entrance. He'd hardly seen Jen at all. Still, he'd had the feeling, after a few months, that Jen was about to descend and tell him Colin was leaving, that things were going to go back to how they'd been before. He'd heard them arguing, more than once, when he'd crept upstairs to get something out of the fridge, and when Colin had banned Jen's cat, a small stray female named Jones that Jag and Jen had brought back with them from a holiday, Jag had thought that would be the last straw—Jen loved her animals. She'd defend them, he'd thought, even if she wouldn't protect herself. Jag still thought it might have happened, Jen might have kicked Colin out, if it hadn't been for the pregnancy. When she'd told him about it, Jag hadn't said anything except, "That's great, Jen." Colin had beamed, then pointed at Jen's stomach. "That baby had better be a boy," he'd said to Jag, "he'll be a man, not a fucking pansy like you." Now, as Jag passed the wide stone laundry sink in which he'd had to both piss and brush his teeth, he felt the return of his adolescent sadness. Christ, how had he stood it?

The basement shelves where he had stored his books were filled with junk—bottles, nails, broken saws—nothing out of the ordinary in the detritus line, but peculiar, given Colin's habits. Even more so were the dozen or so orange garbage bags, stuffed full and tied and stacked against the walls. Two pairs of charred gloves and a bundle of blackened metal rods lay on a shelf nearby. Colin would have cleaned up, Jag thought, if he'd known he'd never return.

Jag pulled out the rags stuffed between door and door frame here, too, and opened the door to his old room; then he tried his best to control the spasm of retching that shook him at the full force of the smell inside. He kept one hand to the cloth pressed to his nostrils and with the other scrabbled for the light switch. He had to blink several times through the sudden brightness to believe what he saw. The floor was layered deep in dead cats. At a guess, there were well over a hundred corpses. Some of these were old, the flesh and fur dried to the bones; others, more recently dead, had been chewed to pieces: limbs were missing, stomachs had been torn out. Shit, entrails, eyes, tails strewed the surface. Bloody claw marks patterned the walls where the cats had tried to climb their way out of the maelstrom. Just in front of him, near the door, rose a pyramid of the dead animals; they had climbed on top of each other trying to reach something that dangled, just out of reach, on a string. The air stirred, the string quivered, the object twirled, reflecting light. Without thinking Jag reached for it, and as he did so he had the sensation that something squirmed in the pile below. His stomach heaved as he broke the small red stone from its cord and stuffed it into his pocket. He slammed the door behind him, hurried to the coal cellar and climbed out of the house.

It was still light outside, although the sky was bleeding pale. He stood and shook, then bent down and vomited into a dead bush at the side of the house. He wiped his face with the rag he still kept in his hand and, sickened all over again by the stench that clung to it, vomited once more. When he was done, he made his way to the broken-down wall of the tool shed, in the lee of which, while scouting for a spade, he had earlier spotted a can of paraffin. He unscrewed the lid, checked the contents, returned to the house and dashed the liquid over every part of the exterior he thought would burn. He soaked the rag in the dregs, stuffed it into the mostly empty container, smashed a window with a brick, set the rag on fire and threw the can into the house. He grabbed his pack and started to run. He heard the whoosh behind him as the paraffin caught and glanced back to see bright flames lace the window. He had to stop to vomit again. He wiped his mouth with a handful of weeds before staggering on down the field to the willows. When he reached them, he stripped off his clothes and jumped naked into the icy water of the rhyne. His feet slithered on the mud on the bottom, and he almost lost his balance, splashing and gulping in panic, for he couldn't swim. The water was unbelievably cold, but he made himself go right under, several times, trying to get clean.

When he had done what he could, and he was numbed to the bone, and he could hear the sirens of approaching fire engines, he climbed out, unpacked a set of clean clothes and put them on. The old ones, reeking of death, he left, after clearing out the pockets, and kicked them out of the way under some roots. Quickly he washed the stone. Seconds after he'd snatched it, he'd realized what it was—the one piece of jewellery that Jen had kept of their mother's. Jen had worn it on a chain around her neck. When he was little, she'd told him it had been taken from the Garden of Eden, and then a whole series of tales of its travels down through the ages in the company of a donkey, perhaps the same donkey that had carried Christ into Jerusalem. They weren't the kind of stories he heard in Sunday school, and he knew not to tell them to the minister when he arrived at the door with a carrier bag of used winter clothing from the Women's Institute. He'd loved the hidden world Jen had given him, a world in which a giant zodiac, a temple of the stars, was supposed to have been built in their part of Somerset more than four thousand years ago. It was laid out in a circle around the point where the pole star would have been. The zodiac was a plan of the stars, the figures of the constellations outlined by rivers and hills and old roadways: pilgrims had quested along the ancient road that still joined the constellations. She'd pointed it out from the Tor, the hill they used to climb. Their village lay within Aquarius, and he'd once found, for himself, Leo, the lion—it was the easiest to identify on a map—with a river forming its underside and its head and mane outlined by streams.

Jen's world. A world dead and gone.

Jag placed the pendant stone with the rest of his valuables in a pouch he wore around his waist. It was a travesty that Colin had ever touched it.

Jag walked towards the sunset. He needed to get as far away from the house as he could. He was sweating, and his heart was thumping the bejesus out of his ribs. The pack began to feel heavy, and he was terribly thirsty. He didn't want to risk drinking from the rhynes or ditches; they were stagnant and full of waste from the waterfowl and other creatures that swam in them. He kept hoping to come across a fast-running stream, but he knew how few of these there were: it had been many years since there'd been anything like a natural waterway here, the land had been so ditched and drained and dyked, and the rivers that had forked their way through marshland to the distant mountains had been tamed. He was walking on reclaimed soil.

Once—how long ago he didn't know—the sea had swept much farther inland, leaving only a few small islets, stranded in the shallows, for people to settle on. Since then, ages since, the sea had shrunk back and the land had risen. Here, on the resulting moor and farmland, there were few distinguishing features other than the long shadows of the willows or other small windbreaks, and the minor undulations people here called hills.

He rested for a while in the shelter of a hazel and spindle hedge, tasted glue in his dry mouth and watched a shelduck paddle sedately through the rushes lining a ditch. The duck quacked as its feet touched mud and it waddled out, lifting and fluffing its feathers. He was glad that Jen hadn't been alive to see what Colin had done to her home. Despair at the images that arose—the ruined garden, the emptiness of the rooms, the final desecration of his bedroom—overtook him. He held his head in his hands. The waiting and manoeuvring and especially the buildup of expectation at getting his home back had worn him out, and it had all been for nothing. More than that, he knew that even if what he'd found in the house were still discernible after the fire, there'd be some palatable explanation found for it. Nobody would consider it proof of the pure distilled malevolence that had been Colin Printer. It was a funny thing about evil: how people went deaf, dumb and blind in the face of it.

Jag stood up. He didn't want to be caught out in the open at night. The temperature could drop quite low by this time in the autumn. He'd have to find shelter. He had his sleeping bag and that would help, but he was thinking that he'd need to ditch his jacket because it had absorbed a strong whiff of the basement fetor and he wasn't sure how long he could put up with that. Sleeping rough without it, though, wouldn't be pleasant.

He'd hefted the pack onto his back and taken three or four steps when the pain struck. He struggled through a few deep breaths but the air caught under his ribs, and his lungs squeezed so hard that even shallow breaths were difficult: it was like something he'd swallowed was trying to punch its way out of him.

A single flat ray of sun flashed over the moor. In its gold he saw, ahead of him, the ditches, black mounds and stripped fields of a peat working. An excavator, its shovel buried in the earth where the operator had left it at quitting time, also turned to gold. He stumbled towards it, thinking that if he could make it that far and climb in, somebody would eventually find him. There was Cathreen to think about: she'd be well on her journey by now and he should be on his way to meet her, he'd intended to, and to have had a home to bring her to. He lurched past the area where the peat, cut into blocks, was stacked in rows and drying and he was crossing the field in which the machine had been working—the ground was suddenly more bog than earth, and his feet kept sinking—when one more step in the abruptly flat light as the ray of light vanished pitched him forward into a shallow pit. He lay on his back, his teeth banging together in shock, feeling the fright in his body shunt itself through the ramming pain of his heart. He thought he was going to die as blackness and nausea revolved behind his eyes, but gradually the pain eased; he felt better lying down, so he stayed that way for a minute and then struggled out of the straps of his backpack. Soon his breath was coming more easily.

He sat up. He was fine. There was nothing wrong with him but nerves. He'd been more upset by the visit to the house than he'd realized, that was all. And why not? Colin Printer had been a bogeyman first class. Finding something like that would shake up anybody. And burning the house down was final. There was no going back, no second thoughts. He wasn't sorry about it. The important thing was that Printer was dead. He couldn't hurt anyone or anything ever again.

A car coughed softly in the distance as it slouched along one of the few bleak roads that crossed the moor: some farmer heading out for the night, no doubt. There wouldn't be many cars, though, and he didn't think much of his chances now of getting one of them to stop—nobody liked picking up hikers on the Levels after dark. The place was old, you didn't want to stir it up. That's how people thought; people who weren't him, who didn't know the Levels and its moods like he did. He heard the distant bray of the moth-eaten beige donkey. The idea that it might have followed him from Jen's brought him comfort.

Jag dug in his pack for the torch. He snapped it on and found the chocolate, matches, extra sweater and sheet of plastic. He took off his jacket, rolled it into a ball and heaved it away. He put the sweater on, ate the chocolate and lit a cigarette. When he was finished smoking and he'd named as many of the stars as he could, he shook out the plastic and turned the torch on briefly again to see the best way to arrange it beneath him. Then he settled himself, in the sleeping bag, into his halt for the night.

He'd been asleep for some time when he jerked awake. He raised his watch to his eyes to check the time—4:00 a.m. As he did, and turned himself on his side, away from the ache in his hip, something in the peat beside him caught his attention. It reflected a soft starlight gleam. He stretched out his hand to it. It felt cool and smooth. He scratched at it with a fingernail and revealed a curve. He scraped a little more until he could see that it was a narrow metal band of some kind. He raised himself on his elbow and cleared away a little more earth and uncovered additional metal until it was plain that he had found at least part of a bracelet. He reached into the sleeping bag for the torch. The metal gleamed warmly. It was gold!

He sat right up and began to dig with both hands. In a very short time he had revealed not only the rest of the gold bracelet but a desiccated arm and hand. He scraped away peat furiously, certain he was about to find more treasure, until he could see most of a small male body. It lay partly on its side with the right arm — the one wearing the bracelet — bent beneath it. The torchlight revealed brown skin, tanned by the bog, and a smooth and well-preserved face. The man had had short reddish hair, and the stubble of a reddish beard was still perceptible over the chin. Wooden crooks had been driven just above the elbows and over each of his ankles to hold him down and stop him from floating to the once-marshy surface. Jag pulled out the pins and gently shifted the body onto its back. He knew what this was: a number of similar remains of men and women, sacrifices of some kind in ancient times, had turned up over the years in the peat workings. The bog acted like embalming fluid. He'd seen, in the local museum, as a boy, some of the artefacts found with them; simple copper or gold ornaments and figurines and other objects meant to accompany the dead on their soul-journeying; but this man had nothing else with him. Jag took the bracelet from the dried arm, polished it on his sleeve and slipped it on. Then he bent to examine the face. The creature looked like he'd been getting ready to say something. Jag noted the line on the neck where the throat had been cut. Poor bugger.

Jag glanced at his watch again: in a couple of hours it would be dawn. He needed to be on his way, hit the road and get on the first bus going anywhere. Sooner or later somebody — certainly the lawyer — would ask questions about the house fire and sooner or later they would think of him. He wasn't sure what to do about Cathreen, but she was a smart kid. Let her come to the village on her own, she had directions to the pub . . . and sort that out when he could. He gathered his things together and stared down in farewell at the bog man.

It was an impulse born of Jen's old tales, and maybe a lingering sense of compensation for the bracelet, that made him bend down, take Jen's stone from his waist pouch and place it in the ancient one's mouth. The mouth slowly clamped on his finger, and a groan rattled from the bog man's throat. Spikes of adrenaline bit Jag's skin. He dropped his pack. There was a definite stir of the rind-covered bones. Jag ran. His feet, as in a nightmare, were heavy and clumsy; they sank into the wet bog; he fell several times, tripped up by lumps of turf as he crossed the field in the dark. He traversed several fields, too terrified to look back, the hot breath of panic warm on his neck. When he came to a ditch he plunged through it, not caring how deep it was, flailing his way through the water. When he had to stop, because he couldn't get his breath, he didn't know how far he'd gone or how long he'd been running. He was removed enough by this time, though, to sense the first stir of a finger of doubt as to what he'd seen, and to feel a little foolish; but he had only a moment to consider this and to know that it was sunrise when he realized that the pain pinching his arms and groin had become an axe head battering his chest and stomach. He fell sprawling to the ground; into his nostrils came the field scents of meadowsweet and clover. He thought he glimpsed the narrow head of a fox, its incisors poised above a small mammal, less than a yard away, before lights exploded in his brain.

Jag awoke from his terrible sleep, ill and shivering. The pain squeezed like wringing hands, as if his chest were a wet shirt being twisted dry.

He fought the urge to struggle against it and lay as motionlessly as he could, forcing his breathing into a rhythmic pattern. He thought of nothing but the count of air entering into and being pressed from his lungs. After a while, he could see his panic, like a figure in a boat, rowing slowly away. His distress eased a little as the boat slipped farther over the sea. The pain still hooked into him, resolute in its mindless toil, but he had taken a step away from it.

He lay on a cot against a wall in a wooden hut. Faint grey light seeped through the cracks in a filthy, boarded-up window in the opposite wall and trickled over his bedding. He'd been covered with a dusty army blanket, a layer of newspapers and another ancient blanket on top of that. Bread, fruit, cheese, water, a note and a container of antibiotics in the name of Merry Wedmore—a name vaguely familiar—had been laid out on a rough table beside him. He took two of the pills and sank back, his nostrils charged with the odours of mice and mould. When he awoke again, it was dark. He took more pills, slept, and opened his eyes to light. This time his waist pouch of money and papers was also on the table. He sat up, checked the contents and found nothing missing, swallowed more pills, then swung his feet to the floor. The dizziness passed, but when he stood, he had to lean against the wall for a moment before he could totter across the dirty plank floor to the door.

The outdoor light, after the gloom of the interior, made him squint. Moorland, green and grey, flowed in a series of low east–west mounds from the pivot point of the hut. Jag eased himself round the back and glanced out at more moorland and what might have been a marsh, stubbled with scrub trees and bush, glinting in the distance. He pissed into the soil. A flake of sunshine sheared from the clouded sky and shattered in pieces over the ground, but by the time he had returned to bed, it was raining, drops spattering on the tin roof like frying fat. He ate a little before sleeping again. When he next awoke, he was ready to get up, and he knew where he was.

Stacked in a corner of the room were newspapers spanning a period of decades. Digging tools, notebooks, wrapped bones and other archaeological finds lay abandoned in boxes in the other two small rooms that made up the remainder of the structure. The back room held a desk and chair, a 1956 calendar and drawings of the site the archaeologists had been studying. Jag had visited the spot as a boy and been chased away after making a brief exploration of it. He remembered the not unpleasant oil scent of screws, drawing pins, broken pencils and fish tins. The project, begun in the first years of the last century, had closed down for good before he'd left home, the excavation of the dwelling places of the original inhabitants of the moor incomplete, the money and interest to do it gone, the archaeologists too old to carry on.

At the time he'd seen it, though, the excavation hut had been maintained in good repair, and was regularly checked on by a caretaker. Now, set as it was among the low mounds, and weathered to the colours of earth and sky, and clearly neglected, it seemed to Jag that few people were likely to remember the hut even existed. If the woman who had brought him here—the owner of the antibiotics— could be trusted, it might not be a bad place to hide until he regained his strength and decided what to do. As far as he could recall, Merry Wedmore was someone he'd served a drink to in the pub, whom he'd had a chat with once or twice from the other side of the bar. He was grateful to her. His good Samaritan had not returned with or sent the police. The criss-crossing of tire tracks in the soft soil outside showed that she'd checked on him several times, always driving away afterwards towards the main road south.

It took Jag hours to walk, crawl and drag himself back to the peat working. The initial strength he'd felt after eating another meal had quickly dissipated, and his fear had returned full force. He'd looked everywhere in the hut for the gold bracelet he'd remembered taking from the bog man. When it couldn't be found, he'd begun to wonder if the entire episode had been part of the lead up to his illness — a hallucination abetted by his experience in Colin's house. He'd decided it was important to check, and to retrieve his rucksack, but as he came to the place where he'd collapsed, and started to retrace the steps of his flight, the details of what he'd seen and heard that night returned to haunt him.

The excavator had been moved away from the soft ground where it had been stuck; more peat had been cut and stacked to dry, but the workers who had been there had left. Jag looked around carefully to ascertain his position and then moved cautiously to the edge of the shallow pit into which he had fallen. One side of it, where he'd scrambled his way out, had crumbled. Ignoring the claw still gripped under his ribs, he jumped down, but he knew, even before he started to dig with his hands, that both bog man and the gear Jag had abandoned were gone. He could see the depression where the man had lain, and small hillocks of peat where his covering had been brushed aside. Drag marks led from the pit side and crossed the tracks the excavator had made in the stripped ground. Jag followed them, wanting to believe that one of the workmen had found the body and had wiped out his own footprints moving it. But then he began to note bunched handprints on each side of the scraped soil and he came at length to the spot where it was evident, without doubt, that the creature had stood to his feet. His footprints — small, with the splayed toes of someone used to walking barefoot — continued until they merged with the grass. Oh, Jesus, he thought, oh, Christ, what have I done?

Three

Galt

I have been gone a long time, I have come from far away. Merry tells me that is why I am tired. She was sitting beside me when I awoke this afternoon in her house. She said that she had come upon me on the moor. She said that after she found me she took me to her car and brought me home. Her house is strange to me. It is long and narrow with thin, hard walls that shake when I hit them. She said that even though I couldn't recall my name, she thought I was an old friend of hers, Galt. I looked like he might have looked by now if things hadn't gone well. She looked sad and sighed. Galt had no luck, she said. She said that Galt — I — had been living in a caravan like hers when the police came. She said we hadn't done anything wrong except camp on somebody's land. She said the police had struck me on the head, I had staggered away and hadn't been seen since, although she and Charlie had looked for me. They'd wondered if a person reported as walking the motorways dragging a cross could have been me. She said I had always liked large gestures. When she said that, she showed me her teeth. I asked her what was a cross. She said I shouldn't worry about not remembering things or her; she said she'd never thought remembering counted for much. She said I had changed a great deal and she would have to get used to the new me. She sent pictures of Galt with her mind. Galt sat in the sunshine, outdoors, in a big chair. I decided to be Galt.

Merry is pretty. She told me so. She said that when you are pretty you can always get by. She said I should try and do something about my looks. She said I had let myself go and people who didn't know me might not understand about what had happened and be frightened of me. Merry has yellow hair that is dark where it grows from her head. Her skin is pale and although there are lines on it, she says she is not old. I asked her what had made the lines on her face and she told me, "Men." I asked her if that included me but she said, "No."

I sniffed at her skin. It smelled sweet. I sniffed my own—it is tighter and thinner and browner than hers—it smelled sour. I touched the blue cloth I was wearing and I remembered where it had come from. It was left for me by my Master. "Where is my Master?" I asked her.

"Master?" Her green eyes flinched like a rabbit's when it is startled. "You've not gone and joined a cult, now, have you, Galt?" She helped me sit up and she held a cup of hot liquid to my lips. I sipped, and the bitter taste of the drink surprised me. I remembered that hot drinks were pleasant. Honey was what I remembered.

"Are you hungry?" Merry said. I told her no. She took hold of my hand and I felt a feeling like warm water spill down my neck and into my groin. With her other hand she touched the scar on my throat.

"What happened here? You haven't done anything bad to yourself, have you, Galt? You've been a good boy?"

"What is good?" I said.

She narrowed her eyes. "I think you're taking the mickey. You shouldn't do that. I'm trying to help you."

"Help me," I said. I touched her throat and she leaned away.

"Phew!" she said. "If you're going to stay here while you get on your feet, you'll have to be clean. Take off your clothes and I'll wash them." I said nothing. I am not certain that it is right for her to touch my Master's things.

"I'm trying to be kind, Galt," Merry said.

She went a little ways away and did something and there were pictures behind a window. "Watch telly while I run your bath and start the laundry," she said. She lifted her arm to pat her yellow hair and I saw the bracelet on her wrist. Once it was my bracelet and then it was my Master's. She saw me look at the bracelet. "Like it?" she said.

"Where did you get it?"

"It was a present."

"What is a present?"

"It's when somebody gives you something because they want to please you."

Merry helped me keep a blanket around myself while I took off my Master's clothes. She showed me where to sit so I could see the telly. I heard water running. I watched telly. My mind began to fill with pictures—animals and a child and a mother and father, and then a house and beds and foods and machines. Everything came into my mind. I knew the names of everything. My groin hardened when a man and a woman touched each other. I wanted Merry to return. Men were fighting. I wanted my Master. I saw red gush behind my eyes. I stood and picked up a knife from the table where

Merry had left it in a bundle of dried flowers and grasses. Merry came back into the room and turned off the telly. The red behind my eyes faded. I sat down.

"You don't have to worry, Galt," Merry said, looking at the knife in my hand. "No one will hurt you here." I put the knife on the floor beside the chair. I closed my eyes: each time Merry spoke, colours brightened and flowed, and I remembered how, when I had been myself, not-Galt, animals would come to me and I knew them by their colours, and I didn't have to hunt them.

"Do you need the toilet?" Merry said.

I opened my eyes. "No," I said.

"Do you know what a toilet is?"

"Yes."

"Well, you must have to use the toilet. I don't care how long you've been living rough, I don't want you peeing all over my caravan like a dog."

I know what a dog is. I looked at Merry through small red flames.

"Don't look at me like that," she said. "Don't you know when I'm teasing? What's happened to your sense of humour, Galt?" She smiled and she came close and pinched her nose with her fingers. "We'd better get you into that bath," she said.

She took me into the bathroom and gave me soap and towels. She put a new razor blade in her razor and said I could shave with it. "Have a good long soak," she said, and she went out.

I got into the bath. I shampooed my hair and soaped my body as I had learned from telly. I ran fresh water in the tub and rinsed myself. I dried myself and then wrapped one of the towels around my waist, and with another towel I rubbed my hair dry. I took the razor and shaved my beard. I found Merry's deodorant and used it. I looked at myself in the mirror. I did not look like anyone on telly.

I am shorter and thinner than my Master, but I know that if I eat the food my Master put in my mouth, I will grow. My Master wants me to be bigger: that is why he gave me large clothes.

I opened the door. Merry was talking to someone on the telephone. She said, "I found him this afternoon. I don't know what happened. Yes, I think you should see him and tell me what you think." She saw me watching her and she put down the phone. "I called Charlie—you remember Charlie—he was at the pub," she said. "He's anxious to see you. He sends his best.

"Well, now! Look at you!" Merry said. "You're almost human!" She examined me with her eyes. I examined her with mine and I found that I could see inside her. I saw that her skin covered old bones. She was not young at all. I understood that she had lied to me. I remembered that I did not like lies. I let the thought show. Merry laughed at the look on my face. "You'd forgotten you could be this handsome, hadn't you!" she said, a hand to her mouth, and laughed some more. I remembered that a woman had left me to die in the bog, but I had eaten my Master's food and I was stronger than I had been, so I said, "I am not afraid of you."

"Afraid of me!" she cried. "So much for thanks. I've just saved your life! Winter's coming, you would have died of hypothermia if I hadn't found you—you were lucky I came by." She kept peering at me. "You must have been very frightened to stay in hiding so long." Her words were tender, but her eyes were not. Her eyes wanted to know more than I wished to say.

"My Master," I said. "I want to know where he is."

"Oh, yes, your Master," she said, smiling. She said, "Why don't you tell me about him?" She went away and came back with clean underwear, socks, a shirt and blue jeans from my Master's pack. I put them on. She cuffed up the shirt sleeves and pant legs. "You know you can only stay with me if you promise to behave," she said.

"I have to find my Master," I said.

"What's his name? Perhaps I can help you look?"

I nodded but I did not say anything more. I understood then that she had lied to me about the bracelet. It was not a present to her from my Master. She does not even know his name. She does not know me. Galt is not my real name.

"I am going," I said.

"We'll go for a walk together, get some fresh air. You shouldn't be out on your own yet. You're not well enough."

"If you come with me, I will kill you," I said. I picked up the knife I had left beside the chair. I went to the window. The light was fading. "Before I leave I will watch more telly," I said. I turned on the telly. Merry sat across from me and began to sort through a sack of dried flowers. She laid out yellow, blue and white piles. When she did this I could not see what she was thinking. She made a screen between us with her work and put her thoughts behind it. It was like looking into deep water: the thoughts were there, swimming, but I could not inspect them closely.

I watched telly until I was overflowing with words and pictures and colours. I turned it off. The words and pictures continued; I followed their stream. They came from wires that went into the wall. I looked out the window again: words and pictures travelled the country. There were more than I would need. Everything was in my mind. The sun had set. It was time to say goodbye. I put the knife to Merry's throat and kissed her. I put my tongue deep inside her mouth as I had learned. I opened the door. I closed it behind me.

Galt walked quickly away from the caravan until the noise of barking dogs had faded and the lights from the cluster of structures where

Merry lived were hidden by brush and trees. When he did look back, he could see only leaves and branches and the oak colour of the sky. The legs of his jeans were wet from the grass, and he had scratched his arm climbing over a barbed-wire fence near a power pole. He did not bleed as Merry had when he'd bitten her lip when he kissed her: nothing thin and red oozed where he had cut himself. The tear in his skin revealed brown tissue dry as earth. He touched the edges of the cut with his fingers and tried to press them together, but the wound continued to gape. He could still taste Merry's blood. He licked his tongue along his lips to remove it; many colours and pictures came, and at the same time he felt his bowels clench and the weakness that he dreaded return. He had to find a place to relieve himself. He needed someplace sheltered and safe to do it.

Galt crossed the field, his stomach cramping and his legs trembling. He came to a path and not far from it, a grove of beech trees. He thrust his way through bushes until he was within the cover of the trees. He squatted. A slice of silver moonlight touched the ground near him. He gazed at it and grunted, and tried not to think of all he had learned in the caravan, or of Merry, or of the black-haired woman who had taken him to the moor before killing him. Such thoughts disturbed him and he did not know what to do with his thoughts. A plug of stool released from his body; he wiped himself with leaves and stood up. The stone that he had felt his Master place in his mouth as he awoke rested in a nest of mucus and fluid between the roots of one of the trees. Galt found fresh leaves, scoured the stone with them as well as he could and went to find water in which to rinse it. His Master's intentions were clear: the stone was his sustenance and it had been clean when it entered his mouth. His Master wanted him to eat clean food. He did not know how long he could last without this nourishment, but he did not think it could be long.

The night was mild and dry. A wind, high up, had swept away the clouds, and in the moonlight it was simple to follow the path. It straggled ahead, worn smooth and raw by use. His feet knew the track, so he let them take him. Sometimes they stumbled where the path had changed, but his eyes recognized what he encountered, and gradually, as he continued slowly along, his brain began to anticipate what would come next: the slight rise of the trodden earth to trace the line of a hill, an open view to the north, the sudden heart-stopping glimpse, between hedgerows, of the breast and nipple shape of the Tor. He cut across tussocky grass to touch a dun-coloured donkey that brayed at him. Its pale coat was a shimmer of softness in the moonlight. He stretched out a hand to stroke its nose, and plucked a fistful of grass to feed it. The damp nibble of its mouth at his palm made him shiver, but the sheer solidity of it gave him strength, and once more he struck out, concentrating on keeping a flicker of light alive in his body.

Ten more minutes of sluggish walking took him to a thickly treed hollow. Anxiously, he stepped to the side of a plankway over the gully. A stream ran dully between fixed walls: he bent and washed the red stone and put it in his mouth. He cupped water to drink, swallowed the stone and sank to his knees to wait for revival. The stone was his life; it was a gift from his Master: but why had his Master had to leave him? When Galt had first opened his eyes, he had seen his Master's face, had felt their minds touch; then his Master had turned away. He would ask his Master about it when he found him.

Regaining the plank bridge, he retied the large shoes his Master had left for him, and adjusted the pack on his back. Mist crawled up the sides of the hollow. He inhaled, and discovered traces of smoke in the air.

Some time later he passed over a stile. A ram, its heavy balls swagging, traversed the path ahead of him. Galt was now near the source of the smoke and he could smell a man. A dog barked and he heard someone swear. A light sprang up on the little rise to his right, illuminating the interior of a small tent. The tent was secured by guy lines to several small trees.

"Who's out there?" a voice called from the tent. "Who's there?"

Galt cleared his throat. "It's me, Galt," he said.

"Galt?" There was a pause, then scuffling noises, as the tent flap lifted and a smallish, bearded face surrounded by long grey hair poked out. "Galt?" repeated the man, staring down at him. He was old, older than Merry. "Is it really you?"

Galt eased himself into the sphere of light, careful not to frighten the old one, then he leapt up the bank to the tent entrance. On the far side of the tent the embers of a wood fire glowed.

"Jesus!" cried the grey-beard, stumbling out of the tent in his underwear. "By god, it is you! Merry said so, but I hardly believed it. I thought you was dead! So the bastards didn't get you after all!"

Galt waited.

"Don't you remember me, lad? It's me, Charlie." Charlie moved close to him, a sour odour wafting from his body. "We was mates, you and me." Charlie burped and covered his mouth. He appeared to be embarrassed. "I'm an old gas bag now, you'd remember me different. I fell into bad company. I drank too much. I don't drink so much anymore except on nights like this when I got to keep warm." Charlie squinted into Galt's face, his red eyes watering. Galt heard a sound like thread breaking in short snaps. It was Charlie thinking. He could hear Charlie think that Galt certainly looked like Galt but that he seemed different, too. The old Galt had been heavier and with fairer skin. Galt heard Charlie's thoughts, and smiled. The thread stopped snapping.

"Charlie," said Galt. "Old friend. It has been a long time."

Charlie's digestion wasn't what it might have been, and the tent was constantly filled with warm farts. Galt didn't sleep. Not because of Charlie but because of the forces running through him. Energy coursed along his veins and sent out leaves. He was a tree with its branches in the sun, drinking in vitality.

An endless supply of pictures and dreams streamed through the air and rattled into him. At first, in the dark, and with Charlie snoring like an old bull, the images threatened to overwhelm him: he saw them, for an instant, as passengers on an infinite train. Face after face, place and incident, one upon the other pressed against glass. Flash and flash and flash. He was in their way, and Charlie's memories and dreams kept pushing at him too, but then he found that he could sort them: Charlie's here; his own there; a handful belonging to the person, Galt, that Charlie and Merry thought him to be; and others that had no origin known to him, in categories elsewhere. Many of these were of women. He scanned them to find which he liked especially. He kept coming back to one.

He had seen the girl on the television in Merry's caravan. Not only the red of her bathing suit, and her long legs, and full breasts bouncing as she ran had interested him but so had the set of her face. It was polished white and hard, a face drawn on porcelain, the eyebrows pencilled thin and high. The face, like the long blond hair, had been defined with cosmetics. But even so, the worm of her real self could be seen: it gazed from the deep shine of her eyeballs, it lay in the shadow of her nostrils and flicked its tongue through her puffed lips. He knew that he wanted to kill anything or anyone that hurt her.

The girl—Pam—ran along white sand carrying an orange rescue buoy. Her strong, smooth feet splashed into the sea, she dove through the waves to rescue drowning swimmers. Galt decided that once he had found his Master, he would look for her.

Galt slipped out of his sleeping bag. It was time to go. Charlie lay squished against the side of the tent, the whites of his eyes slick between half-open lids, his mouth open. Charlie had been kind; Charlie had treated him like a friend.

"Do you still whittle?" Charlie had asked him.

"I don't know," Galt had answered.

"You shouldn't have given it up. You were good."

"It was a long time ago."

"We were both younger then," Charlie had said. Galt didn't know how old he was supposed to be. He read pity in Charlie's eyes. "You've kept yourself in shape," Charlie said, patting his shoulder to reassure him. This had been a lie, but not the kind that bothered him.

Now, in the pre-dawn, he stopped, before leaving the shelter under the trees, to pick up a stick. As he walked, using the knife he'd brought from Merry's caravan, he began to carve.

He wasn't Galt, but after some hours, with the lapwings and plovers flying overhead, and to the whispering accompaniment of his breath, he found that he had shaped one of the swans he'd noticed, sailing a ditch, not long after he'd first awakened.

He walked until noon. Then he was tired with the fatigue that came when the stone was ready to pass from his body. His stomach cramped. He squatted where he was and pushed the stone out, anxious about its passage and the helplessness that would follow. He wiped the stone on the grass and looked around for water. A sheep grazed nearby. He followed it and came to a ditch, but the ditch was dry. When the sheep scrambled up the other side, he hadn't the endurance to trail after it. He sat in a patch of gorse. Why had his Master given him such a hard task? There were so many questions that only his Master could answer, but how was he to find him? He imagined his loneliness and sadness as a gargoyle fixed to his shoulder: he twisted his head to see it and found it there, grinning at him, a mirror image of his own face—lips stretched over broken teeth, eyes like raw meat, a sunken jaw, skin like burned plastic. He observed himself etched on his retinas as his eyes rolled up, and he fell.

Tock, tock, tock. Somebody was chopping wood. The hewing stopped and a shape stood over him. It murmured concern, it brought water in a bottle and held it to his lips. Galt moved his hand, as difficult an action as when, after he'd first been laid in the bog, he had willed himself to blink to show that he was still alive. They had seen his lids quiver. They had pinned him down with wooden stakes.

"What have you got there?" a boy said, touching his hand. Galt could see very little, a leaden film had dropped over the world, but he could tell the fellow was young by his voice. The boy opened Galt's fingers; the smell of excrement rose, warm and rank, but the boy didn't pull back. He poured some of the water from the bottle over Galt's hand to clean it. "You'll be all right, but I can't move you by myself. I'll have to get help. I'll be back as soon as I can." He spread his jacket over Galt, poured a little water into Galt's mouth and left the bottle on the ground.

With the boy gone, the hand holding the wet stone made its way with excruciating slowness to Galt's mouth. The thumb first, still stained, and then the palm, the claw-fingers clenched in terror at the possibility of a slip. The stone dropped into Galt's mouth. He could not swallow, his muscles could not manage that, but he could move his tongue just a little along the facets.

The boy, whose name is Nick, has built a house out of poles and canvas. He and Charlie, whom he found to help him, have moved me inside it. I rest on blankets, still weak because I cannot swallow the stone. "It's Galt," Charlie says to Nick. "You won't know him, he was here before your time, but I run into him last night. He took off this morning. I went after him because he's not quite right yet." Charlie taps his temple. "The police beat him up bad." Nick holds out a cup of soup. Charlie raises my head. I sip, and as I do, at last I swallow the stone.

"I heard you was out here," Charlie says. Nick nods. "You need any help?"

"Yes," Nick says. "Is that an offer?" Nick is handsome and dark-haired like a boy on telly. His clothes—a tweed jacket, olive trousers and a polo shirt—are not like Charlie's clothes. He does not speak like Charlie, either.

"I heard you had some trouble back there with some of those hippies," Charlie says.

"You mean the travellers? Who said that?" Nick takes the soup cup from me.

"You know how people talk. Some folks think you were a fool to let them on your land in the first place. You can't trust 'em—they ain't travellers like travellers used to be."

"I don't care what they think," Nick says. He puts the cup down and goes outside. In a minute, Charlie and I hear the sound of wood chopping. Tock. Tock.

"Now, Galt, old son," Charlie says, "here's what I think. I think you and me can go to work for Nick here and see ourselves through the winter and maybe longer. We could do a lot worse. I ain't goin' back to that bedsit, that's certain. The tent's fine for summer, but I don't know about you, I feel the cold in my bones. This way we'll be warm and fed and maybe make somethin' for ourselves, too."

"What will we do?"

"Nick's a gentleman, and at some point he's had money. He's got big dreams. He thinks he knows how to put the world to rights and I'm not saying he doesn't, neither. But we stick with him, do our bit for this old planet, and fill our bellies. What do you say?"

"What about the trouble?"

"You won't hear me say a word against travelling people—I'm as close to them as a man can be without being one hisself—we was with them, you and me and Merry, that time, weren't we—but they shouldn't have chased him off his own property, not after all he done for them."

"The police beat them. They hurt their women and children. They murdered Galt."

"For Christ's sake, Galt," Charlie says, looking at me disgustedly, "if you want to work for Nick you got to pull yourself together. I'm trying to tell you what you need to know. Nick took in that useless bunch of hangers-on for nothing. The real travellers moved on. What he didn't want to talk about was the fact that those hippies asked him to get off his own land! He brought in a sheep or two for the wool and they said he couldn't, the sheep would ruin their gardens. It's not like they was paying rent or nothing. He said, 'Don't I own the field?' and they got mad. So he told them he didn't want to be anybody's land-lord and if that was how they thought of him they could buy the land from him, bit by bit, with whatever they could pay. So that's what they're doing, and Nick's had to start over out here. Nick doesn't want to be in charge of anyone, he says, but he still likes to get his own way. That's fine with me when he's paying the bills." Charlie opens the canvas flap and I see Nick's jacket flitting between trees as he walks into a thicker part of the woods. He swings the axe at his side.

"This here wood, for instance," Charlie says, letting the canvas drop and coming to sit beside me, "it's called Summerwood, and it's Nick's now. He bought it and the land around it to stop them from cutting down the old trees. Some of them oaks is three hundred years old! Nick heard about the chainsaws startin' in and jumped in his car, drove up and bought it out from under them."

"He bought the wood to save the trees?"

"He did. Now he's going to start a little group of people living here, thinning the old forest and planting new trees, the old way. Coppicing. I heard he just bought a steam mill."

"He's going to cut down the oaks?"

"No, you dumb bastard, he's going to farm trees between the fields and leave the old woods alone, and you and I are going to live here and help him."

I know I am not Galt, I was never Galt, but I can remember him. Galt sits in the sunshine outdoors in a big soft chair. White stuffing oozes from its arms. A cat lies on his feet. A baby in a pram watches him. He is making the baby a toy with his knife. The baby's mother is brewing tea on a fire. Behind him is the caravan where he lives. He stays there with the mother and baby in return for work. He cuts their wood. He hauls water in plastic jugs from the village, hitchhiking in and out every day. The baby's mother trims his hair and helps him shave. She tells him to wash at the petrol station when he goes to the village. She cooks rice and beans, and greens that she collects from the fields. At night she plays the guitar, and the baby and Galt listen. Galt has carved a whistle out of hazelwood. He gives it a blow. Its note is agreeable. He has finished forming the toy. The sun soaks through his long, thick hair and beard. He is happy.

I know I am not Galt, but I watch him get to his feet. He is thinking about his good spirits and that the day will go on like this. He takes the toy to the baby. The baby's eyes are the colour of the bottom of a clear river. They grow larger until they are the mirrors in which Galt sees men in blue overalls, wearing white helmets and carrying black plastic shields, run through the camp. They smash the windows in the caravan. People Galt knows run to hide in the hedges. The mother snatches up the baby and flees, trailing her skirt through the fire: water from the tea kettle splashes the embers. Smoke and steam tower in front of Galt's eyes, but not so much that he doesn't see one of the policemen grab the woman carrying the baby and smash his truncheon into the back of her skull. I, who am not Galt but remember him, see a film of red as the police crash their way into his home. Dishes, clothes and bedding are hurled out the doorway. Children have run inside there to hide.

I, Galt, run through the doorway, screaming. My arms are in front of me trying to reach the children. I hear shrieking. Fire has snaked across the grass and crept into the caravan. I, Galt, know what will happen if the fire reaches the paraffin stove. I find the children and pull them free, although something is striking my head and shoulders, like thick black bees that I do not really feel until I am lying, on my face, on top of the children to save them. I, not Galt, see the blow that crushes the back of Galt's skull, see the police surge on, trampling the woman and baby. I record them not care what happens to the children and the fire and the oil stoves, to the just-finished toy, to the grass thickening with blood. I see this and I lift my arms to stop them.

I am lying in bed. It is morning. Nick is already up and has gone outside. Charlie has put the coffee on and he's out too. When he returns, I'll get up and we'll load boards to take into the village to sell. Last night Nick said Merry was coming to join us. Nick said that Merry was his friend and she was tired of living alone just now. He said he wants women and children to live here, as well as men, and that Merry was a start in the right direction. I asked him, "Why her and not Pam?" He asked me who Pam was and where she was living now, but I didn't know how to answer him.

I have been thinking about Pam, with me, at Summerwood, but I do not know if she would care to live among trees. When I have found her, I will ask. I am almost strong enough to begin my search for my Master. Master first, then Pam. Charlie said to me, "Galt, son, you get bigger every day!" He said it and laughed, but I am not certain that the change in my size pleases him. Most people do not change; they stay the same. My Master's clothes fit me perfectly now: this is how I know it will soon be time to go and look for him.

I am thinking about Pam and waiting for Charlie to return and bring me a cup of coffee. Charlie has started to say, each morning, "You should be bringing me breakfast in bed, you're the young'un." But when the heavy blanket we have hung over the willow-frame doorway is pushed aside, it is Merry who comes in. She strides all the

79

way to the middle of the bender on a wave of cold, damp air. Her hair is wet and tangled. She sets down a sleeping bag and several plastic bags with her belongings slipping out of them and takes off her boots and jacket. She glances over at me in the bed. "Where are Nick and Charlie?" she says. I tell her, and she picks up the coffee pot and pours herself a cup, and then she sits down beside me.

"Hey, how're you doing, Galt?" she asks. Her bones are old and small and light. She is like a little pale bird perched on the edge of the box my mattress lies in. "Listen, Galt," she says, "we got off on the wrong foot a while ago. If we're going to be working together now, like Nick wants us to, we've got to like each other like we used to. Charlie says you're feeling better. He says that maybe what happened at my house was because you were ill. People have been cruel to you, you've suffered and you're angry. I was trying to help, but I think you misunderstood. The last thing I want is to get in your way. I don't need you to say you're sorry, but I do need to know that you will never ever frighten me like that again. Agreed?"

Merry smiles. Her teeth are small, like drops of milk. I show her my teeth. They have become strong and white like my Master's. "Please don't think I do this all the time," she says, peering into my eyes, still smiling, "but sometimes it can help." She raises her arms and pulls her sweater over her head. Her skin stipples with cold like a chicken's. Her breasts are small dipped cones. I touch them. They are as cold as I imagined. I put one in my mouth. I suck the nipple. Then Merry turns back the blanket and climbs in beside me, and as she does, I hear the bracelet that she stole from my Master clink against the bedframe. It makes the sound of an oarlock as the oars are fitted in. Merry slides herself along my body and I reach down to feel her. "Where is my Master?" I ask.

"Shit, Galt, you're not still into that?" she says. I put my fingers into her. "Slow down," she says, but she has not answered my question.

"If you don't tell me where he is, I will kill you," I say. I thrust my hand into her as hard as I can, and Merry screams.

Charlie runs inside, yelling. He hits me on the head and back. "Christ, Galt, let her go!" I can feel the stone slipping through my bowels. I take the bracelet from her wrist and I let her go. She crawls off the bed. Charlie holds her. She is crying. There is blood on her thighs.

"Tell me where my Master is," I say to her. My belly catches; I will have to hurry.

"I don't know what he's talking about," Merry says, sobbing against Charlie's shoulder. But I know that she is lying.

"Bring me my coffee," I say to Charlie. I will need the coffee to clean and swallow the stone once it comes.

"Bugger you, old son," Charlie says, and I know he is no longer my friend.

Four

Nick

Nick was born rich. He didn't have to lift a finger. If there was dust, Nick didn't have to see it. Somebody else whisked it away. His mother had travelled the world digging up bones and pottery shards and thinking about the Bering Strait land bridge and who might have crossed it. His father, a sailor, had slowly sectioned the Mediterranean Sea in his yacht. When the father fell off the back of the boat in the middle of the night and drowned, Nick's mother claimed to have known the moment it happened and to have seen her husband's body lifted and held, turn and turn about, by porpoises. Soon after, she had gone into the hospital with cancer, and died.

When she was alive, his mother had remarked that they were a great family for travelling. Between the pages of their letters you could find wildflowers from the Arctic to the Falkland Islands. Nick's great-grandfather had built railways in Canada, married a Native woman and brought her back to a short life of coughing in a country house. Nick's parents had met in South America; they'd returned there one year for the express purpose of conceiving Nick. "One of us should be a poet," Nick's mother used to say, but none of them were.

Nick's sister, Ann, had turned out to be good at business. She ran an art gallery and then a used bookstore and when she grew bored with the bookshop, she let Nick—right out of school—step in to look after it. The bookstore commanded a corner not far from a tube station on a busy street. Fast-food restaurants jammed together around it, but not far away, across the street, stood a set of houses with neat front gardens and parents shepherding their children through traffic in front of them. Nick lived in a flat above the shop: he adored overseeing worlds from his window, but he found, after a while, that living above two floors and a basement of books disturbed his sleep. The basement shelved law texts, the occult and biographies of missionaries; the main floor sheltered out-of-print fiction, and poetry with its pages uncut. Current fiction in all genres, and ancient history, overran the second floor. In the daytime, when he was busy with customers' requests, Nick enjoyed the sense of controlling a universe of thought within his small building; at night, though, he could hear all the busy, clamorous voices of books, weary of never being listened to, insisting on his attention. He felt it as a miasma, spreading like rising damp; it affected his skin with mysterious rashes; he feared the impossible demands of the unheard.

His sister, checking up on him, spoke to staff and customers behind his back, undermined his authority and elicited a slew of minor complaints. Sensing weakness, perhaps, Ann began to quarrel over the contents of their mother's will. Nick's inheritance of their mother's jewellery, in particular, rankled. What was Nick going to do with it? Nick thought he might sell it.

Not long after, somebody broke into his flat and squeezed toothpaste over the toilet seat. The tires on his car were slashed; his telephone rang at odd hours of the day and night. Nick believed he was being followed. Even after the dispute with his sister was settled in a solicitor's office, and Ann had left town to look after her overseas interests, so many other things went badly in Nick's life that it was clear that forces even greater than his sister wished him harm. In this fragile state he left messages for his friends saying that he was the president of the United States and had done a great wrong. Guilt and depression nearly obliterated him. But over time, and with help— not from the doctor his sister had arranged for him but from an old family friend who worked with the dying—he understood that the illness wasn't personal, it wasn't him. It was a response, like an allergy, to his milieu. Traffic jams, polluted air and water, motor vehicle accidents, senseless violence, slaughterhouses, stock exchanges, shops selling worthless goods as if they were valuable, even the daily, meaningless shuffle of parents and children back and forth across the road—these things made people crazy. Nick had to get out.

He retired to his mother's house in the country. No one had lived there for months. The windows were boarded up, it was no longer supplied with electricity or running water and damp scrolled its shopping lists over the walls, but the decrepitude and isolation suited Nick. He began to feel better. When his sister, on her return from abroad, got wind of his living arrangements and came to see how things were for herself, she said, "That's it. You're out. I'm selling the place before it's worthless."

Soon thereafter, Nick was homeless and with no particular desire to be anywhere. His share of the money from the sale of the property sat in his pocket while he cadged rooms from friends who quickly tired of him. They were investing in the market, looking forward to pressing lawsuits or seeing patients at intervals of fifteen minutes— getting on with their lives. There were only so many times they could reminisce about school. Nick began to wish he *were* still at school. There, as long as he hadn't minded running naked over the moor in the early mornings, winter and summer, and finishing with a cold plunge, as long as he was never last on a climb up a hill so that he could be stabbed in the rear end with a compass until he bled, as long as he disregarded the beatings and wasn't certain about the video camera one of the masters used to film the naked boys in the showers, he enjoyed a kind of freedom: that is, he could believe his enslavement to be temporary. Now he wasn't so sure: the world wasn't what he'd been led to believe it would be, and nobody appeared to think he was vital to it, and what he'd seen of the world, so far, had little good in it. He wasn't so unusual, the family friend, whom Nick went to see again, counselled. Many young men had breakdowns in the year or so after they were first out on their own. Call it a period of adjustment. All he had to do, the friend assured him, was to keep himself physically fit and make himself useful until his niche, whatever it might be, made itself apparent.

Once into an exercise regimen, and rehabilitated with oxygen, Nick searched out a tumbledown farmhouse, bought it and began to renovate. Along with the house came outbuildings and two large fields. While he was still learning the rudiments of carpentry, reading up on small animal husbandry and thinking about what he might do with the land, a troupe of travellers encamped in the pasture. Nick went out to meet them wearing his tie and jacket. Several of the men tugged at their forelocks, called him squire, and then laughed so uproariously that he couldn't help but join in with them. He thought they were marvellous. They didn't keep fixed hours. They didn't have regular jobs. Their clothes consisted of layers of colourful castoffs. The women carried babies in their arms or on their backs all day long. They cooked and sewed, gathered wild plants, doctored themselves and their children and immediately started gardens. The men played guitar or cards, drank beer and smoked marijuana; they rebuilt the engines on their elderly vehicles, they acted as vets to their horses and engaged in a constant swirl of buying-and-selling activity. Once he knew them a little, they told him how they had been chased from their settlement by the police and had moved on, only to be driven out of a series of villages, their children bullied when they tried to attend school, their dogs lured away and shot. They were grateful to Nick for his tolerance.

Soon temporary dwellings seeded the fields, and every room of the farmhouse slept several persons.

Nick put windows, a loft and a stove in the barn and spent the winter there shivering.

In the spring he found that more permanent shelters had sprung up over his land, and there were now a cow, chickens and a piggery. Several women came to Nick to ask him for a loan with which to start a business selling knitted and woven garments and jewellery to passing tourists. Nick gave them the money and approved of their industry. Everyone was happy: the travellers had a home and Nick—at least vicariously—had acquired a sense of purpose. But the fields were churned-up mudholes when it rained and dust bowls when it didn't. Garbage lay in deepening, widening pools, and the stink from the cesspit at the edge of the wood offended the neighbours and frightened them with the prospect of disease.

One day, while driving to a meeting of the local council to respond to his neighbours' complaints, Nick found himself crossly considering what was offensive to him about *their* houses and *their* farmland. He noted that the older buildings he was passing blended into the landscape—they were constructed of local stone, timber, clay and thatch—and that the shapes of the ancient cottages, barns and mills had soft lines, they inclined or wavered, they were at home within their setting of hills or foliage. His neighbours, on the other hand, built their farmhouses and outbuildings out of foreign materials and with rigid outlines; they incorporated mechanical tiling and machined window frames into them. The overall lines of buildings, roads and lawns were obtrusive and overwhelmed the view: you noticed them and not where you were. What if, he wondered, you fashioned an entire community from local materials, and made it small, unobtrusive and temporary—you'd construct it so it could be moved every five years or ten years and allow the land to regenerate; and what if you planned that community to protect wildlife and consume the minimum of non-renewable resources, and linked it to an enterprise that would generate an environmental benefit? Wouldn't that be better than his neighbours' practices of erecting the massive dairy barns and crowded batteries of agribusiness that spewed tons of fertilizers, pesticides, hormones and antibiotics into the water system and atmosphere?

It was suddenly, absurdly, so blindingly obvious what had to be done. Not only were these massive farms hideous and harmful but they employed few people. The countryside had once *benefited* from people like the travellers: they had *fitted into* the old agricultural cycles as fruit pickers, coppice workers and foresters. Nick recalled that during the Black Death of 1348, the poor, alienated and frightened had abandoned the cities; they had made their livelihoods in the countryside from casual work and subsistence production based on access to commonland. On the commons they had found berries, mushrooms, nuts and herbs to eat and marketable goods such as firewood, bark, furze, bracken, reeds, hazelrods, fishing bait and songbirds to sell. They'd been able to set up their cottages provided they could prove they'd resided on the commonland for forty days or more; and they could turn out a cow on the commonland for grazing. Land poor, they still had gardens, yards with stalls or sheds for pigs and poultry or even a couple of sheep or a horse. They consumed little of what they could not produce themselves; they led, for the most part, harmless, useful lives.

Nick stopped the car and began to write down his ideas. What was wrong with what he saw happening around him was that the countryside was being turned into a replica of the industrial wasteland and suburban and urban dystopia he had fled from. He would not stand by and see it happen: over his dead body. Quickly, he drew up a complete program. Nick had been to a very good school.

The manifesto began, "I will plant over twenty trees per acre. I will cooperate with my neighbours over transport, infrastructure, power generation, water disposal, water and commonland. I will build without additional connection to mains water, electricity, sewerage or road systems." He'd started to read it out to the travellers as they sat or stood in front of their dwellings. He'd got no further than the first few sentences when one of the men stepped forward and said, "What's this about a sheep, then?"

"Pardon me?" Nick said.

"You've brought a sheep in without asking."

A woman whose knitting business he'd supported said, "You haven't considered the gardens. It's our work that's gone into them.

What right do you have to bring in a fucking sheep to rip them up, without asking?"

"There's the wool," Nick said cautiously. He caught himself and added strongly, "Well, it is my land."

For the first time since the yacht accident, Nick dreamed of his father. The old man called to Nick from the bottom of the sea. His bones were perfectly preserved. The voice, spiralling through the jaw and eye sockets, setting off spritzers of bubbles, confessed to infidelity, embezzlement and stock fraud. It insisted on forgiveness of its neglect of Nick and his sister. It harangued against Nick's mother in terms that Nick found odious and hurtful: there was no way that Nick could convince the voice that his mother was dead. Night after night the visitations persisted. Nick sweated and shouted in his narrow foam bed in the barn loft and woke up one night to find the police at the door. A neighbour had telephoned suspecting murder. "This is my home, I have to live here," Nick told the phantom of his father when it next appeared. The bitter, nagging voice replied, "I don't live anywhere, why should you?"

In the end, it was as much in hope of ending the dreams as his dislike of being surrounded by hostile people calling him Sir that Nick went to a solicitor to have an agreement drawn up.

The travellers, travelling no longer, would pay him for the land with what they could afford, beginning with five pounds per week. There was a parting of the ways. Nick was banished from the land to a room over the village pub.

He was afflicted with dreams again, but they had changed. His father had settled to the seabed, encrusted with diatoms; whatever was left of him was part of the food chain; there was no more question of a voice; it was a question of the Oneness of God. He dreamed soundless reveries of striking colours and abstract shapes and of a sensation of being suspended in a web, although whether he was spider or fly, he could not tell. For a brief period, infuriating to all who knew him, he imagined he *was* God, and he went about smiling and dispensing blessings.

While searching for the right place to begin his community—a refuge, a secure and affordable place to live, safe for children, where he and like-minded others could tend a garden and keep a few animals and be independent—Nick came upon, in the library, a photographic aerial survey made of the region by the Luftwaffe, when Germany was preparing to invade Britain, in 1940. On it were recorded every tree, hedge, bush, path and pond in the land. Nick took the photos and ordinance survey maps covering his locale to a café, where he spread them over a table. There were still, he saw, vast sweeps of wood, farm and moor in the type of countryside he was interested in, places where there could be plenty of short-term work for the kind of individuals who would join him. They would be a flexible workforce, available, while they were getting started on their path to self-sufficiency, to those who needed help maintaining walls, hedges and ditches, thinning and coppicing woods, cutting reed beds, repairing towpaths, controlling rabbits and squirrels, keeping up the water meadows, shearing sheep, operating tractors, collecting firewood and materials for Christmas decorations; and there would be new work soon in conservation and tourism and the recycling of scrap and other salvageable materials. It would not matter, since they would own land that could provide sustenance and would not have to include the costs of development rights, that such work was poorly paid: it would be enough for them. Certainly it would be better than the life led by the unemployed workers stored in council houses on the edges of villages, who depended not on a pig or a cow but on income support and housing benefit, and who spent their days watching television.

Merry, whom Nick knew from the pub and from her occasional visits to the people who had taken over his land, had come in with new dried-flower arrangements for the café tables, and glanced down at the litter of papers arrayed in front of him. "I suppose you know about the zodiac," she said. She pointed out to him, on both photographs and maps, a circle of gigantic zodiacal figures delineated by rivers, roads and hills. According to this ancient version of the map of the heavens reproduced on land and known as a "temple of the stars," Merry lived within the wing of the dove that was Libra, and Nick's former land was squeezed between Leo and Virgo. "No wonder there was conflict!" she said. Nick was intrigued. All he knew of local history centred on the English Civil War. He remembered a verse his mother had recited to him and Ann when they were children:

> *Heaven above, Heaven below;*
> *Stars above, Stars below;*
> *All that is over, under shall show.*
> *Happy thou who the riddle readest.*

Was the riddle's answer this plan of the stars replicated in the land? Merry emptied a jar of mouldering leaves and seeds into a garbage bag and pushed the maps aside to set out a posy of dried thyme, lavender and poppy in a neatly made wicker cone.

He bought the woods at the centre of the giant zodiac when Merry told him it was about to be cleared of its trees. The very heart of this woods, a grove of old oak, was where light from the pole star (then found in Ursa Minor) had fallen at the equinox sometime around 2700 B.C., so Merry said. They'd arrived just as the saws were making the first cuts. Soon Nick was able to purchase enough property surrounding it, including a good stream and pasture, to begin making his dream of establishing a community a reality. Over the following months, with the help of transients, none settling permanently, he constructed a shelter and storage buildings and moved his belongings to them. Nick was not rich any longer, but he believed, the morning he left the pub for the last time with his remaining clothes and tools and drove out onto a road glistening with spring rain, that his money had been well spent and that he was emerging as a new creature in a new skin.

The airy light of the grey and green dawn found him treading a deer path that wound upwards through the trees of Summerwood, the name he had given to his land. As he climbed the hill towards the woods where the old oaks stood, he was already planning the first stages of the project that would bring prosperity to the nascent community: some thinning of the overgrowth, and milling and selling the lumber, then aggressive planting of quick-growing Douglas fir. His great-grandfather, the one who had adventured in Canada, had brought seedlings home from the North American forests, and had proved the fir to be both sturdy and profitable. But as the low rays of the sun sloped through the shadows to warm him, he heard something moving in the bush alongside. He thought of deer, and then of the panthers rumoured to still roam these ancient hills. The creature came closer and emitted a groan. Nick hefted a stick—but when the thing emerged onto the path, having thrashed ahead a dozen or so yards, it was like nothing he'd imagined. He saw a soldier, exhausted and pale, who wore a mud-caked buff coat and dragged a pike. The raised visor of the soldier's helmet showed blue eyes, and his foam-flecked lips twisted in a grimace of pain. The face, with its unforgiving glare, reminded him of his father. Nick swayed on his feet. The sun's glitter sifted through leaves onto the soldier's raised arm and a flourished, blood-stained sword. The other hand dropped the sack it had been dragging; the mouth of the sack burst open and a large head with long brown curls, the expression of the face almost wistful, rolled out of it and over the ground. Nick closed his eyes against the image of wide, doleful eyes. When he opened them, the soldier and his grisly parcel had vanished.

Nick's heartbeat gradually slowed, and he stood up from the crouch into which shock had dropped him and began to gather his scattered belongings. Bluetits chirruped, insects swam through the warming air; his ears filled with the calming susurration of ash leaves.

He recalled that during the English Civil War, the doomed King Charles I had been harried throughout this part of the countryside. Enemies had scouted for him, but he'd evaded them until he'd glimpsed a dragon who was said to haunt these oaks . . . and then the king had been surrounded and his enemies had closed in. Nick had seen the king's likeness a hundred times in school books and gallery portraits, so there was no mistake about the head's identity. But why had it appeared to him? There was his mother, and the Highlands in her background, and the vivid stream of her grandmother's Native American blood passed. . . . Was that why?

What had he taken on by becoming owner of the zodiac wood?

A sudden noise yanked Nick awake. He listened to a dog barking from the woods, and sat up to check on the others. Charlie sprawled, sleeping, his arms and legs flung wide like a child's; Merry snored, on the far side of the bender, through delicately flared nostrils. Galt's bed was empty. Neither Charlie nor Merry had seemed to know why Galt had left or whether he planned to return. Nick hoped he'd be back. They could certainly use Galt's strength when they were clearing stumps. He lay back thinking. All in all, things were coming together. The drainage ditches were nearly done, and they had lumber to sell. With a little more work, they'd be fairly well set for the winter. The dog, sounding nearer, barked again as if it had no plans to stop. Nick gave up the idea of sleep and got up to take a look.

It was too dark to see much, but he knew what lay all around. They were situated on a rise. The land fell gently away to the west, ahead of him, through neglected fields of thistle, dock and brush to the moor. To the north lay fallow wheat fields, farms with planted hedges, and fences and walls, and beyond these the pale drawings of hills. Behind the bender was the oak wood. As Nick turned that way he saw a glitter of white to his left. He went after it and within minutes he was in amongst the old trees—beyond the new plantation—where the ancient oaks were entwined with mistletoe, and their blunt branches scratched against the sky. He heard soft, padding footsteps behind him. When he stopped, they stopped, so he kept on walking, working his way through the oaks towards a clearing where whatever it was that was following would have to show itself.

The white shape raced by on his right, then paused, caught in a sudden shaft of moonlight near a patch of scrub laurels. Nick faced it, glimpsing red eyes and a white muzzle, and then it was gone. He kept searching, sensing that it was useless—he knew the dog wasn't going to show itself to him again—but as he did so, he noticed the smell of woodsmoke permeating the air. It couldn't be from the bender, which was downwind, and in which everyone was still asleep anyway, and so he worked his way quietly through the trees, following the scent until he came to a small fire smouldering in front of a tent.

Lying next to the fire, its fur bristling, a low growl thrilling from its throat, was the large white dog.

"His name is Breaker," said the Frenchman who emerged from the tent at Nick's call. He controlled the dog with one hand and held out the other one to Nick. "I'm Tomas," he said. Tomas was still young, but older than Nick, probably in his late twenties. His hair was straight, blond and dirty, and he was thin; the hand that Nick shook trembled. A foul odour wafted from his body: Nick had to stop himself from backing away.

"Is he friendly? Can I pet him?"

"I don't know," Tomas said, "you can try. I haven't had him that

l to the dog's level and spoke, extending his fingers, ged sideways, not so much giving ground as simply ntact. "Where'd you get him? I don't think I've ever his."

tain dog. Maybe part Great Pyrenees, I don't know. up." Tomas stuffed his hands in his pockets to hide their shaking. "It was a little strange." He shrugged, and then looked around, changing the subject. "So, this is your land, yes?"

Nick stood up. "We've started a small logging operation—just hand thinning and planting. Not in the old wood, though—I won't let anyone touch those trees. We have lots of plans." He smiled at Tomas. "I don't mind if you want to camp here. You're welcome as long as you clean up after yourself and keep an eye on that fire."

Tomas didn't smile back. His eyes were glazed, and he didn't seem to be taking much in.

"Everything all right?" Nick said. The dog had worked round to

Tomas's side; the young man gripped the hair on the dog's back for support.

"Fine," said Tomas a few seconds too late. He swayed and lost his balance, letting go of the dog. Nick grabbed him by the elbow. When Tomas tried to stand upright on his own, he couldn't. He was sweating and pale; dark circles hollowed his eyes.

"Look," Nick said, "why don't you come back with me? We've got an extra bed, and I can light the stove. You need to get warm. I think you've got a fever. You're shivering." Tomas pulled himself a little away and glanced over at the tent anxiously. "Don't worry. Somebody will come for your things. We'll keep them safe for you." Tomas appeared to be about to say something, but he staggered again and fell hard against Nick. The smell of putrid flesh caught at Nick's nose and throat. He turned his face away, gagging. When he stopped, he eased Tomas to the ground. He could see a shallow, rapid pulse fluttering in the young man's neck.

"It was a small scratch, but now it is very bad," Tomas whispered. He pulled up the loose sleeve of his sweater and showed Nick the inside of his arm. It was swollen from wrist to elbow. A long, shallow wound ran down the centre, leaking a reddish brown fluid.

"What happened?"

"I'm a climber. I was in the mountains with my sister." Tomas fell silent. The dog hove to his feet and growled nervously.

"I'm going to get help," Nick said. "I'll be right back."

He ran, the trees melting out of his way in the rising dawn light as he approached the bender clearing. He woke Charlie and Merry and sent Merry to get the van while he and Charlie returned for Tomas. They carried him between them and laid him, moaning, in the back. There might be a chance for him, Nick thought, but only if the arm were to come off right away. He was sure it was gangrenous.

Nick was just shutting the van door when the white dog, Breaker, jumped in the back. It sat with its head resting on the seat. It's wide face showed friendly interest, and it wagged its long tail.

"I have to tell you something," Tomas said. He was lying, drugged on morphine, in the hospital bed, waiting for the surgeon. An intravenous drip slid antibiotics into a vein of his good arm. His skin was no longer pale—more of a mottled purple—and a runnel of tears tracked continuously from his eyes. Nick sat at the bedside wondering how long he should stay. He'd done everything he could, even called Tomas's sister in France. His stomach rumbled. Merry and Charlie had already gone to a café for breakfast. "I know that I am going to die. I am being punished," Tomas said.

"You're not going to die, you'll be fine. You're getting treatment, your sister will be here tomorrow." Nick tried to imagine what else he should say. "You've got to look on the bright side."

Tomas shook his head. "I know that I am dying, I am not a child. I have to tell you, there is no one else. Please," he begged, as Nick made a move to call a nurse, "there is no time."

Nick hesitantly sat back down. It was impossible to know if he were doing the right thing. His mother would have known what to do. Any woman would have. He wished Merry had stayed.

"Where's Breaker?" Tomas asked suddenly, looking around.

"Still in the van. Charlie and Merry will look after him."

"He won't stay," Tomas said, as more tears flooded his cheeks, "he won't leave me." At his words, a white form brushed low through the doorway, its toenails clicking on the tile, and lay down on the floor, its massive head resting on its paws. A chill crept into Nick's spine. "You see how it is?" Tomas said.

Gingerly, moving slowly, Nick squatted beside the dog. Tomas had insisted that he examine the dog's right foot. "Easy boy," he said. "It's all right." The dog's ears pricked up and it turned its head to examine Nick.

"Lift it up, turn it over, but be careful not to touch the bottom," Tomas said.

Nick slid his hand around the dog's right foreleg. The dog helped him, lifting the paw in a handshake, then letting Nick do what he liked with it. On its underside, embedded in the middle black nail pad, was a clear white stone. Nick thought he could see the pale imprints of pinpoint stitching around it. "Christ, that must have hurt," he said.

"Don't touch the stone, it's very sharp."

Nick angled the paw towards the window. Now the stone swam with blue and orange light. When Nick tilted the paw towards shadow, the stone turned opaque and white. "Do you know what it is?"

"It cut me. It's what caused this." Tomas tried to raise his swollen arm, and winced.

The dog withdrew its paw.

"It wasn't his fault, he was only protecting his owner." Tomas sighed and let his head flop back on the pillow. "You've seen it for yourself, and now I must tell you the rest."

"I was born in the village of Argentière at the eastern end of the Chamonix valley. My sister and I grew up on skis, skiing or climbing throughout the entire region. We climbed Mont Blanc and the Matterhorn, and the Eiger Nordwand not once but a number of times, and we worked with teams, preparing for assaults on the Himalayan peaks, on the Grandes Jorasses overlooking the Mer de

Glace near Chamonix. Our parents were climbers and guides: this was the tradition in which we were nurtured. It meant the world to us, especially after our parents were killed in an avalanche.

"Among climbers there is a code. You rely on yourself, but you go to the assistance of others if they are in trouble, even at the cost of some long-planned achievement of your own. You learn who you can trust with your life, and once you know, you do it without a second thought. You understand that what you see and feel from the top of a mountain makes you different: you believe it is the only place from which the world makes sense, and it is. It doesn't matter what non-climbers think, and you do not talk about it, but it makes every risk you take worthwhile.

"You do not take stupid chances, and you never endanger another. What you have you share or give away to whoever needs it. Do you see? You are the best, you are the luckiest, you are not caught in the webs that trap others.

"No one knew the region better than we did; we were in demand to guide parties of skiers over the glaciers, and climbers up the peaks. More and more of our time was spent like this, on the Vallée Blanche and the Mont Blanc glacier, or up to the top of the Aiguille du Midi and along the arête to a needle where climbers with some modest technical experience could begin to extend themselves. You can see how it would be: in the beginning a pleasure to teach others to surpass their expectations, to instruct in snow and rock techniques and glacial travel and rope management, and by the close of the second season, disenchantment with these 'tourists'—some of whom expected us to carry them, if need be, to the top of whatever height they attempted, and to supply them, along the way, with every possible comfort.

"I began to feel that the mountains were under assault by people with money who climbed only because they had run out of other things to do; I was depressed by the part I was playing in the destruction of the world I loved.

"As always, the mountains extracted revenge. One day, when we reached the top of the Aiguille du Midi cable car, planning from there to gain access to the Refuge du Col du Midi, we learned that a party of eight ahead of us had been killed by an avalanche on our proposed course.

"That night a thunder and lightning storm finished all hope of our attempting the climb in the near future. By noon the next day snow had covered everything and once more the mountains stood in untouched beauty. I told my sister I was finished with guiding. I did not know what I would do for money, but I simply couldn't continue.

"The next season we climbed for pleasure. My sister had found a job in a bank in town, but I could not seem to find any settled employment. There was work available, of course, urging retired men and women, mostly Americans, up slopes their bodies should not go. I suppose I talked about how I felt about it once too often in public: I was told I was a bad influence on the other guides, that I was driving business away, that I was no longer welcome among them. Rumours began to go round that I was bad luck, that people I guided had been injured or died—which was not true; I was proud of my record—so that even if I had changed my mind, by then no one would have hired me.

"One weekend, my sister and I took the rack-and-pinion train from St. Gervais les Bains to its upper terminus and climbed the trail to the hut at Tête Rousse. She'd convinced me to come with her to cheer me up, but she had to pay for everything as I was entirely out of funds. From the hut we crossed a snow slope and then, in increasing mist, followed what we thought was the trail up a rocky ridge. After a while we both felt uneasy—something was wrong—so we stopped. When the mist lifted for an instant we saw that there were climbers on a parallel ridge to our right and realized we had missed the markings. I could see a way to the correct path: a traverse of a boulder-and-ice-filled couloir that would take us out not far below a hut higher up on the Aiguille du Goûter. My sister and I argued over what to do—something we had never done before. She wanted to go back and pick up the right route lower down. I refused; it was my way or not at all. 'What you want to do is a mistake,' she said. 'I will not take the risk. At least if I go back, someone will know what has happened to you,' and she left.

"It did not take me long to realize that she was right. The traverse was much more difficult than I had thought, the ground treacherously unstable. To make it worse, the sun broke through the mist, and the ice in the couloir turned soft. I was very much afraid by then, and unhappy at being on my own, but there was nothing to do but continue.

"Suddenly I saw a piece of turquoise cloth lying in a pool of ice water a few metres away. When I went to see what it was, I found a hand protruding from the sleeve of a jacket. I moved several rocks and chunks of melting snow and ice from around it, and within a short time I had uncovered the body of a woman. She was small; wisps of grey and brown hair clung to a skull that had been half smashed in. She was still clipped to a severed loop of rope, and it was obvious that she had fallen to her death, taken by a rockslide or avalanche, been swept down the face of the mountain into the couloir and buried. Until now.

"I turned her over and found her ice axe. I saw that she wore a pouch around her waist at the back. With only the thought of discovering who she was, I opened it. The pouch was stuffed with American dollars. All my anger at what I had endured as a guide, and at the desecration of what was most sacred in life to me—these mountains— came back. Without another thought I took the money, stuffed it in my pockets and began to cover her up. She had lain there, undiscovered, perhaps for years: leaving her there would make no difference.

"I had almost finished when I heard a slight noise from above. I glanced up. In the freezing air you often see and hear things. I wasn't really expecting anything, but flying through the air towards me, his mouth open in a snarl, was Breaker. I dropped and rolled but he struck me on the arm with his paw. The blow ripped right through my jacket and clothing and drew blood. I knew it wasn't a serious wound; my only thought was that he was going to go for my throat and kill me. But once he was on the ground, he appeared only to be interested in the dead climber. He sniffed all around her and then stood over her looking at me. I was still shaking with terror. I do not know why I knew what I had to do, but I took the money I had removed from the body and I put it down as near to the dead woman as I dared. Still he stood there. I went through all my pockets, I took out every penny I found there. All of it I left with the dead woman, then I turned and continued the traverse.

"The dog followed me.

"When I returned to the lower hut and met my sister, I told her I'd found the dog in the couloir, but said nothing about the woman. It was my sister who, petting him, discovered both the stone implanted in his paw and his name tattooed crudely on the underside of an ear."

Tomas coughed. Nick helped him drink from a glass of water.

"It was so peaceful there," Tomas said.

The dog, who had been lying quietly while Tomas spoke, stood and stretched. In one smooth motion he jumped up onto the foot of the bed. Tomas sighed.

"Why didn't you get the wound attended to?" Nick said.

"I didn't think I was really hurt. I wasn't interested: I knew I had to leave the mountains before I did something worse. I had broken my own code of ethics. Everything was spoiled for me. It didn't matter anymore."

Breaker whined softly and crept forward on his belly until his head lay on Tomas's chest.

"In France, when everybody knows you, you are called a white wolf: *il est connu comme le loup blanc.* People knew me and what I stood for." Tomas kneaded the top of Breaker's head with his fingers. "In spring, in the valley, when the wind blows in waves across the fields, it is the wolf going through." Breaker whined again and licked the salt from Tomas's face.

"Give me some money," Tomas said.

"What?"

"Some money, whatever you have."

Nick pulled some change from his jacket pocket and Tomas took it.

"You've paid for him. Now Breaker is yours," he said.

"I've always wanted a dog," Nick said.

Tomas smiled at him, and then Tomas died.

Five

Cutthroat: *The Early Life of Jones*

When Jones was very small, her mother took her and her three brothers and sisters on a journey. They left the lochside where Jones and the others had been born, just above the little stone circle, and crossed over by Shian and into the Carse. Because it was almost winter, the river was full of silt the colour of blood, and they had to walk a long way before they found a ford by which they could cross. They walked, and they scurried, and they climbed, keeping themselves alive by catching voles and small golden frogs. Occasionally they saw other cats, perhaps on a similar journey, but in the end, when they reached the Hill, there were only themselves.

Jones's mother couldn't tell them exactly why they'd had to make the journey, but it had always been done. They were descended from a line of cats that could trace its ancestry back to the Cait Sith, the cat of the Highland fairies who had mated, once, with a mortal cat. They sat quietly, listening to the wind, and watching damp leaves skirl through the clearing, the great tree at the top of the hill swaying above them. Jones's mother told them that the Cait Sith was their guardian, and would appear to them twice, and that the last time she would grant a favour. She told them some of their history, and they swore to keep this a secret, except from whomever they loved best in the world. At the foot of the tree, tucked into a hollow between the roots, they left a fish they'd caught that morning: it was a fine silver fish, strong and hard fleshed from cold water. Jones had wanted to take one small bite of it, just one to make sure of the taste, but her mother wouldn't let her.

The return journey—by a different route, also traditional—was arduous. It led into mountains thick with pine trees, through steep-sided passes and along ice-edged lochs down which the wind blew without hindrance. One morning, after crossing a frosty meadow, near a stream where they had gone to drink, they saw a horse-like creature rise out of the water. It splashed violently and threw mud and stones at them. They ran off, and when they found a place to stop and rest, Jones's mother explained that the figure was a particularly malignant kelpie, and it was lucky for them they weren't old for it might have frightened them to death: the elderly confronted by this kelpie generally died.

They were exhausted by the time they reached the shores of Loch Tay, and Jones's mother said, after they had rested in a barn for a few hours, "Now I have to leave you. I have a new family coming, so you have all to go out on your own." Since this was the first they had heard of it, there was some crying. Soon, though, the others stopped their tears and went, but for Jones the parting was harder.

Jones followed her mother, mewing and crying, shivering in the rain that pricked right through her fur like pins, until her mother leapt into the water to ford a river. When she was on the other side, she called to Jones not to try to swim after her, that it was too dangerous, she might drown. Jones went in anyway and crossed safely, although she was swept considerably downstream, and by the time she had struggled through the whirlpools to shore, she was far from her mother and in a place she had never been before. She padded uphill past a farmhouse. When she stopped she was in a high bowl in the hills. She ran up one side of it and glimpsed the far slopes where another loch glimmered below. She decided to go on.

It was there, as she descended, crossing through a pine plantation and then up and over a steep of larch, that she paused to formulate the first verse for which she is known. It is said that a pheasant watched her as she composed, and that when she was finished she enlarged a hole in the net that had captured it, letting it go.

The past is shadow, and it grows
From shape to shape and melting blends
Like cloud, like mist, the reaching hills —
It shapes itself to light and goes!

There was wind in the oaks and rowans, hazel and birch farther along, and a fence on which the farmers had strung up shot crows to warn their fellows away. They had a practice, in those days, fortunately all but lost, of setting out a vermin line — a row of dead foxes, crows and voles along the fences — for the landowner to see when he went by on his weekend visits, to illustrate the farm's sound husbandry. All this Jones observed.

Some say that Jones heard music coming from behind a rock, the

"King's rock," and that it inspired further poetry before she followed a path for carrying peat and driving cattle.

The heather was crisp with frost under her paws, and where it had been burned, in late summer, it crumbled to black dust. This practice of burning to give young grouse tender shoots to eat resulted in more rapid regeneration of the plant, but where it was left unburned, it grew tall and rank, and the young grouse, attempting to fly, would hang themselves in the twig forks. Here, so it is said, Jones, foreseeing just such an event, stopped to author that well-known song:

> *Many a cow is without calf,*
> *many a sheep without lamb.*
> *Heart-rending their cry,*
> *and that of the grouse,*
> *on both sides of the Glen.*

She jumped up a wooden stile that took her safely over an electric fence, sprang over sphagnum moss and ran through a field run wild with blaeberry, its golds and reds brilliant even this late in the season. Is it any wonder that Jones's heart was lighter by the time she came to the lochside?

Chance led her, as night fell, to a deserted, windswept moor. When Jones was just about ready to bed down for the night, cold and hungry as she was, with her back to the wind, and huddled against a rock, she heard a faint lowing. Although she couldn't see anything, she followed the exhausted sound and came to a cow caught with its horns twisted in the wire strands of a fence. Jones made herself known, interested the cow in following her movements, and by clever manoeuvring showed the poor thing how to free itself. In gratitude, the cow, sensing Jones's hunger, let down her milk and then allowed Jones to ride on her back as she made her way to the byre. That night, before falling asleep next to the warmth of the large animal, Jones composed the last of the poems of which I have knowledge.

Perhaps one day, more will be found.

> *That kind cow of midnight*
> *Gave me sweet milk on the moor,*
> *Without pail, or cow fetters, or trouble, or calf,*
> *The cow of my heart, cow of my love,*
> *Gave me her sweet milk without stint on the moor.*

We do not know what Jones might have made of herself if she had remained in her homeland. These fragments are the work of her early youth. As it was, she shortly thereafter launched herself into the wide unhappy world to follow her destiny. We are the better for it, but oh that it might have been different.

Lift the Stone and
Thou Shalt find
Me: Cleave the wood
and there am I

Sampler, Maltwood Collection

Six

Cathreen

She was a geological fault, the veins of her mind lay exposed—someone was chipping away at them, retrieving samples. Fragments fell out every time she closed her eyes: her mother rubbed at the smudged rounds of her glasses with a flowered paper towel, Tink yawned, advertising the gold tooth at the back of his mouth, Jag drove a truck down a snake trail of scoured gravel, the trees alongside floured white with dust. Dust hung in the air ahead of them from a logging truck that had passed and all but put them off the road; dust hugged their wheels and let go in puffs.

Cathreen opened her eyes and drank from the bottle of water she'd bought at the airport. Her eyes burned and her throat hurt as she watched the bus she'd just left pass a line of broken-down factory buildings fenced off from the road by barbed wire and nettle and then disappear over a hill. It was still a fifteen-minute walk from here, at the edge of the village, to the pub, but she'd asked the driver to let her off early. She needed the time to think. Jag hadn't turned up to meet her as he'd promised. She'd waited in Arrivals for three hours, had him paged twice and finally called and left a message with a woman at the George and Dragon that she'd take the bus. But what if Jag hadn't got it? What if something had happened to him? What if Helena had phoned him, told him about all the trouble she was in, and he'd decided he didn't want her there at all?

The whole way from London she'd been so cold and miserable, hunched into a ball in her seat to conserve heat, her hands tucked inside the top of her backpack on top of Cutthroat's warm fur, that she hadn't been able to make any plans. Now, as bright sun steamed off concrete and brick and reflected from shards of broken glass, the warmth started to make her relax. She set her backpack down. The cat stuck his paws through the laces and Cathreen loosened off the drawstrings and let him out. He stretched, then ambled off to examine the long grass and weeds that spiked through the rusted-out walls of the tin shed behind them. Cathreen shaped a cup out of a small plastic bag and poured water into it for him. She broke up the remains of the tuna sandwich she'd bought for her lunch and put them on the ground.

She'd found that the cat had come with her only when she'd taken her pack into the plane's toilet so she could wash, change her shirt and brush her teeth before landing. There he was, curled up on her sweater; she hadn't had the heart to disturb him. It was kind of a compliment: he'd chosen *her* over life with Mrs. Hamilton. It hadn't been until she read the signs in Customs about penalties for bringing an animal into the country that Cathreen had realized what she'd done. She'd trembled with anxiety, tried to smile when handing over her passport, prayed that no one would look in her bag. "I'm meeting my father," she'd said when questioned about where and with whom she'd be staying. "My parents are divorced. It's his turn." Another big smile. It wasn't until much later, just before getting onto the bus, that she'd felt it safe to let the cat out. He'd purred, stared at the people and traffic, found some shrubbery in which to do his business and returned to her. When she'd picked him up, he hadn't wanted to leave her arms; she'd had to peel his claws from her shoulder to get him safely tucked away.

"Here, kitty, kitty." The cat ambushed stalks of waving grass near the ruined shed. Cathreen picked up a section of sandwich in her fingers. "Come on, Cutthroat, dinnertime!" He stopped jumping and turned to face her. She could almost see him sigh. He strolled over and brushed back and forth against her leg. "Good kitty, that's a good boy. Want some?" She held out a chunk of the tuna. Cutthroat sniffed it. "You're supposed to eat it, it's food," she said, but he ignored the offering and the water, too. Cathreen reached for him, intending to stuff him into the knapsack so she could get going, but his slim grey and white form slipped through her grasp, and with a few rapid springs he was at the side of the road, then across it and leaping through a field.

"Shit! Come back! Cutthroat!" Cathreen grabbed her things and tore after him, nearly running into the side of a passing car as she looked the wrong way before crossing. She stood, panting, panicked at the prospect of losing him, in the grunge and damp chocolate wrappers and chip bags beside a ditch. The cat roved ahead in the long, untidy pasture, dodging his way through clusters of cows. Beyond the cows, a small hill, wooded on its lower slopes, rose from the flatland and dropped on one flank, back the way the bus had come, to a straight stagnant waterway the bus driver had told her was a river. What she'd seen of the "river" as they'd crossed the bridge was green slime, an upturned shopping cart and half a dozen old tires. She worried that Cutthroat might be headed there to drink. The driver had said the scummy river was where King Arthur was supposed to have flung his sword. If so, she thought, it was probably still there, tangled in bedsprings and car parts.

A memory of a river she'd visited with Jag, one of the smaller ones in the country drained by the Skeena and the Nass, flashed through her mind. It ran deep green, so clear that you could watch the jet black shadows cast by fish fry as they darted over the lava riverbed. She'd sunk her whole face into it to drink, the water pricking ice into her skin. Blue mountains had cut the black distance of the lava fields, and white cloud tunnels had swirled out of far valleys and punched fistfuls of cumulus into the sky.

The cat danced ahead, throwing glances over his shoulder to make sure she followed, skirted the trees and carried on up to the long, turfy back of the hill. From there, red-roofed houses fell away in steps along the southeast slope, and the sun dropped a little lower behind a band of cloud in the west. Cathreen stopped to rest. The sky was dark and light paper all twisted together. The little herd of cows had trailed after them, pausing when they'd paused, trampling, like they did, or at least she did, on knots of cow dung and withered thistle and morning glory. They lowed behind her, as if asking Cathreen what they should do next.

Cathreen had lost sight of Cutthroat, but ahead of her, on a knoll, stood a thorn tree silhouetted against the skyline. The wind crackled the ribbons, surveyor's tape and long strips of paper tied to its branches, and made a noise like popping corn. Curious, she approached the tree.

Jag had told her that people sometimes wrote out wishes and hung them in such trees, but if there'd ever been writing on the ribbons and tape and papers, it was long faded. She leaned tiredly against the gnarled trunk. Perhaps she shouldn't have come; she hadn't expected to feel so lonely. She'd only been thinking about meeting Jag, and living in Aunt Jen's house: he'd described it to her so many times—a stone cottage on the edge of the moor, its doors and window frames painted blue, with a high window that looked west over flatland towards the sea, and Aunt Jen's bright garden spilling over the ground to splash against the cottage walls.

With a skitter of claws, the cat scrambled down from the branches onto her shoulder, startling her. "Don't ever run away like that again!" she said. "We'd better stick together. I'm all you've got in the world, you know."

She stood for ten minutes in front of the pub. It had started to rain, and street lamps splashed gold light over the cobblestones. She'd never been in a pub. Her drinking had been done behind the school with Toni, or in somebody's garage or bedroom when the parents weren't home. This pub didn't look like anything she'd even seen before. She'd waited once in the car, when she was small and Helena was away, while Jag had gone inside a squat building with few windows, not far from where they'd lived. When he'd been gone too long, she'd slipped out and scooted by the open door to see if he were coming. Small round tables, covered with red terrycloth, spotted the floor; beefy waiters carried trays holding dozens of beers . . . a sea of men in work clothes, and no sign of her father. A waiter, catching sight of her, had yelled to her, "Get the fuck out of here!" The smell of beer, sweat and cigarettes flooding through the door had almost made her sick.

What *was* this? It was old, made of stone with a castle-like roof and many small windows of leaded glass, like shiny tears, glistening all down the front. The stone was worn, as if tall people had leaned against it and brushed gently back and forth for a very long time. The entranceway was darkened by an arch, the heavy wooden door propped open within it.

A thin, older woman wearing jeans came out and stood there. She searched in her bag and brought out cigarettes. She lit one and smoked it, occasionally pushing sparse blond tendrils of hair back from her face, looking up and down the street, letting her gaze skim Cathreen's. Cathreen excused herself past the woman and went in.

Several well-dressed couples stood at a curved wooden bar through a doorway to her left; a few others were seated at nearby tables with drinks. As she passed from the flagstone hall into the bar, her feet stumbled over the uneven plank flooring. The ceiling was low, supported by dark oak beams. Bouquets of flowers brightened the tables; candles were lit in the wall sconces. No one paid any attention to her until she placed herself directly in front of the middle-aged barman. "What can I do for you, miss?" he said, continuing to polish glasses.

"I left a message for my father."

The barman glanced over his half-glasses. "And?"

"Do you know if he got it?"

"That would depend, wouldn't it, on who you are."

"My name's Cathreen."

"Why don't you write your name down." He slid a pen and a piece of paper towards her. "I'll post your message over there"—he indicated a cork board beside the washrooms—"but I'm not a tourist service."

Heat suffused her face. The young man next to her, wearing a tie and jacket, looked down his nose at her wet clothing and moved a few feet over. When she handed the paper back, folded, Jag's name prominent on the outside, the barman give her a second glance. "It happens he did come in. If you wait a minute I'll see if I can ring him." She watched him carry the paper with him to the telephone. He wiped his hands on a towel, and without consulting a directory dialled a number. As he spoke into the receiver, Cathreen began to feel uneasy. Jag had said he didn't have a phone, so who was the barman calling?

The woman who'd been smoking outside had come back in while Cathreen was talking to the barman. She reached past Cathreen and dipped her fingers into a bowl of peanuts. "Hurry up, Rob," she called to the barman, "I've not got all day. A person could die of bloody thirst." Hurriedly the barman finished speaking and as he put the phone down, Cathreen saw him refold her message and put it in his pocket before getting the woman her drink. He'd opened and read it. What fucking business was it of his?

The thin woman lifted her pint and gave Cathreen a sharp-toothed smile.

"Why do you think Rob just called the rozzers?" she said. She grabbed another handful of peanuts from the bowl on the bar and tossed them into her mouth. "It's not even Saturday night."

"Rozzers?"

"Police," the woman said.

Cathreen bolted out of the bar, across the street, through a small square and into a parking lot.

Peering around quickly, and seeing nobody watching, she crawled under a tour bus parked next to a public washroom. Small stones bit into her elbows, and the stink of oil swarmed up her nostrils. When she'd dragged her way to the bus's front wheel, she could see the stretch of street that ran by the pub. It wasn't long before a car drew up in front of it, and the reflection of its blue police light shone over the road. "Shit!" she murmured as two policemen got out and entered the George and Dragon: was it her or Jag they were after? Could Helena have figured out where she was already, or was it Jag who was in trouble?

The woman she'd talked to in the pub came out, lit a cigarette and scuffed down the hill in low-heeled boots. She crossed the street and threw the cigarette away. Cathreen watched as she entered the car park and unlocked the door of an old Land Rover. The woman hesitated, glanced over at the washroom and, whistling under her breath, came Cathreen's way. Just outside the washroom door she dropped her keys. Cathreen could no longer see her, but she heard her say as she bent to retrieve them, "Get into the back of my car. Pull the blanket over you. You don't have much time." The door banged behind her as she went inside the ladies'.

The two policemen were at the door of the pub. One of them got into the police car and drove off; the other turned on a flashlight and shone it up and down the street. When his back was turned for a moment, Cathreen rolled out from under the bus, pulling her pack with her, and half ran, half crawled to the Land Rover. Once inside she pulled the old blanket on top of her and tried to control her rapid breathing. The car door opened, the woman started the engine and steered the car to the entrance. She slowed down to make the turn out of the lot and rolled down the window. "Any luck?" she called out. Footsteps approached and a strong light shone into the car.

"You see anything, Merry?"

"No pink elephants tonight, Chris. Sorry."

"You let me know, all right? You on your way home?"

"Straight home, you know me."

"Drive safely." The constable gave the Land Rover a friendly swat as it pulled away.

Cathreen listened as the car went through its gear changes. In a few minutes it speeded up and she could smell the smoke of a cigarette. The odours of dust and straw tickled her nose, and the blanket itched her face. She sneezed.

"You can come out now," the woman said.

Cathreen sat up. Her eyes met the woman's in the rearview mirror. The woman smiled.

"Thanks," Cathreen said.

"Don't mention it."

Little prickles of sweat stood out on Cathreen's forehead.

The woman rolled down her window and threw out the butt. It bounced, sparking across the pavement. Cathreen saw that they were on the same road she'd come in on earlier. Broken-down factories, the bridge, fenced fields edged with trees, little ridges far away, but overall the landscape sloping down to another level and away to the sea. She felt suddenly faint and opened her window. She gulped at the air, trying to get enough of it into her lungs. It was damp, thick with the odour of wet soil. Rows of planted trees sprang up and fenced in the road. They were soldiers, prison gates. She endured the claustrophobia until the plantation square abruptly ended and the countryside once more opened up into peaceful dips and inclines.

When she felt better, she wound the window up and sat back. Again her eyes met the woman's in the mirror. "So why'd you do it?" she said to her.

"Pardon me?" The woman's eyes moved back to the windshield. "Look, I can't talk to you with you back there." She patted the passenger seat beside her. "Why don't you come up here?"

When Cathreen had crawled forward, settled herself in the front and placed the backpack between her knees, the woman said, "My name's Merry."

"Yeah, I heard. The cop said."

"Oh, right. But it's M-e-r-r-y as in Christmas. My mother's idea of cheering herself up." Merry barked out a laugh and took out another cigarette. "Does the smoke bother you?" she asked. "Nobody smokes anymore in America, do they?" When Cathreen didn't reply, she tossed the cigarette irritably onto the dash.

"I'm not American." Cathreen said. "I don't know what they do there. I don't mind if you smoke. I smoke, too, but not when my mom's around, she's allergic."

"What's the accent, then?"

Cathreen shrugged. Merry offered the cigarette pack and matches. Cathreen took one, lit it, gave it to Merry, then lit one for herself. Merry drew in smoke and let it spiral out of her nostrils.

"It's simple why I helped," she said. "Rob's an arsehole. Glad I was there."

Cathreen's eyes stung with the surprise of sudden tears. She'd been scared; she could still be hiding under the bus or maybe, by now, be on her way to jail. "Rob's the bartender?" Merry nodded. "He's always like that?"

"Yeah. You just get here?"

"This afternoon." They'd turned off onto another road, south, she thought, twisting her neck round to look behind the way they'd come. She wanted to keep track so she could find her way back if she had to. The lights of a small village spangled across flat land. Everywhere else was darkness.

"I heard you ask about your father."

"Yeah?" Cathreen tapped a length of ash onto the floor. Merry pointed to the ashtray in front of her. "Oh, sorry," Cathreen said. She butted out the cigarette in the ashtray, then bit at a nail. "He was supposed to meet me. He didn't show up."

"That's too bad. Something probably came up. Men are like that."

"How would you know!" Cathreen said. "Jag's not like that!"

"Oops, sorry!" Merry lifted her hands from the wheel in a gesture of apology. "Didn't mean to step on any toes." They drove on in silence: the headlights swallowed the landscape in bites.

Merry's fingers drummed on the steering wheel. "Listen— Cathreen, isn't it?—I don't know how they do things wherever you're from, but here we take people as they come. I'm not prying, believe me." She gave her head a little shake, setting a gold earring, snagged on a straggly blond lock, swinging. "So, do you need a place to stay or not?"

Cathreen took a deep breath. "I could do with one, yeah. Just until I find my father. His name is Jag Adams. Do you know him?"

"Adams? I remember a family by that name, but it was a long time ago." Merry's fingers on the steering wheel played piano. Cathreen let out a sigh. "Don't worry," Merry said, reaching over to pat her shoulder, "I'll see what I can do. I'll ask around."

Where a few unlit cottages squeezed the road, Merry veered the Land Rover onto a dirt track. They bumped along it and climbed up and down a hill. Warm light splashed through the top-floor windows of a farmhouse. As they passed, a child walked through a room in a dressing gown. Cathreen lifted her backpack onto her lap, pushed her fingers through the opening and scratched Cutthroat's warm ears. Cutthroat purred.

"What've you got there?" Merry said.

"My cat."

"Your cat? You brought it with you?" Cathreen shrugged in reply. "Amazing," Merry said.

The Land Rover's headlights snagged on a tree, then another and another and soon they were driving through a woods. Tree trunks, thick and thin, not in ranks like the plantation but spaced with a kind of rhythm she could almost pick up on, maybe because she was so tired, closed in behind. The track wound a careful way through them.

"It's not far now," Merry said, peering ahead. "Nick will be delighted to have another female in his entourage."

"Who's Nick?" A new stab of fear: Helena's voice prophesying disaster at the hands of strangers.

"Didn't I tell you? We're at Summerwood. Utopia. Nick's pet project. You don't have to worry about Nick. He's harmless." Merry laughed, her narrow face losing ten years. "There's only me and old Charlie here at the moment. People come and go. I've got my own place, but I said I'd give Nick a hand. And anyway, if you want to be where no one will look for you, this is it. People leave us alone: they don't know what to make of Nick. They can't figure out if he's one of them or one of us. They keep hoping he'll just go away."

They jolted to the top of a hill and stopped at a clearing. At the far end, a small fire burned. There was no other light, no electrical buzz, no radio or television. Dense blackness revealed the presence of several dwellings. The scene looked primitive: two men gathered round a blaze, ancient man at his beginnings. Fingers of shadow lunged from the women as they got out of the car.

Cathreen put a hand on Merry's arm. "You won't tell them about me, will you?"

Merry lifted an eyebrow. "What could I tell? Say whatever you want."

Cathreen hugged her backpack to her chest. She didn't move until Merry slung an arm around her shoulders and propelled her forward. A white dog trotted up and sniffed at the bundle in her arms until Cathreen let the cat out. The two animals headed off, side by side, into the woods.

"Will you look at that!" said the old man, Charlie, gazing after the animals. He put down his guitar and stood up to be introduced, a big grin on his face. The younger man, Nick, stood up too, as she entered the ragged perimeter of light. He smiled at her and stuck out his hand. He was tall and thin and stooped. His eyes were a pale sea-blue, striking in his olive-skinned face. A hank of straight black hair fell over his forehead. He was older than she was, but not by that much. Not bad looking at all, she thought. "Welcome," he said. "Have you come to stay?"

"I don't know," she said. "Yes, I guess." She looked at Merry, who explained that Cathreen's father hadn't shown up at the airport, as expected, to meet her. That she'd stay until she found him.

Then Merry sniffed the air. "What's for dinner? It's Charlie's turn to cook, isn't it?"

The old man had reseated himself by the fire. He squirmed on his chair—two slabs of wood set at right angles to form the back and seat, with four short lengths of tree limb for legs, the kind of chair that Tink might have liked—and cast an apologetic grin at Cathreen. "It *was* my turn, but something came up. I'd have tried harder if I'd knowed you was coming." He ducked his head in embarrassment.

"You always skive off when it's your turn, Charlie," Merry said.

"What was it this time?" She lifted a kettle, shook it to see if it were filled with water, and set it on the grate. The old man hunched into his collar.

"We try to share the work," Nick said to Cathreen. "Has Merry told you about us?"

"Not really."

He showed her where to sit, on a log bench next to him. "We're all equals here, with a share in the property and work," he said. "One day we'll have more people, a whole community. This is just a start." His long fingers twiddled a stick, then tossed it onto the fire. "Instead of living separately, like people do on housing estates, we live as a family unit. Eventually we'll produce all the food we and the animals need, and have a small surplus to sell." Cathreen nodded. It sounded to her like a commune Jag and Helena had lived in briefly in the Queen Charlotte Islands, long before she was born.

Nick continued, "We've begun a tree plantation. We've already started thinning the original forest and logging some of the less valuable older trees. We won't log the very old yews and oaks—they'll be preserved. We're planting Douglas firs. They grow quickly and make good wood. The wood brings in cash."

"Nick's an enthusiast," Merry said. She poured wine into three glasses and handed one each to Nick and Cathreen. To Charlie she said, "None for you, you've given up the drink."

Cathreen said, "At home, people chain themselves to trees so the loggers can't cut them down. Tink says you have to leave some wilderness."

Nick raised his eyebrows, but before he could respond, Merry asked, "Who's Tink?"

"My stepfather. Sort of. My mother isn't exactly married to him." Cathreen felt her face tense and her eyes sting. She hoped they'd think her watery eyes were from the smoke drifting from the fire. She coughed and waved a hand in front of her face.

"So, what *is* for tea, then?" Merry said.

Charlie sighed. "You'd better tell her, Nick."

"Tell me what?" Merry glanced at one man, then the other. Cathreen looked away. She hated arguments and she could feel one coming.

"We brought bread, cheese, eggs and fruit. It was all we could carry," Nick said.

"Carry? What about the van? What happened to it? Isn't it parked down below?"

"It broke down."

"Oh, great! What about the parts for the mill?"

"They'll be delivered."

"That will cost money, Nick." Merry threw an exasperated look at Cathreen, who quickly began to dig in her backpack for a sweater. She didn't know whose side she was supposed to be on.

"No, it won't." Nick set his wine glass on the ground. He got up, threw a handful of tea leaves into an earthenware pot and filled it with boiling water. "It won't, Merry. I promised some travellers a crock of cider to bring them out."

"The cider's not ready, Nick!"

"Ready enough," Charlie said with a guffaw. He winked at Cathreen. Merry didn't say anything more but quickly drank the rest of her wine and lit a cigarette.

After Nick had poured the tea and made everyone melted cheese and bread for supper, Charlie fetched his guitar and started to strum. The chords rose like a counterpoint to the sparks, a dance that made Cathreen lift her eyes and catch sight of an owl gliding over the clearing. It settled at the top of a fir to watch them. Where had Cutthroat got to? Out looking for mice like the owl? She thought about getting up to look for him, but there were questions she wanted to ask, things she wanted to know about this place she was staying. She just wasn't sure how to bring them up.

"You didn't run into Galt in the village, did you?" Merry said, as she began to wash the dishes in a basin. Charlie stopped playing. "I don't like not knowing what he's up to. Nick, Charlie, did you see him?"

Charlie said, "You tell her, Nick."

Merry dried her hands on a tea towel. Her face scrunched up; fine worry lines appeared around her mouth and on her forehead. "You haven't said you'd take him back, have you, Nick?"

Nick raised his calm blue eyes. "Maybe we should consider it. We're pretty shorthanded."

Merry spun towards Charlie. "*You* know what happened! Didn't you tell him?"

"Now don't fly off the handle," the old man said. "Maybe it wasn't all his fault, Merry. You can't treat Galt like he's normal or somethin'. Nick here was saying how Galt has nowhere else to go."

"We were lucky he went without a fight," she said.

"I'm just saying, we should have let him have a say. You had yours. You're the one who found him in the first place." Charlie ran his tongue along his lips. "I've been worrying. We should've told somebody about him. It'll cause trouble. He's not 'right.' "

"Of course he's not right!" Merry said. "I could have told you that."

"It's not only that . . ."

"What else?" Merry was so angry she'd gone white. She stuffed the damp tea towel into her back pocket.

"It's just that he might do somethin' when he's with people who don't understand him," Charlie said.

"What's to understand? What about me, don't I count? What about her?" She pointed to Cathreen. "You're not going to have him back with Cathreen here, are you?"

"We didn't find him," Nick said.

"No, but you looked. I can't believe it. You were there, Charlie, you saw what happened!"

"Things aren't always what they seem at first glance," Charlie said. He clutched his guitar by the neck and stared down at the polished wood. "We have to remember how he was. You know, Merry, he was your friend."

"Fine, but we know how he is now, you stupid old fool. Charlie, I can't believe you!"

"In my day people didn't get into bed whenever they wanted with whoever they wanted without so much as an if you please . . ."

Nick said, with a glance at Cathreen, "Don't you think we'd best talk this out in private?"

Cathreen flushed. "I don't have to stay here," she said. "I could go somewhere else." The trouble was, she was curious, she *did* want to ask what was the matter with Galt.

"No," Nick said, "you can stay as long as you like. Please."

"You're welcome to Galt, Nick," Merry said. "He can pull out the stumps by himself with his bare hands and you won't need a horse, I don't care, but I won't be here. And don't tell him where I've gone, don't say anything to him about me." Merry swung on her heel and entered the bender. They heard her inside, stumbling in the dark.

"I think I'll go for a walk," Charlie said. "Give her a chance to cool down. I didn't mean it like it sounded. Sometimes, when you think things over, you see them different, that's all. Merry will come round. Everyone deserves a second chance."

Everyone? Cathreen thought. If so, somebody should tell that to her mother. It would be news to her.

"Not people like that, you old fart," Merry shouted. Charlie set the guitar down carefully and shambled away into the darkness.

"I'm sorry," Nick said. He looked drained, almost sick. "We're not always like this, Cathreen. Usually, we get along. Merry's one of my best friends. . . . I'm not sure I understand what's happened tonight."

Merry stuck her tear-streaked face through the door of the bender. "I just want to say, Nick, before I go to sleep, that I'm out of here first thing in the morning, and whatever you do, don't let that monster near Cathreen." Her head disappeared and she closed the canvas flaps behind her.

Nick gazed around helplessly. His hands dangled by his sides. A sliver of pale blue-green vein pulsed in his forehead.

A thin wail—Charlie's voice or Cutthroat's?—floated from the trees on the hilltop and seemed to mingle with the smoke, then died away. A long silence followed.

"You don't mind about the cat?" Cathreen said, to break it.

Nick smiled at her gratefully. "We could use a cat around here. The mice get into the food stores."

"I wouldn't want to give him up. I've never had a pet before. I always wanted one, but." What was she doing, talking to him about her cat? He'd think she was stupid.

But Nick sat down beside her. "Breaker's my first dog," he said. "I acquired him by accident."

So he told her the story of the young mountaineer, Tomas. When Nick mentioned the pale stone sewn into the dog's paw, and warned her to be careful of it, Cathreen remembered the piece of green glass she'd found at Mrs. Hamilton's. Her fingers searched in her pocket.

Nick turned to examine her, his gaze so direct that she blushed. "My father had girlfriends who weren't my mother," he said. "I heard what you said about your mother and her boyfriend. I want you to know that I understand." He began to gather up his things—the sweater he'd taken off earlier, the cold teacups and teapot.

"It's okay, I don't mind. It's not that bad. I like Tink. He and my father were, like, friends."

Nick paused in his tasks. "I miss my mother more than my father. She was a little crazy, like me. We understood each other. My sister's more like my father. We don't get along."

"There isn't anyone else in my family. Just me," Cathreen said. From the corner of her eye, she noticed Charlie creep down the hill.

Nick saw him too. "That's the only place there is to sleep," he said as Charlie entered the canvas dwelling. "It's not much, but there's a spare bed, and blankets, and sleeping bags and pillows."

"Galt's bed?" She was sorry as soon as she said it. Nick had made it clear it wasn't her business. His mouth tightened. Cathreen had been holding the green stone in her pocket. Now she took it out, balanced it on her palm and held it up to show him.

"That's pretty," he said, taking it. He lifted it to his eye and looked through it at the fire. When he put it down he said, "The force that drives the green fuse through the flower." He grinned at her. "It's from a poem."

"I have to tell you something," she said then, and hoped that this was the right moment. "It's not just that my father didn't come for me, but when I went to the pub to ask, the bartender called the cops." Nick gave the green stone back to her. "I don't want to cause you any problems. I don't know what's going on. What if they turn up here?"

"But you haven't done anything wrong?" he said.

She shook her head.

Nick watched her put the stone away. "Merry was right, there's not all that much we can do at the moment without the van. I'll hitchhike into the village in the morning and look for parts, and while I'm there I'll see what I can find out for you." He caught her anxious frown. "Don't worry. I won't say anything about you."

Cathreen turned over, saw Nick, followed by Merry, push aside the blanket-and-canvas doorway and let in a shaft of early morning light, then she fell back to sleep. When she surfaced again, she lay quietly, thinking over everything that had happened and listening to the noises of wood chopping and Charlie's singing. Cathreen had never before been in a room like this one. Light, soft and filtered, fell through the pale canvas and onto the blue-and-white-checked quilt on her bed. Hooked rugs and Persian rugs were spread on top of a red cloth over the floor. Her face felt cold, her breath steamed, but a fire blazed in a small airtight stove in the room's centre; the chimney poked through a hole in the dome where the poles that formed the circular bender frame came together. The head of each bed was snugged up to the outer wall; the feet spoked inwards. Books, candles, teacups, magazines and clothing distinguished each person's space: Nick's area was immaculate, his sweaters and shirts folded in an open chest; what remained of Merry's clothing and toiletries spilled out of several large canvas holdalls. Charlie's bed was a nest of clothing, boots, tools and blankets. Her own backpack lay on the floor beside the bed that was now hers. She looked around for Cutthroat and the dog, Breaker, she'd met the night before, but couldn't see them.

Cathreen yawned and drew up her knees. To her surprise—she hadn't known he was there—Cutthroat slithered out of the blankets at the bottom of the bed. He stretched, gave a tiny fart and moved away to groom himself.

A hand swept aside the canvas door flap and Charlie stuck his head inside. "Breakfast's ready," he said.

"Yup, there's just us this morning," Charlie said cheerfully when she sat down beside him at the fire. Nick and Merry had left, Merry probably for good, it looked like, and Nick to go into the village as he'd promised. Cathreen felt badly about Merry: the woman had been kind to her, had rescued her from a difficult situation, and from what she'd understood of the previous night's argument, she was in the right. Why should she have to live with someone who frightened her?

Charlie fussed over the eggs cooking in the cast-iron pan, then dished them onto a plate. "I like to see a young woman eat," he said, watching her test, with her fork, the black lace edges, the perfect sunflower yolks. "Come spring we'll have our own hens." He smiled and pushed out his dentures. She needed to pee and wash and she wasn't very hungry, but she ate as much as she could to please him.

When Cathreen finished eating, she took her plate and coffee cup to the table, then followed Charlie's instructions as to where to find water. She brought some back in a pail and put it on the grate to heat.

"There's plenty of water, don't stint," he said as he tidied crumbs into the fire with a broken-off branch. She'd drawn the water from a tap attached to a pipe strapped to a tree. The black PVC piping, Charlie had told her, ran up from the stream in which they'd installed a gravity-powered pump. "That pump's old-fashioned, like me, but she does the job. If you listen, you can hear 'er," he'd said. And she could: a sound somewhere between that of a loud clock and a duck. Tick, quock. Gentle enough to time the swaying tops of the trees.

"What do you do when it gets cold out or it rains or snows?" she asked, wriggling her frozen toes.

"Don't bother us," Charlie said, his rheumy eyes dancing. "We're not like you North Americans . . . spoiled with central heating." Cathreen sniffed through her numb nose and stretched her stiff fingers. Jag's fingers, during cold, damp winters, still broke out in bumps and blisters from the chilblains he'd suffered as a child: there'd been no heating in the house he'd shared with his sister except for a small fireplace in the front room and in each bedroom. People had rheumatism at twenty, he'd said. Cathreen hadn't really believed him then, but she did now. "But," Charlie said, watching her, "if it gets too bad we go up there." He heaved himself to his feet. "Come with me, I'll show you. I'm going that way anyway. I'll be working on the irrigation ditches this morning, so you'll be more or less on your own." Which was fine with her. She was still tired from her journey.

Forty yards or so on, not far from where Merry had parked the Land Rover the night before, stood a canvas-and-pole lean-to, open on one side. A heavy canvas cover was bunched over the opening. Inside it were a large wood stove, tables, cupboards made from crates and old filing cabinets, several couches and broken bench car seats. From the ceiling poles hung two guitars, a mandolin and several sets of rain gear. Nothing was new. It smelled of mice and apples. "Cosy, eh?" said Charlie. "We can close the gap in a storm."

A wave of homesickness surprised Cathreen. Not for Helena or Tink or the house, exactly, but for familiar things. Her mother's waffles on Sundays, the pillowcase of stuffed animals shoved to the back of a closet. And she missed her friends. What was she doing here?

"Where exactly are we, Charlie?" she asked as the old man, carrying a shovel, retrieved string and chalk from drawers of the winter kitchen. "It's the middle of nowhere. There's nothing to do, and it's fucking freezing. Why do you stay here?" She stamped her feet, in their damp running shoes, in an attempt to restore some feeling. At home she could have a hot bath, watch TV, go out to a movie. The old man shot her a look of disapproval, so familiar in its way she discounted it.

She looked around. There wasn't exactly a lot to see except the wet haze that hung over the clearing, the bender and the several small lean-tos; aside from that, there was wet bush and tall trees. Pale grey light threaded through the foliage between gaps in the mist: you couldn't even call it sunlight. Sadness, like beige water spilled inside her, made her feel heavy and thick. Where was Nick? He was the only one anywhere near her age. Everybody else was like sixty. She should've asked him to pick up batteries so she'd at least be able to listen to music. Cathreen caught the old man's eye. A flash of steel in the watery blue and red. He was disappointed in her—why?

"You listen to what Nick said last night about people needing their bit of land?" he asked, his finger pointing. "I planted tea in Malaya my whole damn life, I get back here and what've I got? A bedsit and a telly, a box of photographs, a window the size of a biscuit tin with a view of red brick. How'd *you* like it?" He leaned the shovel against a tree. Cathreen chewed at a ragged cuticle.

Charlie bent his head and busied himself winding the string into a neat ball. By the time she'd bitten the nails of one hand, and he'd finished, the tension had slipped from his narrow shoulders. "You remember to feed your cat?" he said, putting the string in a pocket and looking up. She shook her head. "Breaker and me had breakfast early. I don't sleep much. Used to sleep all the time in the bedsit. Now, I don't need it." His mouth worked. He looked around, then at her, thought better of it, and swallowed his spit.

"Pah! You're young yet," he said. "Go down and feed your cat, then come back up." When she looked back, he'd set himself to wait, his thin legs wide apart, long thighs showing as the wind came up and puffed against his baggy pants. Some of the hairs of his grey beard had caught in the buttons of his shirt.

Cathreen scraped the remains of her eggs into a dish and called for Cutthroat. The cat skittered down the trunk of a nearby tree, sniffed at the scraps and ate. She poured warm water into a basin and washed cups, plates and pots.

When she returned to the winter kitchen, Charlie was crouched outside it, drawing in the earth with a stick.

"It works like this," he said as she came up. "Ancient people, maybe the Sumerians, or maybe not, refugees from Atlantis or maybe Inca priests, nobody knows for sure, built a giant earthwork zodiac around the pole star. Where we are is where light of that star fell thousands of years ago." He glanced up to see how she was taking it.

"I know something about it. My father told me some of the stories," she said.

"He did, eh," Charlie said. "You know the pole star changes? The one we've got now isn't the same as back then. Takes a long time to shift though." He considered the rough figures he'd drawn round the circle. "The Celts said the stars hung like fruit from that pole tree. So I'm thinking, Cathreen, maybe in the first place, further back than we can know, this was Eden. Maybe so, maybe not, but I've got something to ponder, see, and things to keep me busy. That's why I'm here, since you was asking."

"Oh." She wasn't sure about Eden. She'd thought it was just a place that had never existed. "Is that what Nick thinks?"

"Nick speaks for himself," Charlie said. He stood up and dusted his hands on his trousers.

"But where else are we, Charlie? I mean, where is this place?"

Charlie looked startled. "You mean the roads and such?"

"I couldn't see much last night, and I only just got here."

He stooped and picked up the stick again. "There's the village," Charlie said, making a mark at the top of the circle, "here's the road you come on, and that's us." He stabbed at the centre and scratched the shape of a few trees. "There's youth hostels in town if you'd prefer."

"I'm used to camping," Cathreen said. Cutthroat appeared and stepped delicately across Charlie's drawing.

"It's not camping for us," Charlie said. "It's not camping for our Nick."

When Charlie had headed off to work—down in the orchard, over the hill if she needed him—Cathreen returned to the bender. She put on her warmest clothes, got into bed, pulled the blue-checked quilt to her chin and tucked Cutthroat in beside her. The cat lifted his white front paws out and placed them on top of the cover. He purred softly and watched her with his gold-green eyes.

She didn't remember closing her own eyes, but suddenly there was Fawn trailing the skeletal orchard behind her. Now the orchard looked lichenous, scabby and grey, and even more ghostly than before. Cathreen inspected the tall, dazed girl and thought how glad she was not to be her. The space around Fawn was a vacuum; she dared not get too close or she'd get sucked into it. Cathreen shrank away, and kept on shrinking into the core of herself until there was nothing but a dry kernel, tight and hard. It was hardly worth saving. This was not what she'd expected. She was supposed to feel sorry for Fawn and now there was Fawn looking at *her* with pity.

It was like walking into a wall, no less solid for being invisible. Girls—her friends Toni, Judy, Kora and the others—stared at her from the edge of the orchard, turned their heads away to laugh, and she was left standing on the outside of their circle. What have I done? Cathreen asked herself. What is it?

Nothing, I've done nothing, she told herself. She knew where she really was. She was inside that circle with her back to Fawn. With them.

She was out of bed, outside the bender and walking up the hill before she knew it, Cutthroat in her arms, Breaker loping along at her side. The shade of green trees fell over her shoulders, the path wound on, scaled with brown leaves and dropped needles. She stopped, out of breath, her way blocked by a group of trees with grey multiple trunks, giant inter-layered limbs. She flopped herself onto the ground in a patch of fresh pale sunlight at the foot of one of them. Seconds later something cold and wet lay heavily against her neck and shoulder, and her astonished eyes met the lidless saucer regard of a donkey.

She yelped and slid away, scooting over the earth on her buttocks. The donkey stretched thick lips back from long yellow teeth and brayed, its neck still extended towards her. It was mottled and plain looking, its dust-and-tan colour fitting neatly into the background. Its tail switched in matted tufts. It hee-hawed and lowered its head to a clump of grass, which it tugged up with its strong teeth. Cutthroat butted the donkey's legs, and Breaker touched noses with it.

A throaty engine sputtered as it came nearer, then gave several quick machine coughs. "Cathreen!" It was Nick calling. She ran down the hill.

Nick stood in the clearing unbuckling a crash helmet. He placed it on the seat of a handsome red motorcycle. Chrome handlebars, chrome trim, a long black leather seat and chrome back rest.

"What the hell is that?" Cathreen said, grinning as she came up to him.

"This?" Nick did his best to look nonchalant, gave up and just smiled. "I've rented it until the repairs on the van are done. We'll need it to get around."

She circled it, touched the shiny paint job, looked at Nick.

"Try it, get on," he said.

She swung her leg over the seat and bounced up and down. Her hands gripped the handlebars. "You know how to drive this thing?" she said, getting off.

"Want to see?"

"I don't know. Maybe. Yeah, okay!"

He gave her a helmet and she climbed on behind him. He drove down the dirt path that skirted the woods. The farmhouse, in daylight, looked smaller. A dog barked at them from behind a fence, but there were no signs of children.

"I thought you'd be against this kind of thing," she cried into his ear as they turned south onto the roadway. Grey clouds pillowed the horizon, green and brown straggly fields fell far behind them. Her eyes watered until there was no scenery at all.

"The internal combustion engine?" he shouted back. "That's what you mean?"

"Yes!"

"I am!" Nick leaned into the corner. Cathreen leaned with him.

Nick

Nick was being dragged along behind his father's boat, clearly long before his father's death, since both parents were on the bridge, his mother with binoculars raised to her eyes, keeping an eye on him. They were distant enough that he felt lonely and he was fearful of the water rising and falling around him in steep cliffs and canyons and of large birds that swooped low enough to peck out his eyes. This was no Mediterranean cruise on a hot day. Flying fish squirted from the wake his shoulders rooster-tailed from the sea, and a shark cruised lazily in S curves alongside. He couldn't let go of the rope that bound him to the boat: it was tied tight, and if he *were* able to cut it, he'd be left behind to die. Nick leaned his head back, gasping for air, and watched clouds pile up, like mountains, in a magnificent blue sky. Suddenly he could see himself and his parents from above, at a river mouth, steering round stretches of shingle and mud and then disappearing into a deep river gorge.

His parents were lost to him. He grappled, on dry land, in a set of ruins overgrown with weeds and cactus, with a broken bucket, trying to clear out a well. Instead of water, he brought up earthenware and skulls. He watched himself, once more from afar, choked with dust, plagued with flies, scraping charcoal from burned-out trees. Another shift and he was so high up a mountain he could scarcely breathe. Other mountains, far below, were like crusty piles of sand and cinders sloped back from a deserted beach. Then there was a village, an inn of whitewashed mud built round a grass courtyard. He saw hens and little pigs and guinea pigs and he was freezing cold and waiting for his parents at a railway terminus. When he gazed around, there was no limit to visibility: red-tiled roofs, trains of llamas carrying fifty-pound sacks of grain, barefoot Indians in coloured ponchos, a military parade, the men strutting in grand uniforms stretched in a vision reaching hundreds of miles: the sun sank in splendour from crimson to green.

His father, alighting from the train, gave him coffee and a slab of unleavened bread to eat. His mother organized the tent: kerosene boxes for a table, old sacks for a carpet, stores of potatoes, dried meat, beans, a case of macaroni. She waited there while her husband sailed across glaciers and frozen lakes on an aerial tramcar and brought down ore to the mill. Nick could smell llama dung, greasy soup, cocoa, his mother's skin, his father's hair. "Nick, you really shouldn't be here," said his mother in his ear. "It's your birthday."

Nick lay awake in the morning dimness of the bender. Charlie had stumbled in and out several times during the night and had finally fallen asleep in his clothes. Merry's bed was empty. Cathreen lay on her stomach in what had been Galt's bed. Nick missed hearing Merry outside, building a fire, getting the day started. Merry had a kind heart. Maybe things could still work out. He thought they would. Today he'd go out on the motorcycle with Cathreen and look for her father. After that, well, they'd see.

A feeling of richness, like hot cream and honey and cinnamon, bubbled inside him. It was more than he'd expected, it was everything he'd hoped for.

Galt

Sitting still at the small wooden table in the Rainbow's End Café was impossible now that Galt had once more swallowed the stone. The energy that flowed through him made his heart speed. It jammed against his chest wall, a hammering demolition system; he wanted, needed, something to do with the power that surged in his body like a great tide. He could see, behind his eyelids as he thought *tide*, acres of mud flats, and dykes raised over fragments of trees and mammoth's teeth; cold waters mixed with slippery layers of fog, and beneath the waters, silver herring, tons of them, that slid through his bloodstream. With the herring came whales and gulls and the entire resonating response of the floodwaters to the push of the North Atlantic.

Galt blinked open his eyes, wiped sweat from his face and stood up, knocking over the blue wooden chair on which he'd been sitting. The man at the next table stared at him. Galt hoped the man would get up so that he could hit him, but the man shrank away. Galt observed, in the fuzz of blue light in the room, the man's fear, his awareness of Galt's hands clenching and unclenching, then map lines of his own brain, its scrawls like serpents and flames . . . Galt closed his eyes again and tried to slow himself down. He had to be careful; he mustn't do anything that would jeopardize a meeting with his Master.

Outside, in the street, Galt stood with his nose to the wind. A molecule of scent so faint it might have been not in the air, but on a television screen—like an ad for a perfume—skimmed by. He turned his head to catch it and saw Merry driving the Land Rover down the cobblestones, peering sharply around her. He remembered that she had lied to him, that she had stolen from his Master, and he drew back quickly under the café overhang before she could see him. Fear and anger twisted his belly, but he held them in.

Quickly Galt crossed the street. The Land Rover reached the bottom of the hill and bore left at the market cross, trailing wisps of Merry's thoughts like smoke: one of these had caught Galt's interest. He loped past a jumble of shops, some made of painted stone, others of red brick with elaborate facings; he sped by restaurants and candle, book and crystal shops and so many people that he had to close his mind against them lest they overwhelm the fragile notion that Merry had left behind and that he was following.

A handful of boys sat in the market square, drumming on African drums, their noses blue with cold. Galt paused near them; his skin ached as it stretched over thickened bands of muscles and flesh, his too-small clothes hung in rags, and he saw the boys cast cautious looks in his direction. When he'd traversed the Levels at night as a boy and young man, running beside the riverbank, he'd been followed more than once by wolves. The wolves slipped down from the mountains, they ran tirelessly along the secret pathways of the marshes, swimming where you didn't think they could swim, sniffing you out. You never knew if you were going to make it home, but he always had, he'd never been caught by anything or anyone before the woman. And he had learned. But the drums battered at his concentration, threatened to fracture the wall of present time. He glared at the boys, but they kept on drumming. He could almost see, far below the current wash and slop of voices and pictures, the slurry around the living people, the features of his own time. He caught a sharp glimpse of a house made of posts and wattlework and of an old woman crouched by a fire as she placed a lid on a cooking pot, and as he did so, his focus slipped. His body twisted towards the boys, and they stopped drumming, frightened of him, but it was too late. All trace of Merry's passage was gone.

A nearby alley fed into a deserted green parkland set about with ruins. Inside one of the tumbledown buildings, he sat on the wet stone flagging and wished he were human enough to cry.

Galt made his way slowly until he came to the place where he'd seen Nick leave the van when it had stopped running. He would have liked to have helped Nick by fixing it—Nick had been kind to him; it was Charlie and Merry who had sent him away—but he had no tools or money. The van was parked to the side of a lane on the edge of the village, hard against blue limestone slabs that formed a small gorge. Less than a stone's throw away from it, Galt could see men and women, hikers, perhaps, or pilgrims travelling the track to the cathedral at Wells, or round the zodiac. He might have gone with them, but there was suddenly no time. He crouched in a hollow overhung by the roots of trees, dreading the moment when the stone would pass through and leave him empty. In front of him, the figures trudged by without a glance.

When he was finished, and he had wiped and washed the stone and swallowed it, he walked on. As always, inside Galt was his pain at being separated from his Master. There was nothing else, really, no hope or thought or dream, except the growing awareness that he wasn't all that he once had been.

The lane continued between thick hedges. It was one of many that spoked out from the village, one of a dozen footways that unravelled where they met the moors. Galt left the track, climbed a stile and entered a field. The field was wet; several sheep stood staunch in it, heads to a wind that burst suddenly over a hill to disturb the trees and set their tops churning. The roaring gale hurt Galt's ears and he covered them with his hands. When the sudden blow died as quickly as it had arisen, and he lifted his head, he smelled vestiges of smoke and rubbish heaps, and wet ash and charred bone. He swivelled his head back and forth, and there it was, like the faint ring of a triangle, the familiar note that had mingled with Merry's scent and thoughts as she'd passed by. It was his Master.

Galt was made of the oldest materials—clay, stone, water and bone. In the rain that now poured down from the still sky, as he reached the burned house, he could feel a minuscule thinning of his peat-stained skin, the tough sinew and striped muscles of his body gently surfacing towards their covering. A fraction more bone showed in his long hands. He pushed through a gate and walked round the foundation. The rubble stank of wet wood ash and brick, petrol, melted plastic, nylon, plaster and cooked flesh. Rainwater filled his eyes as he looked skyward, grinning. He stretched his arms as if he could push through the heavy clouds to the brilliance of sun and stars he knew lay beyond them. Behind him, lights sprinkled on across the town. It was this way that his Master had come, past houses, down streets, into the yard, then round the back, through a farmer's field and beyond. Galt knelt and grazed his tongue along some of the earth his Master's feet had touched, letting his tongue taste it, filling his emptiness with every atom his Master had left behind him. His Master was present and absent, a veil between them like skin or parchment. It made Galt want to claw at his eyes until he could see him. I, Galt, he thought, have much power, but I do not have Him.

Galt had reached a file of willows next to a rhyne several hundred feet behind the house when he heard the wind-up thrumming of a motorbike. He watched the bike belt up the road towards the house, its headlamp bouncing, then halt in front of the little ruin. Two figures separated from the machine and stood quietly beside it. A girl's voice asked questions and a boy—it was Nick's voice—replied. Galt listened: waves of the girl's anxiety reached him, ripples of how much she missed someone too; he sent out a quaver of feeling in response, but nothing came back. From Nick there was the usual flurry of words, and the dense shadow of the past he dragged with him. Galt squinted: he could almost make it out this time—something tall, but with a blurred outline, and something funny about the neck, and a thick liquid running over the ground.

Jag

The track followed the high ground in from the road, angled across fields and through farms for several miles before weaving its cautious way through the peat workings. A slice of moon crept through the sky, but not enough for him to see by. He'd doused the headlamps a mile back before leaving the road, but had to turn them on now and then to find his way. With only the heaps of stacked peat to give him his bearings, it took him longer than he'd expected to get to the spot where he'd last seen the bog man. He switched the engine off and waited, half hoping for, half dreading what he might find.

He'd revisited the place several times, driven by his need to understand what had happened there, taking long, arduous hikes from the hut that had left him sweating and shaking and, like the last time, almost too weak to make it back. Merry's arrival had been a godsend. He'd been more than exhausted when she, his good Samaritan, had found him again, this time perilously in sight of the road, where anybody passing might have spotted him sitting near the spillway of a small sluice. He'd just crouched there, exhausted, gaping at the green scum of the ditch. She'd stopped the Land Rover and climbed down to him, hauled him up the bank to her vehicle. The wind had sliced across the open field; it was cold and he was wet through. Once back in the hut, she'd unpacked a small propane heater and lit it, turning the damp air of the hut into a thick, comforting fug. She'd also brought a Primus stove with her on which she heated wash water and water for tea. He'd been too weak, initially, to do anything, let alone ask questions or make any objections, so she'd poured tea and soup into him, helped him undress, then bathed him as if he were a baby. When he'd stopped shuddering, and she'd stuffed him into the dry clothes she'd brought, and told him a little about how she'd first found him on the moor and taken him to the hut, she said, "You don't remember me, do you?"

He looked at her more closely. "I do remember you. I've seen you in the pub."

"You went to that boys' school, your sister married that school-teacher. It was sad about her and the baby."

Old grief washed over him like a wave of seawater. "Did you know Jen?" he said.

Merry nodded. "My father ran a farm. She used to come out to the dairy sometimes when I was still little. Then later, after I left home, I saw her in the village a few times." Merry shook her head. "I couldn't believe it when I heard what happened."

"What was that?" he said. "What did people say?" He felt more naked at that moment than when she'd pulled off his wet trousers. He didn't remember her from those days at all. But then she was a girl, and younger, and had probably gone to the village school.

"Well, what she'd done, drowned herself and the baby. Her body turned up, what was it, after a week? Did they ever find the baby?"

Jag didn't say anything.

"Jen lived a dog's life after she married, didn't she," she continued. "You were lucky to get out when you did."

"Yes," he said. "I was lucky."

"Was that before Jen died?"

"Just before," he said.

Merry began slicing a loaf of bread. "So why'd you come back after all this time? Looking for your roots, is that it?"

"Something like that," he said.

"You were a good-looking boy," Merry said, giving him a glance from behind the little table where she sliced cheese to go with the bread. She came round the table and handed him a plate. Jag shrugged off the blanket Merry had draped around his shoulders. "My boyfriend would have put my eyes out if he'd known I was looking at other men."

"I never saw you," he said.

"No, I don't suppose you did. Nobody looked at me and Neil unless they thought we were stealing." She smiled. "Neil was a traveller. His family had a camp outside the village."

"So, why are you doing this?" he asked her, waving a hand to take in the clothes and food and blankets and medicine, all the trouble she'd gone to for him.

"Maybe I owe you something. Neil, my boyfriend, used to say that a home and food and a bed was enough for anyone. I said it was, but it wasn't. Not for me. I could tell you were going places, you weren't going to stay here forever. I used to wonder what you'd make of yourself. It gave me ideas." She shrugged.

"But you're still here," he said.

"I left not long after you did," she said.

"But you came back."

"Well, there were good reasons, and when I did, it was on my own terms."

Jag lay back on the cot, not so much ill as spent. His guts were in ferment, and he felt weak. "You said Jen lived a dog's life . . ."

"Everybody knew it. Colin Printer was scum." She crouched beside him and let her hand graze his face.

"Nobody said anything," Jag said, fighting not to cry.

"They wouldn't, would they? Frightened of him, weren't they? I know I was." Jag closed his eyes and let her stroke his forehead. "Turn over," she said, "you're all done in. I'll rub your back." She helped him roll onto his stomach, then knelt astride him on the cot and gently massaged the knots from his neck and shoulders. Her fingers had drawn a slow line down his spine and onto his buttocks, kneading there softly. It felt good. Even grief, even anguish and guilt, apparently, had their limits.

Jag stretched and turned on the radio. The station played oldies, beach music from his youth. He tapped out the melody on the steering wheel. Merry had kept her promise to return to the hut with more food and bring whatever news there was of Cathreen. She'd told him she'd found her and had her tucked up safely in the countryside, away from the prying eyes of the police. It was best for them all, now, if Cathreen didn't know anything about him until he'd sorted himself out and got the stone back: he owed it to Jen and to himself, and to Cathreen. It was his responsibility. His mistake, if it was one. He'd been over and over the sequence, hoped sometimes that he could have only imagined what he'd found at the house—the stench, the dead, tortured cats, the red stone vibrating to his breath on its string—and later, his flight, the flutter of life in the bog man when he'd placed the stone in its mouth, and then the drag marks from the pit, the footprints leading away. But it wasn't his imagination; he had seen it all.

So here he was again, this time in comfort, out of the wet and wind, hoping, somehow, to recover Jen's stone. Merry hadn't even asked why he wanted to borrow the Land Rover, just handed him the keys. "Anything you want, Jag," she'd said.

Those other times he'd reached the digging, he'd had to lie on his belly on the ground while he watched for movement near the pit or the stilled machinery. Fear walked his spine; cold drained the energy from his body. Each time he'd thought he'd seen something—the glow of eyes, or some stirring out of the cavity—but he'd been wrong.

The desire to find the stone made him restless, his skin itched with it. He made himself not think about what he could do with it if he had it, if all the old stories were true. He drifted, the music on the radio knitted time, the car was a womb, the moor a screen for pleasant thoughts. For once there were no bad dreams, no terrifying thoughts from which he'd have to pull himself coughing and retching, then stumble away to be sick. This time, not a thread of distress.

Then the figure rose, not twenty feet from him, water streaming from its shoulders, out of the black ribbon of a ditch and shook itself. Jag's belly turned to ice. He switched off the radio and hunched down in hiding. The man was huge, his head like a lump of stone with a thick mat of hair stuck to it. The creature shook himself again, like a big dog, threw a shy glance at the parked Land Rover, and shambled to the pit edge where he sat down, his large back curved towards the car. He wore what was left of one of Jag's flannel shirts, taken from the mislaid rucksack. Jag had seen the hanging rope ends of the makeshift belt, the jeans undone and held up only by a few loops, as the man walked. Jag felt the crackle of energy. He sat up and stared.

What had happened? He knew it was the same man, the one he'd glimpsed in the bog, but that body had been a shrunken thing with cords for muscles and skin tugged tight over bone. The brown skin and tea-coloured hair, the flare of red eyes—these were the same. The feeling of intimacy. The man was waiting for him.

Jen, help me, Jag whispered. He eased open the car door.

"Don't turn around," Jag said when he was standing right behind him. He'd stuck his hand in his pocket so that if the man looked, he'd think Jag had a knife or a gun. Although the creature didn't move, there was a quick shimmering in the air. Jag could feel its intensity, a probing at his thoughts. He did his best to shut it out. He wished he'd told Merry where he was going. "I don't know who you are, but you've got something that belongs to me, and I want it back. I won't hurt you if you give it to me now." His voice was thready with fear.

"Master!" the man said. The deep voice was joyous.

Jag's knees trembled, he felt faint. "You know what I'm talking about?"

"Yes, Master!"

"The red stone is mine. It belonged to my sister. Put it down behind you and I'll pick it up. I'll let you go free."

"I am here, Master. Everything I have is yours." Again that voice like a bell, ringing with happiness.

Jag was still terrified, but he also felt foolish. His mind searched for and failed to find any logic to the man's response. Jag struck a match and held it up. Slowly the man turned his face towards him. The dazzled red eyes were full of tears. "Who are you?" Jag said.

"I am Galt now, Master," the thrilling voice said. "I am yours. You made me. Who else would I be?"

Flames stroked Galt's hands as he reached in and out of the fire he had built, but they didn't appear to hurt him. They'd moved to the shelter of a small coppice. Galt had caught a rabbit, broken its neck, cleaned and roasted it. He'd torn off pieces of the cooked flesh for Jag, but he ate nothing himself. Jag swallowed what he could, and threw the rest away when the man wasn't looking.

Twice more Jag had asked for the stone, but each time the bog man—Galt—had evaded answering.

Theirs was the only pinpoint of light, these small flames on the heath dwarfed by darkness. No other people existed; there were no houses, cars or history. Jag felt himself straying into lostness—too light for his body. He put a hand close to the flames so that the heat would make him feel real. He drew back from the pain, but the sense of unreality persisted, the knowledge that he'd been cut loose from his normal moorings. The rain that drizzled on his head was tangible, as was the soft earth beneath his haunches, and his muscles ached with damp, but not *him*. He'd taken a turning.

Jag blew on his stiff hands. Galt moved close to him. Jag nerved himself against the repulsion he felt at the man's nearness and asked for the stone again. He forced himself to smile and meet the red eyes.

This time Galt stared down at him, baffled. "My Master doesn't mean it," he said. A strong, fetid odour came from the bog man's mouth.

"I wouldn't ask for it if there weren't a good reason," Jag said.

"I searched for you, Master. Sometimes I thought I saw you passing across the Levels, searching for me. Was that not true?"

"Yes, it's true. I sought you out."

"But once you have the stone, I can no longer serve you, you know that." He shook his head as if this would clear his thoughts. "My Master wants what's best for me. My Master loves me," he said. "My Master wants me to keep the stone."

"If you loved me in return," Jag said, "you would give it to me when I ask."

Galt bowed his head, tugged at the mat of hair on his head, then looked up slyly. "I do not think you mean what you say."

"I do mean it, Galt, I'm only asking for what's mine," Jag said. He stretched his arms, and rotated his neck to ease the kinks, then he got to his feet. He glanced casually at his watch, then over at the Land Rover. "Well," he said, "I'd best be going. See you around."

Galt stepped in front of him. Jag could feel the heat that radiated from Galt's body: its fingers moved inside him, searched out his hidden repugnance, sniffed at it. Galt flexed his hands.

"Master," Galt said, "stay with me awhile." The bog man took his hand. "Don't be afraid. Killing the loved one is not love, Master," he said gently. Galt pushed Jag into a sitting position. "Let me tell you how I know.

"When I was a man, I lived in a village on an island in the marsh not far from here. The islands were made out of cut-down trees, reeds, bracken and clay. The marsh gave us protection from our enemies. I grew barley on a smaller, nearby island that my father had farmed before me. I had a dog for protection from the wolves that sometimes came down from the hills in search of prey.

"In those days, the sea reached far inland, even here. There was no flatland but that which lay underwater. Salty reed beds and fen formed most of the world. Yet one day a strange woman found a path across the marshland to our village." He paused. Firelight played over his features. It was like witnessing the development of a print, the image arising from within the paper and overlaying the blankness.

"The woman gave me presents of apples and hazelnuts. She said that a god had sent her. She told me that light falls from the stars to the earth and impregnates it, each star transmitting life of a different type, and of the great wheel that spins and unravels the universe. I knew nothing of these things. She told me she had followed a star to find me.

"I stopped my work to be with her. I loved her, and she loved me. I thought our love would last forever. One day, in midwinter, she gave me a drink. After sipping it, I dreamed I smelled the wet of the marshlands, heard the drip of water from a paddle. I drank more of the bitter tea. What I saw was there and not there, what I felt was behind a wall, only the wall was transparent. Like on telly.

"I saw myself dragged by the arms like an animal into the marsh. The woman pulled a rope tight around my neck, kissed me and raised a knife. I understood only at that moment that my life was to be a sacrifice. Is that love, Master, is it?" Galt waited until Jag shook his head. "I thought not," he said. "That is how I know I am right not to give you the stone. If I give the stone back to you, I will die. Then I will have to ask myself, Why did my Master give me such a gift just to take it from me? If it is taken back, it is not a gift. I am as you have made me: everything I do is for you."

"Yes," Jag said.

Jag dozed and sweated and dreamed until early morning, waking once to see Galt stumble away into the trees, and then return and stretch himself out on the damp, oozing soil. Jag waited for him to fall asleep, thinking that he could search him then—the creature's clothes were rags, there couldn't be many hiding places. Galt's chest inflated and deflated as regularly as if he were attached to a respirator, but each time Jag shifted a muscle, Galt's eyes fluttered open. Jag must have nodded off first, for when he awoke, Galt had relit the fire and was standing over him. It would go on and on if he let it.

Jag pushed himself to his feet. He began to walk. Short marsh grass splashed his shoes and wet his pant legs. He had to school himself not to run. The sopping pant legs slapped his calves and he stumbled over an undone bootlace. He dared not look behind before he reached the Land Rover. As he climbed into it, Galt called after him, "Master, you must tell me what to do!"

"Make me happy," Jag said over his shoulder as he shut the door behind him and started the engine.

"What would make you happy, Master?" The bog man had stopped a few feet away, his face screwed up in puzzlement.

Jag locked the doors and opened the window a crack. "I've already told you. But failing that, you could get my wife and family back for me, I'd sure as hell like that." Anything to get the creature off his tail. Helena was thousands of miles away.

"Get them back?"

"My wife doesn't love me anymore, Galt. It happens. She's found someone else." He permitted himself a smile. "It could happen to you. You ever lose someone you love, Galt?"

He drove away.

When he arrived at the hut he didn't go right in. He scrutinized the undulations of the surrounding moor. Nothing. The few spiked trees, shadows chasing the wind. He pulled down the visor and looked in the mirror. He hadn't changed. The same thin face, and blue eyes puffed with fatigue, but he couldn't even hold his own gaze. His eyeballs shook, his whole being.

Inside the hut, Merry slept, sprawled on top of the cot blankets. She'd taken off her boots and jeans but kept on her T-shirt and underthings. He eased a blanket over her legs and stared at her creased, freckled face. It looked crumpled and used, but not unfriendly. Should he ask for her help? What could he say that would make sense to her? Maybe Galt would do for a woman what he wouldn't do for him—give her the stone—or maybe, judging from the woman he'd talked about, a woman would scare him off completely.

He sat on the chair and took off his boots. He unbuttoned his shirt and placed it over the back of the chair. What would shake the stone loose? Where had Galt hidden it? What would make Galt give it to him? He stepped out of his trousers and padded in bare feet to where Merry stirred on the bed, her jaw slack, a trail of drool glistening at the corner of her mouth. It was lovely, in its way, that saliva. He reached out a finger to touch it. Merry snorted and swallowed and turned away from him.

As he watched her, Jag remembered his hand at the bog man's mouth, recalled the feeling he'd had when he'd placed the stone inside it and felt the sudden clench of the jaws on his fingers. Merry coughed and swallowed again, and he had it, he knew what had happened. He remembered looking back, as he'd run away in his panic, at a sudden noise from the bog man's throat and seeing the limp grey mouth open, empty.

Oh, Christ, Jag thought, turning from Merry to the window. That fucking stone was inside him. What the fuck was he supposed to do now? He yanked a piece of cardboard from a broken windowpane and took deep shuddering breaths of cold air.

A band of rain had topped the line of trees and pushed strongly east. Jag's nostrils filled all at once with the fust of dust and ozone, a whiff of rotted meat, and Galt's face appeared in the opening. Jag's heart stopped, then reluctantly took up its march. His instinct was to cover his nakedness, but he forced himself to stand still.

Galt grinned. He waved a piece of paper—a letter—in his hand. "Master, I understand now," he cried, putting his lips to the broken pane, his great voice only slightly thinned. "I am going now, but I will return. Master, your happiness is in my hands!"

Jag waited until he was sure Galt had really gone, his body frozen, his mind petrified, then he made himself search. His wallet was in his jacket pocket where he'd left it, money, bank and credit cards, driver's licence—all were there—but the letters and pictures of his family that he kept with the banknotes were missing.

Cutthroat

We had walked the whole night through and at daybreak we came to a house on the edge of the moor. I knew what was in the house, although the red stone, strictly speaking, was Knowall's business. The green stone lay on a shelf in the village library cloakroom, wrapped but not mailed, forgotten by the archaeologist who had dug it out of the ground. The white stone remained where it had been stitched, long ago, into Breaker's paw. His master at the time, a local poacher, lay drunk in the road miles away.

I scratched at the door, looking only for food and rest for the three of us. A tall woman with brown hair opened the door to let a cat out—not us in.

That was Jen.

The cat, a small tabby, stared at me, licked her paws, then fixed me with her emerald eyes.

That was Jones.

Cathreen

On the way back to Summerwood, Nick turned off the main road and drove to the top of a hill. He parked the bike and led Cathreen through long wet grass and thistle until they were standing at an edge. Nick pointed northwest. "On a good day you can see from here to the Bristol Channel," he said. Unrelieved blackness stretched westwards, although for an instant Cathreen thought she'd seen a small glimmer of light in it.

"I can't see anything," she said.

"This hill is the back of the Aries lamb in the zodiac Charlie drew for you," Nick said. She'd told him what Charlie had said to her. "Over there," he said, pointing to other dim hills in the distance, "are Taurus and Gemini. Also way over there"—he shifted her to face seaward again—"was where the last English battle to be fought with pitchforks took place. People still dig up pieces of armour and bones." Nick stuffed his hands in his pockets and hunched his shoulders. Cold, heavy clouds had blown in. "They cut off his head too," Nick said.

"What are you talking about?"

"The Duke of Monmouth, after he lost the battle, just like they did to Charles I thirty-six years earlier."

"Doesn't anything nice ever happen around here?" she said. "Let's go, Nick. This isn't helping my father."

"We'll find him, Cathreen."

"But how? He could be anywhere!"

"He won't be, he'll be searching for you. He knows you're here."

"I can't even go into the village now, I can't ask anybody if they've seen him! Nick, I'm getting scared!"

Where they'd just come from, the shell of Jen's house, its black crumbling brick and stone, the damp stench of wet ash that still clung to her hair, the crunch of unrecognizable objects underfoot—the utter absence of anything to show that Jag had ever lived there—had shocked her. Until then, she'd believed that life with Jag was a picture postcard she could just step into—the house with the room upstairs and a gable window for her, a little kitchen that looked out to the moor, the moor itself, Jen's garden, Jen's animals. It had been worse than finding nothing at all. What could have made him—as they were saying in the village—burn it down?

"Here's what I think," Nick said. "Your father doesn't have a car, so he'll be on foot. We should be on foot, too. We'll pack enough gear to stay out in the countryside for a few days and give him a chance to find us."

"What about the police? Won't they think the same thing, too?"

Nick snorted. "Constable Chris? He won't get out of his car if he doesn't have to. If your father keeps away from the roads, he'll be fine. We'll do the same."

"But where do we start?"

"Near the house, because we know he *was* there. Even if he didn't set it on fire, like the police think, he was seen in the area, and he won't have gone very far away, because of you."

"You've got better things to do, you won't want to babysit me."

Nick, about to climb on the motorcycle, paused. "I want to do this, Cathreen," he said.

After Charlie had ferried them to their starting point at the ruined house—Charlie, who had been horrified at first sight of the red motorbike as it had thundered into camp, had perked up when Nick had told him he'd have to use it himself to get around until the van was fixed—they'd walked back to the Aries hill. In daylight, Cathreen could see that Nick was right: you *could* see the sea from there. It looked like a piece of wrinkled hide, spreading west, bleached to near white. Nick dropped down beside her on the grass where she had stopped to rest. "Give me that stone you've got," he said. "I want to have a look."

She scrounged in her pocket and handed it to him. He held it in front of his eye for a minute, then returned it and pointed down at the valley. She put the glass to her eye. First there was nothing but the normal greenish undulations of the landscape, but then a shaft of sunlight illuminated the lower fields and she saw the shape of a ship and its masts outlined by the dykes criss-crossing the land. The image was as clear as if it had been drawn there; then the sky clouded over and it disappeared.

"What is it?"

"King Solomon's ship. They say the real ship made its way around the islands along the old coast until it foundered here. Farmers still dig up ship's timbers from the marshlands."

She put the stone down. "But that thing's huge!"

Nick shrugged. "They say that the same people who built the rest of the zodiac put it there so that the world would remember the original."

"They say, they say," she said mockingly. "Doesn't anybody know? Why would the ship come in the first place?"

"Bringing treasure, maybe," Nick said. "I don't know. Nobody knows. Wasn't that what Solomon did, bring treasure, know things?"

Cathreen held the green stone up once more, but the image was no longer there. "It must have something to do with the light, Nick. I can't see it now. But why would looking through it at all make a difference?"

"It acts as a filter. It'd probably work with a piece of cellophane too." Nick took the stone from her again and turned it over in his hand. "This could be valuable, Cathreen. My mother had an uncut emerald that looked something like it."

Cathreen felt herself flush. "I wouldn't know, Nick—my mother never had any emeralds." She snatched at the stone in Nick's outstretched hand, put it back in her pocket and jumped to her feet. "Go ahead, why don't you ask me where I got it?"

Nick gazed at her in amazement. "Cathreen, I didn't mean . . ."

"Go on, ask me."

"All right," he said quietly, "where did you get it?"

"I took it from the house where my mother works as a cleaner. I stole it."

Nick's face showed surprise, dismay, sadness. Tiny cold fingers that she'd almost forgotten existed dug into her arms. *Tell the whole truth, Cathreen.* "I didn't plan to give it back; I didn't know it was worth anything."

She turned as the dog, Breaker, streaked by, passed between two small oaks and disappeared over the brow of the hill. "Is that the way we're going?" she said. She lifted her backpack and took after the dog, picking up speed as her feet caught the rhythm of the downward slope.

Galt

When you love someone, you want to be with them. When you love someone, you don't kill them. When you love someone, you do what you can to make them happy. You bring them what they want most in return for the love they have for you. You make them love you more.

Love is not selfish, love shares.

It was the fault of his extended absence that he'd forgotten such things: the long sleep in the bog had placed holes in his feelings that the telly hadn't yet mended. He'd have to go back to Merry's and watch telly, or stand under the wires, or simply pay attention to the deluge of information washing the air that he'd grown far too practised, in his busyness, to listen to. Take Pam, for instance. How was it that he hadn't taken the time to consider what would make *her* happy?

Quickly, he scanned all the images he had of her: Pam in red, swimming, Pam running. He let out a breath in relief. No happiness yet. In all the programs, she was on her own. Just like his Master, just like him. Pam needed a family, everyone needed a family. That's what his Master was telling him. They'd have children. The boys and he would hunt in the marsh, he'd teach the girl to snare rabbits, she'd cook soup. Teach all of them to paddle the dugout. When Pam came home they'd have supper.

The scent from one of the letters Galt had taken from his master's wallet led him back to the burned house where he'd first encountered it. It belonged to the girl he'd seen there with Nick. He should have known she was his Master's daughter. They might have found his Master—her father—together. Nevertheless, gratitude for the opportunity he'd been given to reunite father and daughter swept over him. His Master wanted him to be a success, to prove his love; he'd been given a second chance. He wiped his nose clean with the back of his hand, then raised it to the wind.

The trail led, as he soon realized it would, all the way to Summerwood, where Charlie, lonely and garrulous, tried to make him stay. "Where the hell've you been, you old bastard? I've missed you!" Charlie clapped him on the shoulder. "Let's start the mill up and get rolling. I got the parts run out by the travellers Nick's let camp by the stream. We'll fix it up and surprise him. It'll take no time at all with the two of us. We'll get the whole lot cut up. Whad'ya say?"

Galt pushed him aside and roamed the clearing, sifting on hands and knees through the dust and mud, the rubbish heap and the ashes of the cold fire; then he entered the bender. He stayed inside for no more than a minute, just long enough to tear the place apart and find Cathreen's blanket. He stood outside with it pressed against his face.

"C'mon, old son, calm down!" Charlie cried, watching him. "What's got into you? I've got Nick to take you back, and I just cleaned up in there, it took me all morning." Charlie was keeping his distance; he picked up a chunk of firewood. Galt lowered the blanket and laid it on the ground. He breathed heavily. There was a tear in his arm where he'd caught it on something sharp. The open wound leaked tissue. Charlie's eyes fixed on it.

"Where is the girl?" Galt asked.

"Is this some kind of a joke?" Charlie said, wrenching his gaze from Galt's arm. "If it is, chum, I don't think it's funny. This is me, Charlie, your pal. I'm on your side." The old man gummed a grin, but rank sweat oozed from his pores and stained his clothing.

Galt smiled back at him. He pushed his tongue against his bottom loosening teeth. There was time to listen to the wild ringing call of a swan from down in the Levels.

Charlie said, "That's better, I'd knew you'd come round." He shuffled forward, one step at a time, then reached out to pat Galt's hand.

Galt took Charlie's wrist and twisted it. "You will tell me about the girl," he said. He twisted it harder and Charlie fell to his knees.

"There's no need for that! Let me be!" Galt let him go. Charlie cradled his arm. "What's got into you? You been drinkin'? You never were good with drink." He began to get up.

"Tell me," said Galt, raising a fist.

"No problem, give me a minute." Charlie struggled upright and wobbled to a seat near the dead fire. "I've had the DTs myself, I know how it is, boy, I'll get you somethin' to help." He stood again and moved towards the wood pile where he kept his bottle, but Galt blocked the way.

"Tell me or I will kill you," Galt said.

Cathreen

They crossed a mesh of dykes though a maze of fields and paths, treading where she'd spied the outline of the ship, and headed towards the mass of the hill in front of them. Although she'd packed as lightly as possible, the weight of the backpack and sleeping bag tied to it pinched into her shoulders. "How much farther, Nick?" she asked after they'd been walking in silence for over an hour.

He didn't answer, but he glanced at the quickly darkening sky and picked up the pace. When they came to the base of the hill they took a narrow lane that climbed to an even narrower path that wound its way upwards. At the top, inside the raised earthen walls of what Nick briefly told her was an ancient hill fort, he built a small fire while Cathreen cleared away debris from a hollow, filled it with dry leaves and branches and set out their sleeping bags on a sheet of plastic. They said nothing more as they worked, but while Nick dumped a can of beans onto a tin plate and placed it at the edge of the fire to heat, Breaker appeared and tugged at Cathreen's sleeve. The dog led her to a spring where Cutthroat was already lapping water and delicately grooming himself. Cathreen went back for the empty tin, filled it, made a handle for it by twisting a length of broken fence wire, and set it wedged between stones at the fire's side.

When they'd finished eating, and had made tea with the boiled water, Nick built up the fire for light. The sky was salted with stars. "I want to show you something," he said. "Come on." He held out his hand, pulled her up and led her away from the blaze towards the earthwork walls.

"The shape of the hill fort makes the spiral shape of the inside of an ear," he said as they walked. "We're camped inside the figure of the giant Orion, lying on his side, listening to the heavens. From up here, you're supposed to be able to hear the music of the spheres." He was whispering.

Cathreen, relieved that he was speaking to her again, whispered back, "Can *you* hear it, Nick?"

"Just look up and keep quiet," he said. He helped her to climb behind him onto the earthen bank. "Walk along the top with me. I'll go first. It's safe. You won't fall off."

She inched slowly after him, testing her footsteps, but the wall was firmer than it looked and knitted through with grass. Several times she had to push aside bushes that had grown right through, or step over clumps of thistle, and once she came to a full stop, her heart drilling into her chest as she saw a thick pale shape shuffling towards her.

"It's just a sheep. Keep going."

She went on, and gradually as she walked, she began to discern the design unfolding: the wall coiled in on itself. They were deep inside the ear.

"Now listen," Nick said.

She listened. She heard the distant crackle of the fire, the soft footfalls of Breaker padding along at the bottom of the wall, the rush and pause of Cutthroat's progress as he hunted voles through the grasses. Cathreen felt space all around, the stars above reached for her. The vast emptiness made her ache for everything she'd left behind, and with the shame she'd felt earlier when she'd let Nick know what she was really like—a thief—and still worse than he knew. Then it lifted and she didn't think about it anymore.

Once, after Cathreen had managed to get to sleep, she woke up thinking she was being watched. Nick had told her, when they were settling in for the night, that the hill was supposed to be haunted by the ghosts of King Arthur's knights still searching for the Holy Grail, so maybe that was it, her imagination acting up. But the air was ribboned through with a feral smell. Like skunk, or bear. She glanced round for Breaker and found him awake and sniffing nettles nearby. Cutthroat, tucked into the sleeping bag with her, purred. This was reassuring; they would know if anything were wrong. She scanned the ash trees that straggled over the hilltop. Many of them were dead, killed by ivy, as unlike as could be from the vibrant, towering sweet-scented forests of cedar and fir at home. These bare trees concealed nothing. She tested the air again, but the odour of decay remained. She tossed and turned, but returned to sleep eventually, her ears strained to hear music that evaded her, her dreams filled with just-missed meetings with Jag.

Galt

He had found them on top of the hill. He had watched and waited until all was quiet and he was certain they slept. He knew he had to make the girl come with him, but he wasn't sure how, or if the "how" mattered. Surely, since his Master could bring his daughter to life if he wanted to—as he had with himself, Galt—he needn't worry about taking her alive?

Galt moved forward quietly. A few sturdy frogs, rattled by the night chill, croaked from the wetlands below, and several dragonflies, half dead with cold, feebly whirred their wings as he crossed the distance between himself and Nick and the girl. He cursed as he stumbled into a wire that fenced off one side of the earthworks: his night vision had failed just when it should have been at its best. The stone newly in his stomach crowded energy through his veins. Why had he missed seeing the split strands? A white blur, nebulous at first, like a cloud, but giving off the essence of ice, moved in a circle round the bodies of the boy and girl. When Galt's vision steadied, he saw that it was a dog.

Galt stopped. He bared his teeth in imitation of the animal as it passed near him, retaining its circle; he felt the hairs on the back of his neck, and on his arms, stand up. He remembered the wolves that had skulked from the mountains to kill cattle he'd raised, wolves that had slaughtered the pigs he'd kept and counted on for food to feed himself and his mother through the winter. He remembered his mother's hunger. He peered through the white circle to where the girl and boy lay. His eyes prickled. Despite the great power within him, he could not get past the dog.

He tried again to cut near the sleepers, and forced his way almost to the boy, but the circle held, the white dog stood over the girl and growled. He was strong, his Master had given him everything he needed to succeed, but for a reason he did not understand, he was not as powerful as the dog and the girl together.

Galt hung his head. He did not know how he would find the courage to do it, but he'd have to tell his Master that he had failed.

Nick

Nick lay waiting for dawn to spark the birds to life, and for his heart to return to its usual quietness. It didn't matter that he knew he was being irrational, his heartbeat wasn't listening. In his dream he had seen himself as Charles I brought back to London to face trial as a tyrant, a traitor, a murderer and enemy of his country. He'd watched himself ascend the scaffold at Whitehall. As the face of the executioner—his father?—leaned over him, axe in hand, he'd lain rigid with fear, aware of himself in the sleeping bag, but waiting for the blow to fall and sever his head.

Across the remains of the fire, Cathreen slept on. Breaker stood over her. "Deserted by you too!" Nick said softly. The dog came to him and nudged the sleeping bag until Nick reluctantly got up. His heartbeat had finally slowed, but he found himself looking around carefully as he searched for kindling and firewood.

Once the fire was going and he could smell the coffee as it came to a boil, he shook Cathreen awake.

She stretched. "You hear anything last night, Nick? Did you sleep all right? Something kept me awake." She slid out of the bag and hung it, wet with dew, over a branch. "Stupid, eh?" Nick squatted by the fire and stirred cornmeal into a pot. "Is that all we've got to eat?" she said.

"Why? What do you want?"

"Bacon, eggs, toast, orange juice, waffles."

"Fine," he said. "First you walk to the shops—" She threw a pair of dirty socks at him. "Watch it, they almost went into the pot!"

"Too bad! Won't make much difference." She threw a T-shirt.

"Cathreen! Stop!"

"Not until you say you're sorry."

"For what?"

"For making fun of me."

"I wasn't!"

"You were! You know you were!" When he didn't say anything more, she stood over him and watched him stir the yellow mush with a teaspoon. "How far away did you say that store was?"

They came down from the hill and walked along a track that skirted the backs of farms. In one of the fields, not too far away, Cathreen spotted the donkey she'd seen at Summerwood. It hee-hawed when it saw them, and swished its tail, the tuft on the end showing pale. When they reached it, the donkey snuffed its nose over Cathreen's jacket pocket and toothed out a lint-covered pack of gum. "Hey," she said, "that can't be good for you!" She bent to pull up a handful of grass to feed to it instead.

"Charles I was a very stubborn man," Nick, who had told Cathreen about his dream, explained as they continued on. The donkey had surged ahead up another hill, the swing of its tail just disappearing in front of them into some trees. "Even when he knew it was all over, and he was imprisoned, he thought that divine right would see him through. Because God had made him king, no one would really harm him."

"Sounds dumb," she said.

"Not really. His friends begged him to make his escape, but he said that he had promised not to, and his foes had promised not to harm him, and so he stayed. Morally, it was the right decision."

"He was stupid to stay if he could have got away," Cathreen said. They had come out of the trees onto the hilltop. The land fell away steeply to both sides of a narrow, windswept path that stretched along a rocky spine. Nick still felt ill. He'd thought, several times, he'd seen the executioner—could it really be his father?—waiting with the axe in the bushes. Once he'd even said, "You didn't see anyone there, did you?" And Cathreen had answered, "No, there's no one there." He could sense her frequent glances of concern and hoped he looked better than he felt.

"Where's this supposed to be?" Cathreen asked, looking down the narrow path.

"Taurus. We're walking along the bull's horn."

"Oh, right, of course," she said. "What else."

Farther along the path stood a stone monument topped with the replica of a ship's fo'c'sle. Its base was entwined with ivy and surrounded by broken iron palings. When they got close to it, they saw that there was an inscription listing famous battles. The letters *Mad* had been painted red in the word *Madras*. Nick traced the letters with his fingers.

"He refused to accept the jurisdiction of the court at his trial," he went on. "He said they had no authority to try him—how could they have when God had put him where he was?—and to show his disdain he kept his hat on during the whole proceedings."

Cathreen picked up a stone and threw it between the railings. She picked up another and hit them. The noise rattled through his brain. "If it was me," she said, "I'd have escaped, I'd never go back, or I'd kill myself."

"When he was beheaded, the crowd groaned and people ran to dip their handkerchiefs in his blood as a memento. The executioner died insane." Nick gazed balefully at the candy-bar wrappers, drink cups and torn crisp bags near the base of the monument. "Things happen to people that they don't plan," he said. "Take your father, for instance." He looked around vaguely as if Jag might appear round the corner of the memorial.

"What did they do with the head?" Cathreen asked him. Nick stared at her. "Charles's head."

"I think the body was embalmed and his head sewn back on. Why?"

"I don't know. Something Jag said once about heads in a well."

"Isn't that a fairy tale? A girl goes to a well, dips her hand in and feels a skull. It speaks to her but she refuses to listen and she's given snails and slugs instead of the gold and wheat she expected?"

"Helena didn't do fairy tales," Cathreen said.

Nick noticed a couple walking towards them from the far end of the horn.

"Maybe there's a reason that you're thinking about Charles I," Cathreen said. "Something logical."

"I dug up several relics from the Civil War when we were clearing brush at Summerwood."

"Well, that's it, then."

"Funny, isn't it," he continued, "there were good people on both sides." His father's face seemed to swim up at him suddenly out of the landscape mouthing—what? A greeting? A warning? But when had the old man done anything other than threaten him? The image, a trick of the light, bleached out to nothing. The couple, a fair-haired woman and a dark-haired man, were coming closer, swinging their joined hands.

Cathreen glanced over her shoulder to see what he was looking at and froze. Then she grabbed his arm, and dragged him around the monument and down the slope behind it, and ran through the underbrush at the bottom of the hill. After a few minutes' rapid walking they came to a semi-derelict church half overgrown by brambles.

"Can we stop, please?" Nick said. "I'm not going any farther until you tell me what's going on."

Ivy and nettles joined with the brambles in a scroll over the outside walls of the pale stone building. Nick pushed the jumble aside and squeaked through a wrought-iron gate that led to a porch speckled with bat and pigeon droppings. An unlocked battered wooden door opened into the nave. They stood in the unswept central aisle on the uneven floor, and looked up at the carved beams where doves flew, taking turns bumping each other from their perches. Dust motes scattered as Nick cleaned off a short section of bird-limed pew and they sat down.

"Well?" he said.

Cathreen pulled at a tuft of her hair and bit the fingernails of one hand. "That was my mother and Tink back there. They're looking for me, Nick. Tink saw me, I'm sure of it."

"So? They're not going to hurt you, are they? Why are you so frightened?"

Cathreen chewed her lip and looked down, and suddenly he understood. "You didn't tell them you were leaving. You ran away." He watched Cathreen pull at the loose balls of fluff that clung to her fleece. "What about your father? I thought you were supposed to be visiting him."

"I am." She nodded vigorously. "It's just that . . ." She looked away again.

Nick sighed. "You'd better tell me all of it, Cathreen. I'll help you if I can, but I don't want to be lied to." He didn't say "again" but he knew it was in his voice.

"I didn't see why I should stay at home, the way Helena treated me. She didn't tell me Jag had sent me a plane ticket, she hated my friends. She wouldn't let me see them anymore. I liked being with them more than her." She had spoken with her back to him. Her unhappiness was palpable. Nick felt a surge of panic at the memory of his own not-so-distant suffering.

"Why come here, then? Why not go to those friends?"

Cathreen began to cry. "Everyone hates me, they think it's all my fault. You'll hate me too."

"Why would I hate you?"

She was going to say she didn't know why, that her father was the only one who cared about her, that it wasn't fair, but instead, with Nick sitting quietly beside her, she told him the story of Fawn and Timmy, how she had stood by and let it happen. Of how unfinished it was, with Timmy's brain locked into its state of injury and Fawn's body lost in the murk of the lake.

Nick rubbed at his eyes with his fingers. He felt tired. "I don't know, Cathreen . . . ," he said.

Cathreen wept harder, then doubled over and retched. Nick held her head and scanned the walls for shadows. The nerves at the back of his neck were tingling. "All these little hills, every last one of them floating on the marsh out there," he said, "is a door to a world where a year can seem like a day. The world is made of stories, Cathreen. You'll have to choose among them."

Galt

Forgive me, Master. I kneel to you as one of your creatures — the small and the great, the spiders, frogs, newts, mink, otters, the carp that swim in shoals in the rivers — and I am less than the least of these. The herons that nest in the woodlands, the black-tailed godwit probing with its beak in the soil, the copper butterflies, deer, foxes, badgers, all are greater than I. I am a creature of the soil. I have lain within the passage of time, I bear the record of pollen, the vegetational history, the stamens of the legions of plants that have blanketed me, and I have learned nothing. I have taken your great gift, given freely and without condition, and I have not even done the one thing I could to make you happy. I have not brought you your loved ones.

"Master," Galt said, as Jag glanced round to see Merry, yawning in the hut behind him, sit up in her crushed T-shirt, "these will be my last words. I ask only that you return me to where you found me. It is all I deserve." Galt took a long shuddering breath. His faded hair straggled over his face as he bent his head. He dug his fingers into the earth as he squatted, as if to retain a hold there. A fingernail flaked into the dirt.

"For Christ's sake," Jag said. "What's this about?"

"The stone is beginning to leave my body. I will give it back. Because I have failed you, I must return your gift."

"What's going on, Jag?" Merry said, coming out in bare feet and squinting into the sunlight. She saw Galt and drew back with a gasp.

"I tried to do what you wanted, Master," Galt went on. "It was easy to find the girl—she has some of your scent." Galt gave a racking cough and strained to move his bowels. "I tried to take her as she slept. I crept close in the darkness but before I could reach her, I was stopped. The girl has a wall around her."

"Girl?" Jag said.

"Your daughter," Galt said.

Merry screamed.

"Shut up!" Jag said to her. "You told me she was safe!"

Galt gave a groan and a weak shudder and the stone slid from between his buttocks onto the ground. Merry bolted, running straight from the hut. Galt couldn't help himself. He shifted and reached out and grabbed her ankle as she fled past. She screamed again as she fell.

"Tell me where my daughter is," Jag said, launching towards him.

The smell of himself, even to Galt, was terrible. He knew that he stank of putrefaction, that his clothes were stained from weeping wounds where his skin had split. Perhaps that explained his Master's anger? Galt tightened his grip on the struggling woman, his eyes roved over her, remembering, in the midst of his distress, his pleasure at her pain. "See, Master," he said, pointing to the stone, "my loyalty to you is stronger than life itself."

Jag was two steps away when Merry's hand snaked out and grabbed the stone. Galt let go of her leg and lifted his fist to smash her, but she was on her feet in that second.

"Run!" Jag shouted.

Merry ran. Galt gave Jag a reproachful look from over his shoulder as he struggled to his feet and lurched away.

He would have caught her in another few steps, weakened as he was, but the cat he had seen with the girl got in the way. Galt tripped over it, and Merry sped out onto the Levels. He grabbed the cat and squeezed its neck. The cat went limp, but Galt knew it wasn't dead—its heart puffed out the fur on its breast—so he kept holding it. He would have kept on squeezing, but it occurred to him that Pam might like cats. He could keep this one and look after it and be its Master if it stayed alive.

He let the cat go and followed Merry's scent. After not very far, Merry's increasing fatigue rushed back at him in shreds of salt fragrance, irritating his nostrils; she slowed step by step. He could tell, as he watched the sun spin light behind the clouds, that she was heading for home. Then on top of a hill, when he knew he could go no farther, he heard Merry try to stifle her sobs as she hid in a windbreak. He laughed. Merry thought she was safe.

Merry, hearing him, called out, "Can we strike a bargain, Galt?"

"What is a bargain?" he said. He glimpsed the cat again. It pleased him that it had followed.

"A bargain is if I give you what you want and you give me what I want."

Galt watched the cat as it crouched, belly to the earth in stalking position. He knelt and held out his fingers to it. "What do you want, Merry?" He could feel the fear emanating in drifts from the thicket. He breathed it in and felt a little stronger.

"I'll give you the stone back and you let me go," she said.

"Yes," he said.

"Promise?"

He almost said, What is a promise? but stopped himself.

He picked up the cat and rubbed his face against it so they would be friends. Inch by inch Merry emerged from hiding; it amused him to watch her with the cat snuggled in his arms, purring. When she stood upright she gave him a quick glance, then threw the stone—not very well—as far as she could and pelted off. He set the cat down, fetched the stone, cleaned it and swallowed it. He could still see Merry as she limped, in the distance, across damp grass, her shiny red heels kicking up at each step. He began to follow her, his pulse racing as he drew near without her knowing it. One quick run and he would have reached her, but again the cat ran across his path and he stumbled and fell. With a roar he was on it, his hands poised to snap its neck, when a blur of white vaulted at him from the side and at the same time he heard the throaty growl of the dog and saw the glitter of its paw just before it struck him above the eye. Pain screeched through him and the cat surged away. The dog wheeled to face him and stood him off as Merry skittered on her way.

Galt brushed his hand over the wound. It was only a scratch, but cold spread from it, a poison he could sense spread rapidly inward to his brain and downward to his heart. Galt had felt death pitch into him before, so he knew what was happening, but suddenly its progress stopped. There was a delicate probing at the barrier set up by the red stone lying in his stomach, then the see-saw settled and he lived.

Galt touched the wound again. He tried to pinch the laceration closed, but the skin was tired, stretched and brittle; it gaped. What would happen now when the stone left his body as it must? He wished his Master were there to advise him. He watched the dog and cat slip away.

Not far off a car was parked to one side of a lane. Settling around it, like the falling leaves, was another scent of interest. Galt sniffed at it and found a hint of Jag and of the girl, as well as something else. He plucked his Master's letters and photographs from the pocket of the shirt his Master had given him, flipped through them and found what he'd remembered. A fair-haired woman stood, in a photograph, between the girl and his Master. This was his Master's wife. The new note in the air was hers. His master had said he wanted her back. Galt smiled a smile that stretched his mouth and cracked the skin at the corners. Galt had failed with the girl; he would not fail with the woman.

There was also, in the air, the smokier whiff of a man. This too meant something, for the man's odour conjoined that of the woman. Surely this wasn't right? Galt opened the car door. Two suitcases were stowed inside. He snapped the locks and explored, his frown deepening.

His master had said that his wife had found someone else. Was this the man? He sniffed again, and the hackles on the back of Galt's neck rose.

A few last leaves twirled on branches, some letting go to flutter and skirl in the air. A footpath jogged downhill through a break in the vegetation. Galt took it, detecting that it was this way that the car's passengers had gone, but partway down, a small beige donkey blocked his progress. He pushed at it roughly, but it seemed to flow aside like water only to stand in front of him again.

"Get out of here!" he shouted at it, waving his arms. The woman's scent grew fainter as he stood there. He struck at the donkey's back, but it stepped away, let him lurch after it and led him from the path into an open field near a crossroads in time to watch the woman's car speed down the hill towards him and drive quickly away.

Galt squatted and strained. The stone seemed to have acquired new edges, every one of which scored his intestines. He lay on his side in the grass and put his head as close to his crotch as he could. The stone was coming now. He didn't know how much time he'd have to ingest it again—certainly there wouldn't be much before icy numbness flowed right through his limbs: he didn't even know if it could be done. The donkey yanked at a mouthful of grass and looked him closely in the eye as it chewed. Then the stone, glistening with mucus, was on the grass, then in his hand, and he was clawing it to his mouth.

Cathreen

It was late afternoon. The weak sun had turned to a small silver disc that showed through a line of pollarded willows. Long broken shadows stretched eastwards. The sodden ground beneath her feet sucked at her shoes. Cathreen's eyes were wept dry. Her head hurt. Nick strode ahead with Breaker. There were little rises here, between the small rhynes that they could mostly jump across, that made it hard for her to walk. She couldn't set a pace or be sure of her footing. Nick waited for her on top of one of the higher of these and they looked across silver meadows. The wet Levels shone under the darkening sky all the way to the woods. Only a few stiles, and a sheep or two fleeing heavy cloud blowing down from the north, interrupted the view. "We'll have to find shelter," Nick said. A squall rushed towards them, turning the earth black beneath it. She could hear it as it spun through trees and flattened the grass. Nick took her hand.

Ever since they'd fled the hill and stopped in the church, she'd had the shivery feeling: it strayed in front of her, giving her the sensation of someone holding an ice cream cone in front of her nose, or of a taste of sugar on the tongue just before it burst into sweetness. She glimpsed the donkey she'd seen earlier, running as hard as it could away from them.

It might be a long, sad walk, Cathreen, the silvery voice said in her ear.

Why would it be sad? Even if Helena found her and made her go home it wouldn't be sad. She'd just run away again. Cutthroat dashed up, wet, and scrambled onto her shoulder. She thought he looked a little worn out, so she put him in her backpack as she and Nick hurried along.

Lightning crackled across the sky. She could smell wet earth and ozone. Lightning again, to the south, then so nearby that the thunder slammed on top of them.

They could scarcely see in the thick darkness that fell as the tempest drove the rain in. They were soaked through within seconds. Breaker ran off, a slick white streak through the torrent, and then returned, barking. "Maybe he's found something," Cathreen shouted into Nick's ear. She checked that Cutthroat was safe in the backpack and then, holding on to Nick's arm, fought her way, after Breaker, against the storm.

Galt

The storm struck just as Galt caught up to the donkey. He reached for it, and his vision flooded with rain; there was a roaring in his ears like the sea. While he was blinded, one of the donkey's hooves struck him in the forehead; it bit through to bone and sent him reeling backwards, his hands full of the donkey's coarse hair. When he could see again, the donkey waited in the blowing downpour, just out of reach.

A war waged inside him. His heart pumped valiantly, but while the stone had been out of his body, the cold poison had advanced a little farther from the wound. He staggered against the storm's onslaught, moving jerkily through the lightning flashes, over the rough ground.

He kept the blowing pale tail of the donkey in sight, and followed her as she crossed a farm track. The wind climbed to a fresh fury— Galt glanced up as the gale snapped a pole between a farmhouse and a barn, and a power line fell. It brought down everything with it: the pole, and telephone and electrical wires, struck Galt across the back of the head and knocked him flat to the soaked earth.

He smelled his flesh burning. Electricity jolted through him; his body convulsed and flipped like water dropped into a hot pan. He expected to fall into unconsciousness, or to leave his body, but it was nothing like that. He felt himself—his life—crawl into his head and crouch there. In front of it—it was definitely a creature, small, round, covered in fur—played a film of spectacular colour effects, red, yellow, green, blue, indigo, violet zigzags, lightning bolts, peaks and valleys; and then rippling light waves and pulses that translated what he could hear—the sizzling and popping of his flesh and joints—into motion. He was a hare, hunched before the glories of the aurora borealis, he was a rat gnawing at a bone just as a cat took it by the back of the neck. Pain and pleasure. The out-of-control body simply a medium.

Then there was something different: a code blinked through his bones, on and off in a bewildering yet orderly pattern; deep, satisfying draughts of information, transmitted along the power lines, flooded his brain; the entire network spread out on the screen of his vision so that he could see it from farmhouse to town to the next town, to London, breaking, branching until the veins and filaments covered the world. He knew all there was to know, or so it seemed to him—except the answer to the question that meant everything: how could he secure his Master's love?

Then the knowledge current went dead.

Galt stirred and groaned, his nostrils filled with the reek of charred flesh, scorched wire and earth, and he rolled away from under the broken wires and sat with his head in his hands. Would he never have an answer? He would do his best to make his Master happy by restoring his family, of course, but the question of love? Even now, it seemed, filled with knowledge as he was, it was closed to him. Despairingly, Galt examined his new riches and posed his question fruitlessly, opening and closing files and finding no answer until a figure strode towards him across the steppes of Central Asia. "There is a way," the figure said. The figure, Genghis Khan, had killed and raped and looted; he'd drunk milk and blood from horses; he'd established a great civilization and imposed a code of laws: adulterers were put to death whether they were married or not, retreat was impossible, meat was taken from animals whose hearts were squeezed by hand until they died.

"What is the way?" Galt asked. His breast fluttered in anticipation.

"What could show greater love than to defeat what he cannot defeat himself?" the Khan said.

"Yes," Galt said.

"You must bring him the head of his greatest enemy," the Khan said. The Khan peered at Galt closely. "If you had not committed great sins, God would not have sent a punishment like me upon you. Give me the red stone so that I may live."

"Yes," Galt said, but he shut all the Khan's files, and erased them.

Cathreen

After crossing a track, they came to a farm where a dozen sheep stood, heads down, facing the wind, and a few cows formed a knot against the wall of a small barn. The farmhouse was dark, there was no car or truck parked in the yard, and no dog barked at them.

"There's nobody home," Nick said. "Let's see if we can get in." The house was locked, but they swung open the barn door and let the cows push inside ahead of them and into their stalls. It took all their strength and several minutes before they could shut and bar the door against the tearing blast. Nick checked the cows to see if they needed milking, and then he and Cathreen stripped off their wet things and piled hay on top of themselves to keep warm.

It was dark inside the barn. Cathreen reached out to touch the glimmer of Nick's face. His skin was damp and cold. "Are you all right? Are you warm enough?" She had taken Cutthroat out of the pack and he'd burrowed in next to them.

"I'm fine," he said. "It's just these thoughts. I don't know where they come from. Sometimes I can't stop them."

Thunder hammered more distantly, but still the walls trembled and the cows moaned, conveying their uneasiness, although the barn was warm and dry, ripe with the smells of milk and dung. As Nick's breathing evened and he fell into a troubled sleep, Cathreen thought about Helena and Tink looking for her. She didn't want to go home, she would never go home again, they could go to hell. They'd never find her. She'd stay with Nick.

She moved a little closer to him, and Cutthroat eased out of his nest and resettled himself against her neck. "I'm tired, Cutthroat, I'm wet and I'm sad," she said. The cat gave a dry cough. The cat purred in her ear. She was thinking that she would like to know more about her parents, how they'd met, when they'd fallen in love. They must have loved each other at some time in order to have had her.

When they began walking once more, in the morning, everything had changed. They could see, a short distance away, that last night's onslaught had knocked down the power lines. The landscape was eerily quiet, the sky full of still, yellow light, and instead of continuing to look for her father as they had been—and as she'd assumed they'd keep doing—they were on their way back to Summerwood.

Nick had said he was worried about damage to the camp and trees and about Charlie, but she didn't believe him. It was because of her. He hadn't forgiven her at all; he was going to turn her in.

The sky was heavy, the ground sodden with rain. Cathreen stepped over a puddle, noting as she did a knot of worms pink and writhing on the surface. Cutthroat jumped down from her shoulder, where he'd been riding, to tackle them, and Nick, who'd been striding ahead, waited for her to catch up to him. His face was grey.

"Do you smell it?" he said.

"What?"

"It's stupid, I know, but that smell wasn't here before."

"What smell, Nick?"

"I've remembered something I read about Charles I written by somebody who'd known him. 'I have seen the waistcoat you allude to, and it has a stain upon it from some of poor Charles' blood.'" Nick brushed his hands over his clothing. "You can't see anything there, can you?"

"Jesus, Nick, would you stop it!" She shook her head and walked on. Breaker had reappeared and ranged along the horizon. Then she thought, for a second, that she saw Fawn and Timmy, but it was only a trick of the light on the sun-struck earth. Cathreen wiped cold sweat from her brow as panic seized her throat and she understood that she was tied, forever, to everyone she knew by long, dark strings.

She would have called for her mother, but Nick would have heard her.

Seven

Helena

A small northern B.C. town arranged in squares on a river plain and set about with spindly spruce, the trunks no bigger than your wrist. Marshland and boggy lakes where moose splashed and sank and bellowed for their calves; pale birch, gnawed by mice and deer and stripped like finger bones, fringing the edges of everything—bog, lake, roadways, the narrow city lots, wherever there was a scratching of clear earth and some moisture.

The sky was always white with heat or snow, the mountains surrounding the plain too high to reveal sunrise or sunset. In winter it was dark most of the time, in summer too light. All year round logging trucks from the coast ate up the gravel roads into the town on their way to the pulp mill and all year round the chemical stink of the pulp digester liquid permeated her hair and clothes. She couldn't get rid of it no matter how many times she washed her hair in Herbal Essence, her clothes in washing soda: she walked through the streets to church and to school, nose pinched, as if through a stagnant river with a body in it. When she complained to her mother, Garnette, about it, Garnette said it was "the smell of money." When the mill shut down, all the men were out of work, including Helena's father, Sailor.

Sailor worked in the mill when he could, but he was low down on the union roster. His "real" work was the ministry, the Lord's work. He travelled, weekends, to the little church he had built, up north, with his own hands. The hope was that one day, when there was a congregation large enough to support them, the family would move there together. Sailor was building the congregation one at a time, it seemed, bringing them home from bars or ditches or from under the bridge over the Nechako, home to Garnette to feed and put up for a night or two, helping them find work away from the city. There were always one or two recovering drunks in the minuscule living room. Helena—only she wasn't called Helena then, but Belva, after Garnette's long-dead mother—learned to play cards from them when her parents were out, and how to stop a man from hurting himself during delirium tremens. How to keep her bedroom door locked with the back of a chair, after she turned eleven.

Garnette was the one who had gone to Bible school: she should have been the preacher. Sailor was just as happy chopping wood for a widow or playing with the neighbourhood children; but he was always on call to fill in for some reverend's Tuesday-night prayer meeting, Wednesday visiting, Friday "Young People's" or Saturday communion for shut-ins. Only Sunday school and morning service and evening singsong in the small wooden church he'd built were his own. He was a gentle, humorous man, the best kind of father, a storyteller, a throwback to a riverbank childhood in a softer clime, a round peg in a square hole in this one. Helena (Belva) thought she recognized him when she read *Huckleberry Finn* and *Tom Sawyer*, although the country was wrong, the accent, the presence of Negroes. There were no Negroes in Prince George, but there were Indians.

Garnette, a proud survivor of the worst kind of prairie poverty, where flat-out want had pushed her farming parents to near madness, had trouble with the potbellied Native children eating chips solemnly outside the bars, and the big Native women, laughing with each other, pushing, not wearing bras. She thought they could have done more with what they had. Sailor didn't seem to notice man or woman, white or Indian: if someone needed his help they had it. Of course Garnette supported him always, whatever she thought, sat in the front pew whenever Sailor ministered, cheered him on with her "Praise the Lords" and "Yes, Jesuses." She cooked pies furiously and put up fruit all summer. The little she kept back for them, Sailor managed to give away. "The Lord will provide" was his only defence when she remonstrated, and what could she say to that? She scrubbed the kitchen linoleum till it wore through, she cut down her old clothes for Belva, and Sailor's for the little boy who would come one day, surely. Her hands grew knotted and sore looking; she had a winter dress and a summer dress and neither fit, anymore, around the middle.

Sailor didn't slack off, he worked his heart out, but he was a child in some way, the burden too much for him. He grew thinner and grey, as if slowly wearing out from the inside, all through Helena's — Belva's — childhood, until, when she was sixteen, he faded right away, dying considerately in bed on a Wednesday night with no one to disappoint on Thursday, his day off.

The funeral, held in the little northern church, with hymn singing and the twenty or so there coming up to shake Garnette's hand, was held on Saturday. Sunday, for the first time ever, Garnette didn't go to church, not even in town, but she sent Belva off to represent the family. When Belva got home, having walked from the bus in the rain, in the dark, with the pulp-mill effusion condensed into fog that felt acidic and ate right into her lungs—or maybe that was her grief over Sailor—Garnette told her there was no money. Nothing. Not a scrap of insurance or a dollar in a bank account. Garnette would go out cleaning, and Belva would have to quit school and get a job.

There is no way to know what is inside a person's heart, what dreams there are, what sense of a life that might be lived. Nobody had ever, not once, not even Sailor, asked Belva what she might want for herself, although Sailor had looked at her sometimes as if he wanted to ask but was frightened to, since anything she might ask for he certainly couldn't provide.

Where they lived, in winter, it was cold and dry, the inside of a meat freezer, so mercilessly frigid that your nostrils stuck together when you tried to breathe. If you struck a moose on the road and gutted it and dressed it and tied it onto the hood of the car right there, it would be frozen by the time you limped your way home. In summer, dust from the unpaved roads caught in your throat and choked you. Once or twice, in spring, before the mosquitos swarmed out of the river in fat clouds, or in fall before the snow fell and rain froze on branches and grass, turning the landscape into an ice palace, and with the wind blowing the pulp smell away, you could imagine what life could be.

This was what Belva wanted. Just cleanliness, temperance, stillness.

She wasn't a girl who read, not then, so she had nothing to model a dream on, but when Garnette told her what she had to do to save the family, the sacrifice it was her duty to make, she sucked in her breath, thought of air so pure you could see across the plain, over the mountains and clear beyond the continent, and feeling Sailor's warm arm around her shoulder, his gentle voice whispering courage, she said, "No. No, ma'am, I will not."

"You will not what, Belva?"

"I will not be called Belva, for one thing. My name is Helena. Please don't call me Belva again, for I will not answer."

Garnette said nothing for a minute. Then she threw off the afghan she'd wrapped herself in, sitting on a kitchen chair with her feet in the oven to keep warm. "What God has joined, man may not put asunder," she said, and stood up. Helena saw how red and bumpy her feet were, the toes half curled under and crippled with bunions. You would never know, for Garnette always wore dress shoes when she went out and good solid house shoes—nurse's shoes—indoors.

"God didn't join me to my name," Helena said. "I will not be called Belva any longer. Helena is a pretty name. Helena is me."

"You're as plain as an old boot," her mother said, tears springing from her eyes. Garnette hadn't cried for Sailor—he'd slipped away so silently she couldn't have said when he'd really gone—but this parting—that it was, a parting—she at once recognized. "And," she continued, "you'll make the best of it like we all do, and lump it."

"No," Helena said again. If Sailor had been alive she couldn't have done it, couldn't have shown him up like that, couldn't have left him behind. "I *will* finish school. I will not leave this town without a high-school diploma, but leave it I will, as soon as I can." She left the kitchen and went to her room, put a chair back beneath the door-knob and waited for the rattling that would follow.

"Belva! Belva! You come out now!" When Helena didn't answer, Garnette went down on her knees and prayed, groaning to the Lord and reciting Bible verses all night. In the morning, Helena stepped over her sleeping body and went to school. And so it went, Helena studying at the school library until late, coming home, frying pota-toes and onions and a sausage for dinner, not attending church, not answering her mother who insisted on calling her Belva and praying loudly for her salvation whenever she saw her.

Garnette cleaned houses for other church ladies and brought home food: bacon ends, half-rotted apples, dented tin cans, and once, used tea bags.

One Friday night, a week before her graduation, when Helena arrived home, she was met by a delegation in the living room. Young people, people Helena used to know from the town church, girls with long dresses and bangs, boys wearing neckties. They formed a prayer circle around her, praising Jesus, calling on his name to heal their sister from her backsliding. Helena kept her eyes open and stood rigidly face to face with the stranger in the middle of them who appeared to be their leader.

"Who are you?" she asked him. He had curly auburn hair and looked cheerful.

"I'm the travelling evangelist," he said. "Are you the sister in trouble?"

"No," she said, "that's Belva."

"Then who are you?"

"Helena." She looked into his hazel eyes and didn't dislike what she saw. There was a glitter there, a gleam of clarity.

"Why don't we step outside and see if we can straighten this out?"

he said. She got into his car without a second's thought as to where he might take her. They drove to the train station and he said, "You're the first good thing I've seen since I got here. I'm leaving tomorrow and I'll never come here again. If you want, you can come with me. We'll have to get married though. I've been called to the mission field in the Bahamas. You can come as my wife."

She leaned a little closer and smelled Brut and whiskey and a little smoke, but it was the light in his eyes that made her say yes. They sat there until morning when he unloaded his luggage and bought their tickets. She didn't say goodbye to her mother, she didn't go home for her clothes. He left the car with the keys under the mat for the fellow it belonged to. She held her breath until they were over the bridge and were miles across the northern plateau on their way east.

What Clayton hadn't told her was what she would have to do in return for the rescue. Really, it was a job, though unlike any she'd seen advertised. Not that she minded it. The first part was easy: buy new clothes, wear stockings, not socks, and high heels instead of flats, shorten her skirt enough to show her legs, have her hair cut, styled and sprayed, apply discreet makeup. Clayton was relieved when she said she could play the piano enough to accompany him on his accordion.

When he made love to her, she was astonished. Never, in all the sidestepping from the wavering hands of drunks in that little 10th Street house, had she imagined what it would be like. Clayton adored her white, smooth skin, her thinness, her long arm and leg bones and pink fingernails, her small untouched breasts, her hip bones like rounded hooks, her little bottom. He held her hand in public, he told her she was wonderful . . . He liked everything about her, apparently;

she could do anything she liked, as long as she expressed no opinion and didn't speak about herself. She had found that out like this.

In Saskatoon, the third stop on the tour that would take them to headquarters in Toronto for outfitting and briefing, and from there to "Mission to the Bahamas"—where, given the chequebook she'd found in Clayton's jacket pocket, he already had a bank account—they were met at the station by the principal of Prairie Tidings Bible School. "The little woman's in the car," he said after shaking Clayton's hand. "I didn't know you had your wife with you, Clay, or I'd have brought my wife. She's in a delicate condition, and in this heat . . ."

"Oh, that's all right," Helena said, stripping off the white gloves Clay had made her put on before getting off the train, "I've had enough company. I don't mind being alone for a while." The dry heat didn't bother her at all. She looked forward to it, and to the dust that blew in with the trains along the tracks. She'd sniffed the air first thing—no smell. Whatever this was like, it wasn't like home.

"We're hoping to start a family of our own soon," Clay said, putting a heavy hot arm around her. The arm was damp, even through the summer-weight jacket. Helena gave a little shrug to make him lift it.

"That so?" the Reverend Styles said, showing his teeth to Helena but addressing her husband. "You take good care of this little lady, Clay. You're going a long way from civilization. She's young, you've got plenty of time. Put it in the Lord's hands. The Lord will supply."

"I don't want children yet." Helena said, "Why, I haven't even done high school!"

"Yes, you have, sweetheart," Clay said, squeezing her hand. Their bags had been unloaded onto the platform. The Reverend Styles hefted one up. "Don't joke like that, you'll have Ray here believing you."

"But it's true," she said, unable to understand why Clay would want her to lie, "I left a week early to marry you. Maybe they'll still give me my diploma, but I don't know for sure and I certainly am not going to be a mother before I finish my education." She turned to the Reverend Styles, who was looking a little uncertain. "When my dad died I promised myself I'd make something out of my life so I wouldn't end up like him. He was a disappointed man, my father."

"He's not been gone long," Clay said. "She's still grieving." The Reverend Styles nodded. Clay picked up their other bags and they walked along.

"He was a minister without a real congregation," Helena said. "He would've been happier as a mechanic—he could fix or build anything—or a teacher, maybe. He was good with children."

"Times were hard, Helena. Young people now don't know how it was. Not many of us were able to fulfill our ambitions. But the Lord knows best. He doesn't give us a burden we can't bear."

"Praise the Lord," Clayton said.

"Maybe so," Helena said, "but he gave us brains to think with and hands to work with and arms to love with." She looked at Clayton, walking beside her, with affection, and saw that his face was tight with fury.

"Well," the Reverend Styles said as they approached the Studebaker where Mrs. Styles waited, green complexioned, stupefied by heat, "all we need to know is in the Good Book, isn't that so?" He smiled at Clayton. Helena had a few more things to say but Clayton squeezed her upper arm so hard it took her breath away. She gasped, and Clayton put his hand at her back.

"Feeling faint, sweetheart?"

Later on, in their room in the married quarters of the Bible school, in the half hour they had before Clay was to deliver his lecture, "The Call of the Lord: Will or Surrender?" as Helena was hanging up her new dresses, she said, over her shoulder to Clay, who was washing up at the sink, "You hurt my arm back there, you know. I'm going to have a bruise."

Clay crossed the room, grabbed her shoulders and turned her to face him, his hot breath right against her face. She could only think that without his shoes on—did he wear lifts and she hadn't noticed?—he wasn't as tall as she'd thought. He gripped the muscle over her left breast so hard she thought she'd faint. She fell to her knees with the pain, his fingers still bunched tight at the muscle, making five black marks that would stay for weeks.

"You keep your mouth shut," he said. "Nobody cares about you, you're nobody, you hear?" He pushed her away. "I'll tell them you've got a headache." When the door shut behind him she cried, lying on the floor, calling for Sailor and, when he didn't come, for Garnette.

She fell asleep, waking only when there was a soft knock at the door.

"Mrs. Fernie? Are you all right? It's Mrs. Styles here. Your husband said you weren't feeling well."

Helena got to her feet, straightened her dress and opened the door.

"My dear!" Mrs. Styles said. "You don't look well! May I come in?" At her sweet smile and the gentle inquiry in her eyes, Helena fell into her arms and sobbed. "Whatever is the matter? Can I help?" Mrs. Styles said, patting Helena's back.

"We think we're pregnant," Clayton said, appearing behind the principal's wife. He separated the women and shepherded Helena over to the bed.

"The reverend said," Mrs. Styles replied, not taking her eyes off Helena's tear-stained face as she shrank from Clayton's touch. "How old did you say you were, dear?"

Helena didn't even try to open her mouth. Clayton wrung out a washcloth and placed it on her forehead. "Twenty-one next birthday, although you'd never know it. I'm a lucky man, Mrs. Styles. My wife is one of those women who'll age well."

Two weeks later, in Toronto, in another Bible school's married quarters, the humidity pressing its damp thumbs into her eyes so that they ached, she lay under a single sheet waiting for Clay to return. A street lamp shone onto the wall by the bed. When he came in smelling strongly of sweat and coffee, she tried to pretend to be asleep, but when he got in beside her, she turned her head away.

"So you're awake. I thought so," he said. He pulled her to him, and not even knowing that she would, she said, "Clay, I want you to go."

He stopped. "Did I tell you to talk? Did I give my permission?" His hand rose on the words, then fell back weakly. "You've spoiled it now," he said, "you've wrecked it." He threw back the sheet, dressed and went out, stamping loudly down the stairs.

He was back in an hour or so and sat on the side of the bed. "Helena, I'm sorry, I shouldn't have raised my voice like that. I love you. But we can never be away from each other. You understand that, don't you? We are one in the sight of God and man. We're together until we die."

When he finally wore himself down and fell asleep, she wiped herself with the sheet, dressed in the first thing she could find and went out. It was pre-dawn, the street quiet except for a sweeper truck rolling along, its brush pads down, cleaning the roadway. Water sprayed from a rod at the back, laying the dust.

Helena didn't know anyone outside the Bible school. She had no money and no place to go. At the telephone booth on the corner she closed herself in, frightened to look behind in case he had followed her. She dialled the number collect, her hand shaking, her world at an end.

"Garnette? Mom? I have to come home."

There were worse things in life than being a waitress in the Dingle Pot Café on 3rd Street. Waitressing in a bar, for instance, or living with Clay for the rest of her life. She was only seventeen. She asked her mother if she were still married to him, and Garnette said, "Where's your marriage certificate?" Since she didn't have one, had never seen one, and since Clay had performed the ceremony himself the second day after they'd left, in an unlocked church in Edmonton, with no witness but "God himself," Garnette thought it wasn't something Helena had to worry about. It was probably why Clayton hadn't come after her.

Her day began at 6:00 a.m., when the highway and construction workers came in for breakfast. She had a break at 10:00, missing the office workers drinking black coffee, but was back in time for the lunch rush from 11:00 to 2:00. Hamburgers, club or western sandwiches and ham omelettes were the most popular choices, with liver and onions for the truck drivers, and for the secretaries, bacon, lettuce and tomato sandwiches, easy on the mayo, fruit cocktail for dessert. She was finished then and could go home, if she liked, to the 10th Street house, darker and dimmer and sadder than when Sailor had lived there. Garnette was never home before 10:00 p.m., when she finished cleaning at the school.

That first week, Helena stayed inside during her breaks, drinking coffee and eating stale banana cream pie for lunch. Her feet hurt. The only shoes she had were the white pumps she'd run off in. Clay had bought them for her. Garnette had offered some house shoes with the toes cut out for bunions, but Helena still had her pride.

There was no one to train her how to remember an order or carry plates, or to tell her how the cook liked the orders to be given—he shouted at her every time she put one in. She had to keep the salt, pepper, sugar, milk and napkin dispensers filled, but so discreetly that the customers didn't notice what she was doing. She'd almost lost her job when she'd refilled the ketchup bottles at the tables: they were labelled Heinz but the red sauce came from a plain plastic gallon jug. Her tips were split with the busboy and manager; she was paid $1.10 an hour. At the end of the week she put her head down on her arms as she sat in the back booth and would have cried, but she was too tired. Serving meals, talking and smiling when she didn't want to, making coffee and milkshakes . . . Her day off she spent stopping herself from calling Clay.

The second week she put a coat on over her uniform, despite the heat, so no one would know where she worked, and walked down the street to the bookshop, even if all she had was ten minutes. She didn't read the books or even touch them, just pulled a chair over from Office Supplies and sat and stared at the stacks of new volumes.

While there she found herself considering what had happened to her, how Clay had come into her life when she'd been desperate for change, as if she'd set out to summon him, how she'd learned a little about leaving home and what life might have in store for her. As a bonus, he'd taught her the perils of sex: that just when you thought you'd found what you'd been looking for, what you were born for, that was the very moment at which you could be destroyed. It was a lesson of a certain kind, one that Sailor and Garnette couldn't have taught her.

In this mood, one day, she saw a small book of Byzantine icons on the remainder table. The text was in French, and she couldn't read it, but she was drawn to the rich gold and reds of the illustrations, the calm haloed faces, the dragons, horses, visions; the sense of time passed and passing that had gone into these paintings of bearded men and gaunt men and draped women. She turned the pages trying to see if she recognized anyone, but soon saw that each face, almost a mask, was a pool in which, if you looked long enough, you might recognize yourself.

When she got home, she gave in and asked Garnette if she could borrow her shoes.

Tink

He was too old to fall in love with a waitress. He was twenty-six, he had a job in the high school teaching English. That morning he'd showered and dressed as usual in the teachers' annex near the school, gathered up his papers, walked outside, and stopped. Overnight a wall had come between him and his work. Beyond it was the middle class he'd been heading towards, behind it was his village on the Nass River. He wasn't sure where he stood, exactly, in relation to each, but he felt that the wall bisected his heart. So he turned away from the school and walked all the way downtown instead.

He passed the bars and the Indians heaped in front of them waiting for opening, he passed the shoe stores and small grocery and hardware outlets and the library that was likely to remain empty all day. He thought about all the fights he'd been in; he thought long and hard about who and what he was trying to become. He had a cheque for two thousand dollars in his pocket and summer vacation coming up—a stretch of emptiness so profound, when he considered it, that the earth might as well have been cleared by the atomic bomb, and he the only person left on it.

When he'd walked long enough to be thirsty, he went into the Dingle Pot for coffee.

The waitress, though young, wore nurse's shoes with the sides cut out. Her hair was darkening at the roots. Her eyebrows drew together in a frown and her lips pinched as she waited for his order. Sticking out of the pocket of her uniform, at the waist, was a book. Tink looked at the vivid colours of the painting on the cover, and then he looked more closely at her. The pieces he could see—the shoes, the book, her age—didn't fit together.

He might have been an archaeologist: as he watched her he suspected fossil life, bones, ruins; he saw in her the evidence of a layered, complex life, and all this without their having exchanged a word.

"Will you come with me, just for today?" he asked her. "I'd like to show you something."

Helena

She didn't know why she said yes. She didn't bother to change or make excuses to the manager. She put on the heavy coat she always wore and they walked together to the highway. They got a ride in a pickup truck right away and spent seven hours in the back, bouncing over gravel roads, the wind stripping away any words they might have spoken. When they got out to hitch again, they were stiff and thirsty and sunburned. A jalopy, fenders missing, engine steaming, the driver drinking his way through a twelve-pack of beer, took them the rest of the way. It was midnight by the time they walked across the suspension bridge over the river to Tink's village. An ancient wooden figure guarded the settlement at the bridge's far end, its shoulders carved with faces, its hands at its sides, its mouth open in a frozen "O."

The dirt streets were dark and empty. They slept on the floor of the unlocked Salvation Army Citadel, a small empty white wooden building with a pitched roof. In the morning they slid down the steep banks of the river and washed their faces a hundred feet from where a grizzly bear dipped its paws into the water and fished. Tink took her to see a field of totem poles aged to silver, and then they walked across a lava bed, the black stones a wide, rough road leading to blue snow-capped mountains.

They stopped after an hour or so and gazed at the sky and the heavy weight of clouds over the valley. When they returned to the village there were still no people in sight. A few skinny dogs stared and didn't bark, paint peeled from boards, cars rusted. It was, she said to him at last, after slowly looking around, as if they were survivors of a flood: everything around them was stripped and old and bleached; or as if there'd been a fire and they and the lava valley and the totems and the river were all that were left unscathed.

"Why would we be the survivors?" Tink asked her with a smile.

"That's what I'd like to find out," she said, looking beyond him.

She called Garnette from a telephone booth to tell her that she wouldn't be coming back for a while. She was heading as far west as she could go, she'd call when there was anything to report. "I'm sorry about the shoes," she said. "I'll mail them back."

"What about me?" Tink asked her when she hung up. "We just got here. There's more to see. What's your hurry?" His face bunched in perplexity.

And so they lost each other. He returned to being a teacher, at least for a while, before he gave it up for good to work with his hands, building houses, boats, cupboards—whatever he could that was useful, and she landed in a small hotel in the Queen Charlotte Islands, a waitress again, but working in the bar this time.

On Friday nights she sang a little with the local band and drank the beer the loggers bought her. She lived in a room full of mice on the third floor. She sat at her window and saw the moonlight as it crossed the only street in town and watched the rain blow through on Saturday mornings, her morning off.

Sailor wept through her dreams. He said even the angels falling from heaven were on their way towards something, they still were, despite time passing. He said we only have our parents' word for where we've come from, we only have our own for where we're going.

Jag

The girl from the Cameroon, who lived across from the toilet, took everything out of her room once a week. Furniture, rugs, bedding, all went into the hallway. She tied her hair in a scarf and got down on her knees with a bucket of water and lye. She scrubbed every inch of her room, smoked cigarettes while it dried and then moved the furniture back in. Jag wondered where she had learned to do this, and why she bothered. Five rooms shared the single toilet on their floor.

There was no bath. His own room was farther down the hall, near the stairs. Inside it was a mattress on the floor, a chain strung across a corner on which to hang his clothes, and in an alcove, a couple of chairs, a small table and a hot plate. He'd heat milk, look out the small window at the Eiffel Tower and drink his morning coffee. His other meals he found through connections on the street—students selling their meal tickets or willing to exchange invitations to receptions, at which there was always food, for whatever Jag had to offer. Clothes were more of a problem. His best clothes were gifts. The handbasin in his room was a haven for roaches. When his linen and sheets and towels were filthy, he threw them away.

On his seventeenth birthday, at the end of his first year in Paris, Jag sat in a park and told himself how lucky he was to be there. The trees, newly in bud, faded into the distance in perfect rows. The sand at his feet was swept clean of debris. Small children wearing good wool coats with velvet collars ran back and forth holding balloons. Their socks, perfectly white, were folded down to touch the tops of their shoes. The only people sitting on the grass were foreigners. They appeared drawn, exhausted. Jag knew he could sell to them, but for today, this one day, he chose not to. When he had finished smoking a cigarette, he kept the butt in this hand, and waited until he neared his own neighbourhood to throw it away.

In the evening, he went to a workmen's café. Here the tablecloths were torn lengths of white paper on which the waiters tallied the bill. Jag ate bread and drank wine and waited for someone to approach and buy him dinner. Today, though, no one came. When the wine was gone, Jag got up, ready to start on the circuit from the square to the newsstands where businessmen, late leaving work, gathered, to the bridge, the deserted flower market and, if all else failed, the public urinals. Jag was not a queer; neither were most of the men he had sex with. They did not care about the gender of their partner, they simply sought sexual pleasure. They met in public because only the rich could afford privacy. Jag did it for the money, and because, otherwise, he was lonely. He knew exactly what he had to do to look after himself. He had several girlfriends, but none of them knew where he lived.

At the petrol station at the edge of the village, the night he'd left home at sixteen, he'd gone into the gents to wash himself. The blood flecks came off his hands and face and neck, but he could do nothing about the stains on his clothing. He removed his sweater and shirt, and then his socks, and splashed water over his skin. His face, in the polished metal mirror, belonged to a boy he had never seen; it wasn't him. He stared at it with interest. His legs, on their own, had taken him through the streets to these lights above the tarmac, to the door propped open at the back, to the weak bulb from the gents shining on a worn path into the field. Burrs stippled his trousers. He plucked at them, and his hands came away wet and sticky from the fabric. He removed his one remaining sandal and heard its metal buckle clink on the concrete floor. When he stepped outside, a man waited there, watching him.

The man asked, in the car, "Have you ever been to Paris?" Jag replied no. "Would you like to go there?" Jag nodded.

"You must be cold. You can change into some of my clothes." The man reached into the back for a small case. Jag took out a pair of corduroy trousers and a polo-neck. He stripped off his own trousers and underwear, balled them up and threw them out the window, aware of the man's glances when the car's interior lit up with oncoming headlights. The man's skin was coloured blue-white. He was made of that cold colour, and long dark shadows, and softly padded bones. Jag smoked the man's cigarettes—there was an endless supply of them. When they finished a pack, the man would stop and get more from the boot.

They arrived at a farmhouse near Dover. Here Jag's photograph was taken. When it was dry, from the darkroom, it was pasted into a passport. Jag signed where he was told. Outside again, the man fitted amber shields over the car's headlamps, put a Paris parking disc on the windscreen and changed the plates. He didn't eat or offer Jag food. They slept in the front seat.

The man said, later on, "Men live close together aboard ships and in army camps, they spend their days together in their workplaces, close friendships are highly valued. How are you off for friends, Jag?" He said, "If you'd been in the army you'd understand. I am not a pederast, I love women, I am not a woman inside."

Despite himself, when the man touched him at last, Jag cried out. He did not know if it hurt, he thought not, but in any case, once they were done, the man bought him breakfast.

"My relationship is to divine love, to God," the man said while they were eating. "I should have lived in ancient Greece where I would have been understood."

Soon they were on the ferry to Calais. Clearing Customs on this cold day was easy. The man was known. Jag's new passport, which wasn't even checked, said that he was French, the son of the man's business partner. Jag's feet were freezing. He had no socks or jacket. The man kept talking and talking. He said, "I love you, I'll take care of you," but he didn't.

In Paris the shops were closed on Mondays. Lunch was at 12:30 and dinner at 7:45. Food shops were open on Sunday mornings until 12:00. In Paris you shook hands with people when you met or parted. Tobacconists sold postcards, carte-lettres and postage stamps, but Jag didn't write to anybody. The push-button minuterie in the stairwell illuminated the landing for a minute—long enough to see a face and money, long enough, sometimes, to run away.

You could do anything, Jag believed on his seventeenth birthday, if you worked hard enough, and if you were willing to work at whatever you found. When he had children, he would teach them this, although he would also ensure that they wouldn't have to do the things he'd had to.

Jag's connections to businessmen hadn't panned out this evening, but he found a drunk seaman in a wooden toilet under a bridge and brought him up the stairs and into the hallway off which the girl from Cameroon lived. The girl helped him drag the sailor into his room to sober up. In the morning, the seaman bought Jag eggs and pickles from a street vendor and offered to find him a job on a ship.

So it was that Jag learned to coil rope and place it neatly in a locker, operate an anchor winch, move a pallet, take soundings the old way with a weighted knotted line, carry coffee to the steersman in the middle of the night, serve the captain's table and do laundry, wash himself or vomit when he was seasick, using a handbasin the size of a soup bowl.

At Colón, on the Atlantic side of the Isthmus of Panama, Jag came down with a fever. He sat out on deck wrapped in a blanket, shivering and sweating while the ship took its turn in the lineup of ships waiting to enter the canal, then sailed from the outer anchorage to the inner anchorage. At dawn, they moved again: the land was blurred with mist, the vegetation an insipid green, the American barracks, warehouses and a church steeple painted white, the ghost shapes of a faded colony. Near the shore were two wrecks, rusted warnings, as Jag's ship ploughed by towards the blue lights that showed the gap in the hill where the canal ran.

It was here, as they waited outside the locks, that a shore party came on board to handle the mules—the engines that ran on tracks along the lock walls—that would guide them through the locks. One of the men came up to Jag as he sat wrapped in his blanket, watching. The man had attended a Spanish-speaking college, he explained bitterly. His brother had gone to an English-speaking one and now had a good job and only two kids. He, on the other hand, had no job and five kids. It had cost him forty dollars American to come out to the ship with the mule crew. He gave Jag a cigarette and sat with him while a Danish ship entered the transit channel lane ahead of them. Two sailors moved slowly along the deck towards them, using long rollers to paint the ship's side down to the waterline. By the time they reached the spot where Jag and his new friend sat, Jag had bought a hammock, sandals, a T-shirt, souvenirs and, so he thought, the chance of a lifetime.

It was still dark when the ship skirted close to the Gatun locks. A cadet, coming off duty, had awakened Jag so that he could carry breakfast to the pilot. When he'd done so, Jag peered at the lights, set just above the water, that illuminated palm trees and giant ferns, and listened to the rising cacophony of insects and birds as daylight began to leak over the lake. A rain cloud scudded towards them and a large black bird circled as the rope crew clambered on board from the lock and loped forward to the fo'c'sle. Jag eased himself forward, too, to where several of the men were working, throwing ropes to the square-shaped mules that would tow them, and where the others had lain down to sleep. One of the men was late in hooking up and the ship slipped too quickly towards the lock gate. There were shouts and cries; a flourish of cockatiels rose from the jungle; Jag stooped and took a package from one of the sleeping men and threw it into the rope locker.

"Be careful, son," the pilot said later, sniffing and wielding his handkerchief over his nose, when Jag brought him a second glass of bourbon before noon. "You get caught down here, you'll never get out." He gazed into Jag's face. "You know what I mean?"

Jag knew. The fever continued to flicker through him. The vegetation swam down to the water through mangrove swamps, the trees burst at their tops with purple flowers. The soil, where the banks had eroded, was blood red. There were red flags along the shoreline, and a darkening blue sky was blotted with cumulus cloud, and the wind was blowing up. Then the shoreline was yellow, orange and pale green, with stick-white trees, branching out at the top, standing straight up from the water. Yellow grasses trembled at the water's edge, vultures circled; Jag saw a jaguar swimming away from a brush fire.

Fires burned all night along the cut, and then there were flares and star shells and the far-off wheezing of guns. When a new rope crew came on board, after Pedro Miguel lock, Jag threw another plastic bag into the locker. A band played "Lights Out" as they passed the infantry barracks near Panama City.

"God created all races, so he must have known what he was doing," the pilot said when Jag brought him coffee. He motioned Jag to follow him onto the monkey island, where they could look down on the rope crew below.

"You know their game, I hope," he said. "They come on board to sell drugs and after they do, they inform U.S. customs. They get money at both ends. They try it on with everyone new. If someone gets caught, it's not just them, but the whole ship in trouble."

For dinner there was poached eggs Florentine, sirloin roast, onion pudding, mixed vegetables and scalloped potatoes. Jag ate slices of meat standing up in the galley. The cook didn't like it, he thought it set a bad tone, but Jag told him a story of letters to write home and no time for a proper meal. He took coffee and brandy and a large fruitcake the cook had spent the afternoon decorating to the officers' table. Des, the chief steward, was saying that there was scientific benefit from the Nazi medical experiments, and Dave, the third officer, was denying it. Jag turned to go, but Des caught his arm. "Tell Cookie to come on out and bring the rest of the kitchen staff. I'm buying the drinks."

So Jag told the cook and the second steward and the young cadet. When they sat down, Des said, "We're discussing murder, Cookie, and how to dispose of the body."

"There's the sharks," said the mate. "You've got your white, your tiger, your hammerhead."

The pilot came in then. He wore a string tie with a little rectangle of wood as its clasp, and he flipped it up as he sat down.

Cookie said, "About your question, Des? Well, there's two things you could do to get rid of the body. There's your patient approach where you cut it up and bake it bit by bit into the bread." He turned to Jag. "You've seen how much bread we make. It could be done." Jag nodded and took a sip of brandy.

"Christ, Cookie!"

"Then there's your more obvious," he said.

"What's that, the soup?"

"No," said Cookie, turning his small, wizened face to Des. "You'd dress and butcher it and hang it in the freezer."

"I was locked in the freezer once for three hours," said Keith, the second steward. "It was pitch black in there. The light came on automatically, but only when the door was open. I couldn't see to find the alarm—some silly bugger had put boxes in front of it. If it hadn't been for Cookie here who came looking for something—"

"That's what I was saying," Des said. "We know how to treat

hypothermia because of the Nazi experiments. You have to warm up the core.

"If you wanted to disguise murder," he went on thoughtfully, "you'd put the alarm bell out of action by taping the hammer so that it couldn't strike the bell loudly."

"If he's dead he's not going to pull the alarm!"

"He's not dead when he goes in," Des said crossly. "He becomes dead. That's the whole point, it looks like an accident."

"Not if you tape the hammer."

They were quiet for a minute after that. So Jag said, "If it were me in that freezer, you know what I'd do?"

"I hate to even think!" Des said. Cookie gave him a look.

Jag said, "I'd take something, anything I could find, and wrap it around the probe of the heat-sensing mechanisms. That would raise the temperature. The engineers would see it on the readout and go and check."

"That's true," said the mate, who had been quietly listening. "Even five degrees C could ruin thousands of pounds of food. Good thinking, lad."

Forked lightning danced over the land, and sheet lightning lit up towers of clouds. Jag sat at the bulbous bow to watch the flying fish. Some flipped over, some crashed into the waves, but a few took off flying forty feet or more at great speed.

Somebody was jogging round the deck behind him. He found himself counting the laps without thinking.

He asked if he could be of more help in the galley. He was bored and he didn't drink or gamble. There was little to do in the cabins after making the beds. So he was set to cutting up vegetables for soup. When he had finished that, Cookie sent him to the freezer for

fish. They would be having crumbled fish and roast and boiled potatoes as well as the vegetables and salads. Cookie weighed the fish and
meat and entered the weights in a logbook, then set Jag to skinning
the fillets of frozen haddock, working from the head down, letting
Jag use one of Cookie's own knives.

Later on, when Jag came back from taking coffee to the bridge,
Cookie let him try his hand at icing. He had made a white icing base
for a cake and set a fine pink latticework over the top. He showed Jag
how to add scrolls and rosettes at the edges and then thin chocolate
piping on top of the scrollwork. Cookie finished it with rice-paper
roses he had made himself and a sprig of lavender. "What do you
think?" Cookie asked.

"It's perfect," Jag said.

The night before they docked at San Pedro, south of Los Angeles,
Jag woke up sweating.

At 4:00 a.m. he took coffee to the bridge. The mate was checking
the radar and charts and they were waiting for the pilot. It would be
their first landfall since the canal. In the engine room they were
beginning to burn the oil out of the system and powering up the
diesel generator to operate the winches they'd use to unload cargo.
On his way back to the galley, Jag detoured to the fo'c'sle. He
watched the crew place the pilot ladder midships on the starboard
side, and he could now see the yellow harbour lights reflecting on
cloud just over the horizon.

By the time breakfast was over, the ship had stopped to test the
stern gear and was proceeding slowly towards the breakwater after
taking the pilot on board. The sun touched a line of white buildings
on the docks, a row of palm trees, a hill and several tractors. The dock
was a kaleidoscope of colours—containers, vehicles and ships. When

the tug had dropped them and the ropes were secure, the second the gangway was down, Jag saw the men sprint from their hiding places behind the white buildings.

There were twenty-five searchers and two sniffer dogs, a golden Lab and a black Lab. Within the hour, they had arrested a steward and the steersman. One of the sailors had been seen throwing something overboard, and drugs had been found in the rope locker, in the library behind a row of books and taped to pipes in the engine room. None of it was Jag's.

Jag left the ship in Prince Rupert after another stint of helping Cookie, which took him into the freezer to retrieve his packages. He sold the drugs in the bar on the first night. By the third night he'd spent half the money.

Still, sometimes it doesn't matter what you do. There's a kind of loneliness so deep it doesn't have a name. It comes when you've gone in the wrong direction for a long time. You're going west when you should be going east, or you've left home when it's home you need, or you've stayed too long in one place and you've forgotten how to dream about any place else. You wake up and the hole is in your chest and you don't think it will ever go away and you just have to not be alone anymore, even when your luck has changed.

Jag hitched a ride on a fishing boat from Prince Rupert, stopped off in the islands and went out drinking with the crew. In the hotel lobby you had to go to the desk and the man behind it looked you over, and if you seemed all right to him, he'd buzz you through the steel door between the lobby and the bar. There was a lock-up for weapons.

He said to Helena, "You ever been out of the country?" and she shook her head. "You ever been to Vancouver?" No again. "You married?" Another shake no. "You want to dance?" He put his face against her hair during the third song and held her hand as if it were fragile—a broken wing, a precious object, something loved.

They left for a walk on the beach, but they had to cross a bridge, stroll down a road, pass by a graveyard, trek through woods and over sand dunes. By the time they arrived, they were cold, so they built a fire, and then because they were too warm, they went for a swim in the clean north Pacific. Salt prickled their skin. The cold was incalculable. They'd each come as far west as it was possible to go and not fall off the world.

He moved into her room that night, and because she was finished with the place, they left town. He flew out on the next plane, and to save money, she rode down on a freighter that delivered supplies up and down the coast. By the time she arrived in Vancouver to meet him, he had everything arranged.

So, how did they fall out of love? Who says they did? What makes you think it? There's Tink, of course. When Jag left, Tink returned. But that doesn't tell you everything. Sometimes people just hurt, almost from the beginning, and nothing goes right until the end.

You are between two influences. Earth and spirit
   mingle not. . . .
Assimilate and combine both forces. Stand in the
   market-place and cry your wares
but listen for the still small voice in the silence of
   your chamber.
Work in the sun. Listen in the starlight.

Frederick Bligh Bond,
"The Gate of Remembrance"

Eight

Helena

The car shook under the wind that punched at it from the open sweep of fields. Helena rolled down the window and leaned out, letting the wind pry at the fear she'd carried ever since Cathreen had run away. The days since then had been filled with the terror of what might have happened to her daughter; in Helena's dreams, her parents castigated her for her neglect—Sailor especially—and that was hard to bear. She'd traced Cathreen to Jag's village, and she and Tink had scraped up the money to come only to find that Jag, too, had disappeared and there was no further word of Cathreen. In the pub the night before a blond woman selling willow baskets and dried flowers had given her some hope. She'd spoken of a place called Summer-wood, the kind of place a lost kid might go. But overnight, maybe it was because of the storm, that spark of hope had faded. Helena couldn't have explained the uneasiness she felt, and so she hadn't said anything about it to Tink when they'd set off.

Crows flew into the wind and let themselves be blown back and down, then they lifted up again from the ground. Acres of grass-land, dotted with a few bedraggled grazing cows, their rumps sten-cilled with numbers, slipped by. The fields were bounded by ditches and willows. The few houses sat on slightly raised ground. They passed a farmer cutting reeds from one of the flooded ditches; his tractor idled nearby, attached to a load of hay. Sailor would have liked it here. She could see him pitching in, going out to look after the cattle, clearing nettles and brambles, planting fruit trees, always lending a hand.

Clouds smeared the pale sky and skidded away from them as they drove. A knot of horses browsed behind a row of willows planted as a windbreak, then the road veered and followed a peat cutting. A man cut peat blocks by hand and set them out in small piles to dry along-side the trench. A partly full wheelbarrow waited beside him.

"Do they still burn that stuff for fuel?" she asked Tink. "Sailor used to put it on the garden."

Tink shook his head. "I don't know." Then, after a minute, he pointed out a sunken corner of another field, tangled with fresh greenery, that marked one more small peat cutting. "It's mostly given up, I think, except by the old people." When the car had climbed a small hill and skirted a quarry, they could see, in the dis-tance, a cutting machine plodding through a field, leaving a black channel behind it. The land was striped with trenches, water and the delicate green of reeds.

A few more hills rose up as they drove southward, some dotted with pine and hazel wood, and then the road slewed off into a deep lane so overhung with trees that Tink had to turn on the headlights. When they emerged, they ran through a veinery of narrow lanes hedged with hawthorn and sycamore. Helena read out the directions so that Tink had time enough to make the turns.

They knew they were on the right road when the lane crossed a little stream spurting out of a wooded bank. Several travellers' wagons were parked in a clearing. The pub woman had told them that there might be squatters living on the fringes of the commune. The owner of Summerwood, Nick, was well known for standing up for their rights.

A piebald dog ran out from the wagons to bark at them as they slowly bumped along the rutted drive. "It shouldn't be far, now," Tink said. "See, there's the orchard she mentioned."

On their left, a dozen acres of long-neglected Russets and Bramleys straggled up a hillside. "Sailor'd have that pruned in a week," Helena said. The long, thin branches of the apple trees trailing from the short trunks made her think of seaweed, the shrivelled apples like water-fat seaweed pods.

"We're here," Tink said, pulling up at a fence. They got out of the rented car and Tink locked the doors. Somebody had entered the car the previous afternoon and smashed up their suitcases. These things happened, you had to be careful, even here in the countryside where you thought you were safe.

The woman had told them of two entrances to the place, one that led directly into the heart of the camp on the hill, and this one, which passed the outpost of sheds that Nick had acquired with the property. By taking the longer way, they could approach quietly on foot. In case . . . Well, in case, as Tink had suggested, Cathreen, if she were there, wasn't too pleased to see them.

"You mean sneak up on her," Helena had said. Tink had just winked, but there was more to it, Helena was sure, although Tink, when she'd tried to probe, had just shrugged his shoulders and looked away.

A log shelter with a sod roof held bags of fleece; a tool shed contained trunks, harnesses, cardboard, old clothes and a neatly arranged box with slots for mail. Helena couldn't stop herself from looking for Cathreen's name on the tags: she tried not to feel disappointed when it wasn't there.

"The lady said not many of them stay long, it's a hard life," Tink said. "Don't get your hopes up too much, Cathreen might not be here at all." He lifted a tarpaulin tied round a large circular steam saw. "Looks like they're getting serious about that logging," he said.

"Why do you have to poke fun at everything!"

He raised his eyebrows, and let the tarp fall back into place. "I wasn't."

Helena stalked away—anger, but mostly dread, fluttered in her throat—and gazed at a pile of cut yellow stone. Behind it, in a bush, a sparrow flapped, trapped in a tight weave of branches.

Tink had moved on. "Come look at this, Lena," he called. So she went over and squinted into another small shed, at a table set out with balances, a few boxes of yellow apples, a big wooden cider press, and several barrels and crocks stacked against the wall. The shed was damp and musty, dust lay thick on the surfaces, and the canvas strung under the roof beams to catch leaks was a nest of spiders' webs.

Tink caught her eye. "I didn't say anything." But it was clear that whatever enterprises the community had undertaken were struggling. It was the same everywhere. They passed a crumbling kiln set into a clay bank, a couple of haystacks covered with tarps, and a pile of logs through which grass and nettles grew. It all spoke of work suspended or stopped, of odds too overwhelming to overcome. "They've had lots of good ideas," Tink said.

"Where is everybody? It's so quiet." Helena took Tink's hand and they followed a path into a dark forest of spindly fir, the earth fine and dry under their feet, the trunks bare for the first thirty feet or so of their height and then the brown branches joining overhead to shut out light. They paused when they heard the mechanical ticking of a pump.

"I'll go that way," Tink said, pointing in the direction of the distant clatter, "and see if anybody's working down there. That'll be at the stream we crossed. Maybe one of the squatters can tell us something."

"I'll follow the path and see what's up there," Helena said. She didn't want to go alone, but couldn't think of any good reason why not to.

"You be all right?"

"Of course!"

He squeezed her shoulder, patted her bum and loped downhill through the trees, in and out of view, before blending once and for all into the shadows.

A little more light leaked through as she mounted the hill. At one spot she could see through a break in the trees to a small valley. A fence, a partially ploughed green field, a few reassuring sheep composed a pastoral view. She pressed on, feeling the cold. Some falls and snags had been cleaned up and piled together to one side of the trail, and then suddenly she was at a clearing with enough space in it for the camp. A stew pot bubbled on a grate over a small fire. She looked around, and seeing no one, sat on a chair made from slabs of wood nailed together, to wait.

A few minutes later, an old man emerged from a canvas shelter, his grey hair on end, his hand scrubbing at his beard. "If I'd knowed there'd be company, I'd have baked," he said.

Charlie introduced himself and pointed out where he kept the cups, sugar and fresh milk—"I paid a visit to a cow this morning," he said—and she went to fetch them. She was fascinated with the set-up—dishes stacked in racks, pots hung overhead, a basin to wash dishes, all on a pole contraption in a shelter built from tarps. She set the tea things on the ground. "Did you do all this yourself?" she asked.

"Some."

"Are there any women here?"

"They come and go."

"How many people live here?"

"It depends."

Helena watched smoke twirl round the iron tripod on which a kettle simmered. She took a photograph of Cathreen from her wallet and held it out to the old man. "This is my daughter. I just want to know that she's all right."

Charlie looked at it, then handed it back. "I used to live in a bedsit," he said and got up to pour boiling water over tea leaves in a black teapot. His eyes narrowed in the smoke. "It might not look like much to you, but you can't beat freedom."

Helena could hear somebody moving through the woods on the far side of the settlement. She caught a glimpse of a tall, gaunt figure moving quickly through the trees.

"Don't pay any attention to him," Charlie said, after his own swift glance, "he don't much like women. If he comes any closer, I'll chase him away." He coughed.

"That's not Nick?"

"Nick!" Charlie scoffed. "Naw, Nick's a different kettle of fish."

He rose to pour the tea. "You can put in your own sugar and milk," he said.

"You see," he went on, as if she'd asked him more questions, "it's no good telling the Third World what to do when you can't take care of your own back garden. What have we got to offer? Greed and selfishness! We tell them not to cut down their rain forests, and what are we doing? The same bloody thing, cutting our trees! Nick has the right idea: we cut trees, we plant 'em. Now, I don't know, I don't go out much anymore—look at them motorways, roads to nowhere. But you can't store veggies in a flat even if you've got an allotment, and you don't need to worry about the electricity going off and spoiling things when you've got none to start with." He took a sip of his tea. "I only came back here to retire," he said.

"What were you doing?"

"Planting tea. Hot bloody climate."

She placed her cup on the ground beside her seat. "Do you think I could look inside your shelter?"

She knew, at once, that Cathreen had been there, although it took her a minute to understand why she was so sure. The beds—mattresses on wooden platforms on the floor—were neatly made; colourful rugs and blankets lined the floors and walls, books lay open, ready to read, coal lamps stood prepared on shelves. It looked peaceful: the white canvas stretched over the poles gave the interior a sense of space and light. Then she saw that one of Cathreen's scarves had been tied around a post.

Charlie said, from the doorway, "I'll show you around the rest of the place, if you like." He blushed. "Maybe you'd like to join us? We're getting a horse to pull the logs."

"I don't want to join. I don't want to stop you working. I'd just like to talk to my daughter."

Charlie coughed into his hand. "Everyone does manual work on Mondays and Tuesdays. The other days they do what they want."

"Have you seen her?" Helena untied the scarf and held it out. "This is hers."

"People come and go," Charlie said, avoiding her eyes, "they pass through. Not many of them stay once they see what's involved. Not many like to work hard." Charlie glanced over his shoulder, then back at her. "Let's you and me talk quietly," he said.

He took her by the elbow, ushered her outside and showed her the path to the deeper woods. "You just go on ahead. I'll follow in a minute. There's something I have to do, then I'll see if I can help." He swung away, his shoulder blades showing sharply through the ragged grey wool of his sweater.

She entered a mixed wood where the earth underfoot was soft and dry and carpeted with fallen leaves. The canopy of branches let light through to the forest floor in small pools and smatterings of coins. There were little hazels and larger ash, poplar and hawthorn, as well as several ancient beech trees and a wild pear. As she moved further towards the centre of the wood, several paths branched off from the main track. She crossed these, following Charlie's directions, and arrived, as he had said she would, at a ring of giant oaks and yews. Several of the oaks were entwined with ivy.

She seated herself on a fallen tree. The wood was quiet. She was cold and slightly damp, and she rubbed her hands together to warm them. Something made her look up. The pale shape of a large white dog moved in and out of the trees.

Tink

Tink followed the clicking sound to the pump, crossed the stream and walked round the orchard and back to the road without seeing anyone, then he cut upwards to the hill where they'd spotted the encampment of travellers when they'd driven in. No one but the motley dog answered his first shouts. It wouldn't come to his hand, but backed away, its tail down, and stood near the door of a wagon, snarling. Tendrils of smoke drifted into the air from the ashes of a fire recently put out; a few broken-down chairs, and, beneath a tree, a drunkenly leaning baby carriage completed the outdoor furnishings. Ten or twelve yards away, heaped in brush as camouflage, he found a brand-new Harley. He put the disguise back, but not before he'd discovered, in a saddlebag, a large lump of hashish, still bearing its number and gold stamp. When he returned to the wagons, a girl stood on the steps of one of them, squinting at him. She wore jeans and a torn sweater, and her long hair was tied at the nape of her neck. She yawned, showing a set of neat silver fillings in her teeth. She looked to be, at most, seventeen. She held a very small infant in her arms.

"Nice baby," he said.

"You don't want the men to find you here," she said. "It's kind of tribal. They won't like it." She crouched, tucked the baby under an arm, and got busy with a kettle and a small gas stove she'd put out on the step.

"I'm looking for a girl a little younger than you. I wonder if you've seen her."

"It's all family here," she said. She finished with the stove and sat down on a step. Tink had squatted down several yards away so that he'd look smaller, so she'd know he intended no harm.

"I need to talk to her. I want her to come home."

"She your daughter?" the girl said. "Weren't you good to her? She run away, then?"

"I miss her. Maybe she's in trouble. I'd like to help."

"My parents didn't come looking for me when I left," she said. "Nobody gave a toss." She scrounged in a box beside her for an apple and held it out to him. "Help yourself. We got lots." Tink eased to his feet and took it. He'd known plenty of places like this, with the same litter of ketchup bottles, mugs and plastic basins outside, the hand-to-mouth living that was fine when you were young and not so fine as you grew older. Stones tied to a rope slung over the canvas roof of the wagon weighted the roof against storms.

"I didn't have my baby in hospital," she said while he ate. "I had him here, just me and Tom."

"Tom?"

"The baby's father. He's got this tattoo," she said, pointing to her shoulder. "I was going to get one, but . . ." She jiggled the baby enough to wake it and slid it under her sweater so it could nurse. "Did you come from Nick the landlord? We told him we'd go. We don't stay where we're not wanted. He thinks we're dealers, but we're not. He's taken against us 'cause Tom's just out of jail. He doesn't mind, normally, he said, but somebody said we were dealing heroin. We're not. We're not killers. So we're looking for a place. You can tell him from us."

"I don't know Nick," Tink said. "I'm looking for a girl. She's four-teen—almost fifteen—kind of medium build, brown hair? Her name's Cathreen."

The girl shook her head. "I haven't seen anyone. I just stay here with the baby."

Tink heard movement behind him in the trees. He stood up, threw the apple core into the bush and backed away to show whoever might be watching that he was no threat to the girl. "You have a horse to pull that wagon?" he asked her.

She snorted. "Where do you come from? Of course we've got a horse. Old Strider, in the field over there." She examined him up and down. "There was another guy around here who talked funny but he was a Frenchman."

"So you're sure you haven't seen her?" The movement had stopped, but he could smell rotted flesh. He swivelled his head and caught a glimpse of a big man at the edge of the clearing. His clothes were too small for him and they hung in rags; pieces of what looked like loose skin flapped where his flesh was exposed. The girl, preoccupied with the baby, had noticed nothing.

"You look after that baby, then," Tink said. He started to walk away, concerned now to draw the man who was lurking there away from the girl and her child.

"Merry might know," she called after him. "Merry knows everything. If I see her, I'll tell her you were asking." The baby cried briefly as she shifted him to her other breast. "We won't be here if you come back, you can tell that to Nick."

Tink listened hard, attempting to keep a clear sense of the direction from which the big man was coming. Tink was being herded, given leave to go only where his tracker wanted him to. He headed once more for the woods, anxious to warn Helena and get her out of there, but the figure suddenly loomed in front of him, swinging a machete. Tink made a wide turn and ran downhill to the road and along to the car, but when he got there, he found that its tires had been slashed. He vaulted the fence into a field and ran straight through it, uphill, in the direction of the Summerwood camp, parallel to the track Helena had taken. He could see smoke rising at the top, a lazy drift that touched the crowns of the thin brown trees. He was still running, thinking that he was going to make it to where there was someone to help him, when he heard the shrill warning scream of the donkey just breasting the hill ahead.

The figure rose out of the ground as if it had been waiting behind that small hillock of tufted grass and cow parsley all along. Tink lifted his arm to ward off the blow. The metal blade bit deeply, cutting instantly through to bone. He had no time to cry out, no time to say any of the important things he might have wished to say, no time to think anything other than "No!" before the creature swung again, and the blade caught the sheen of the weak sun before dulling, in an instant, with his blood.

Galt

The landscape had emptied. There were no birds, no field mice, no grasshoppers or diving beetles, no late dragonflies or darters. In the distance, only, could be seen fleeing lapwing and snipe. Sound dropped away as Galt finished cutting the head from the body, then rolled the body into a ditch. The donkey stood nearby, its chest heaving, its head shaking, white froth falling from its lips. Galt wiped his hands on the grass.

Now the head swung from his hand, cradled in a rope sling, the only sound the quiet spattering of Tink's blood on the meadow. Galt went slowly, the donkey following, silent now, stepping carefully over the ditches as he came to them. Ferns and sedges, milfoil and duckweed floating in the rhynes, became part of the grey haze that slipped over Galt's eyes. A greenish fluid leaked from his nostrils and mouth.

Still, laughter bubbled inside him: he had done what he'd set out to do, despite his increasing difficulties. Now he needed to get the timing right. He didn't want to be weak when he caught up with Jag. A clock inside him counted out the seconds as the red stone ebbed through his intestines. He took a firmer grip on the head—its weight was making the rope knots slip.

They passed hawthorn, blackberry, beech and hazel hedges, and then Galt stopped. Not far away, behind a wire fence separating several old oaks from a caravan park, brightly coloured clothing had been pegged out on lines to dry. Not just Merry's clothing, but Jag's. Galt smiled.

Good, his Master was here.

Galt heaved himself into one of the oaks and tied the head there, then he let himself down carefully. The swift urging of his bowels sent him into the lane.

Galt knocked on the caravan door. He waited a few seconds, and when no one answered, he put his fist through the sidelight, slipped the lock and went in. The shower was running. The bathroom door was open. He slid back the glass tub-door.

"Master," Galt said, "I have something to show you."

Cathreen

Cathreen and Nick lay in the long, rain-flattened grass at the edge of a ditch across the road from the entrance to Summerwood. Flood-lights strung between trees scraped bald flat open holes in the night. Cathreen counted four police cars and two ambulances slewed across the roadway, doors left open, lights flashing. Nick quaked beside her.

"I've got to go and see what's happened," he said.

"I'll come with you."

"No! You stay here. I'll be right back."

She grabbed on to his arm. "Nick, please."

Gently he pried away her fingers. "Take Breaker. He'll look after you. If anything happens and I'm not back in an hour, meet me at the barn where we stayed last night." Nick called the white dog and made him lie down beside Cathreen.

Nick started to go, crawling on his knees, then returned, took her face in his hands and kissed her. She stared after him as he took off in a running crouch and made a wide turn, angling across the field. He'd come out, going that direction, above the camp, where the floodlights didn't reach. She kept on staring long after she could no longer see him. When she stirred, intending to follow despite what he'd said, Breaker growled a warning.

Galt

Mist rises from the ditches and lies a foot or so above the surface of the ground. Cattle scatter through the fields ahead of me—they bawl and don't look back. Only their heads and the top of their rumps show, the rest is lost in the grass and vapour. I run so quickly that I, too, must appear to be floating, cresting the haze when I leap the ditches, then falling back into the white wave.

When I was a boy, and if I had come this way, I would have drowned. The trackway was two rails of wood laid on crossed pegs floating on mud. If you slipped off, you were caught in the marsh and slowly sank, or you splashed like a fish in a great ocean before going down. There was nothing here but the glitter of light or the pattering of rain on water. When I was a boy, and I went out along the trackways, someone always came with me.

Now the sea has been forced behind walls of earth and rock. A belt of clay fringes the coast, and peat fills the old river valleys. Although little is the same, the rivers still flood when the tide, pulled by the moon, flows inland as far as the pumping station and the opened drains. The water spreads, and softens the grasslands.

I run over dry land westwards. I know where I'm going.

Soon I will excrete the red stone and return it to my mouth. Life enters my body through my mouth and leaves it through my rectum. Nothing in this is new. If you do not eat, you starve.

I am bone, I think, and shreds of flesh and the will to live. Life and death howl through me. One chases the tail of the other. Neither can quite catch hold. I did everything I could for my Master, and still he sent me away. I do not know why he gave me life, I do not know why he doesn't love me.

My village was at the centre of a maze of marsh and overgrowth. Our forebears had built the islands with wood and wattles and clay; you could hear the noise of rafts and boats arriving and departing and always the questing sounds of the animals held in pens. There are drier patches now where there used to be thick clumps of birch and alder. I have a map in my mind, and in my feet and in my heart. I know the way.

In the fields in front of me are low mounds covered in long grass. I can tell by the drop-off of land where the island boundaries lie. The water in the little pools makes mirrors. Their light flares at my eyes, and I scrub away tears so that Pam, if she is watching, will not see that I am sad. I helped build the fencing that sheltered us from wind, I kept the landing stage, where we unloaded the dugouts, in repair. I cut and carried reeds and rushes for thatch. I brought clay from the quarries a mile away and smoothed it over the floor of our house.

Nick says that the land has become a factory. The cows are part of it, and the damaged peat moors, and the fields of rape and ryegrass. No more pelicans or sea-eagles fly the marshes.

Nick is right about many things, but he does not understand.

No one understands. No one but Pam.

There the wise Merlin whilom wont (they say)
To make his wonne [dwelling] low underneath
the ground,
In a deep delve, far from the view of day,
That of no living wight he might be found,
When so he counselled with his sprites encompassed
round.

Edmund Spenser,
The Faerie Queene

Nine

Cathreen

When Cathreen awakened, it was already late afternoon. She lay in sweet hay, the arched roof of the barn high above her. She could sense, more than see, the flutter of birds in the bracing. Lower down, soft light filtered through cross-shaped slits and the trefoils placed in the end walls. Her clothes were still wet, except for where she was curled around the cat. A deep purring came from its throat, but the reassuring rumble and the relative warmth comforted her only until she sat up, looked for Nick and saw that he hadn't arrived, as she'd hoped, while she was asleep. Breaker lay a few yards away, guarding the doorway.

She'd waited for Nick for hours, afraid to go nearer Summerwood — there'd been more cars, more activity — in case the police were there because of her, in case Helena and Tink had reported her missing. That wouldn't have explained the ambulances, but still . . . She'd stayed hidden until she was almost too cold to move. When Cutthroat had returned from wherever he'd been, he'd jumped onto her shoulder, and then Breaker had nudged at her until she'd finally stood up from the ditch, her feet porridge at the end of her legs, and started walking, stumbling over fields and dragging through hedges until at length she'd arrived at the barn, crying all the way because she'd felt so alone.

Breaker gave a growl, and the white hair bristled up along his spine. Cathreen dumped Cutthroat to the floor, ran to the door and pushed the big wooden gateway open. "Nick!" she cried into the stream of twilight, but it wasn't Nick who stood there, the light turning his figure silver, it was Merry. "What are you doing here?" Cathreen said. "Where's Nick?"

"Nick told me where to find you."

Merry brushed past her and sat down in the hay. Her face was splotched with bruises.

"Christ, Merry, what happened?"

"What am I going to do? How am I going to tell you?" Merry sobbed. She removed a clump of damp tissue from a pocket, blew her nose, wiped her eyes on her sleeve and began.

While Merry went outside to start the Land Rover, Cathreen held tight to Cutthroat. She felt empty. She couldn't remember what Tink's face looked like or what they'd last talked about. She tried to imagine it — the head in the tree — the way Merry had described it, but it wasn't real yet. She'd asked Merry why Galt had let her go, but she didn't know. She'd asked her where her father was now, and Merry had said she'd take her to him.

Tink had come looking for her and she'd run away from him. He'd only ever tried to help her. If it hadn't been for her, he'd be safe at home.

Cathreen's stomach heaved, and she ran outside to be sick. When she was done, Merry offered her a handful of tissues and a drink from a water bottle.

"There, that better?" Merry said.

It wasn't, not really. Cathreen's stomach was a hard knot of pain. Her mouth tasted foul.

"Where's my mother? Why isn't Nick here?"

"Your mother's gone. She went back home."

"She left without me?" Even at the worst, Cathreen had always thought that Helena loved her. It was her job. The emptiness inside her became an abyss.

"She has to make arrangements, I guess."

"But what about me!"

"She said you ran away because she and her boyfriend were going to get married. She said you wouldn't want her, you'd want your father."

'No," Cathreen cried, "I loved Tink, how could she even think . . . ?"

Merry put a spindly arm round Cathreen's shoulders and lifted her to her feet. "You can stay with me tonight. You need to eat and clean up. I'll take you to Jag in the morning." She steered Cathreen towards the Land Rover.

"What about Nick? Didn't he say anything?"

"Nick's gone too. He went to his sister's. He asked me to look out for you, that's all."

"I don't understand." Cathreen stumbled against Breaker, who had padded over next to her. Sharp pain clenched her guts.

"Both me and Jag could have been dead last night, Cathreen—your father was there, like I said, but I didn't tell that to the rozzers. Don't you say anything, either." Merry opened the Land Rover door. "You coming?"

"You've known where Jag was all along!" Cathreen said, suddenly sure of it. "I've been looking for him ever since I got here, you knew that, it's the first thing I told you!"

Merry touched a finger to her bruises. "The police wanted him. You'd have led them right to him. What else could I do?"

"You could have told me he was all right. He'd know I'd be worried!"

"You were fine. You met me and you met Nick." Merry dug in her pockets for cigarettes, tapped one out of the pack and offered it to Cathreen.

Cathreen pushed her hand away. "Don't you care? None of this would have happened if you'd let me see Jag in the first place. Tink wouldn't have had to come here, he'd have known where I was. It's all your fault. Why didn't you mind your own fucking business!"

Merry lit the cigarette, narrowed her eyes and blew a smoke ring. "So, it's all my fault?" She blew another ring. "It wouldn't be the first time you couldn't face up to things, would it?"

Merry dropped the cigarette and ground it out with her heel.

"What do you mean?"

"It's nothing, forget it," Merry said. "I've got a daughter—she's grown up, but we went through hard times, too, and it's all worked out."

"You talked to my mother," Cathreen said. "What did she tell you?"

Merry got into the car and started the engine. "Half the world's screwed up, Cathreen." She looked around the farmyard at the low sheds with tile roofs, the stable, the stone granary, the farmhouse at the far end. Pine, ash and fruit trees had been planted round the perimeter. "I grew up on a farm, not one as nice as this. Maybe I'll tell you about it sometime."

Cathreen's teeth rattled; she couldn't control their juddering.

"Here," Merry said, reaching into the back seat, "take this," and she gave Cathreen her red sweater.

Jag

It was a hard landscape, a hammer-and-nails view. The trees, banged into the spongy soil, slanted black and leafless against the pewter sky. It seemed brittle, the whole of it, ready to shatter like a mirror if you looked at it the wrong way. You could examine it a thousand times and nothing, and then that one glance and you'd see yourself coming back at yourself, stepping over a rise, leaning out of the picture, floating to the top of the surface, restored to life. You'd keep thinking—just because of where you were—that you'd get another chance.

Jag shook his head to dispel the image. There'd be no resurrection for him. He wouldn't get back what belonged to him, or put the pieces of his broken life together; there'd be no mending. There was no peace, no enlightenment, only horror. All he'd managed was to endanger himself, his daughter and his wife, and to bring about the cruel death of his friend. How could it be explained? How forgiven?

The only good thing he had ever done was to run from this place the first time.

He'd come straight back to the hut. Merry had said that if the police found him at the caravan it would make things worse. How worse? What could be worse? "Think about Cathreen," she'd said. "She can't lose you, too." For now, the police would be too busy figuring out who Tink was and where to start looking for Galt to worry about him, but they would soon. It wouldn't take them long to make the links. And then what?

His feet hurt; he had blisters. He'd had to walk all the way in the dark, up the lane and through a series of red-brick and yellow-stone villages, past more lace curtains and garden gnomes than he'd known existed, before striking the path onto the moor. It was nearly dawn by the time he'd arrived at what was now his only semblance of a home. Merry would have to help make the arrangements to get him out of there. The police wouldn't have an easy time tracking him—none of them knew the moor, just the roads to the next big town—so he might have a little time, but sooner or later somebody local, frightened of Galt, would start helping them.

He'd been a fool to come back, an idiot to believe that anything could change.

Jag turned away from the light that reflected off the ditches in sharp silver spikes, and rubbed his eyes. They were red, sore and watering. He hadn't slept; he hadn't shaved or washed or had anything to eat or drink. He'd been afraid to sleep. Every time he shut his eyes he saw Tink. Jag staggered a little, suddenly dizzy. He took a couple of deep breaths to steady himself, and fixed his eyes on the horizon. Somebody out there, a figure like a pin on a felt board, was digging peat by hand, the spade dipping into the greenery and turning up black ink. Already a little pile of satin black peat bricks stood in a pyramid to one side of the distant man, just the right size for a wheelbarrowload back to a cottage. Most of the land around was owned by some company with headquarters in London, Brussels,

Bonn or Amsterdam. But peat smoke rose from every chimney on the Levels, scenting the air, the smoke making spirals, curling the horizon. A small victory for Everyman.

It was cold back inside the hut. Jag opened a tin of beans for supper. Since there was no more fuel for the little stove, and he didn't want to light a fire or a lamp in case somebody saw it, he squatted, huddled in his jacket in the dim doorway, and ate the beans from the tin with a spoon. A church spire and several lights showed from a far village. He could smell the wet grass and earth. When spring came these same fields would be pink with orchids. He closed his eyes, hearing the night noises of animals and the palest of sounds, like rain pattering, that he thought must be the stars as they lit up the clear sky.

Something clattered through the branches in a line of pollarded trees. Jag started up and stared out into the darkness. The noise stopped, but he kept on listening until the quiet turned into time, and time lapped around him. Time he hadn't even known he'd spent or lost or missed. He supposed it was to do with grief, but it was funny how what you felt didn't finish you off like you thought it would.

In the nightmare, he smelled burning, and saw a boil of greasy smoke spread from behind his sister's husband's face until it swallowed the sky, and he fell or was pushed. He awoke, sweating and disoriented, and felt the weight of the night pour through the cracks between the sheets of paper taped over the window next to the cot. He thrust off a blanket with his foot, took a drink from a bottle of water and tried to get back to sleep. If there were any justice in the world there would have to be a reason for the things that had happened. It couldn't be for nothing that Tink had had to die, or Galt had been allowed to live, could it? Please, God, please, Jag prayed into his rising tide of despair, but he didn't know how to finish, he didn't know how to say what he wanted.

Galt

The dog had barked nearly all night, a continuous rasping that set his teeth on edge. That, and the weakness that came so suddenly as the stone made its rapid progress through his body, frightened him. The emotion of fear was new, but he recognized it for what it was: he had seen it on the faces of people as they ran towards cameras on TV, their hands raised over their heads, and something like it on the faces of those who drowned or almost drowned at Pam's beach.

Galt's bones hurt where they stretched apart at the joints. The inside of his skull felt splintered, as if there were bone shards embedded in his brain, as his body, worn by the quarrelling forces in it, continued to disintegrate. Yet, despite the fear and pain, despite the sadness that seeped through him drop by drop, without apparent end, because of his Master's rejection of his gift, there was a sweetness to life.

Across the field, a puff of crows fell into a huge oak. The crows cawed from the branches. From beneath them, at the drip line, where the grass began, a fox embarked on a measured trot. It went on a way, stopped, sniffed the earth, licked a paw and continued. Galt admired the rust of its coat against the more muted colours of the faded wet field. He watched until it passed under a fence and into a coppice.

Thirst made him gather his bones once again and move. He patted at the flaps of skin that hung from his arms as he walked. Thin sheets, shapes of vellum, they were shiny, with a polished brown richness not unpleasing on their own, even though he now knew how they would make him look to others. This was recent knowledge. It had entered his mind as he had neared his birthplace. Here, in this place, he could remember what it had felt like to cross a field with a sense of measureless strength in his legs, at ease with his breath; and then, when he had bent to a pool to drink, he had seen not only that his hair stood out in matted tufts from his head, that liquid seeped from his eyes, his nostrils, his mouth and ears, that the membrane within which he existed had thinned to near transparency, but that his internal organs were as brittle as dry leaves. He had worried, briefly, that Pam, when she saw him, might be bothered by his appearance, but he'd recalled, "Man looketh on the outside, God looketh on the heart," and Pam was not a man.

Here, where he'd been raised, he could clearly recall those who had been part of his life's path—his parents and friends, and those who had taught him important skills. His mouth tasted of apples. There'd been an orchard, just a small one, on the uplands. He'd gone there with his father in the late autumn, falls squishing underfoot as they'd walked: the odours of sweetness and rot were the odours of the earth itself. In the spring there would be new shoots on the trees, and then blossoms. Galt sighed. Where were they now, those who had entangled him in a human package, who had lived, with him, love for field and swamp and forest, and who had taught him to conduct himself with ceremony? They were gone—the strings of that parcel had been cut for centuries. But once, they had *been*.

Galt spent the day searching through the long grass for the particular mound that marked the site of his village. There had been perhaps thirty or so houses on it, and the landing stage for boats that plied the channels through the reeds. On the dry slopes of the upland, farther away, they'd planted wheat, barley and oats. Galt—only that hadn't been his name—had worked the fields and supervised the pasturage for sheep and cattle. His mother had been a potter. His father had drowned in an accident. The dead were laid on the sacred island when the time came.

When he had cleared the grass from as many of the mounds as he could, he sat in a small depression at their centre. He could feel the turning around him, the run of daily activities, people crossing the marsh by boat to hoe plots or to hunt wildfowl in the reed beds, or to search for birds and berries on the raised bog; there was also the strain of the longer, harder journey to the woodland and back. As he sat, rain swept in, followed by wind and sun and more rain. He could hear the bees in the skeps kept in the pasturage and feel the gentle hands of his mother as she cared for him when he was ill, and also remember how he'd felt a surge of power and greed when he'd been chosen over all others by the woman who had later taken him to the bog to kill him. The pain in his head worsened, and he began to wonder if all that had happened to him since was a punishment. Surely he wouldn't be allowed to suffer as he was unless the suffering were deserved? *Had* he done something wrong? Could his Master have had a reason for sending him away, even after he had done his best to please him?

Pam would know. He'd ask her.

He had never been to the sea, although its tides had governed his homeland as it had spilled into the rivers inland. The log boats of his boyhood were only for poling through marsh, not for powering through waves. Beyond the moors and the filled-in hollows of the old river valleys was the wide coastal clay belt, but when Galt imagined the shore he saw a curve of silver-white sand set between rocky headlands where eucalyptus scented the air. While he breathed in air rusty with damp and cold, he felt warmth flood through him. He looked up and saw the stars, the planets and the moon rising along a watery white path.

In his mind, the red stone had become a signal waving from a shark-infested ocean: he knew that sooner or later, Pam would see it and find him.

He was so still that the fox didn't see him, or he the fox, until it was nearly upon him. He stared into its vivid eyes. It backed away slowly, its fur shining in a thread of moonlight, and then trotted swiftly away through the mounds.

During the night Galt dreamed what had happened to his village. The windward side, towards the ocean, where his house had been, had been abandoned after the whole site was washed by floodwaters. Perhaps fifty people, only, had survived. Soon after, the entire site was overwhelmed, the houses collapsed, the fences loosed, and the village had disappeared under layers of silt.

In the early morning Galt stirred a little as the deep ache of his bones penetrated the misery of this awareness. The stone continued to slide from his body, but it was no easy matter, lying curled as he was, to swallow it again. He was not sure any more why he bothered, except that what he was to become if he didn't was all too evident: upon the low peat surfaces, small birds, hungry in the cold, pecked for worms, seeds and insects that were slow in burrowing. The birds fluttered to him, their bright eyes travelling the ravages of his body for opportunity. Fiercely he swatted at them, scraps of flesh flying from his fingers; the birds dashed up in a flourish of wings, circled and returned.

Then his mouth was full of water and silt, he was lying on the ground and drowning. The stone, rough-edged and painful, had lodged in a pouch in his gut. It burned. If he allowed himself, he could turn an eye to it and see right back to the beginning, to a small tree growing on a river delta, the stone hanging from it like a fruit. Life spread its warm fingers from that tree, branching, investigating, incorporating: it pushed all the way through the earth and out the other side, grubbing after the stars, and he felt his cells replicate and die, he was filling up with cellular debris, becoming a garbage heap. He clawed at his stomach, trying to get at the stone, aching to rid himself of it, to be finished with pain.

But there was news! He turned his head to try to find where it was coming from.

He heard the hum of wires, the static of voices, there were signals of all kinds, but out of the mass of information, he managed to find her. Boys and men stood all around her. Hundreds of them, in a swarm: they would tear her to pieces and not even know what they'd done. She grabbed a T-shirt from a bag beside her and pulled it over her head. She put on her sunglasses. Hands reached for her, one boy's arm snaked out and touched her breast. She flinched.

"Pam!" he screamed. Pam looked up! Just for an instant the crowd drew back, the wave was broken. Then she tucked her head down, covered her bright hair with a ball cap and in seconds was gone behind the palm trees and into a car that had driven onto the beach to fetch her. The sun was so bright on the green water it made a necklace of pennies over the ocean, but there was nothing where she'd been but a puff of exhaust. Just back from the beach were the rollerbladers, ice cream vendors, cappuccino bars. Galt blinked. The men and boys ran into the water and were drowned. Or so he wished them. In any case, the signals had stopped, the pain was gone. Pam was safe because he had done something. Galt, his body dissolving, leaking, tendons dried and popping, smiled.

He stood, his thinness risen out of the weather-flattened grasses, brown as old sticks, rags tied around his joints to hold them together. The wisps of mist and smoke that dawn had drawn from the earth melted as he reached out his arms.

Galt opened his eyes. He'd heard a door slam and the stepped whine of a car's engine as the car drove away. He closed his eyes. He wanted the scene on the beach back, or the one where he was in his mother's hut standing next to his dog. He groaned as the stone moved again, slipping along his gut another few inches. Then it came to him, a nugget of information unwrapping itself in his brain, a surprise. The figure he'd seen in the distance wore red.

Fearfully, he opened his eyes again. It had circled him and edged nearer. His eyes, dull as moss, followed it. He shifted painfully on the ground. "Pam?" he said, hardly daring to believe. The stone ground its way out of him. "Pam!"

Cathreen

The hut where Jag was staying, just as Merry had said it would be, was several hundred yards or so away at the edge of a series of low undulations in a field. It sat, a small grey smudge against the morning sky, invisible until Cathreen had climbed over and down the little ridge that rose up from the track where Merry had dropped her off.

Cathreen had spent the night at Merry's, had eaten what was given her, showered and gone to bed—not that she'd slept much. She'd watched the curtains over the small window ripple in the night breeze, the hemmed edges making little waves that almost lapped her into restfulness. But when that happened, and for a half second she forgot Tink's death, the next second the pain slammed into her fresh, took her breath and tore her heart anew. She'd made herself stay awake, on guard against it, preferring the constant nausea of knowledge to the repeated onslaught of anguish. Only when Cutthroat had jumped in through the open window in the middle of the night had she allowed herself to relax at all. The cat's purring, its measured kneading of her chest as it lay on her breast, had sent her for an hour or so into dreamless sleep.

The cat ran ahead of her in the grass. It scuttled, then halted and flattened itself to the ground with its ears back at each new sound. Breaker, who had followed her first to Merry's and then here, ranged over the moor. She watched him run back towards her from a stand of willows not far from the hut, but when the dog was only a few yards away, he dropped from view. Cathreen walked slowly onward, puzzled, until she came to the brink of the hollow in which Breaker lay. There he was, and lying in the bottom of the bowl with him was a creature she knew could only be Galt. Despite her instantaneous fear, she couldn't look away. He was more rags than human. He was brown and grey and plant green and she could see the links and claw forms of his bones.

"Pam!" the strange man said. "I knew you would come." He smiled, his lips drawing away from the points of his few brown teeth.

Cathreen slid to her knees, trembling, and reached blindly for the cat, who had paused beside her. Galt tried to lift himself to beckon her closer, but his strength failed and he fell back across the white dog.

"Pam," he said again, a slight frown creasing his forehead. "I've waited for you so long, where have you been?" The frown deepened and he groaned. Although Galt still looked in her direction, his gaze had filmed with milk. He groaned again and turned to lie curled away from her on the ground. A small red stone, glossed with mucus, pointed from between the sharp bones of his naked buttocks.

"Please, Pam," Galt said, his voice muffled against the earth, "I don't want to hurt anymore. Please help me."

Cathreen could hear her father calling her name from somewhere behind her. Breaker now lay with his paws on Galt's body. She heard Jag yell something more, but Galt was trying to speak, and she pitied him, and so she eased herself a little way into the hollow to hear him.

"I'm so grateful, Pam," he said. His fingers fluttered as if he wanted to touch her.

It wasn't that the silvery voices said anything—although they were there, somewhere, in the background—but she knew what she had to do. She had a quick vision of Fawn's body slipping through deeper water, farther and farther away from any possible place she could be reached. Cathreen couldn't listen to anybody else, not when it mattered, not anymore.

"Cathreen!" Jag shouted from the top of the hollow. She glanced up at her father, smiled at him, grateful that he was there, then took the green stone from her pocket and put it in Galt's hand. His fingers cupped to hold it. Then she picked up the moist red stone with a handful of grass, cleaned it as well as she could and placed it beside the other in Galt's loose fist. Breaker whined as the two stones met. Cathreen stared, transfixed, as the hand holding the stones flexed, and the hand and the rest of the arm filled out over straight bone and smooth muscle, and the skin became taut and clean.

It was as if a stream ran through Galt, healing where it flowed from his hand and arm through his shoulder and neck and down into his chest. His face softened and plumped; dark, luxuriant hair spilled from his scalp; his belly tightened, the hips rounded, the thighs grew strong, the calves hardened and the toes stretched and curled. She could hear her father's shallow, ragged breathing from above her as it caught in his throat. Then Galt took several deep breaths. Slowly he pulled himself upright, using the dog's back for leverage. He gazed at her through bright eyes and held the stones to his breast.

"Thank you, Pam," he said.

Galt grew taller, so that she found herself sitting with her head craned back, squinting to look at his face against the bright backdrop of sunlight. She felt bathed in his gladness, happy for him and for herself. Not afraid anymore, not worried or hurt or sad.

She scrambled to her feet and backed away, still gazing at Galt: he was muscular, radiant, perfect. She threw a look of joy at her father as he clambered down to her and hugged her. She was watching his face as it suddenly gave a tight, small grimace. Wordlessly, he pointed over her shoulder. She turned, and even as she did she began to feel cold. The sun sped through the sky, the shadows flying behind it quickly touching the darkness that slammed towards them from the eastern horizon.

Ice formed on the grass, on the glittering branches of trees: even the tears that had begun to flow from her eyes halted, frozen. Galt's body had already diminished. It had shortened and thinned, the dark hair was silvered. Soon he was old and frail, his hair white, his breathing difficult, and he eased himself onto the frozen ground. Only his eyes remained kindled. He breathed deeply one more time, sighed, and his eyes dimmed; the stones fell from his hand. A puff of air brushed by Cathreen, light as a leaf.

"Oh, no, don't do that!" she cried. Galt's head lolled and his body toppled sideways. Cathreen pulled herself away from her father. She knelt beside Galt and pushed at him and tried to make him sit up. "Please don't, Galt, not now. Please stop," she said. But it was too late. She cradled his beautiful old man's head in her arms and smoothed a hand gently over his cheek. She looked up at her father. "You saw, didn't you?"

"I saw," he said. He bent, a little cautiously, and picked up the stones. He held each up to what had returned of the light, then he dug through his jacket pocket until he found his knife. He scratched at the surfaces with the steel tip. He turned back to Galt's body, but Breaker bared his teeth and barred his way. Again, her father examined the stones; he jiggled them in his hand, looked thoughtful and put them into his mouth. His eyes closed. Cathreen waited. Her heart, so briefly at ease, was now pinched with dread. After a while, he opened his eyes and spat the stones into his palm.

The world looked different, dusty and faded. Cathreen closed her eyes and hoped that when she opened them the dull film would be gone. But it wasn't. She watched a fox run across the grass and disappear under a fence. She thought she saw its rusty tail as it entered a circle of beech trees then darted out towards a farther patch of ferny woodland near a ditch. But there was no following splash of water, no wake, as far as she could see, where it might have been swimming.

A few cold flies rose up from the turned earth. Cathreen and Jag had rolled Galt's fragile body onto a piece of sacking and dragged it all the way across the field to an oak tree. Jag had wanted to conceal it with blocks of cut peat, but Cathreen had said no, that wasn't good enough, and they'd dug him a proper hole. After they'd tipped him in and covered him, Jag walked away and Cathreen stood there alone, the sky clear and empty, until a storm of hail and sleet swept in and drove her after her father.

In the morning they set out, trudging across the scraggly fields through mist as heavy and nearly as impenetrable as a blanket of snow. It reminded Cathreen of her mother's tales of her childhood, of Helena as a girl, gripping the hand of Sailor, the grandfather Cathreen had never known, as he walked her safely through a blizzard to school, his clasp all that connected Helena to her future.

Jag had awakened Cathreen in the night to question her. Why had she put the stones into Galt's hand? he'd asked her. She'd shaken her head, she really didn't know. "He needed them, that's all," she'd said. She'd twirled a strand of hair around her finger, something she hadn't done since she was little. He'd asked her more and more questions—Where had the stones come from? What did she know about them?—and finished, finally, by giving her back both of them. She'd pushed his hand away—she didn't want them—but he'd insisted, pressed both into her hand and squeezed her fingers shut around them. She'd slipped them into a pocket.

"The story says three stones, Cat," he'd said then.

"It's Breaker, Dad," she'd said, tiredly. "Look at his paw."

Cathreen's fingers trailed through the wet branches of a hedge. Crumpled leaves, many of them dark with mould, still clung to twigs of ash, elder and hawthorn. She pricked her finger on a wild rose thorn, lifted the finger to her mouth and sucked it. He father walked ahead, occasionally turning round to urge her on. The dust-beige donkey she'd glimpsed on and off for days stepped through the fields shadowing them, stopping, when they rested, to put its head down to graze.

They passed farm buildings and a pen where chickens pecked the cold, hard earth, and where the surrounding fields were abandoned to rubble. They crossed the sluggish water of a ditch where barbed wire on the banks, screened by long grass, caught and tore at her clothing. They crossed a field dotted with black cattle. She spotted Breaker rolling in ivy at the base of a tree. An old wooden cart, stacked high with peat, pulled by two drays, rattled up behind them. Cutthroat jumped down from it as it passed, scrambled up to her shoulder and then into her backpack.

It was dusk, and she was very tired, by the time Jag said they were nearing their destination. The sky was thick with cloud. A line of pale white light crawled along the horizon.

They skirted a green hill with a tower on top of it—the look of it was familiar—and she asked Jag what it was, but he only had eyes for the road.

They passed along a valley and turned into a lane bordered with yews. Jag hurried ahead of her and climbed a short slope through a scattering of bedraggled sheep. One kicked its heels sideways in its hurry to be gone, and baaed to the others, who watched, too cold to care. Then they came to a small locked gate in a high wooden fence. Jag climbed the fence, opened the gate from inside and let her in. They were in a garden.

Jag reached for her hand and led her to where a set of stone steps descended into the grasp of deep sheltering trees. From there, a further set of mossy steps led them to a glade. Here Jag let go her hand to wrestle the stone lid from a well. He rolled the lid out of the way and wiped his hands on his shirt. Cathreen slipped off her pack and looked for a place to sit.

"Call the dog, Cathreen," he said.

Ten

Jones

It is a requirement, as you well know, Cutthroat, for those of us who have been given conscious life to leave an account of how we have spent our time. What is done with such notes? Are they kept for reference? Perhaps the soul is permitted a browse through the stacks to weigh up, consider its options, before choosing its next life? Possibly it is read by those it most concerns? They say we cats have nine lives, but I, Jones, only know this one of mine. Some things in it I would not choose again, but I would always want to find you, dear friend.

For nearly four hundred years my family has lived with a blessing and with a curse. The blessing is to know when death will come and to be given time to prepare for it; the curse is that the death will be hard. I did not tell you this before because I did not want you to worry. You will grieve for me when I die, and because you are immortal, your grief may last. How I die—its difficulty and pain—is likely to make things worse. I would not tell you even now, but the dream in which I saw the Cait Sith says that I should: it will make a difference. How this could be, I do not know. I do know that I am very much afraid. I have loved my life and do not want to leave it. But I'm luckier than you, Cutthroat: whatever happens to me will be over relatively quickly and it won't happen again, at least not to me.

In the dream that presages death in my family, the fairy cat, the Cait Sith, who is our guardian (and ancestor, if my mother could be believed), comes to say that she can no longer protect us. I have had that dream. In my case, the Taghairm, the ancient Highland rite used to summon the demon cat, Big Ears, has been begun, and I, in some way, will be its victim. This wicked ceremony, which has not been performed for some three hundred years, requires the demon to grant the summoner his wish. To call Big Ears, dozens of live cats are roasted on spits for twenty-one days. It sounds almost funny, doesn't it, Cutthroat, the name Big Ears? And can you imagine our summoner skulking through bushes and pouncing upon kittens in barns? He'd have nets, and baskets with lids, and traps to clap over unsuspecting catnappers. . . . But there is nothing amusing about the suffering that follows. Out of the seam of darkness this opens, the giant demon cat enters.

It is said that the summoner will never see the face of God, and indeed it seems unlikely to me that he would. Why would God want to look on him?

My fate, as I said, is linked to the Taghairm, but I will not die *that* way—no warming paws at bonfires for me!—the Cait Sith has promised, and I am grateful, for I've inherited the family horror of burning.

A little history might help you understand this. Bear with me, friend. I won't take long.

On the night of November 16, 1680, during the reign of the Catholic King Charles II, one of my forebears, a wanderer like me, who had made his way from the Highlands to London, was caught and stuffed into a huge sack with a hundred other homeless cats. The next day a crowd of anti-Catholic Protestants made the sack into an effigy of the Pope. They built a fire near the statue of Queen Elizabeth, and more than 200,000 people watched as the effigy was thrown onto the flames and my relative and the others screamed and writhed in their agony. It may not have been a formal Taghairm, Cutthroat—it took a long eight years before the crowd got its wish and the Catholic kings were expelled in favour of the Orangeman— but the whiff of the demonic lingers. (I am not a bigot—I believe there are those on the other side who would have done the same, given the opportunity—but it is a fact that the Whigs had Highland Scottish nurses who could have taught them what they never should have learned.)

In the midst of his torture, my ancestor called on the Cait Sith, our guardian, to ask what he had done to deserve such a fate, and to entreat her to explain what lay behind his death and to reveal its meaning. He begged that none of his descendants would go to their deaths as he had, unforewarned, tormented by flame, and with no opportunity to say goodbye to family and friends. The Cait Sith granted him this blessing, but in his final anguish, my kinsman cursed all his descendants with a hard death, so that we would not forget him.

I do not blame him. How can any of us know what we might have done or said in the extremity of such pain?

I know who has begun the Taghairm, Cutthroat, and I begin to guess why. I will do my best to stop it in the time I have remaining, but I cannot avert my fate; I can only entrust this account to you, who of all living beings will, sooner or later, know what it means.

I was born on a hillside in Scotland near the north end of Loch Tay, above Croftmoraig, a small holding in the river plain, and near the road. My mother's yowls made the hens scatter cackling through the circle of standing stones that had lain nearby for centuries and were upright centuries before then. By the time she quietened, there were four of us, two sleek grey, one black like my mother, and me—ringed tail, striped, and patched brown and grey and white all over. Not a pretty conglomeration for a female, even in my mother's opinion! She named me Jones after a Welsh poet she'd met in her travels, and made some predictions about my future poetic talent. Whether or not Jones was my father, she didn't say.

She carried us, one by one, higher up the hill and onto the wild moor that first day, and there we stayed, hidden under a wall. The only colours I knew were greens of all shades, and pale golds, purples and silver, and moonlight with a sharp red glitter to it. When I looked out from the wall, fearful of the golden eagles that hunted the moor, I'd see mist and rain and enough sunlight breaking through mazy cloud, from time to time, to reveal shadows where the peat dipped away. The moor stretched forever, its hollows were on the move, alive with birds, and haunted by those who had once lived there and been forcibly removed. I don't believe in ghosts, Cutthroat, but when you're "cleared" from what you love, as these Highlanders were, the best part of you, whatever you want to call it, doesn't let go, it stays. We chased those shadows, and the mice and voles, when we felt brave, but if they turned to face us, we raced back to our mother.

The first frost lit up the roadway when she took us down the hill, past the light at Tombuie Cottage to the loch. She made us learn to swim in those cold waters, and when we came out, crying, she sprang at us to make us run ourselves warm and dry. We went with her on short excursions to Acharn, to Ardradnaig and Achmore. We were growing stronger, I thought I would be there forever. I didn't know it then, but the world I'd been born in was about to fall away.

After the journey of which I have already told you, at the end of which I was on my own, and during which I found my vocation, I ventured out of the byre where I'd spent the night. I stood on a little hillock thinking about breakfast, and watched the cattle clop by. Their breath steamed, their great heads bobbed, and their kind brown eyes bade me good morning. I heard a boy whistle after them and then I was caught from behind.

I was glad enough, once I was over the fright, to be taken inside a cottage where it was warm. A peat fire burned, a young dog sniffed at me then left me alone. I was given warm stew to eat and a corner to sleep in. The wind moaned down the chimney that night: the wail in its voice was like the sound of the water in the river where I'd lost my mother. I heard the people talking and laughing and I thought over to myself everything I knew, which didn't take long.

I knew how to earn my keep; my mother had taught me well. I chased mice and rats from the house and barn, I was clean, and I soon grew strong on the food they gave me. It was an excellent arrangement: they didn't mind what I did with the rest of my time as long as I didn't bring in snakes, and I had relative freedom and comfort— what more could I want? I might be there still, Cutthroat, except for one thing. The postman, who passed by nearly every day in his van, brought a boy with him who liked to throw stones. The postie would leave the van running when he came to the door, and the boy would scoot out and look for me. One day he had a slingshot with him and the stone he slung struck me on the side of the head. I lay nearly dead the rest of the morning. The next day I was ready for him, and when the van stopped and the postie jumped out with the mail, I leapt in the window and scratched that boy across the eyes. How he shouted and carried on! It didn't bother me, he deserved it, but I knew I would have to go. The farmer was already out with his shotgun. So that is how I took to the road.

Sometimes, when I was lonely, I wished none of it had happened, that I could return to the hill above Loch Tay, but mostly the outside world called to me, saying I would accomplish great things. Every now and then I had news, as cats do, brought by other travellers, of how my mother was keeping. She was growing older, spending less time in the hills and more in Croftmoraig cottage, but she sent her love, not forgetting us as they say our mothers do. I would have liked to see her again.

In a while, by following the road and avoiding the villages when I came to them, and by leaping into the backs of lorries when they stopped at a turning, I made my way to Edinburgh.

I slept in a wood off the Queensferry Road for two weeks, but there was little to eat there and I did not see myself turning over garbage.

My life has been a little thing, Cutthroat, not like yours, so busy with the doings of the great. I have watched an old woman card wool, spin it, dye it the colours of the bracken in autumn, and of the moon and its rings the night of a hard frost, and of the bees as they putt and flurry over the heather in August: this is magic, too, Cutthroat, this is the fame of the small world. If there are other worlds, as you say there are, it is by these things they will know us. What must we look like to them? Like our seas and our forests and the great deserts where cats have thrived forever; like red and green eyes in the dark. We look like our wildness, not the civilizations about which you know so much. This is not a criticism, Cutthroat, but another point of view. There is one, you know.

The city is built on seven hills, of which Arthur's Seat is the highest. One of the smaller hills overlooks the whole town. My friend and I (I wouldn't be what I am, flesh and fur and bone, if I hadn't had loves, but I am old enough now not to cause needless pain. So let it suffice to say that in the woods, as the traffic rumbled by day and night, in my hunger and strangeness, I was not alone) . . . we made our way there through the busy traffic, down into the long gully of the railway line, and then up through the brush and briar to the hilltop. We did so because we had heard of a woman who went there twice daily to feed the city strays. (You see how far I had descended— a Highland cat who could not feed herself!)

The side door of the old observatory was open and we slipped in. You could smell the cats at once. There were too many ill-nourished bodies confined in too small a space, and it was dark and damp inside. I doubt that a ray of sunshine had ever fallen there. The tower was built of stone and without windows, and with no heating of any kind, not even a coal fire. I imagine it had been assumed that astronomers would don overcoats, boots, hats and gloves in all weathers when they made their observations. This was spring, and in the tower it was cold as the grave, musty, stinking of urine. (Not unlike the old folks' home in the village, Cutthroat, where they put old Mrs. Morkill after her "turn" and we went to visit her.)

We climbed the crumbling stairs. Up there, on a platform littered with leaves, cigarette ends, sweet wrappers and, oddly, pages torn from pornographic magazines and science texts, was a mat of cats. A thin drizzle fell onto them from the open crack of the dome. I had never seen anything like it. It was quiet except for the crunching of teeth on bone and the lapping of tongues in water and milk. The "cat woman" had spread the floor with meat scraps and gruel. When I got to know her, I learned how much effort went into collecting those leftovers—a labour of love, indeed, going door to door, asking housewives to scrape out breakfast pots, staying up late for the closing of restaurants, hours spent at the doors of the big sheds at the slaughterhouse in Gorgie. But what I saw that first time was Hell, what I smelled was decay, and what I felt was raw despair: so heavily did it lie over those bobbing heads you could have cut it with a claw. What drove me and my friend to join in, despite this, was hunger. We dove in with the rest of them until the floor was clean and all the other cats had slipped away.

I wanted to scuttle off too, but I was too well brought up. So I waited, and when the coast was clear (I didn't want to be noticed by the others) I sidled up to where the woman sat on an old rug that jumped with fleas. "You've come to say thanks?" She put out a hand to pet me. "Not one in a hundred does, did you know? Years ago, it was every one." She sighed, and I sighed with her to think how standards had slipped. "We're not born with manners," she said, "so would you please pass on my thanks to your mother, God hope she is living."

We went through this ritual a number of nights. Each time I stayed a little longer, until I was there to observe what she did when the rest of the world slept. A crank operated the dome. On clear nights, she turned it and sat in the starlight as still as a rabbit when it has given up to its prey. Some nights, when there was moonlight, she took out a pencil and paper and drew on it. "This is my work," she said, when I poked my head over her arm to peer at it. She took the trouble—how few of them do!—to explain what the work was: she cast horoscopes for the rich. She told me things I would never otherwise have learned.

I'm sure you laugh at my lack of education, Cutthroat—next to you I know nothing. But did you realize that Dante's *Divine Comedy* is astrological? It begins with the Sun in Aries, which rules all new beginnings. He arrives in Purgatory when the Sun is in Scorpio, the sign of regeneration, and he comes to the top of Purgatory when the Sun is in Taurus, the sign of Earthly Paradise. In the *Paradiso* he journeys through the seven planets. I found this inspiring, and as you know (if you've had time to look at the manuscript), I've used it as a model for my recent work. I learned why Charles I, who consulted the astrologer Lilly, did not profit from his advice. "I told him to go east, and he went west," Lilly said. Most of all I learned that the chart tells what my intuition had already informed me: there is a real plan in our lives. Sorrows and afflictions are merely the factors employed to shape, to alter the crude materials of ourselves: our joys and happinesses come when we make contact with the great harmony of the spheres.

Well, these are excellent themes for a poet.

One night, when there was sufficient moonlight but she had no work, the old woman cast my horoscope. Danger lies for me in the house of dreams, the occult and secret enemies. Something very old is given to me to guard. Death waits for me in the house of secrets. Love will come, but a life together isn't to be. I'll have a chance to die for what I believe in, though, and it will be in the nature of a payment for something owed.

You see why I'm telling you?

Did you know that *zodiac* is an Arabic term for animals? Haven't you wondered what we're all doing here?

"Wondered," I say, not assumed that you knew?

One day, as the winter hardened, we were scooped up in a raid on the observatory by the R S P C A. Our benefactor was taken away too, to be "looked after" by society. That is, they took her life's work and purpose from her and placed her in an institution. (That's how it's done, if you rock the boat they drop you over the cliff of insignificance. If I were to start over, in politics, Cutthroat, I'd be an anarchist, because once "they" are organized, there's no stopping them.)

We were institutionalized, too.

It was a three-step process. First, admission, second, sterilization, then a two-week reprieve in a cage, and if no home were found— euthanasia. Be grateful you've never been inside such a place. The worst is that there's no one to tell you what's going on. They feed you, you're warm, so you think it's not so bad, all you've lost is your freedom. Then they take you out in groups of twenty. You know what an assembly line is, Cutthroat? Like what Mr. Morkill does when he lines up his cider barrels for filling. That was us, only we weren't to be filled, we were to be emptied. We were held in a long, narrow cage, so narrow we couldn't turn around. They didn't bother to keep us in another room. We watched while those ahead of us were anaesthetized, sliced open, and their organs removed. There's nothing but fear until the needle goes in and then nothing at all until you wake up in pain.

You know what's inside a hole, Cutthroat? Nothing. Not past or present. Nothing.

We were set out in rows on a mat on a large table after the operation. I believe they never thought we'd chance it, ill and groggy as we were—and it was cold! They left the door of the recovery room ajar while they put out the trash for collection. So it was—alert my friend, crawl to the edge of the table, fall to the ground, pray that the stitches would hold and stumble out behind the back of the shelter worker onto the ice of the cobblestones, trying not to cry out. No one bothered to come after us. I expect they thought we'd freeze to death.

We were lucky. We were close to the train yards and we found an empty, heated passenger car to sleep in. When we awoke, luggage was stacked around us on the rack, a little girl sat winking up at us from her seat, and we were on our way south.

We were starving and still ill when the child took us off the train at Berwick. Her mother spotted us, chased us away, and we hid beneath the platform of the train station. During that wait in the bitter cold my friend took a chill and died. I did not care what happened to me after that, but thirst tormented me. When it began to rain, I thought I would just get a few drops of moisture on my tongue . . . so I crept into the open . . . and it was there, while she and her brother were waiting for a train to take them home from their holiday, that Jen found me. Colin had paid for their trip! A few days away for Jen to think over his marriage proposal, a little time off from her poorly paid job at the library; time to consider that her young brother, Jag, was in need not only of a home and schooling but of male guidance. A long weekend to gaze at a grey sea from behind a dun-coloured sand dune, to walk back and forth over the railway bridge, to contemplate the coming years of bleak financial prospect. For Colin had noticed, even if few others did, that no matter how capable the two looked from the outside, they often went hungry, and they had to share their winter clothes, and for how many years the dead mother's and vanished father's leavings had done for them.

Jen wrapped me in her scarf, bought warm milk for me with her few pennies, kept me alive on the journey, and when we were home, nursed me with steam and herbs. It was a condition of her acceptance of Colin's proposal that I be allowed to stay. Later, when Colin's true nature became evident, she poured out her heart to me. When Jen fell pregnant, she was thrilled. Everything was going to change with the birth. But it was a daughter she bore and not a son, and this her husband couldn't accept. Why this was, dear Cutthroat, I could not say—some point of arcane honour or desire for immortality, in name?

Colin railed at the doctor, he accused both Jen and the midwife of switching the baby to spite him; he cursed Jag incessantly, as if it had anything to do with him. You could see the boy sicken under the onslaught of poison.

One night while I lay nestled next to Jen in bed, Colin came in. He said right out that he had tried to exchange the baby for a male infant in the village, but that the boy's mother had thwarted him. He stroked Jen's hand while she shuddered and he said, "Never mind, Jenny, there's another way." He leaned forward and put out his hand to take the pendant from around her neck. "You won't deny me, Jenny, will you?" he said to her, reaching to unclasp the chain. "There's a good girl." I snapped out a paw and raked him over the eye. He fell back with a yell, and I leapt out the window. I heard, even as I hit the ground, the sound of his fist as it struck Jen's face.

He couldn't have taken the stone from her without her permission, but I didn't know that then: in trying to help, I only caused Jen more pain.

I have found where the ceremony is being done, Cutthroat. Done. Not *conducted*, not *performed*—those words are too kind, and there is nothing kind here. I'm giddy with terror, exhilarated that I wasn't caught, destroyed that I escaped as so many did not. What an inadequacy of words. Can you understand? The sun of our birth casts a shadow, the cat woman told me, and in the shadow lies evil, sleeping until it wakes. How long will it rest? Until the next time. Ha!

Do you remember the barn with the carved wooden ceiling? We slipped in there once out of the rain. You strolled up and down, gazing at the gable ends with their trefoils, and the arches linked by a beam with small pairs of arches on top. You paid no attention to me!

but discoursed, as usual, about history—how the barn had been built by monks and had escaped the general destruction of the Dissolution. How wonderful that it was saved, you said. Saved—and for what, for this?

The barn is only a stone's throw from a farmhouse let out to a poor family, but it is enough out of the way of passersby, masked by outbuildings, for the purpose.

Inside the farmhouse live the farmer and two children—there is dog faeces on the floor, potatoes boiling in their skins at all hours, the steam condensing on the dirty walls and running in streaks. Filthy clothes lie piled up on chairs; tables and chairs sprawl overthrown; crusts of bread, dead flies, rodent droppings litter the cupboards. The children have dark circles under their eyes from bad food and too little sleep, and they're up at all hours to work. They start early in the dairy to light the fire in the boiler, then they have to watch it the whole day and stir the milk for hours. When it's warm out, like this, they also have to pump water to cool the milk so it doesn't turn sour. It is a cruel life. By the end of the day, their hands, which have been in some form of liquid on and off the entire time, are puffed and raw. I sit and watch from the shade of a weeping ash tree. The little boy, Jamie, comes and pets and feeds me when he can. Today he whispered that his sister had run away for good, then he picked me up and said, into my ear, "Come and see," and crawled with me across the courtyard (we pretended to be ducks) and into the wagon shed. We stayed there quiet as mice, the little one going, "Shush!" until not five minutes later I saw him, Jen's husband, Colin—why did she have to marry him!—come creeping round the cowsheds carrying sacks.

I knew, at once, what was in them. The farmer followed with more sacks, swore at the child absent from his work in the dairy, and then the two men went inside the barn. A minute later the farmer came out, counted money into his hand and put it in his pocket. Jamie, beside me, was trembling. The farmer scoured round the courtyard, shouting, "Jamie, you bastard, c'mere!" then got into his van and drove away.

When the coast was clear, the little boy carried me to the back of the barn where he'd scraped mortar from between some stones — there must have been a door there once — and removed them. He pushed me through and I was in.

It took me a minute to get my bearings. Smoke hazed the room. The stink of burned flesh was nauseating. In one corner broken machinery and old wagons sagged in a heap. I ran there and hid. I waited, made the breath flow evenly in and out of my mouth, then tried looking again. In the centre of the dirt floor, Colin had built a fire. I was glad to see, when he turned my way, that claw marks cross-hatched his face and arms. His shirt was in ribbons. He removed what appeared to be charred wood on spits from the flames and tossed the remains aside. Then he put on heavy gloves, reached into one of the sacks and extracted a cat by the scruff of its neck. They were drugged, Cutthroat, but not enough.

He thrust a clamp into the poor thing's mouth and picked up one of the metal spits. I didn't even know I had jumped until my claws were deep in Colin's back! Ha! Ha! Ha! He danced and screamed. Jamie, who had been watching through a crack in the door, ran in while I kept Colin busy and opened the sacks. There were cats every-where, staggering, vomiting, but the little boy collected them up and drove them outside. I hung on, too frightened to let go, until Colin, cursing, whirled and tried to slam me, still on his back, against a wall. I leapt onto his head and went for the eyes, but he caught me a blow in the throat and I fell. That would have been the end of me — I saw his foot come down towards my skull — except that the child returned and grabbed hold of Colin's hand and bit it. Brave soul! We both ran, one after the other, out of the barn and across the courtyard, and hid together in the field, lying flat in the wet grass, while Colin searched for us. "It'll be all right, Jamie, you come out. It was just a joke. You can take the kitties home." Jamie never budged.

If only there were something I could do.

Why, Cutthroat? Why do the innocent suffer? Why do some have life who don't deserve it?

I'm almost out of time. Darkness lies heavily on my limbs; I am heartsick. He has moved his set-up. I slipped back to try once more to stop him, but he had gone. The farmer will have helped him shift everything. The boy is safe. He came with me to the tinker's caravan where his sister now lives with her boyfriend. The father won't go there to get her or Jamie, he's afraid of the boyfriend and his mates. And of those dogs!

I have searched for hours—nothing! Silence everywhere. Not a cat in the streets. You can almost hear the dying, and you can smell it. Everyone knows without knowing. They are saddened and quarrelsome. Jen sobs, sitting on the bed, still in her nightdress, holding the infant who cries too. I huddle on the windowsill and watch her choking on tears.

Colin came into Jen's room this morning. He stripped off his evilsmelling clothes—they hung in shreds, each fibre ripped by a cat fighting him—and dropped them on the floor. He's not a tall man, although he's strong and solid, but he looked big then, swollen, his eyes huge and red, red nostrils, hair greased with sweat. He reeked of blood, sulphur, too, Cutthroat, I swear it. He dressed, then turned to Jen, who sat up, staring and frightened, and clutched the baby to her. "I'll take her now, it's time," he said, and pried the infant away, pulling on her hard so that Jen had to let go.

I sprang out from behind the curtains where I'd hidden and ran after Colin to see where he would go. He met Jag, who had heard the commotion, on the stairs, pushed him aside and kept on to the bottom and out the door. "He'll kill her!" Jen screamed, beside herself with terror. She would have pursued Colin herself, weak as she was, but Jag stopped her. "Stay here," he said. "I'll go."

Jen tore the pendant from around her neck, "Give it to him," she said, "it's the only thing he wants."

For a second I closed my eyes and the Cait Sith showed herself once more. We cannot stop the wheel of time, Cutthroat. I'm about to spin off it for good.

Do what's best.

Farewell, dear friend.

The Faiery beame upon you,
The stars to glister on you;
A Moon of light
In the Noone of night,
Til the fire-Drake hath o're-gone you.
The Wheele of fortune guide you,
The Boy with the Bow beside you,
Runne aye in the Way,
Til the Bird of day,
And the luckyer lot betide you

Ben Jonson,
"The Jackman's Song"

Eleven

Cathreen

"Call the dog," Jag ordered for the second time. Cathreen shook her head. He wouldn't tell her what they were doing there. He wasn't interested in anything she had to say. Something wasn't right. Jag's face was grey and drawn. His eyes skittered frantically round the clearing as she stood there, obdurate, wishing she were back at Summerwood, and with Tink still alive. The dun-coloured donkey stumbled through a clump of bushes and brayed. In the seconds that Cathreen looked round at it, Jag snatched her backpack from the ground, untied its strings and lifted out Cutthroat. He clutched the cat by the scruff of its neck, stepped over to the open well and dangled the cat above the opening.

"No!" she cried. "What are you doing!"

He held her eyes, and with his free hand tossed the pack into the opening. She heard the sigh of the fabric as it brushed rock on the way down. Jag swung the cat over the well mouth. "I mean it, Cathreen. Call the dog."

It was madness appearing out of nowhere. But then she thought back to their conversation in the night and the uneasiness she'd felt at his questions, and before that to his strange behaviour with the stones at Galt's death. Something in Jag that she hadn't yet understood had changed. She felt dizzy and hot. Sweat poured into her armpits. Her vision filled with the white fur of Cutthroat's exposed belly. She took a breath and tore her gaze away. It was nearly winter; dark flowed over the hills. Broken paving stones glistened with dampness, beads of moisture daubed the bare branches of trees, and she could just make out, at the top of the path, the sharp wooden spikes of the gate. She wished, suddenly like a child, for snow to smooth the fields and make space like a clean handkerchief, but a wish couldn't change a thing.

"Breaker, come," she said.

The dog burst from the green and brown trees in an explosion of white muscle and sprang straight for Jag's throat. Jag threw up his arms to protect himself, dropping the cat. Cutthroat's claws scrambled vainly at the lip of the well mouth. Jag's arm swiped hard at Breaker's back and sent the dog plunging after the cat into the well.

"Shit!" A trickle of blood ran down his forehead from where the dog's paw had scratched it. He smeared it away with his sleeve. "Why'd he do that? I wasn't going to hurt him, I wouldn't hurt anything on purpose!

"Don't look at me like that," Jag said as Cathreen stood there, rigid with shock. She listened for the animals' cries, but all she could hear was the whistle of Jag's rapid breath. She could scarcely believe what had happened.

"It's not as bad as it looks, Cathreen," he said. "We were going down there anyway, and there's a ledge to stand on. I know it's safe. I've been down there before. I was going to take you."

"We've got to get them out!" she said, at last finding her voice. She stumbled forward, scraping her shins against rock as she ran to the well and looked in. It was too dark inside, she couldn't see anything.

"You'll have to go by yourself now because of the dog. I can't trust it—you saw—but it likes you. Once you're there, I'll tell you what to do."

She looked at him. "What are you saying?"

"There's a bit of a drop at first, but it's not far, then your feet will find the shelf."

A whimper rose from her belly, even though she knew he had to be kidding. "Jag, what do you mean?"

"We know what the stones can do, Cathreen, we have to try. I want this more than anything." He wiped a sleeve across his forehead again. "It's why we're here, Cat. It's the reason for everything."

"Let's go back, Jag," she said. "It's getting late. Look, it's almost night—we'd better leave right now." She tried to go, but he held her fast. It was so dark that even the shadows had vanished.

"My little niece's down there, Cat. I can't just leave her, not after what we've seen. I can't do that." Cathreen began to cry. Jag dabbed at her tears with a handkerchief. "She'll be like a sister to you. It's Jen's baby, Cat! You'll see. When we're done here, we'll go home."

He kissed her forehead and brushed her hair back from her face. "Don't slip off the rock or I won't be able to get you back up. Just feel for the opening to the small room at the side. You'll find her. Use the stones, Cathreen. Just do what you did before."

He pressed her backwards, one hand holding both her wrists, then he gave a quick shove, swept her legs over, and she was dangling into the blackness, pain scalding her arms. She kicked, trying to find some purchase in the walls, but there was none. "Don't be afraid," he said to her, and he let her go.

There is nothing to a fall. It is only the dream you have dreamed since birth. It is only the loss of before.

Her shoulder snagged briefly on a protruding stone. She hit the ledge and crumpled onto it long before she expected to: pain smashed into her thigh. She'd crashed on top of Breaker. Fear had hammered her thoughts blank but she saw that Jag's face hung over the opening and blocked out the sky.

"Can you find it?" Jag shouted. Cathreen's hand travelled Breaker's form. When it reached his muzzle, he licked her palm. Then she heard a soft mew and searched until she discovered Cutthroat lying stiffly on top of her backpack. She eased him off, stood shakily to her feet, picked up the pack and felt around the outside of it until she found, attached to the pull ring, the key chain with miniature light and whistle and compass that Tink had given her. "It's so I don't lose you," he'd said. She hadn't even thanked him.

Together, in the tiny circle of dim light, the dog limping beside her, the cat pressed against her ankles, they edged into a small side room. It was narrow, built of giant stone blocks with sloping edges. What had it been used for? Nick could have told her. Maybe Nick would have seen this coming.

"Did you find her?" Jag shouted. They edged round a corner; his voice, when it called again, was muffled.

Breaker, who had gone on ahead, whimpered. Cathreen inched along, shuffling one foot after the other, a hand braced on the smooth wall. When she reached the dog, she knelt next to it, seeing something heaped just beyond where the dog had stopped. There was another deadened shout from Jag.

Cathreen aimed the tiny light at the shape, took a breath, and moved the light away. It was a small skeleton. Stuck to the bones were shreds of skin and hair. The niece, Jen's baby, Jag had spoken of? She felt sick.

What was she going to do? She put a hand out to touch the cat for comfort. She was sure that her father, in this state of mind, wouldn't let her out unless he thought she'd done what he wanted, but she didn't know how, she couldn't.

The cat's eyes, huge in the darkness, stared up at her, and it nudged the hand holding the light so that it lit the skeleton again. She held the little light steady with both hands to still its shaking. The illuminated image settled. It wasn't the skull of a child! The shape was wrong, and it was too small. There was also, attached to the pieces of bone and dried skin, some mottled fur and a collar. "It's a cat," she whispered. "I wonder what happened to it." She let the light play over it. Cutthroat bumped her arm again and she leaned close enough to read the small engraved plate on the collar. It read "Jones" and gave Aunt Jenny's address.

Aunt Jenny's cat? She looked at Cutthroat. It was a funny thing, but she had the feeling that the cat had known all along what it was.

She tried to lift Cutthroat onto her lap while she thought, but he would have none of it. He crouched nearby, his tail slowly swishing. She could see the way spiders had made use of the remains, weaving silk between the bones. With a sigh, Cathreen took the red and green stones from her pockets and examined them. Pieces of glass, that's all they looked. "I think you only get to do this once," she said to the cat, "but maybe it's okay to try again for Jones. I'm not sure. I don't know what's right or wrong, but I wouldn't mind. I don't know why I did it before."

But she did know. She'd followed her heart; and Galt was at peace now, no longer a monster. He couldn't hurt anyone anymore.

They heard the noise of rocks dropped into the well. "All right, then," Cathreen said. She whistled Breaker away from his explorations, and he padded forward, sniffed at the shell of bones and lay down next to it. She edged ahead on her knees, both stones now in one hand. Her heart flipped, then steadied. She placed the stones within the skeleton's rib cage. The cavern seemed to draw in its breath. They waited—seconds, half a minute, longer.

"I'm sorry, Jones," Cathreen finally whispered to the glimmering, web-wrapped bones. Soft, plaintive mewing sounds came from Cutthroat. "I'm sorry for you too, Cutthroat. I wish I could help, but I don't know what else to do." She reached to pet him, but he hissed at her and so she left him alone. The dog stretched and began sniffing out the back of the cell. There was more here than she could fathom, but it must have been terribly lonely for Jones, here by herself.

More dampened shouts from Jag. He'd want to know what she'd found, what she'd done. She returned to the chamber opening.

"Help me back up, please," she called. "There's nothing here."

"There is, there has to be!" She could sense his disquiet, hear his feet and knees and elbows as they scraped against the stones of the well mouth; he was leaning forward dangerously.

So she told him about the ledge and the dog lying on the shelf, and her bag that had cushioned the fall of the cat. "There's a very small skeleton, but it's not a child."

"That's it!" he cried excitedly.

"It isn't a child."

"You can't tell for sure."

"I know what it is, Jag. It's a cat."

She could almost hear the rattle and jumble and clamour of his thoughts. She tried to stifle the giveaway of her quickened breathing.

"I'm coming down," he said. "Stay out of the way."

"What about the dog?"

"Push him over, do it now."

"No!" Cathreen looked over: Breaker stood at the edge of the shelf, looking downwards.

"Then keep him out of the way. If you don't help me, you'll stay there, Cathreen, I swear it."

It was quiet above. She could picture the circle of stones in which the well was set, the nearby steps, the shelter of the trees, the path and the locked gate. She wished Jag climbing the fence, disappearing round the body of the hill. Gone. The dog gave a low whine and she shone the light past him and down into the well. About six feet below, a metal buckle and what looked like the remains of a sandal glittered on stone.

A dark mass loomed over the well opening and a rope fell straight from its coils. It swung between the walls.

"All right!" she called. "Give me a minute."

"I'm coming down now. Hold the rope steady."

"Wait! I said I'd do it!"

There was still so much to do. She winced as she felt the hard tugging in her hair. It had started up again, more strongly than ever. There was the yanking, and the tickling in her ears and on her neck, the sensation of minute breath on her cheeks. She realized suddenly that she had felt this sensation not twice or twenty times, but a thousand times before. It had been there at every moment of danger, or of decision, at every point of choice. She'd felt it at the lake when the others were throwing stones at Timmy and Fawn, and when she'd thought she should go back to help them. Always, she had known what she should do.

Her heart skated between her ribs. Jag had begun his descent, swearing at her because she wasn't holding the rope for him; but he was tall enough to brace his feet against the walls as he tested the rope's strength.

She dug in the pack for a T-shirt. Moving as quickly as she could, she returned to the chamber, grabbed Cutthroat and, over his objections, tucked him into the backpack, then gently wrapped the bundle of bones in the shirt, put them in next to Cutthroat and struggled into the pack straps. It was time to go.

"Cathreen!" Jag was having trouble with the rope's sway as the sides of the well widened. His voice sounded tight and frightened. "Help me!"

She eased herself over the edge, and held on to the ledge with her fingers as long as she could, and tried to feel for cracks in the wall with her toes, but it wasn't very long before her fingers gave way and she fell—and landed almost immediately on the small platform below. She held her arms up and whistled for Breaker. He seemed to take aim for a point just behind her—his shoulder grazed past and he almost knocked her over, but she was soon steady on her feet. She followed the glimmer of the dog's body into a low tunnel.

She had only just stepped off the ledge when it gave way with a sharp crack. Debris showered into the depths and plashed somewhere below. "Don't try to follow us," she shouted back to her father. But Jag didn't answer. He had already entered the dark alcove above.

After a lengthy climb between crumbling blocks of limestone, a waft of fresh air blew in on them and they emerged from behind a screen of bushes onto a hill.

Stars pebbled the sky above and gradually paled to almost nothing within the glow cast by the rising moon.

She was tired. She knelt and rubbed Breaker's head and muzzle and scratched between his ears. Weariness blunted the awareness of what she'd just been through. What mattered was that they were safe. She let Cutthroat out of the backpack, watched him stagger a few steps, then carried him over to the stream so he could drink. Once she'd set him down, the dog poked his nose back into her hand. She petted him awhile longer while she watched the cat lap at ripples of water, then she squatted to wash herself. When her face and hands were clean, she scooped water into her mouth. Then she picked up Cutthroat and made a nest for him on top of the backpack, and a bed for herself in the grass, using her fleece for a pillow and her extra clothing for warmth.

In the dream, in which, unlike most dreams, she knew about her other life, the one that slept on near the stream, she met Galt. He walked along the old track through the marshes, a creel on his shoulder, a sack on his back. "Cathreen!" he cried when he saw her. He looked well and strong and young. She was glad that he didn't still think she was Pam. It was as if they were old friends. He put down the creel and sack. The creel was full of fish. "You must come and eat with us," he said. The sack bulged and wriggled, and she could hear, coming from inside it, much cross mewing.

"Galt!" she exclaimed as he opened the loosely tied top and kittens began to climb out. "Where did you get them?"

"Someone put stones in here and tried to drown them."

She lifted up a small tabby with a ringed tail and pressed it to her cheek. Its fur was like down, its blue eyes showered her with angry sparks.

"Do you know anyone who needs a cat?" he said, taking the kitten from her hands.

"Yes, I do! I'd love to have one!" But he had picked up his bundle and gone.

Cathreen opened her eyes, glanced around for Breaker and Cutthroat, found them lying not far off, beside the stream, and got up and made her way through trees and bushes until she stood at the hill's edge. The wind roared up its steep sides and shoved at her. She could see cows on the next hill, and in a far hollow, she recognized the caravan park where Merry lived. A familiar donkey gnawed its way through a meadow.

She didn't realize her pack was gone until, ready to set off, she went to get it. She turned round and round, scouring the little clearing with her eyes, but there was no sign of her belongings. There were, however, several footprints in the mud edging the stream, and Tink's key chain glittered on a low branch where it had caught and torn from the pull ring. A few steps through the bushes in that direction brought her to the track she hadn't known was there, and a glimpse of a boy on a bicycle pedalling furiously down the road.

Her money, passport and ticket were in the backpack, and so, of course, was poor Jones. Cutthroat, when she lifted him, felt heavy as stone, as if his bones, while he'd slept, had had cement poured into them. He opened his eyes briefly, then closed them, so dispirited and sad looking that it made her smile. She could sense the cat's indignation.

"I'm not laughing at you, Cutthroat," she said, but as she bent over and set him down, tears of laughter or pain, it didn't seem to matter, spilled from her eyes and onto the ground. She wiped at her running nose with a hand, then lay down in the grass, ignoring the cold. A pale green light fell on her and she was cushioned by moss and swathes of wet clover. The long blades that forecast bluebells swam between the trees.

It's over, she thought, I have to go home.

Twelve

The Tale That Needs Telling

The round canopy of the stars, the round world, the Atlantic Ocean like a broken blue plate, just like it would look from space. It's warmer than it should be this late in the season: the trees stripped bare, the wind violent and clean, scouring away the mist that has crept in from the Bristol Channel. Below, muddy shallows give way to the silver river, canal and rhyne veining of the Levels, the hawthorn- and willow-hedged fields. You can see the grassy purple contours where there were once islands before the waters surrounding them withdrew and the marshland was drained.

Seven islands, like the seven stars of the Great Bear constellation, now girdled with trees: hills and rivers and ancient paths that outline shapes sleeping in the landscape.

Lower down now, a kestrel beats about over the water-pocked surface of the fields, then drops with a flash of red; a marsh harrier hunts the reed beds, then rises and soars until it has a view of cows punctuating the meadows. Below the wind, a rancid trickle of smoke begins to wind itself in knots around the hills and to thicken in hollows. The dying sun lights the path to a tinker's caravan tucked into a recess on one of the seven hills-once-islands. Shadows elongate, but inside the shelter a young man takes a young girl in his arms. There's one more ray of sunlight to locate a dragonfly spinning above the blade edges of peat cuttings, its darting iridescence like a jewel . . . then it's dark.

The girl glances out the window, but the jet stream swirls onward heading hard across Europe and Asia and the paint splash of the Pacific, towards autumn on the coast where one day, decades later, Cathreen will wake up and set out to find her father.

But now, the girl, who must be Merry, for it is Merry's story to which Cathreen, dozing, listens, thinks she sees something move, out there, in the withies, hidden beside a river of spectres. . . .

Cathreen blinked hard and stifled a yawn, doing her best to stay awake in the warmth of the gas fire in Merry's caravan.

Merry had stopped speaking. Her face screwed into a frown. Rain spattered the windows. Although it was only lunchtime, it was dark enough that Merry had turned on the lights. Now they guttered and went out as the wind picked up and a hard gust shook the trailer. Merry got up and went into the kitchen for candles.

Cathreen had arrived an hour earlier to find Merry saying goodbye to a dark-haired woman who'd elbowed by her down the stairs. The woman had slammed the door of her car and sped away.

"My daughter, Joan," Merry had said. "She came down from London to see if I was still alive. She'd heard about what happened to your mother's friend. But after one look in here, she decided she was needed back at the office."

"I'm sorry," Cathreen had said.

"Don't be. She gives me financial advice. We don't owe each other anything."

They were in the little kitchen. Drawers and cupboards were open, their contents dumped onto the floor. The wind puffed at net curtains pulled back from an open window. A draught pushed down the hallway through the open back door. Containers of flour and sugar had been spilled everywhere.

"What happened?" Cathreen had asked her as Merry picked up several tins. "Did your daughter do this?"

"Joan? Never! She wouldn't say boo to a goose. No, this is your father's work. I only left him alone for a few minutes after Joan arrived and I went out to meet her. He'd asked who Joan was when she drove up—he said he didn't feel like seeing anyone—and I told him. I'd decided it was time. People have to face things, Cathreen. I thought we could go somewhere for dinner together and discuss it." Merry had gone to the back door to shut it. She was still talking as she returned to the kitchen. "When I told Joan who *he* was, she wanted to meet him, of course . . . but by the time we got back inside he'd gone and, well, you see what it's like." Merry bent to pick up cutlery.

"Did he say anything about me?" Cathreen asked. She felt weak with relief—Jag was safe.

Merry straightened and gave her a sharp look. "He said there'd been an accident, but that you were fine, something about you having protection. It didn't exactly make sense. He looked frantic, half out of his mind, but he kept saying you'd be all right and not to worry. That's why I told him about Joan, you see, so it would put his mind at ease and I could find out what was going on. Do *you* want to tell me?" She'd put the kettle on after Cathreen had shaken her head no. "Then maybe there are things I should tell you," Merry had said.

"He didn't say anything else about me?" Cathreen had persisted, watching Merry fetch a tray and teacups.

"No. Should he have?"

She'd led Cathreen into the sitting room, poured each of them a cup of tea, then started in on a story that began with her birth and childhood on a tenant farm. Cathreen had listened as well as she could, trying to show interest, considering how tired she was, but she kept thinking about Breaker and Cutthroat out in the weather, and hoped they'd found shelter.

Merry returned with lit candles and placed one in front of her. "There, that's better," she said. "Now where was I?"

The young man holding the girl was Neil, a tinker Merry had run away from home to live with because of the cruelty of her father. Their caravan was in Gypsy Lane at the back of the Tor. Neil had been a kind man, making his living from poaching, content with his lot, teaching Merry how to set snares and cook game, and had offered to care for Merry's little brother, Jamie, as well, but Jamie had refused to come. He looked after the smaller animals at home on their father's farm and was afraid to leave them to the wrath and neglect of their father once he was gone. Only Neil's strength and Neil's dogs and Neil's friends had kept the father from coming after Merry.

"I was fifteen," Merry said. "I'd never even owned a pair of stockings."

But this night, the night of the heat and wind and tarry smoke blackening the land, Merry had heard a sound outdoors, gone outside to see what it was and found Jamie, mute and shivering in the reeds and withies. She'd brought him in and warmed him up and fed him, but he hadn't settled. He'd kept going to the window until Neil, giving up on him, had drunk a glass of whiskey and gone to bed. Merry had waited up with the child, and had just fallen asleep in the chair when she heard Jamie cry out, "There she is!" He was out of the caravan door in a second, barefoot and in his underwear and shirt. Merry slipped on her shoes and ran after him, seeing as he hared ahead that he was following a little tabby cat he'd befriended and had often fed with scraps at the farm.

"Jamie, wait!" she called, but he wouldn't turn back.

On they ran: across the ditches and round the far side of the turfy hill that loomed behind the caravan. Merry puffed and stumbled, and yanked at her damp skirt as it clung to her legs as she ran.

Through her closed eyes, Cathreen could see the two—the little boy and the cat ahead of him—leading Merry across the rippled terraces. The sky was mackereled with cloud, black and grey, that gradually suffused with pearl moonlight. The dimple shape of the Tor overhung them now as they entered a lane that wound between rustling hedges and skirted the boundaries of small groves of trees. Into a valley and up a slope, then racing downwards towards a wide knot of tree and bush surrounded by a wood-and-wire fence. Jamie slithered after the cat between broken wires, and was gone. One more glance to see the curve of the round moon emerge, another at the gate where Merry stood, searching for a way in, and Cathreen knew where she was. She'd been here, too, with Jag.

The warm wind made her shiver as she climbed the fence and entered with Merry, who searched for the lost boy, her nostrils assailed with acrid fumes. From within the knot rose solid fists of smoke and showers of sparks. Men's voices, urgent, hushed, drew Merry along a pattern of hedge, the overgrown garden rotting in the heat and damp underfoot, her footfalls muffled in mouldering leaves, then silently down moss-covered stone steps. Merry halted at the edge of the clearing.

"The well!" Cathreen said aloud.

Merry glanced at her, her face shifting through the wavering candlelight. "You know it?"

Cathreen nodded: she could see the whole of it, the outer stones of the octagonal opening, the square shaft of worn stone down which she'd fallen, and the shelf with the inner pentagonal chamber to the side of it, and down below, the unceasing flow of the spring that fed the well.

In front of where Merry crouched, hidden, to one side of the well, stood her father and Colin Printer. A low fire stank and roiled and sent up scarlet spikes of flame from a barrel. In his arms, Merry's father held a child. Colin Printer lifted a sack and threw it onto the blaze. Even while the whimpers and cries of the pitiful animals inside died away, and before Merry had fully realized what they were, Jag came pelting through the trees. Merry's father looked up, shocked to be found there. His long, drunken face leached in shadow, the bristles of his unshaven beard like a pox, he took one stumbling step away, then set the baby down, shouting at Colin to beware, and ran.

Colin turned, saw Jag aiming towards the child and snatched it up. He raised it over his head and smiled. The infant, surely cold in its shirt and nappy, never stirred; it wasn't dead, though, as Merry heard a cry no louder than a mew leak from its mouth. It opened and closed drugged eyes. "No!" Jag screamed, and as Colin held the child over the conflagration, threw something small and red and glittering into the air. Colin stopped, his face a study of anger and surprise, let the child fall to the ground and caught what Jag had thrown. Behind him, the fire, as if drenched, went out.

At this, Colin gave a roar, lunged at Jag as he stooped for the child and snagged him with one thick arm round the throat. Jag twisted and struggled, but he couldn't breathe and he was only sixteen, tall and slight, no match for the older man. Merry watched, in horror, as Printer dragged the youngster backwards, Jag's heels scraping trails in the soil, wrestled him over the well opening and pushed him in. Merry heard the thud of Jag's landing, then nothing more but the "huh" of Colin's panting. Once more the madman picked up the infant, and holding it like a package under an arm, took a stick and scraped at the fire's coals. He threw the stick down and lifted the child.

"Oh, Cathreen, all praise to Heaven for what happened next," Merry said.

"It was Jen's baby, wasn't it," Cathreen said dully. "That's how it died."

"No," Merry said. "You're not listening."

Jamie's little cat streaked into the clearing and leapt for Colin's eyes. Her claws scored deep tracks across his cheeks and eyelids, and blood streamed as Colin once more dropped the child and smashed the cat to the ground. It rolled and twitched and staggered to its feet, and as Colin wiped the blood away and bent to the infant once more, it sprang at him, hissing, scratching, biting his arms and hands, and again swiped at his eyes, sending Colin reeling back and blinded.

Merry crawled from behind the well, grabbed the baby and ran. She looked back as she reached the sheltering trees to see Colin catch the cat by its tail and swing it headfirst against the side of the well. The sound of the wet smash of its skull had made her sick. She'd remained watching long enough to see Colin throw the cat's body into the well.

Jamie waited for her, shivering and crying just outside the gate, and she carried both him and the baby home.

"Jen's baby? You took Jen's baby home?" Cathreen said. Tears splashed down her face and into the corners of her mouth.

The lights came back on. From the rear of the trailer came country music, softly playing on a radio.

The three figures, Jamie on Merry's back, the baby in Merry's arms, made their way to Neil's caravan. Merry put the child to sleep in a drawer on a folded towel, then made Jamie a cup of tea with poppy in it to help him forget, and laid him to sleep on the settee. Then she went out into the pre-dawn with a rope she'd found among Neil's tools and ran back with it to the well, where she knotted it to make it easier to climb, fixed an end to a tree and threw it into the well, so that Jag, if he were alive, could get out. The clearing was empty, the barrel gone, Jag's heel marks smoothed over, all signs of a struggle swallowed up by time; even the last tendrils of smoke had dispersed in the returning mist.

"You didn't say anything? You didn't call to him? You didn't tell anyone what you'd done?"

Merry shook her head. "Only Neil. He went out in the morning and came back to tell me that Jag had been seen at the petrol station in the early hours and was gone, and that Colin had reported Jen's suicide. He'd staggered into the police station a short time before, covered in cuts and bruises, saying he'd done his best, but Jen had fought him, taken the child, run to a rhyne and drowned them both before he could stop her."

"But all these years, Jag's believed his sister's baby died because he couldn't save her! He thought the body that came down the well on top of him was hers!"

Merry shrugged. "If I'd said anything, Colin would have come and taken her, and then what? Neil and I left the next night—nobody in the village cared about us or what we did—and we raised Jamie and Joan together. Neil was good to us. He died ten years ago in a pub fight. I still miss him. I moved on with some traveller friends and came back here once both Jamie and Joan were on their own."

The boiler in the cupboard grumbled, the clock, the refrigerator, the electric stove droned. Out of the corner of her eye, Cathreen saw Cutthroat's small grey face at the window.

"Why didn't you try to find him and tell him the truth?" she said.

"Jag? What would have been the point? You can't go back. What's done is done."

Cathreen drew her knees up and hunched over them. "He was a good father to me, we had good times, he built a whole different life, he took me camping, he told me stories, he did his best. . . . What you did to him was unbelievably cruel."

"It wasn't me," Merry said, getting up to put away the teacups, "it just was."

Cathreen spent the night in the little caravan, going to bed as soon after Merry gave her supper as she could. They'd been polite to each other, but they'd said little more beyond commonplaces for the rest of the afternoon and evening. Cathreen had asked, and Merry had told her that she had no idea where Jag had gone. The room was tiny, only about six feet wide, with the end of the bed tucked beneath the window, but there were clean sheets and a warm downy, and despite everything she fell asleep at once.

When she awoke, it was because she could not breathe, and she could not breathe because of the waves of grief that filled her chest. She was overwhelmed with loss, so much had been taken from her.

Jag was gone, Tink was dead, her mother had left her behind, even Nick, her one friend—what other real friends did she have?—had deserted her when it counted.

In the dream, she and Helena had run towards their burning house. It was nighttime, flames shot high into the air and singed the trees and went higher, carried by the wind until they seemed to scorch the sky itself. Rain fell and soaked them as they ran down the shabby, endless street from orange street lamp to street lamp. They could see, as they ran, Jag standing in the kitchen at the stove where he'd been cooking breakfast, the way he always had when he'd lived with them. The walls crackled with fire and collapsed, his body was on fire, his clothes flaked from him in charred sheets, the tallow of his skin spat as he burned. His face was lifted to the sky, but in a last howl of wind it too caught fire and a tall tongue of flame consumed him.

Not until that moment when she saw there was nothing left of him did she know how much she had loved her father. A few brittle, damaged leaves clattered overhead. The moon uncovered itself, and under its lamp Cathreen and her mother began to rescue a few old toys, books and dolls still identifiable in the remains of Cathreen's bedroom.

Now awake, concentrating on dawn's light seeping in, hearing the wood pigeons from the oaks, the larks starting up from the fields, she noticed what she hadn't the night before when Merry had ushered her in to the unlit room. On the long radiator set against the wall at the foot of the bed was draped a set of men's underclothing: underpants, a T-shirt and socks. Cathreen got out of bed, picked up the undershirt and sniffed it. It was fresh, washed clean. It was the right size for Jag.

Thirteen

Cathreen

It was cold on the road for the first hour, but a few birds sang from the oaks and rustled the bushes as Cathreen walked past. The sky would be grey later on—heavy slabs of cloud were piled up to the north—but for now a line of silver tinged the horizon with luminescence. Although she'd looked for them where they'd parted the day before, there'd been no sign of Cutthroat or Breaker or of the donkey that morning. She wasn't worried about the dog—he could fend for himself—and the donkey had gone its own way ever since Cathreen had first noticed it, but Cutthroat's absence bothered her. He was used to being with her. Still, she trusted that Breaker wouldn't leave the cat on his own and she knew the dog could always find her.

The world without them was quieter; the temperature had fallen several degrees and all creation appeared to be resigned to the coming months of frost and hibernation. She could use the calm to reflect on what had happened to her, but her bones ached and her heart felt dry after all the feelings that had washed through it. She was a little numb and older, but not so numb that she wasn't still heartsick because of, and afraid for, her father.

Other feelings lurked in the wings: guilt and sorrow over Tink, sadness at her estrangement from her mother, and confusion when she considered all she knew about Galt, whom Merry had told her she'd met, years ago, with the travellers. There was so much to think about that she was grateful to be tired. She knew where she wanted to get to today, and that was enough.

A sparrow hawk roamed above the wet fields as she stood on the roadside. Swans bugled in the distance: a big flight, wintering over, had skimmed past when she was following the river—its banks were choked with weed, its waters high, on the verge of flood, the river path sodden. Her boots were wet through from where she'd traversed it, and her toes made squishing sounds in her socks. She wriggled them, trying to get them warm as she waited, with her thumb out, for a truck heading her way.

The driver had a daughter about Cathreen's age; he wouldn't have wanted his own girl out here on her own; he drove her all the way to Summerwood.

It took all of Cathreen's courage to go through the gate, past the broken-down trucks and a van she thought might be Nick's, the sheds and half-built kiln, and to walk up the hill. The woods, their thin brown trunks making a palisade, were bad enough—they made her feel trapped—but just below, to the right, at an opening between them, yellow police tape still marked the perimeter of the field in which Tink had been murdered. She had to stop, force air in and out of her lungs, and squat down because of dizziness. She concentrated on the rust-coloured fir needles scattered over the earth, the sound of the rushing stream on the far side of the hill, the chuk-chuk of the pump, and the smell of woodsmoke and cooking that assured her that someone was home, higher up, in the Summerwood clearing.

When she felt able, she looked down at the pasture. The low morning sunlight, clouds closing in on it, licked flecks of gold from the grass. In the damp earth, insects burrowed, and snakes slithered from their holes for a last examination of the outside world before real cold set in. . . . Cold.

Tink was cold. He'd never warm up.

Her heart clenched, but she kept her eyes open. You could think, with those splashes of light promising the bright side of the seasons, that nothing bad had happened here. There was no dark patch to show where Tink's body had fallen, there were no footprints in the grass—rain and wind had swept the signs away. It would be easy enough, too, to forget about Galt: his strangeness had melted back into the earth when they'd buried him, and even to her, now, he was almost past imagining.

You might think, in fact, when you saw nature getting on with it— morning dew, frost, sun, plants growing and dying—that human beings were like skaters on a pond, leaving little behind to show what they'd done but a few surface scratches, certainly nothing that would last long. That everything essential happened without them.

It was a thought she couldn't contain, and she let it pass.

Nick had described plans for flooding the field temporarily to bring in fertilizing silt for an intended garden. Would he do that now, or would he believe the field was ruined? Would he go ahead with anything, or was Summerwood a lost cause? He'd described to her how the field looked in spring, with dandelions and Queen Anne's lace, and creamy meadowsweet, and red sorrel brushing against you as you walked, its copper dust coating your clothes and skin. Maybe he'd just leave it as it was. Maybe one day she'd get to see it like that.

She walked on, hardly aware of doing so, and was quickly at the top. There stood Nick tending a smoke-blackened pot that hung from a tripod over the open fire. He looked up.

"Charlie told me you'd come," he said, staring at her. "But I wasn't sure if you'd want to." He wore a flannel shirt with frayed collar and cuffs, over an old sweater; his eyes were tired and he was growing a beard. She found herself noticing how many places he'd set for the meal—only one.

He squinted at her through the smoke. "I didn't know what had happened to you," he said. "When that boy turned up with your rucksack . . ."

"You found my pack?"

He nodded. "Listen, Cathreen, I don't know what to say . . ."

"Can I sit down?" Her legs wobbled. The sense of relief at finding him here as she'd hoped, but not quite dared to believe, weakened her. Until this moment, she hadn't been absolutely certain that he was okay.

"Yes, of course." He pulled forward two of the stools that he and Charlie had made out of wood lengths. Cathreen sat, and he settled next to her.

"I don't know where to start," he said. "I've told everyone, even Charlie, they can't stay here anymore. I've got to think things over. Summerwood belongs to me, I'm responsible for it, but when Tink was killed, I didn't have the courage to stay, I ran away, back to my sister's." He took Cathreen's hand and pressed it to his cheek. "I couldn't even stay for you.

"Cathreen, it should have been me and not Tink. I'm the one it was supposed to happen to, that's why I had those dreams."

"No," she said, "that's stupid!"

He let go her hand and stared at the ground. "Then I thought, seeing your belongings, that you, too . . . that I'd done it again."

"Look at me, Nick. I'm here, I'm fine." She stood up and turned all the way around. "See? All in one piece." She sat down. "You're not responsible for the whole world. Tink wasn't anything to do with you. You're not the centre of the universe."

He looked up, anxiously. "I've been so worried, Cathreen, about you, about myself. I didn't know how to find you."

"I waited for you in the barn, where we said."

"I couldn't stand it at Ann's. She started phoning trauma counsellors . . ." He flashed Cathreen a grin. "When I got back here, I went to the barn, I asked everyone. No one knew where you'd gone. The only good thing was I knew you had Breaker, I knew he wouldn't leave you."

Not like me, his eyes said, and clouded with shame.

"Galt wasn't your fault. He was like . . . like an accident. He just happened. You couldn't have done anything."

Nick stood up. "Come with me, I want to show you something." He reached for her hand and pulled her up. He towed her past the table on which the single plate and cup were laid and around the teepee-shaped stripped poles that formed the outdoor dish and pot rack. The cookware was blackened and corroded.

They came to the winter kitchen, draped in tarpaulins and open on one side to the elements, the rusty airtight stove in one corner, the basket of apples, the oil lamps and old jackets. Nick kept going. A little farther up the hill stood Charlie's unfinished bathhouse. "It's almost done," he said. "Charlie put the windows in before he left." He squeezed her hand. "Once I install the stove and boiler we'll have hot water. Maybe I'll finish it while you're here?" He glanced at her, but she was gazing at the far end of the clearing where you could see through the fringe of trees to the next hill. Beyond that was Merry's, and behind Merry's, the well, and Jag's hut, and Galt's burial place. Another world.

"See that frame over there?" He pointed out a square of poles tied together and anchored by ropes to four trees. A tarpaulin drooped over part of the structure and one wall had been filled in with hay bales. Another score of bales lay scattered around. "He'd already started to build his house. He was going to stay the winter. I thought he was a runaway, he said he had nowhere to go, so I took him in."

"Who, Nick?"

"The boy, the one who had your rucksack." He kicked a damp bale out of the way. "I told him it wouldn't work. As soon as hay gets wet, it rots and lets in the cold. There'd be rats, he'd get sick. He said he didn't care.

"The thing is, Cathreen, I knew something was wrong, but I didn't know what. Then, when I was leaving for the village with a load of wood, I saw Breaker down by the travellers' wagon at the stream. It worried me. I'd told him to stay with you. Breaker headed into the wood, so I came back up to look for him.

"A truck blocked the road on the far side—the way you came with Merry that first night—and a man was up there with the boy. They'd taken off the tarp and moved some of the bales. When they saw me, they both took off. I walked on up to have a look. They'd had television sets, stereos and computers hidden behind those bales. Stupid buggers, the mice would have had the wiring out in hours. And they'd stuffed in carrier bags full of jewellery. Wedding rings, silver brooches, pearl necklaces—old people's things. When I moved some of the bags out I found your rucksack." He rubbed his hand over his face. "I can't tell you what I thought when I saw it. If anything had happened to you . . ."

"But it didn't," she said. She slipped an arm through his.

"I've worked so hard to make this a good place. It *should* work here." He turned sad eyes on Cathreen. "Maybe I couldn't help what Galt did, I can see that, but I let the boy move in against my better judgment, and I left you behind when you needed me. Both things were wrong, but I did them anyway."

"It's more complicated than that, and you know it, Nick. You did your best." She held tight to his arm to keep him with her.

"Right up there," he said, pointing deeper into the woods, strain distorting his face, "was where the pole tree touched the earth. At the top it was hung with stars. The stories say it's guarded by a knight and a dragon. Everything winds together here, I've seen it for myself, wars and dreams and death . . ."

"And my backpack?"

She thought he would pull away, but he said, "I go too fast, I'd better slow down or I'll get myself in trouble again. It's hard to stop, sometimes."

When it grew dark, they went inside the bender. The sky had cleared, and Nick had opened the canvas smoke hole so they could see the stars—white holes in the quilt of sky that spread over the forest—as they rested on his mattress. They lay under the damp duvet fully clothed against the cold. She'd kept on her jeans and heavy shirt, and he'd given her dry socks and his sweater. His hands were clasped under his neck.

"You still awake?" he asked.

"I was tired before, now I can't sleep."

He felt for her arm under the covers, followed it down and folded his hand over her fingers. "I looked in your bag. Your ticket and passport are there, but if you had any money, it's gone. If you need some to get home, I'll help you."

"Nick?"

"But if you're not going home, I want you to stay here. We could do this together, we could build Summerwood. We wouldn't need anybody else."

She rolled over to face him, hoping to buy thinking time. "It's a good thing you're doing here, Nick. You give people a home and work and something to believe in. There's nothing wrong with that, it's important. Don't give up on it. There's hardly anybody like you anywhere. Most people don't care about things the way you do, or they care about the wrong things." She took a deep breath. "I don't think I can stay here just now, there's still some shit at home I have to deal with, but I'll come back later on if you want me to." She waited for what he'd say next. She knew what else had been in the pack, what he hadn't mentioned yet. Nick's thumb made little circles around the pulse on her wrist.

"I don't know if I should've or not," he said quietly, "but it looked like you must have put that skeleton in there for a reason and I guessed it needed to be buried, so I dug a hole beneath the pole tree and put it in. I tried to do it properly, Cathreen, the way I thought you'd want me to. I even said a prayer." He was looking at her, not questioning, just asking for her blessing. "I hope I did the right thing." He added, a little defensively, in the ensuing silence, "We used to say prayers at school, I do know some." She nodded.

He stared up at the stars again. "Your cat turned up when I was finishing, and then Breaker came along and that donkey. We stayed there, together, for a long time. Tell me I didn't do anything wrong?"

"You did good, Nick," Cathreen said softly. "That was Jones, Aunt Jenny's cat." Her mind lurched back and forth between the different ways there were of looking at things—the way it would make sense to someone who hadn't been there, and the way it had really been—and then it decided. She told him everything.

When she was done, Nick's eyes were liquid, inches from hers. She could almost hear the wheels of his thinking and worrying. "Jones would have liked to be buried up there," she said to reassure him.

"That's what was wrong with your cat," he said. "I took up food and water and he wouldn't touch it. He'd lost his friend."

He was quiet for a minute, then he said, "I might have been King Charles I, but I wasn't. I didn't get beheaded. King Charles I had a trial, not a very fair one, but he did have a chance to explain himself. That was just, wasn't it, in a way?" He bit a fingernail. "I might have been the Duke of Monmouth, though. He was beheaded too, later, after the Restoration."

"Nick, what are you talking about?"

"Yes, it could be Monmouth."

Cathreen held his face in her hands. "I didn't mean to upset you, Nick. You're my friend, it helps me to talk to you—but maybe it's not so good for you."

He shifted and put his arm under her shoulders. "It was just a thought, Cathreen. I get these thoughts, I don't know where they come from." He shook his head.

"But you have other thoughts?"

"Yes, of course."

"Then think them." She wiggled her frozen toes. "You could think, for instance, how to make this place warmer."

"Yes, I could." He kissed her gently. "I wasn't serious, it's just how I talk. I yammer out whatever story pops up." Nick looked thoughtful. "Monmouth wasn't even that smart. He lost the battle and ran away. He dressed up as a shepherd but was found shivering in a ditch. He'd kept the Order of the Garter in his pocket — not an object normally in the possession of shepherds — so they took him to Tower Hill in London and executed him for treason. They botched it. It took the executioner five blows with the axe, and in the end he still hadn't severed Monmouth's head from his body, so he cut it off with his knife."

"Nick!"

His fingers touched her mouth. "You're beautiful, Cathreen."

"I like you a lot, Nick. I don't think I've ever liked anybody as much."

"I won't do anything to make you stay."

"You mean you don't think you should sleep with me because if you did I'd be powerless to leave?"

"Yes, something like that." She felt her heart, so dry and tight with all its troubles, loosen. "I have to go home," she said. "I don't know what I'll do after that. I should finish school, and my mother's not very good at looking after herself."

"I'll wait for you," he said. He kissed her again. When he drew away, a shadow, the familiar shade of Nick's anxiety, crossed his face. "You'll forget all about me, though," he said.

"I will?"

Nick lay back and once more put both hands behind his head. " 'But his fame is gone out like a Candle in a Snuff, and his Memory will alway stink.' "

"What's that?"

"Winstanley, talking about Milton. He held Milton partly responsible for the death of King Charles I."

She propped herself on an elbow and leaned over him. "You promised you were going to think about other things."

He began to laugh. "You don't know who Milton is, do you! You're trying to stop me finding out!"

"I'm not that ignorant!"

"Tell me, then!"

"You'll have to wait for it. I'll finish school . . . I'll catch up to you, Nick." She grinned, lay back and curled her body to his.

In the morning, before they left for the airport, Nick took her to see Jones's grave. He had buried Jones in the earth between two large roots of the old oak said to be descended from the original pole tree. Cutthroat lay miserably on top of the small burial mound. His coat was matted and filthy. Breaker stretched out nearby. His paws quivered in half-sleep but his eyes remained fixed on Cutthroat. The tawny shape of the donkey drifted in and out between the trees.

Cathreen stooped to pet the cat. "I should take him with me," she said, "but I don't know if he'd come with me now, he seems to want to stay here." Cutthroat's skin twitched beneath her fingers, but he didn't otherwise respond. "Nick, what should I do?"

"He can't go with you. They won't let him on the airplane."

As she opened her mouth to argue, a soft cry escaped from the grieving cat and she felt his unmendable sadness. "Will you look after him, Nick? He can't do much for himself."

"I'll look after him."

"You'll look after Breaker, too, won't you?"

"I'll take care of them both."

"Breaker," Cathreen said, kneeling beside the large white dog, "stay with Nick." She put her arms around the dog's neck and hugged him.

The music on the plane told Cathreen it would soon be Christmas. Her birthday had slipped past unnoticed and she'd turned fifteen without knowing it. Last Christmas she'd been with Helena and Tink. Last birthday she and Toni had got drunk, and Fawn—somewhere with her family—had still been warm and alive. Would Timmy even know it was Christmas?

They were flying down from the north over frozen lakes rimmed with cliffs and forest. The long white sweep of the big lakes, and the dozens of smaller ones, green and blue in their centres, fled below them. On one lake, a spread of black dots, maybe a wolf pack, followed the criss-crossed tracks of a snowmobile. She dozed with her head against the chilly glass of the window until they landed.

No one came to meet her in Vancouver, so she headed straight from Customs to the gate of the little commuter plane to the Island. The waiting room was almost empty. She sat for an hour, hungry and thirsty, on a hard plastic chair. She examined the soundproofing tiles in the ceiling, the fluorescent lighting, the dull ugliness. It was a very ordinary world to which she was returning.

When the flight was called, she walked down a set of steps into a passageway. The wind blew through the sweater Nick had given her. She crossed the tarmac in the rain, went up the stairs of the little DASH-8 and sat next to a window. The clouds had lifted enough to show the moon in a black and silver sky. The clouds were like crumpled paper. Once the plane was airborne, she watched the wrinkling of the sea, islets on it like scraps of rumpled carpet, and the few lights that showed from small bands of shoreline houses gathered in villages.

Her hair was dirty, her clothes soiled, damp and smelling of woodsmoke. In the orange light of the bus, her face, reflected in the glass, looked old and drawn, a bit like Jag's and her mother's squashed together. She could smell diesel and disinfectant and gum. The only people on the bus were old people, or teenagers like her. She'd tried, before catching the bus from the airport, to call Helena at home, but there'd been no answer. She got off at the rec centre where the buses changed.

They told me to meet them at the pool. They said it was an initiation. Fawn's voice. Fawn right at hand, and nothing changed.

The house was dark. Tink's car sat in the driveway. The living-room curtains were open. Cathreen peered in. Enough light splashed from the street lamps to show the mess inside: newspapers on the floor, a blanket and pillow on the couch, a plate of half-eaten pizza, apple cores, orange peel. And open file folders overflowing with letters, drawings and photographs. The drawings were hers, from when she was little. The letters, she thought, were from Tink. The photographs glimmered at her, many of them faces sunk just a step too far away in time for her to recognize.

She sniffed the air: leaf smoke, plastic smoke, different smoke from that which still clung to her clothing.

Helena stood at the bottom of the garden. The bonfire beside her was surrounded by heaps of junk that had been dragged over to it: broken lawn chairs and ladders, bicycle wheels, boxes of papers.

Helena scraped a rake at the ground, trawling for leaves, morning glory, blackberry runners. A scrawny kitten pounced at the rake each time she lifted it. "Go on," Cathreen heard her mother murmur, "go on, out of there, you'll get hurt."

"Can I help?" Cathreen stepped close to the firelight so her mother could see her. She put down her pack.

"Oh!" Helena dropped the rake, then wiped the back of her hand across her forehead, leaving a streak of dirt. She wore an old jacket of Tink's and a pair of his rubber boots, far too big for her. Her hair hung in lank strands around her face. "I wasn't expecting you," she said. Her mother scarcely looked at her, didn't hold out her arms in welcome. She bent to pick up the dropped rake. Cathreen had to do something with her own arms so she folded them across her chest.

"I don't like to be inside," Helena said. "I can't seem to sleep. I don't mind tidying at night." She scratched the rake back and forth over the same spot, although there was nothing left on the bare earth for it to collect.

"I'm glad to see you, Mom. I wanted to come back. Maybe I can help?"

"Maybe," Helena said. The kitten, frightened off by Cathreen's sudden arrival, crept out of the grass to sniff at her running shoes. Without stopping work Helena said, "I don't have a job anymore. Mrs. Hamilton died, she was quite old, so I'm not that sad, she'd said she was ready, but I didn't get a reference from her. There wasn't time."

"You'll get something else." Cathreen crouched to catch the kitten but it shied away. She'd planned to return the green stone to the old lady.

"No," her mother said. "I doubt that I will. I'm tired, Cathreen. I've had the wind knocked out of me. Oh, I know I'll have to start again, sometime, I'll have to, but I can't see it now."

When she realized that Helena wasn't going to listen to the things she wanted to tell her, Cathreen took her mother inside, made her tea and put her to bed. She placed a hot water bottle at her feet and tucked the covers around her with a sense of loss so profound she wasn't sure she could bear it. She telephoned and left a message for Nick at the George and Dragon, as they'd agreed, so he'd know that she'd arrived safely. After that, there was no way she could sleep, so she put on a heavy jacket and boots and went out. The air had turned thick and cold. It felt like it might snow.

The dingy streets, the still marshland, the roof of the Chinese restaurant were dusted with frost. Cathreen crossed the bridge and made her way to the path to the scout camp: a new gate with a new lock barred the way. She poked around and found a route down through the underbrush and woods and across a wedge of swamp to the lake; she walked to the end of the slippery black plastic float dock and stared at the water. Timmy had moved to live with his mother in the Maritimes. He still couldn't talk, but he could blink his eyes for yes and no and squeeze a hand. Divers had tried a number of times to search for Fawn, but the water was turgid and brown, choked with weed and constantly stirred by rain. Come summer, when the water level went down, they'd try again. At the mooring post, where Cathreen, Toni and Judy had found Timmy's shoes, somebody had tacked up a shrine: faded yellow and white ribbons, wreaths of flowers, a water-damaged photograph of Fawn, a dozen pink rosettes.

Just before she'd gone out, Cathreen had called Toni's house to see if she would come with her. Toni's mom had answered and said, "She's not here. I don't know where she is. I think she's at a party. You might try Judy. They spend a lot of time together." Cathreen tried to tell Toni's mom some of where she'd been and what she'd done, but Toni's mother interrupted and said, "Look, I'm kind of busy just now. I'll tell Toni you called."

The chill wind bit into Cathreen's skin. Her lips dried and cracked, her eyes stung. Small foamy waves splashed at the plastic lip of the jigsaw blocks under her feet. She wriggled her toes to get them warm. The air was weighted with car exhaust, mill smoke, town detritus; a pinkish spillover of light from houses and street lamps dirtied the leaden sky. People would still come here to picnic or drink or make love or learn to swim, and some would stand here like she did to ask forgiveness. To wonder what they'd do if they didn't get it. Cathreen closed her eyes so that she could feel what was left inside her, she, the lucky one. There was loneliness and sadness, but also something like hope—she discovered herself thinking about Nick and what things could be like when they met again, if she could manage it, in the summer. That was in another landscape, and on the other side of shame.

Cathreen removed the gloves she'd borrowed from her mother's drawer and felt deep in her jeans pocket. The two stones were still there. She took them out, polished them on her sleeve, and held each, one at a time, to her eye. Through the red one, her surroundings looked wavery and unfinished. The stone pulsed between her thumb and forefinger; it sent red shifts of blood that flooded through arteries, branches, veinlets of everything in sight: all of it was tunnelled through with life. The green one revealed fluid, amoebic edges and clusters with dark dots—she thought of frogs' eggs: the trees were hung with them, the shoreline weeds dipped under their weight, even the distant, almost unseen sketches of houses and streets bore great strings of them.

Where was Breaker and the white stone? Still with Nick, she hoped. She didn't like to think of him, or Cutthroat, or the donkey who'd shadowed them, on his or her own. Roaming the world, friendless. She held both stones in her palm until they were warm, and then she drew back her arm, holding the stones high over the lakewater, and threw them in.

Epilogue

Those stones wake the land up, Knowall. Look around you. It's more like it used to be, the horses awake by 5:00 a.m., swishing their tails through the fog and nosing up to the sheep; and the frogs—like a green carpet snapping over the moors; and there's Breaker, lying under a bush, his paws making running motions even in his sleep.

When Jones was here, we'd keep the farm dogs away from the cattle—we'd leap out of the grass to frighten them. Then I'd crawl through the fields and search for peewit eggs to give to her at lunchtime. When the moors were flooded, wild swans flew in—they had the most wonderful calls. Happy times, Knowall.

The geese arrived early that winter and stayed through. You could hear them honking to each other, and they'd walk out in groups and stroll across a field just to take a swim in a different pool. With hard weather at the coast, the ducks came in. The farmer got out his gun and Jones chased the milk cows so he'd run after them instead, and I'd be scanning for ducks over her shoulder, directing them.

I knew where I belonged, Knowall. I knew who I was. But to know yourself is to follow the Creator's will, and the Creator's will includes life and death for all living things. . . . Where does that leave us?

(Sigh.)

Think of the earth as wound round by three bright ribbons, like those in Cathreen's hair when she was little, or as circuited by the rings of an astrolabe: the colour and movement of one affects the others, and the end, the Great Purpose, is to restore them to a single essence. As they were in the beginning, when living things were perfect.

Not that we would know it if it happened. . . .

Or, look at those stars, Knowall: you can't count them, you can't even begin to think of their possibilities, and there's the Milky Way—Breaker, you're yawning now, waking up and peering round to see what's coming next—it's like a ribbon of its own, or as Jag described it, a river, and if you look hard, you can see, where it spills into moonlight, even now, at day's beginning, someone travelling to be born.

Acknowledgments

I owe a debt of thanks to many friends, family and colleagues for conversations about various aspects of this novel. These include Liz Gorrie, James Carley, Chris Black, Ariel O'Sullivan, Ellen Godfrey, Heather Spears, Patrick Grant, Ed Carson, Rob and Betty Cairns, Jeffrey Green, Martha Spice, Xan Bowering Elcock, Michael Elcock, Liz Lochhead and the staff of Special Collections, The McPherson Library, and the staff of the Maltwood Gallery, both of the University of Victoria. My especial thanks for assistance from Special Collections in accessing the Katherine Maltwood archives and to the Maltwood Gallery for allowing me to view the complete Katherine Maltwood collection. The discoveries of Mrs. Maltwood concerning the Glastonbury Zodiac were crucial to the writing of this book. I also received assistance from the staff of Little St. Michael's at the Chalice Well, Glastonbury.

Thanks are due, as always, to my family for their patience and understanding, and to my editor, Iris Tupholme, for her counsel as I trod this extraordinary maze. I owe much to the intrepid and tolerant Linda Taylor, and I'm indebted to my brother, David, for the good name of his cat.

In Chapter 5, Jones's poems are adapted from *Folklore and Reminiscences of Strathtay and Grandtully* by James Kennedy (Perth: The Munro Press, 1927). "The hills are shadows . . ." is unattributed. "Many a cow . . ." is attributed by Kennedy to "a cattle stealer." "That kind cow . . ." is attributed to "the dairymaid of Meggernie Castle when a prisoner of the Macdonalds of Glencoe."

Many of Nick's ideas can be discovered in *Low Impact Development* by Simon Fairlie (Charlbury, Oxfordshire: Jon Carpenter, 1996).

I wish also to acknowledge, with gratitude, the Canada Council and the British Columbia Arts Council for their support during the writing of parts of this work.

MARILYN BOWERING is an award-winning author, poet and playwright. Her first novel, *To All Appearances a Lady,* was a *New York Times* Notable Book of 1990, and her second novel, *Visible Worlds,* winner of the Ethel Wilson Fiction Prize and finalist for the Orange Prize, received widespread acclaim in Canada, the US and Great Britain. Born in Winnipeg, she has lived and worked in the US, Greece, Scotland, Spain and now makes her home in Sooke, BC.